Debbie Macomber is a #1 *New York Times* bestselling author and a leading voice in women's fiction worldwide. Her work has appeared on every major bestseller list, with more than 170 million copies in print, and she is a multiple award winner. Hallmark Channel based a television series on Debbie's popular Cedar Cove books. For more information, visit her website, www.debbiemacomber.com.

New York Times and *USA TODAY* bestselling author **Lee Tobin McClain** read *Gone with the Wind* in the third grade and has been an incurable romantic ever since. When she's not writing angst-filled love stories with happy endings, she's probably Snapchatting with her college-student daughter, mediating battles between her goofy goldendoodle and her rescue cat, or teaching aspiring writers in Seton Hill University's MFA program. She is probably not cleaning her house. For more about Lee, visit her website at www.leetobinmcclain.com.

#1 *New York Times* Bestselling Author

DEBBIE MACOMBER

READY FOR ROMANCE

**HARLEQUIN
BESTSELLING
AUTHOR
COLLECTION**

**HARLEQUIN®
BESTSELLING
AUTHOR
COLLECTION**

ISBN-13: 978-1-335-74498-2

Ready for Romance
First published in 1993. This edition published in 2022.
Copyright © 1993 by Debbie Macomber

Child on His Doorstep
First published in 2020. This edition published in 2022.
Copyright © 2020 by Lee Tobin McClain

For questions and comments about the quality of this book,
please contact us at CustomerService@Harlequin.com.

Harlequin Enterprises ULC
22 Adelaide St. West, 41st Floor
Toronto, Ontario M5H 4E3, Canada
www.Harlequin.com

Printed in U.S.A.

CONTENTS

READY FOR ROMANCE   7
Debbie Macomber

CHILD ON HIS DOORSTEP   197
Lee Tobin McClain

Also by Debbie Macomber

MIRA

Blossom Street

The Shop on Blossom Street
A Good Yarn
Susannah's Garden
Back on Blossom Street
Twenty Wishes
Summer on Blossom Street
Hannah's List
"The Twenty-First Wish" (in *The Knitting Diaries*)
A Turn in the Road

Cedar Cove

16 Lighthouse Road
204 Rosewood Lane
311 Pelican Court
44 Cranberry Point
50 Harbor Street
6 Rainier Drive
74 Seaside Avenue
8 Sandpiper Way
92 Pacific Boulevard
1022 Evergreen Place
Christmas in Cedar Cove (*5-B Poppy Lane*
and *A Cedar Cove Christmas*)
1105 Yakima Street
1225 Christmas Tree Lane

Debbie Macomber's Cedar Cove Cookbook
Debbie Macomber's Christmas Cookbook

Visit her Author Profile page at Harlequin.com,
or debbiemacomber.com, for more titles!

READY FOR ROMANCE

Debbie Macomber

For Jessica,
who caught the wedding bouquet first

Prologue

Jessica Kellerman looked both ways, then slipped around the corner of the Dryden four-car garage. She flattened her body against the wall and moved cautiously, one infinitesimal step at a time. It was vital no one see her.

Evan's vehicle, a fancy sports car, was parked just outside the garage—and in direct view of the house. She needed to be quick.

Squatting down by the side mirror, she withdrew a bright red tube of lipstick from her pocket, opened it and heavily outlined her lips. Taking a soft white rag from the pocket of her jeans, she wiped his mirror clean and then kissed it several times. The imprint of her mouth was left in bold red.

Jessica sighed with satisfaction as she carefully

opened the door on the driver's side and crawled into the front seat. The mirror over the dash was next. Her heart was pounding hard and fast, but it wasn't entirely due to her fear of being discovered. Her heart rate tended to accelerate whenever she thought about Evan.

There wasn't a man in all of Boston who could compete with Evan Dryden. To think she'd lived next door to him all these years and hadn't noticed until recently what a gorgeous hunk he was! As far as Jessica was concerned, he was the handsomest man in the universe.

She remembered the exact moment she had realized her destiny. She hadn't been the same since. The Dryden estate, Whispering Willows, was next to her own family's, and she'd often spent time in the huge oak tree spying on the two brothers. Damian was in law school now and Evan in college. Being an only child, Jessica was left to invent her own amusement, and spying on the Dryden brothers had always been great fun.

Jessica had been sitting in the tree one day when Evan had walked to the pond and stood on the footbridge tossing rocks into the water. His back was to her and she held her breath, wondering if he'd seen her hiding in the thick foliage.

She must have made a sound, because he turned abruptly and stared into the tree.

"Jessica?"

She didn't dare move or even breathe.

He stared upward and the sun cut across his shoulder, highlighting his handsome features. It was then that she realized Evan wasn't just an ordinary boy. He was an Adonis. Perfect in every way.

After that she started having dreams about him. Wonderful dreams about him falling in love with her. Dreams about them marrying and having a family. It seemed so…so right. It came to her about a week later that fate had thrown them together. They were meant for each other. The only problem was that Evan had yet to make this discovery for himself.

Jessica had recently turned fourteen and Evan was much older. Six whole years, but it might have been a hundred for all the notice he gave her.

That was when Jessica decided she had to take matters into her own hands. She was a woman of the world, and when a woman knew what she wanted, she went after it. It, in this case, was Evan Dryden.

Jessica soon discovered she wasn't nearly as dauntless as she would have liked. She must have phoned him ten times or more, and each time he answered, she lacked the courage to so much as speak, much less tell him about her undying love. Each call had ended with her replacing the receiver and stewing in frustration.

She'd always been better at expressing herself with the written word, so she'd taken to writing him love notes, pouring out her devotion. She let her best friend read one such note, and the girl claimed it was the most beautiful love letter she'd ever seen. Unfortunately, Jessica hadn't found the courage to sign her name.

This latest trick, planting kisses on his rearview mirror, was sure to accomplish what nothing else had. He'd know it was Jessica and he'd finally come for her, and together they'd ride into the sunset in his sports car.

Outlining her lips with a fresh coat of brilliant red, Jessica was about to kiss the interior mirror when the car door was flung open.

"So it *is* you."

Her heart sank all the way to her knees. Slowly she looked over and her eyes connected with Damian Dryden's. He was taller than his younger brother, dark and handsome in his own way. She was certain the day would come when some girl would feel as strongly about him as she did about Evan.

"Hello," she said, pretending it wasn't the least bit out of the ordinary for her to be sitting in his brother's car kissing the mirrors.

"You're the one, I bet, who's been phoning at all hours of the night."

"I've never called past ten," she denied heatedly, then realized her mistake. It probably would have been best to pretend she didn't know what he was talking about.

"The notes on Evan's windshield have been from you, too, haven't they?"

She could have denied that, but it wouldn't have done any good. Feeling trapped in Evan's car, she swung her legs around and gingerly climbed out. "Are you going to tell him it was me?"

"I don't know," Damian said thoughtfully. "How old are you now?"

"Fourteen," she said proudly. "I know Evan's older, but I was hoping he'd be willing to wait for me to grow up so we could get married."

"Married!"

Damian made the word sound ludicrous and Jessica

bristled. "Just wait until you fall in love," she challenged. "Then you'll know."

"You aren't in love with Evan," he said gently. "You're too young to know about things like that. You're infatuated with him because he's older and—"

"I most certainly do love Evan," she flared, stuffing the lipstick tube in her pocket. She wasn't about to stand there and let him ridicule her. She might only be fourteen, but she had the heart of a mature woman and she'd made her decision. Someday she would marry Evan Dryden, and nothing Damian could say or do would stand in her way.

"I'm sure my brother's flattered by your devotion."

"He should be. The man who marries me will see himself as the luckiest man in the world." Her words were fed by pure bravado.

Damian laughed.

Jessica had been willing to overlook his earlier statements, but this was unforgivable. Hands braced against her hips, she glared at him with all the indignation she could muster, which at the moment was considerable.

"You might be older than Evan, but you don't know a thing about love, do you?"

Her question appeared to amuse him, and that only served to irritate her further.

"When a woman makes up her mind about a man, nothing can change the way she feels. I've decided to marry your brother, and not a thing you say or do will have the least effect, so save your breath. Evan is my destiny."

"You're sure about this?"

At least he had the courtesy to wipe the grin off his face.

"Of course," she said confidently. "Mark my words, Damian Dryden. Time will prove me right."

"Does my brother have a say in this?"

"Naturally."

"What if he decides to marry someone else?"

"I... I don't know." Damian had zeroed in on her worst fear—that Evan would get married before she had a chance to prove herself.

"There's something else you haven't considered," Damian said.

"What's that?"

He grinned. "I just might want to marry you myself."

Chapter 1

Jessica Kellerman's time of reckoning had arrived. For the first time in eight years she was about to face the Dryden brothers. Evan didn't concern her. She suspected he wouldn't even remember what a nuisance she'd made of herself. Then again, he just might. But Damian was the brother who worried her most. He was the one who'd caught her red-handed. He was the one who'd mocked her and suggested her devotion to his brother was a passing fancy. Now she was forced to face him and admit he'd been right. She sincerely hoped Damian would have the good grace not to drag up the past.

Swallowing her dread, Jessica walked into the highrise office building in the most prestigious part of downtown Boston. The building was new, with a glistening black-mirrored exterior that towered thirty stories above the ground. The Dryden law firm was one of the most distinguished in town, and in Boston that was saying something.

Jessica's footsteps made tapping sounds against the marble floor in the lobby. Although she'd been in this part of town often—the university wasn't far from the business section—this was the first time she'd been inside the impressive building.

She was nervous, and rightly so. The last time she'd spent any time with either of the Dryden brothers she'd been caught kissing rearview mirrors.

Looking back, she knew she'd been a constant source of amusement to the brothers and their respective sets of parents, as well. Young love, however, refused to be denied. Risking her family's censure, Jessica had diligently sought Evan's heart all through high school. It wasn't until Benny Wilcox asked her to the graduation dance that she'd realized there were other fish in the sea. Sweet, attentive, good-looking ones, too. Yes, Evan had been the man of her dreams, the one who'd awakened her to womanhood. She held her love for him in a special place in her heart, but was more than willing to forget the way she'd embarrassed herself over him, praying he did, too.

Although Jessica had let her infatuation with Evan die gracefully, neither set of parents had. Particularly, Lois and Walter Dryden. They thought the way Jessica felt about Evan was "cute," and they mentioned it every now and again, renewing her embarrassment.

When Walter Dryden heard that Jessica had recently graduated from business college with a certificate as a legal assistant, he'd insisted she apply with the family firm. In the beginning Jessica had balked, but jobs were few and far between just then, and after a fruitless search on her own, she'd decided to swallow her pride and face the two brothers.

She was warmly greeted by the receptionist, who gave her a wide smile. Jessica smiled back, hoping she looked composed and mature. "I have an appointment with Damian Dryden," she said.

The woman, who appeared to be in her early thirties, with large blue eyes and a smooth complexion, glanced at the appointment book. "Ms. Kellerman?"

"That's right."

"Please have a seat and I'll let Mr. Dryden know you're here."

"Thank you." Jessica sat in one of the richly upholstered chairs and reached for a *People* magazine. She'd dressed carefully for this interview, choosing a soft dove gray suit with a double-breasted jacket. The silver-dollar-size buttons were made from mother-of-pearl with flashes of deep blue and white. She wore high heels, hoping to seem not only professional, but sophisticated. Her glossy brown hair was sophisticated, too, cut in a flattering pageboy. She'd grown up, and it was important Damian know that.

Jessica hadn't even scanned the magazine's contents page when the elder Dryden brother appeared. She'd seen Damian often, from a distance, but this was the first time they'd spoken in months, possibly years. She'd forgotten how tall he was, with broad shoulders that tapered to slim hips. She remembered how much he enjoyed football as a teenager, and how good he was at tackling the opponent. From what she remembered about Damian, he preferred to tackle problems head-on, too. She knew him to be aggressive, hardworking and ambitious. He'd taken over the leadership of the law firm upon Walter Dryden's retirement three years earlier, and the firm, which specialized in corporate law, had thrived under his leadership.

"Hello, Jessica. It's good to see you again," Damian said, stepping forward.

"It's good to see you, too." She stood and offered him her hand.

He clasped it with both of his own. He wasn't an especially large man, and at five-eight she wasn't especially small, but her hand was dwarfed in his. His grip was solid and strong, like the man himself.

"I've come to talk to you about a position as a legal assistant," she said. The direct approach would work best with Damian, she felt.

"Great. Let's go to my office, shall we?"

She was struck by the rugged timbre of his voice. It exuded confidence, sounding deep and firm. Little wonder Damian was one of the most sought-after corporate attorneys in Boston.

He motioned her to be seated, then walked around behind the deep mahogany desk and claimed the black leather chair. He tilted it back slightly, conveying ease and relaxation.

Jessica wasn't fooled. She sincerely doubted that Damian knew how to relax. His mother, Lois, had often voiced her concern about her elder son, complaining that Damian worked too many hours.

"Thank you for seeing me on such short notice," Jessica said, crossing her legs.

"It's my pleasure." He rolled a pen between his palms. "I understand you recently graduated from college."

She nodded. "I have a degree in early American history."

The motion of the pen between his palms froze and a frown creased his brow. "Unfortunately we don't have much call for historians here at the firm."

"I realize that," she said quickly. "About halfway through my senior year, I realized that although I love history, I wasn't exactly sure what I planned to do with my degree. I toyed with the idea of teaching, then changed my mind."

"And you want to be a legal assistant now?"

"Yes. I was dating a law student and I discovered how much I enjoyed law. You see, we often did our homework together. But rather than register for law school and invest all that time and effort, I decided to work as a legal assistant—sort of get my feet wet and then decide if becoming an attorney is what I want to do. So I went to business college and got a certificate." She said all this in an eager rush. "Your father suggested I come and talk to you," she added, winding down. She opened her purse and produced her certificate for his inspection.

"I see." The pen was in motion again.

"I'm a hard worker."

Damian smiled fleetingly. "I don't doubt that."

"I'll work any hours you wish, even weekends. You can put me on probation if you want." She hadn't meant to reveal how much she wanted the position, but despite her resolve, she couldn't keep the anxiety out of her voice.

"This job means a great deal to you, doesn't it?"

Jessica nodded.

"I think," Damian said casually, "you're still infatuated with my brother."

He spoke as if it had been only a few days since she'd all but thrown herself at Evan. Heat radiated from her cheeks. "I... I don't believe that's a fair statement."

Damian smiled shrewdly. "You've had a crush on Evan for years."

"Perhaps, but that has nothing to do with my applying for a position here." She closed her mouth and collected her composure as best she could. She should have known Damian wouldn't conveniently forget their encounter all those years ago.

"It's true, though, isn't it?" Damian seemed to take delight in teasing her, which infuriated Jessica. She clamped her mouth shut, rather than argue with the man she hoped would employ her. "I was there the day you put kisses all over his rearview mirror, remember?"

Not trusting herself to speak, she nodded.

"I watched you look at him with those big worshipful eyes. I've seen plenty of other women do the same thing since, all gazing at my younger brother as though he were an Adonis."

Jessica's eyes widened at the use of the term. That was exactly the way she'd viewed Evan. A Greek god.

"It's true isn't it, or are you going to deny it?"

Jessica's mouth refused to work. She opened and closed it a number of embarrassing times, not knowing how to respond, or if she should even try.

Cathy Hudson, her best friend, had claimed it wasn't a good idea to apply for work with a family who knew her so well. Jessica was about to concede that Cath was right.

"I did have a schoolgirl crush on your brother at one time," she confessed, "but that was years ago. I haven't seen Evan in…heavens, I don't remember. Certainly not any more often than I've seen you. If you believe my past feelings for Evan would hinder my performance as a legal assistant, then there isn't anything more I can say—other than to thank you for your time."

Damian's smile was slightly off-kilter, his eyes bemused as if, despite himself, he'd admired her little speech. Slowly a look of sadness crossed his face. "Evan's changed, you know. He isn't the man you once knew."

"I'd heard from my mother that he's been unhappy recently." She didn't know the details and hoped Damian would fill in the blanks.

"Do you know why?"

"No."

Damian gave a soft regretful sigh. "I might as well tell you, since you'll find out soon enough yourself. He was in love possibly for the first time in his life, and it didn't work out. I don't know what caused the rift, and neither does anyone else, not that it matters. Unfortunately, though, Evan can't seem to snap out of his depression."

"He must have loved her very much," she whispered, watching Damian. He was genuinely concerned about Evan.

"I'm sure he did." Damian frowned, apparently at a loss as to how to help his brother, then shook his head. "We've ventured far from the subject of your employment, haven't we?"

She straightened and folded her hands in her lap, wondering if Damian would take a chance and hire her. She was a risk, too, fresh out of school, with no job experience.

"You're sure you want to work here?" he asked, studying her with a discerning eye.

"Very much."

Damian didn't immediately respond. His silence made her uncomfortable enough to want to fill it with something, even useless chatter. "I know what you're thinking," she said breathlessly. "In your eyes I'm a love-struck fourteen-year-old, convinced your brother and I are meant for each other." She shook her head. "I don't know what to say to convince you I've grown up, and that nonsense is all behind me, but I have."

"I can see that for myself." A glint of appreciation sparked in his eyes. "As it happens, Jessica, you're in luck, because the firm could use another legal assistant. If you want the job, it's yours."

Jessica resisted vaulting out of the chair and throwing her arms around Damian's neck to thank him. Instead she promised, "I won't let you down."

"You'll be working directly with Evan," he replied, still studying her closely.

"With Evan?"

"Is that a problem?"

"No... No, of course not."

"Just remember one thing. It doesn't matter how many years our parents have been friends. If you don't do your job and do it well, we don't have room for you here."

"I wouldn't expect you to keep me on if I didn't pull my weight," she said, trying hard not to sound defensive.

"Good." He reached for the intercom and glanced at her. "When would you like to start?"

"Now, if you want."

"Perfect. I'll ring Mrs. Sterling. She's Evan's secretary, and she'll show you the ropes."

Jessica stood and extended her hand. "You won't be sorry, I promise you." She pumped his hand enthusiastically until she realized she was overdoing it.

Grinning, Damian walked around to the front of his desk. "If there's anything I can help you with, let me know."

"I will. Thank you, Damian."

She hadn't meant to call him by his first name. Theirs was a professional relationship now, but it *was* difficult to think of him as her boss. A personal bond existed between them, but until this interview Jessica hadn't realized it was there. To her surprise she found she had no such problem regarding Evan.

She and Damian walked out of the office together and down the corridor to a door with Evan's name engraved on a gold plaque.

Damian opened the door for her and allowed her to precede him. Jessica's gaze fell on Evan's secretary. The woman was middle-aged, with sharp, but not unattractive, features. She seemed to breathe efficiency. One look and Jessica was confident this woman could manage Evan's office and the entire law firm if necessary.

"Mrs. Sterling," Damian said, "this is Jessica Kellerman, Evan's new legal assistant. Would you show her around and make her feel at home?"

"Of course."

Damian turned to Jessica. "As I said earlier, come to me if you have any problems."

"Thank you."

"No, Jessica," he said cryptically on his way out, "thank *you*." The door made a small clicking sound as it shut.

Mrs. Sterling rose from her chair. She was a small woman, barely five feet, a stark contrast to tall and slender Jessica. Her salt-and-pepper hair was cropped short, and she wore a no-nonsense straight skirt and light sweater.

"I'll show you where the law library is," Mrs. Sterling said. Jessica glanced toward the closed door, wondering if Evan was in. Apparently not, otherwise

Damian would have made a point of letting his brother know Jessica would be working for him.

The secretary led the way out of the office and down the hall. The library was huge, with row upon row of thick dusty volumes. Long narrow tables with a number of chairs were scattered about the room. Jessica knew she'd be spending the majority of her research time here and was pleased by how pleasant it was. She noticed the faint scent of lemon oil and smiled as she saw various types of potted plants set here and there, including a speckled broad-leaved ivy that stretched across the top of one large bookcase.

"This is very nice."

"Mr. Dryden has worked hard to make sure our work environment is pleasing to the eye," the woman remarked primly.

"Damian's like that," Jessica murmured.

"I was speaking about the younger Mr. Dryden," came the surprised response.

"Oh, of course," Jessica said quickly.

By the end of the first day, Jessica felt as though she'd put in a forty-hour week. She'd been assigned a small desk in the corner of the room and her own phone. Mrs. Sterling seemed to feel it was her duty to keep Jessica occupied with a multitude of tasks which included taking lunch orders, organizing file cabinets and hand-delivering messages throughout the office.

Just when she was about to think she wouldn't even lay eyes on Evan her first day, he breezed into the office, stopping abruptly when he saw her. He was as tall as Damian, at least six-two, with chestnut hair and dark soulful eyes. To Jessica's way of thinking, it wasn't fair that any one man should be so breathtakingly handsome.

"Julia," he whispered, as though he'd stumbled upon a treasure chest. His eyes suffused with delight. "What are you doing here?"

"It's Jessica," she corrected him, refusing to be offended by his failure to remember her name. "I'm here because I'm working for you now."

"Your brother hired Ms. Kellerman as your new legal assistant," Mrs. Sterling explained.

Evan stepped forward, gripping Jessica's hand in his own. "This must be Christmas in July! Why else would Damian present me with such a rare gift?"

"Christmas in July," Jessica repeated, having a difficult time not laughing. What she'd heard about Evan was true, she decided. He was a flirt, but such a pleasant lighthearted one that it didn't seem to matter. She knew he wasn't serious.

"There are several matters here that need your attention," Mrs. Sterling said stiffly from behind Evan.

"I'll be with you in a few minutes," he said.

"I know you will," Mrs. Sterling said. "Just don't leave before these letters are signed, and while we're at it, there are a few items we need to discuss—when you have the time."

"I promise to get to the letters first thing," he said as if he had no interest beyond studying the young woman who stood before him. "Just put everything on my desk and I'll look through it before I leave."

"You won't forget?"

Evan chuckled. "My, my, how you love to mother me."

"Someone has to look after you," his secretary said, her eyes crinkling above a bright smile.

Jessica watched in amazement as Evan charmed the older woman. Mrs. Sterling had been the picture of cool efficiency until Evan walked in the door. The minute he did she turned into a clucking mother hen. Before Jessica had a chance to analyze this reaction, Evan grinned. "You love me, Mary, and you know it."

"It's just that you've been a bit forgetful of late," Mrs. Sterling said with a concerned frown. She reached for a stack of letters and leafed through them. "It doesn't hurt to offer you a little reminder now and then, does it?"

"I suppose not," Evan said and, taking the letters with him, walked into his office as if he hadn't a care in the world.

"Have you been working on the brief for the Porter Corporation?" Mrs. Sterling asked, following on his heels.

"The Porter Corporation," Evan repeated as if he'd never heard the name before. "It's not due anytime soon, is it?"

"Yes, it is," the secretary said, and Jessica heard a hint of panic in her voice. "First thing Friday morning."

"I'll have it ready by then. What day is this, anyway?"

"Mr. Dryden, you've got to start coming into the office before closing time!"

"Don't you fret. I'll have everything ready the way I

always do," he said as he ushered his secretary out the door. He paused when his gaze fell on Jessica and he winked. Then the door closed and Evan disappeared.

Mrs. Sterling shook her head and glanced toward Jessica. "Mr Dryden's been going through some rough times lately," she explained.

"How long has he been without a legal assistant?"

"Quite a while now. He didn't seem to think he'd need one. Damian's cut his workload and, well, things just haven't been the same around here for quite a while."

Jessica was leaving for the day when she happened upon Damian. Looking dignified and businesslike, he was talking to his secretary. A few silver hairs at his temple added a distinguished air. He made a striking figure, and she wondered briefly why he hadn't married. Tagged onto that thought came another. One that took her by surprise. She realized she was *happy* Damian hadn't married.

He must have seen her in his peripheral vision, because he straightened, smiled and walked toward her. "Well, Jessica, how'd your first day go?"

"Really well."

"Mary isn't working you too hard, is she?"

"Oh, no, she's great."

"Mary's one of the best secretaries I've ever worked with. She may be a bit abrupt, but you'll get used to that." He was walking with Jessica now, their steps matching, his hands clasped behind his back. Mary was abrupt perhaps, Jessica mused, but not with Evan.

"I'll always be grateful to you for being willing to take a chance on me," she said conversationally.

Damian's smile was rueful. "You may not be thanking me later. My brother can be a handful, but if there was ever someone who could get him back on the straight and narrow, it's you."

"Me?" she asked, not understanding.

Damian broke eye contact and looked away. "Everybody needs to be looked at with wide worshipful eyes now and then, don't you think?"

"Ah…" Jessica didn't know how to respond. One thing was becoming abundantly clear. Damian hadn't hired her because of her high test scores at business college.

Chapter 2

"You actually got the job?" Cathy Hudson said over the telephone line, her voice raised with astonishment. "You were hired, just like that, by one of the city's most prestigious law firms?"

"It helps to have friends in high places." Jessica was excited about this job, but she felt mildly guilty knowing the only reason she'd been hired was that their families were such good friends. However, Damian had made it plain she'd need to pull her own weight. Jessica was determined to prove herself; she'd be the best legal assistant the firm had ever hired. It was a matter of pride.

"Why is it everything comes so easy for you?" Cathy lamented. "You set your sights on something that would give Norman Vincent Peale second thoughts and—"

"Me? You're the one trying out for a lead in *Guys and Dolls*. Talk about setting your sights high."

"All right, all right," Cathy said with a dramatic sigh, "you've made your point."

"So how did the tryouts go today?"

"I...don't know. It's so hard to tell. I would kill for the part of Adelaide, but then I watch the others, and they're all so good. I came away today thinking it's just a pipe dream. David, the director, is wonderful. Working with him would be one of the highlights of my career, but I don't dare hope I'll get the part."

"I have faith in you. You're a natural, Cath." It was true, her friend had a knack for the dramatic, and that had always made their friendship so interesting.

Cathy laughed softly. "How can I fail, when both you and my mother are convinced I'm destined for stardom? Now, before we get off the subject, how did the interview with Damian go?"

"Really well, I think." Damian had dominated her thoughts all afternoon. He'd changed, she decided, or perhaps she was the one who was different. Whichever, she found herself enthralled by the man. The thought of working with him excited her.

"What about the younger brother?"

"Actually I'll be working directly for Evan."

Cathy must have noticed the hesitation in her voice because she asked, "Does that worry you? What's the matter? Do you think you're going to make an idiot of yourself over him—again?"

So much for Jessica's delicate ego. "No way. I was fourteen years old, for heaven's sake."

After she'd hung up, Jessica slipped a CD into the player, choosing an invigorating medley of jazz hits, and set about fixing her dinner. She whipped together a hot chicken-and-spinach salad and stood barefoot in her kitchen, humming along to the music, her heart singing its own melody.

Later that evening, she relaxed with the paper. Despite her best efforts, her thoughts drifted to Damian. The last thing she wanted was to make a fool of herself over another Dryden.

To the best of her knowledge, the source of which was her mother, Damian wasn't currently involved in a relationship. Joyce Kellerman said that Lois Dryden had complained that her elder son didn't take enough time for fun in his life. What Damian needed, Jessica decided now, was to fall in love with a woman who would take his mind off his work. Someone fun. Someone who would make him laugh and enjoy life. Someone who appreciated him.

An hour later, as she was getting ready for bed, Jessica realized she'd spent most of the evening thinking about Damian. Well, quite understandable, she rationalized. After all, he was head of the firm she was working for.

The following day, Evan didn't show up at the office until well after eleven. As she had previously, Mrs. Sterling fussed over him as though he were the prodigal son the moment he waltzed in the door.

"Good morning, Mr. Dryden." Mrs. Sterling gushed,

nearly leaping from her chair. "It's a beautiful day, isn't it?"

Evan seemed to need time to think about this. "I hadn't noticed, but you're right, it is a gorgeous day," he said as he reached for his mail and leafed through the envelopes.

He was on his way into his office when he noticed Jessica sitting at her desk. She felt his scrutiny and was pleased that she'd dressed carefully, choosing a smart-looking flowered silk dress with a blue jacket. In her heels, she was nearly as tall as he was.

"Good morning, Mr. Dryden," she offered.

"Evan," he insisted. "You can call Damian Mr. Dryden if you insist, but I'm Evan."

"All right. Good morning, Evan,"

"It is a good morning, isn't it?" he asked, giving her a roguish grin. Jessica couldn't help but respond with a smile of her own. She hadn't noticed it so much the day before, but there were definite changes in the Evan she remembered. He was thinner and his smiles didn't quite reach his eyes. Another thing she couldn't help notic-ing was the way everyone walked on eggshells around him. Mrs. Sterling had made a point of letting her know Evan's work load had recently been cut, and Damian had said Evan hadn't yet recovered from a broken rela-tionship. It must have been pretty serious, she mused.

"It's been a long time since we've had a chance to talk, hasn't it?" Evan asked, walking over and sitting on the edge of Jessica's desk.

"A very long time," she agreed, praying with all her

heart he wouldn't resurrect her girlish antics. It'd been embarrassing enough to have Damian do it.

"I think we should make up for lost opportunities, don't you? Tell you what—I'll treat you to lunch." He checked his watch and seemed surprised at the time. "We'll leave in half an hour. That'll give me enough time to clear whatever's on my desk."

"You want to take me to lunch?" Jessica asked. "Today?"

"It's the least I can do," Evan said with a shrug. "I'll have Mary make reservations."

"But—"

"That's an excellent idea," Mrs. Sterling interjected, clearly pleased.

"I… I've only just started work," Jessica said. "I'd enjoy lunch, perhaps in a week or so, after I've settled into the job." The last thing she wanted was to give Damian the impression she was already slacking in her duties.

Evan pressed his thumb to her chin and gazed deeply into her eyes. "No buts, and no arguments. We're going to lunch and you can fill me in on what you've been doing for the last five or six years."

Mrs. Sterling followed Evan into his office, looking inordinately pleased with the turn of events. She returned a few minutes later, casting a delighted look in Jessica's direction as she picked up her phone and called the restaurant to make reservations. Evan chose Henri's, one of Boston's finest, well-known for its elegant dining. It also happened to be a good fifteen-minute drive from the office, which meant they were going to be out for lunch much longer than usual.

"I doubt we'll be back in an hour if we have lunch at Henri's," Jessica felt obliged to say.

"Don't worry about it. You'll make it up another time, I'm sure."

"But this is only my second day. I don't want to give the wrong impression."

"My dear, Mr. Dryden is your boss. If he wants to take a leisurely lunch with you, don't argue. You should be counting your blessings, instead."

"I know but—"

"From what I understand, you two are old family friends," Mrs. Sterling interrupted. "It's only natural for him to want to personally welcome you into the firm."

It seemed the reservation had barely been made when Evan reappeared. "Are you ready?"

Jessica blinked back her surprise. "Yes, of course, if you'll give me just a moment." She finished typing her notes into the computer, stored the information and pushed back her chair.

Evan took her elbow and told his secretary, "We'll be back in a couple of hours."

They were on their way through the corridor leading to the front of the office when Damian appeared. His gaze shifted from Evan to Jessica.

"Jessica and I are on our way out to lunch," Evan explained. "Do you need me for anything?"

"No. You two go on ahead. I'll talk to you later."

Damian nodded, and it was all Jessica could do not to blurt out that this lunch date hadn't been her idea, but there wasn't the opportunity and she doubted it was necessary anyway. Damian must have known she hadn't invited herself out to lunch. Nevertheless, she didn't want him to think ill of her.

"We'll probably be late getting back," Evan said to his brother, guiding Jessica out of the office.

They arrived at the restaurant by taxi and were seated immediately. The ambience was formal, with soft chamber music playing unobtrusively in the background. The waiters, who dressed like diplomats, were attentive, the tables were well spaced, and the meal was served with a good deal of ceremony.

Evan seemed disinclined to talk about himself, asking her a series of questions about school, her friends and activities. He appeared attentive, but she suspected his thoughts were far removed from her and their lunch. At least he didn't dredge up the past and her infatuation with him. She could have kissed him for that.

After their dishes were cleared away, Evan took out a pad and pen. "I'm going to be working on a civil suit that'll demand a fair amount of research," he told Jessica. His eyes were bright with an enthusiasm she hadn't seen before. "The case involves Earl Kress—you might remember reading about him."

"Of course." The unusual details of the case had filled the local news for weeks. The twenty-year-old former athlete was suing the Spring Valley School District for his education.

Jessica wished she'd brought along a pad and pen herself. She listened, enthralled, as Evan explained the details of the suit. It seemed Earl was a gifted athlete and the key figure in three of the school's biggest sports—football, basketball and track. In order for him to participate in these sports he had to maintain a C average. Unfortunately Earl had a learning disability and had never mastered reading skills. Although he'd graduated from high school and been awarded a full scholarship, he was functionally illiterate.

Evan explained that the school district had pressured Earl's teachers, and they'd been forced to give him passing grades. After he graduated from high school, he went on to college, but a severe knee injury suffered during football training camp effectively ended his career. And within the first two months of school, Earl flunked out.

"That's so unfair," Jessica said when Evan finished. If Damian was concerned about his brother, she thought, then offering Evan this groundbreaking case was sure to take his mind off other things. It would give Evan purpose, a reason to come to work in the morning, the necessary incentive to look past his personal problems.

"There've been a number of similar suits filed in other parts of the country," Evan continued. "I'm going to need you to do extensive research on the outcome of the cases previously tried."

"I'll be happy to help in any way I can."

Evan grinned his appreciation. "I knew I could count on you."

So this was the real reason for their lunch. The case clearly meant a good deal to Evan, and consequently to Jessica. She was grateful for the opportunity to prove herself.

By the time they returned to the office, their lunch hour had stretched to three. It seemed everyone in the office was staring at them, and Jessica felt decidedly uncomfortable.

She walked directly to her desk, keeping her face averted when she passed Damian's office. His door was open, and when he saw her walk by he stood up, called her name and then glanced pointedly at his watch. It was all Jessica could do not to tell him it had been a *business* lunch.

Damian had made it painfully clear that he expected her to do her job. He wasn't paying her to romance his brother during three-hour lunches, and Jessica didn't want him to have that impression. She longed to explain, but she'd look ridiculous doing so in front of Evan. The only thing she could do was stay late that evening in an effort to make up for the time spent over lunch.

Although it was after seven when she started out of the office, a number of others were still there. With her sweater draped over her arm, she was on her way down the long corridor when Damian stopped her.

"Jessica."

"Hello, Damian," she said. He was standing just outside his office.

He relaxed, crossed his arms and asked, "How'd your lunch go with my brother?"

"Very well, but..."

"Yes?" he prompted when she didn't immediately finish.

"I want you to know it was a working lunch," she said, rushing the words in her eagerness to explain.

"We discussed the Earl Kress case. I didn't want you to think we'd spent three hours socializing."

"It wouldn't have mattered."

"But it does!" she insisted fervently. "The lawsuit was the reason Evan asked me out. He wasn't interested in renewing an old friendship."

Damian's frown was thoughtful. "Did he seem pleased with the assignment?"

"Very much so," Jessica recalled Mrs. Sterling's saying that "things just haven't been the same around here for quite a while," implying *Evan* hadn't been the same. She wondered if Damian realized the extent of his brother's unhappiness.

Damian grinned; Jessica had the feeling he didn't do that often, which was a shame. The grooves in his cheeks and the sparkle in his gray eyes were very attractive. "I thought he might need a change of pace. Did you two have a chance to talk about old times?"

This was a casual way of asking if she'd noticed the changes in his brother, Jessica guessed. "A little. Evan really was hurt, wasn't he?"

Damian nodded. "Generally he disguises it, but I wondered if you'd detect the changes in him."

"I couldn't help noticing." She'd seen it almost from the first moment. Even though she hadn't seen Evan for years she could see how hard he was struggling to hide his misery. No wonder his parents and brother were so concerned.

Damian glanced at his watch and arched his brows. "It's late. We'll talk again some other time. Good night, Jessica."

"Good night, Damian."

As she waited for a train in the subway station, Jessica at last understood what Damian had meant when he'd told her that everyone needed to be looked at with wide worshipful eyes sometimes. It made perfect sense now that she thought about it. Damian still viewed her as that teenage girl infatuated with his younger brother. If ever there was a time that Evan needed a woman to idolize him, it was now. She'd been hired, not for her legal skills, but to help his brother forget the woman he'd loved and lost. Damian was looking to her to heal Evan's pain.

The following morning around ten, Evan, his smile bright enough to rival the sun, breezed into the office and presented Jessica with a bouquet of a dozen bloodred roses. Their perfume filled the room.

Jessica was speechless. "For me?" The flowers took her completely by surprise. Mrs. Sterling, too, from the look the secretary cast her.

"I need a favor," Evan said, leaning against the edge of her desk, his face scant inches from her own.

"Of course." She was holding the flowers against her like a beauty queen, inhaling their heavenly scent.

Evan reached into his jacket pocket and withdrew a folded sheet of yellow paper. "I need you to do some last-minute research for me."

"Certainly."

"There're some statutes I need you to look up and report back to me on as soon as possible. This stuff is as dry as old bones—I'm sorry about that."

"Don't worry about it." Jessica looked at the items Evan wanted her to research and her heart sank at the number. "How soon do you need this?"

"Yesterday," was his frank reply.

Mrs. Sterling made a small tsk-tsk sound in the background, which made Jessica smile. Evan's eyes twinkled and he whispered, "There's nothing worse than a woman who can't let 'I told you so' pass. Remember that, Jessica."

"I will," she said with a small laugh. "I'd best get started. I'll have the information for you before I leave tonight."

"Good girl."

Mrs. Sterling produced a vase for the roses, and after setting them on the edge of her desk Jessica got down to work. She ensconced herself in the library and kept at her research straight through the lunch hour. She didn't notice the time until it was after three, when her stomach rumbled in protest. Even then she didn't take the time to sit down to eat, but grabbed an apple and munched on it while she continued to search for the required data.

The next time she looked up, the clock on the wall said seven forty-five. She'd heard the others leave, but that seemed like only minutes ago. She stood up and, placing her hand at the base of her spine, arched her stiff back and breathed in deeply.

Her eyes felt tired and her back sore as she carried her paperwork into the office. She stopped, surprised to find the room dark. She flicked on the lights and looked around, certain Evan had left a note for her.

He hadn't.

Picking up one of the roses, she held it to her nose and closed her eyes as she tried to battle down the weariness—and the disappointment.

"Jessica, what are you doing here?"

"Damian." She could ask the same question of him.

"It's nearly eight o'clock."

"I know." She rotated her overworked shoulders. "I guess time got away from me."

"So I see. I had some reading I was catching up on, but I assumed I was here alone. There was no reason for you to stay this late."

She glanced toward Evan's office. "What time did Evan leave?" she asked casually, not wanting him to know how abused she felt.

"A couple of hours ago. Why?"

"He said he needed this information right away." She'd been in a frenzy attempting to finish the task as quickly as possible. She'd assumed he would wait until she'd collected the data he seemed to need so desperately.

"I believe he had a dinner engagement," Damian explained.

"I see," she muttered. In other words, he'd cheerfully abandoned her.

"You sound angry," Damian said.

"I am. I worked through my lunch hour getting this stuff for him." And dinner hour, too, she thought, feeling even angrier. She realized too late that she probably also sounded jealous.

"I'm sorry, Jessica."

Evan's thoughtlessness wasn't Damian's fault and she said so, then asked bluntly, "Is there anything to eat around here?" She blinked back unexpected tears. Hunger always had a strange effect on her emotions, but it was embarrassing, and she tried not to let Damian see.

"You mean you haven't eaten since lunch?"

"Not since breakfast, unless you count an apple, and if I don't eat soon I'm going to cry and you really wouldn't want to witness that." The words rushed out and she felt a sniffle coming on. "Never mind," she muttered, turning away from him. She wiped her nose with her forearm and returned to the library. Several ponderous law volumes were spread open across the tables. She closed them and began lugging them back to the shelves.

"I found a package of soda crackers," Damian said, coming into the room.

"Thanks," she said, ripping away the clear plastic wrapper and sniffling again. "I'm sorry, I don't mean to act like this." She ate a cracker quickly and managed to hold back a sob. "Don't look so concerned. I just needed to eat."

"Let me take you to dinner." Damian lifted a couple of the volumes and replaced them for her.

"That isn't necessary." A second cracker had made its way into her mouth and she was beginning to feel more like herself.

"We owe you that much," Damian countered. "Besides, I'm half-starved myself."

"The least he could have done was waited," Jessica fumed.

Ignoring her comment Damian suggested a popular seafood restaurant nearby.

"He made it sound like it was a matter of life and death, and then he doesn't even bother to tell me he's leaving," she continued to fume. "You're right," she said as Damian cupped her elbow and led her out the door. "Evan *has* changed."

Damian didn't respond to this comment either.

They walked the three blocks to the restaurant. It wasn't too crowded, and they were given immediate seating at a wooden table near one of the windows. Even better, the waitress brought hot bread and chowder no more than a minute after it was ordered. Damian must be a regular here to get such service, Jessica thought, her good mood restored now that her stomach had something warm and filling.

"This is excellent," she said. "Thank you." She sighed in contentment as she spooned up the last of her chowder.

Grinning, he finished his own soup, then reached for another piece of bread.

"What's so funny?" she demanded. How like a man to keep something humorous to himself and then feel superior about it.

"I think I might just have averted a lawsuit. Can't you hear it? 'Woman Sues Boss over Lost Meals.'"

"I'd get a huge settlement." The corners of her mouth twitched with a smile. Her eyes met Damian's and soon their amusement had blossomed into full-blown grins.

He had very nice eyes, Jessica mused. They were a dark gray and revealed his keen intelligence, his sharp insight. She wanted to clear away any lingering misconception he had about her and Evan, but she couldn't think of a way to do it without sounding as if she was jealous of whatever person Evan spent his personal time with.

Jessica wondered what Damian saw when he looked at her. Did he see the woman she'd become, or did he view her as the pesky kid next door who'd adamantly declared that his younger brother was her destiny?

The waitress arrived then with their main courses. Damian had ordered oysters and Jessica baked cod, which was delicious. By the time they'd finished, she felt completely restored.

"I said some things I shouldn't have back at the office," Jessica began, feeling self-conscious now but eager to explain. "You see—"

"You'd worked far longer than necessary and were starving to boot," he interrupted. "Don't worry about it."

"I just wanted to be sure I hadn't provoked you into firing me."

"It'll take more than a demand for food to do that," he assured her, hardly disguising his amusement.

The June sky was dark and overcast and the temperature cooler as they came down the stairs and into the street. "It looks like rain," Damian said. No sooner had he spoken when fat raindrops began to fall. Taking Jessica by the elbow, he raced across the street. Neither had thought to bring an umbrella.

"Here," Damian said, running toward an alcove in front of a bookstore. The business had closed hours earlier, but the covered entrance was a good place to wait

out the cloudburst. Jessica was breathless by the time
they stopped. A chill raced over her and she rubbed her
arms vigorously.

Damian's much larger hands replaced hers, then he
stopped and peeled off his jacket, draping it over her
shoulders.

"Damian, I'm fine," she protested, fearing he'd catch
a chill himself.

"You're shivering."

The warmth of his coat was more welcome than she
cared to admit. No doubt about it, Damian was a gentleman to the very core.

The downpour lasted a good ten minutes. Jessica was
surprised at how quickly the time passed. When the
storm dwindled to a drizzle and eventually stopped, Jessica discovered she was almost sorry. She was talking
books with Damian and discovered they both shared an
interest in murder mysteries. Damian was as well-read
as she was, and they tossed titles and authors' names
back and forth without a pause.

"Did you drive to work this morning?" he asked.

She shook her head. She'd taken the subway.

"I'll give you a lift home, then."

"Really, Damian, that isn't necessary. I don't mind
using public transit."

"*I* mind," he said in a voice that brooked no argument. "It's too late for you to be out on the streets alone."

How sweet of him to worry about her, she thought.
"But I already have enough to thank you for."

"What do you mean?"

"I was just thinking—I seem to be continually in your debt. You've got a heart of gold."

He chuckled. "Hardly, little Jessica."

"You hired me without any real job experience, then you fed me dinner, and now you're driving me home."

"It's the least I can do."

They returned to the office building, walking directly to the underground parking garage. Damian opened the car door for her and she nestled back in the leather seat.

One thing she'd learned during their time together was the fact that Damian was protective of his younger brother, though she doubted Evan appreciated that.

"You're worried about him, aren't you?" she asked, without clarifying her question. Damian knew who she was talking about.

"Yeah," he admitted.

"Evan's the real reason you hired me, isn't he? You think I might be able to help him through this…difficult time." It wasn't a responsibility she welcomed or wanted. She was about to explain that when she noticed the way his mouth quirked into an amused smile.

Instead, she told him sharply, "I'm not a silly fourteen-year-old infatuated with an older man. What I felt for your brother was just a crush. It was over years ago." That was the simple truth.

His shrug was noncommittal.

"Nevertheless," she forged on, "you hired me because of Evan?"

It took Damian a long time to answer. "Sometimes I wonder," he finally said. "Sometimes I wonder."

Chapter 3

Jessica arrived early the following morning, hoping to have an opportunity to thank Damian again for dinner and more importantly to let him know how much she'd enjoyed the time they'd shared. But when she passed his office, the door was closed and his secretary was searching urgently through a file drawer. It didn't look like the time to pop in unannounced.

Not surprisingly, Evan was nowhere to be seen. Mrs. Sterling arrived ten minutes after Jessica, greeting her with a small approving smile, and set about sorting through the mail.

Jessica spent the first part of the morning organizing the material she'd researched the day before and typing up her notes. That way, Evan wouldn't be forced to waste time deciphering her hasty scrawl.

She'd just completed printing out the results when a breathless Evan entered the office. From the look of him, he'd raced all the way up from the parking garage. Briefcase in hand, he marched up to her desk.

"Do you have those notes ready?" he asked, reaching for the file before Jessica had a chance to present it. She stood up, intending to discuss a number of points with him, but he brushed past her and hurried into his office without a word. She would have followed him, but he closed the door.

Jessica was taken aback; unsure of what to do, she looked at Mrs. Sterling. The secretary sighed and shrugged. "Working for Mr. Dryden can be a real trial," she muttered, then grinned and added, "No pun intended."

No sooner had Mrs. Sterling finished chuckling over her own little joke than Evan reappeared, looking composed and confident. He'd removed his raincoat and was leafing casually through the file. He looked over at Jessica and his face relaxed into a broad smile.

"You're an angel," he said, kissing her cheek as he walked past. Jessica had seen him kiss Mrs. Sterling in the same affectionate way.

"I'll be in a meeting with Damian this morning," Evan announced on his way out the door.

As the morning progressed, Jessica found herself wondering exactly what her role in the office was. Although Evan had recently been assigned the Earl Kress case, his workload had been light in the past few months. Now that she'd finished the research project, there was barely enough to keep her busy.

From various bits and pieces, Jessica had learned that Evan's interest in corporate law had waned recently. Surely Damian hadn't hired her expecting miracles! Since he was so closemouthed about Evan's troubles, Jessica wondered if Mrs. Sterling could fill in some details. She didn't want to be obvious about asking, which could prove tricky since the woman was so clearly devoted to her employer.

"That Evan's a real charmer, isn't he?" Jessica began conversationally.

"He always could charm the birds right out the trees," Mrs. Sterling answered proudly.

"He's different now from the way I remember him. More…intense."

Evan's secretary nodded and muttered, "I'd like to shoot that woman."

Jessica's heart leapt with excitement. "What woman?" she asked, hoping to hide her eagerness. She was about to learn what had happened to change Evan so drastically from the man she'd known.

Mrs. Sterling glanced up, as if surprised that Jessica had heard her mumbling. "Oh…it's nothing."

"But it *must* be something. Evan isn't anything like he was a few years back. Oh, he's charming and sweet, but there's an edge to him now. A sharpness, I guess. Something I can't put my finger on." She looked expectantly at the other woman.

"That's true enough," Mrs. Sterling reluctantly conceded.

"You say a woman's responsible for the changes in Evan?"

"Isn't it always a woman?"

"What happened?" Might as well try a more direct approach, Jessica thought. Tact wasn't getting her anywhere.

"It's a pity, a real pity."

"Yes, Evan just isn't the same," Jessica said, hoping to encourage the other woman to continue.

"It shouldn't come as any surprise, really. Yet it does, Mr. Dryden being the charmer he is. Plain and simple, he fell in love with someone who didn't feel the same way about him." Then she clamped her mouth closed as though she'd already said far more than she should—far more than was circumspect for a secretary to say about her boss.

But this much she already knew. What she was looking for were the particulars. Who was this woman who'd hurt Evan so badly? Her back stiffened at the thought of someone rejecting him. The man she'd worshiped from afar during her tumultuous teenage years. Whoever this woman was, Jessica decided, she was a fool.

About eleven Evan walked into the office. He smiled as he strolled past Mrs. Sterling's desk to hers. "The research you did was wonderful, Jessica. Thank you."

His appreciation caught her off guard. She wondered if Damian had said something to him and was momentarily speechless.

"I appreciate the effort that went into your report," he continued. "I'm very pleased by the quality of your work."

"I… I was happy to do it. That's my…my job." The words stumbled off the end of her tongue. Jessica was amazed that his praise could fluster her so. She was embarrassed now by the way she'd overreacted last night when she'd learned he'd left the office. It was her own fault for not taking time to eat lunch. Evan's disappearance wouldn't have bothered her in the least if she had....

"Damian said you were here till almost eight."

So Damian *had* mentioned that. "As I said earlier, I was only doing my job."

"Mom and Dad are having a barbecue this weekend," Evan continued, "Saturday, around four. I'd like you to attend it with me."

His invitation threw her. She wasn't sure what to say. Although she hadn't had a lot of work experience, she knew that dating the boss could lead to problems.

"This shouldn't be a difficult decision," Evan said, grinning.

His pride had already suffered one blow, and Jessica discovered she was unwilling to deliver a second, no matter how slight. "I'd enjoy that very much," she said. "Thank you for thinking of me."

He smiled affectionately. "You always were a sweet thing."

As a teenager, Jessica's daydreams had been filled with such scenarios. She'd close her eyes and pretend Evan had asked her out. Now her dream had come true, but Jessica was left wishing it had been Damian issuing the invitation, instead of his brother.

"I'll pick you up. You are living in the city, aren't you?"

Jessica nodded. "Wouldn't it be simpler if we met

at the party? As it happens, I'm spending the weekend with my parents, and I can walk over with them."

Evan seemed a bit surprised by her suggestion. "You're sure?"

"Positive."

"Then that'll be fine. I'll look forward to seeing you there."

There'd been a time in her life when she would have gladly walked across a bed of hot coals to attend a party with Evan. Any party. Anywhere. Hadn't Damian been counting on that when he hired her—even if he claimed to know she was long over her crush?

"The festivity's in honor of some dignitary," Evan went on. "Mom's worked herself into a tizzy for the event. I can guarantee this will be the most elaborate barbecue Boston has ever seen. The last I heard, Mom hired a country-and-western band."

"It sounds like fun."

"Considering all the effort that's going into it, I'm sure it will be. You can do the two-step, can't you, sweet Jessica?"

"Of course." How easy it was to stretch the truth. In fact, she'd only done the two-step once or twice before. "Well, I'm pretty rusty," she amended.

"Me, too. We'll leave the fancy footwork to Damian."

Damian, she thought with a sigh. There was definitely something wrong with her, something psychological, something rooted deep in her childhood, she guessed, if she could agree to date one brother while longing for the other.

The hours flew by and before Jessica knew it, the

workday had come to an end. Mrs. Sterling had just
stepped out of the office when Damian strolled casually in.

"Evan's left for the day," Jessica said, a little flustered to find him standing in front of her desk. Especially since she'd again been thinking how much she'd
have preferred to attend the family barbecue with *him*.

"I'm not here to see my brother."

"Mrs. Sterling will be right back."

"I came to see you," Damian explained, his eyes dark
and intense as they settled on her.

Jessica tensed. Did he have some complaint with
her work?

"Don't look so worried. I came to tell you my parents are holding a party this weekend. A barbecue."

"Yes, I know. Evan mentioned it earlier."

Jessica swore Damian's eyes brightened with interest. He crossed his arms and leaned against her desk.
"What did he say about it?"

"Not much. Apparently it's in honor of some dignitary."

"I see." He hesitated as if he was unsure, which Jessica knew was completely out of character for Damian.
"I was wondering…" he began, then straightened and
buried his hands deep in his pants pockets. "Would you
like to come to the party with me?"

Her shoulders sagged as she opened her mouth to
explain that Evan had already invited her, but before
she could respond, Damian added, "I realize it's short
notice, but I didn't hear the details myself until this
morning." A hint of a smile turned up the corners of

his mouth. "Mother phoned, wanting to be sure I'd be there. She seems to be taking her duties very seriously."

"Ah…"

"There's a problem," he guessed.

She nodded glumly. "Evan's already invited me to the party—as his date." She wanted to tell Damian she'd much prefer to attend with him, but she couldn't. "I'm sorry," she added.

"He did?" Instead of looking displeased at this turn of events, Damian sounded positively delighted. "Don't be sorry."

His reaction annoyed her.

"It isn't like a real date," she said, wanting to make that clear. "At least, that wasn't the impression Evan gave me. The invitation was his way of thanking me for working so hard on the research project."

"My brother wouldn't invite you if he wasn't interested in your company," Damian insisted. "Besides, I wouldn't want my brother to think I was cutting in on his territory."

His territory.

Damian must have guessed her feelings, because he said, "Evan asked you first."

He was right about that, she thought, but little else.

Damian turned away, and it suddenly became important to Jessica to explain herself. "I don't think you should put much stock in Evan's invitation. It really *was* just a way of thanking me."

"It's a start, though, don't you think?" Damian said over his shoulder. "A good start, at that." He left her then before she could say anything more.

Jessica was upset, and it wasn't until she got home
that she figured out why. Damian hadn't invited her to
the party out of any real desire for her company. He'd
assumed that Evan hadn't asked her—and he was looking for an opportunity to throw her and his brother together socially.

Jessica arrived at her parents' house early Saturday
afternoon, after spending all morning shopping for the
perfect outfit. Cathy had come along to offer encouragement and advice.

She might not be attending the barbecue with Damian, but when she showed up looking like a movie
star, he'd wish she was. This was her mission, plain
and simple.

Evan had casually mentioned the country-and-western band, but he'd also said the barbecue was in honor
of some dignitary. These somewhat contradictory snip-
pets of information served to confuse her about how to
dress. Nothing in her closet seemed suitable, but then
little in the shops did, either.

In one outfit she resembled Annie Oakley, and in another Jackie Kennedy. There didn't seem to be much of
a middle ground—until she found a long denim skirt, a
red shirt decorated with rainbow-colored fringe sewn
about the yoke and white cowboy boots. A white silk
scarf tied around her neck lent a touch of elegance.

Her mother's eyes widened with approval when Jessica modeled the outfit. "I wish now I'd gone shopping,
too, and bought something new myself. You look great."

"Thanks." Her mother's praise gave Jessica confidence. Cathy, who tended to dress like a character in a sci-fi movie, had also said she looked great, but Jessica wasn't sure she trusted her friend's fashion sense.

"It was so sweet of Evan to include you," Joyce Kellerman went on to say. "Not that I'm surprised, his being your boss and all. Life is certainly full of little twists and turns, isn't it?

"It sure is," Jessica said without elaborating.

"I'm thrilled that you're working with Evan."

"He's a nice person."

"He's *wonderful*. It's always been my dream, I know it's silly, but well, we're such good friends with the Drydens... I've hoped you'd grow up to marry one of Lois's boys."

"Whatever you do," Jessica said quickly, "don't say that in front of Damian or Evan."

"Why not, dear?"

"Mom, it'd embarrass me to death!"

"But you were so keen on Evan a few years back, and I thought... I hoped..."

"Mother, I was only fourteen!" Her old infatuation with Evan was turning into the proverbial albatross around her neck—thanks to Damian and her mother. If it wasn't for them, the whole thing would have been forgotten by now.

"You'll make a beautiful bride," her mother said, adding the finishing touches to her own outfit. Suddenly she changed the subject. "Lois has worried herself sick over this silly barbecue."

"But why?" Mrs. Dryden had thrown a hundred parties more elaborate than this.

Her mother sat on the bed and leaned back on her hands. "I don't suppose there's any reason to keep it a secret. Walter's been approached about running for the Senate."

Walter Dryden had been active in community affairs for years. Although he'd never held public office, he'd often managed the successful campaigns of others. He'd taken an early retirement from the law firm, and, from what Jessica understood, had grown restless with inactivity. Running for office would doubtless come as a welcome challenge.

"Has he decided he's going to run?"

"Your father and I think so. He hasn't declared his candidacy yet, but we're confident he will. He's testing the waters with this barbecue tonight. Several people from the political arena will be present. This is probably the most important party of Lois's marriage. Little wonder she's a nervous wreck."

Even before Jessica and her parents arrived for the barbecue, the pungent smells of tomato sauce, spices and roasting meat mingled with the afternoon sunshine and drifted over the fence.

As they were greeted at the front door, Jessica was reminded, by the way Lois hugged her mother, what very good friends the two women were. Their friendship had spanned twenty years, and they were like sisters. Jessica felt the same way about Cathy. They'd met in college, where they'd been roommates for three years.

When Jessica didn't immediately see Evan or Damian, she wandered outside. A series of round tables decorated in red-checked tablecloths were scattered across the lush expanse of lawn. The day was perfect, warm but not hot, and the sky was cloudless. A soft breeze ruffled the leaves of the large shade trees that lined the property. This was New England summer at its best. The smells of food were heavenly, too, reminding her how hungry she was. Shopping and preparing for the party hadn't left time for lunch.

Several dozen guests had arrived, and Jessica scanned the crowd. She spotted Evan standing next to a lovely blonde in a chic white fringed dress with a turquoise belt and silver buckle. Jessica didn't recognize the woman, and a few discreet inquiries got her nowhere. She became all the more curious. She attempted to make her way to Evan, since she was officially his date, but in actuality, she was seeking an introduction to the lovely blonde. Perhaps this was Evan's new romantic interest, she thought hopefully. But before she could reach Evan, she was waylaid by some family friends. Most of the Drydens' guests were older people, established names Jessica had known or heard all her life.

"Hello, Jessica," Damian said from behind her. She turned to find him in the sort of suit he wore at the office. He'd made an attempt to dress to the theme with a black Stetson, which, Jessica thought, looked entirely out of place on his very Bostonian head.

His eyes glimmered with appreciation. "You look—" he hesitated as though he didn't know what to say "—good."

Jessica wagered that it wasn't often Damian was at a loss for words. It lifted her spirits considerably.

"I imagine you're wondering who that blonde is, the one draping herself all over Evan," he suggested casually.

Jessica pretended she was, although she couldn't help being grateful to this unknown woman for keeping Evan occupied. Otherwise he might feel obliged to pay attention to her, and she'd much rather spend her time with Damian.

"Who is she?" Jessica asked, playing his game.

"Do I detect a small hint of jealousy?"

"Of course not." The question irritated her.

"That's Romilda Sidonie."

"Who?"

"The European dignitary's daughter."

That explained it. Naturally Evan considered it his duty to make Romilda feel welcome. Jessica was pleased to see him apparently enjoying himself.

"Would you like me to introduce you?" Damian asked.

"No," Jessica said, noticing Evan and Romilda moving toward the dance area. "Evan's having a good time. I don't see any reason to interrupt him."

"You're his date."

"But only because you prompted him into asking me."

Damian's eyes narrowed. "What makes you say that?"

"I'm not completely naive, you know. I think the reason you came into my office to invite me was that you didn't think Evan had—you wanted to make sure the two of us were together in a social situation so you could see what happened. Am I right?"

He joined his hands behind his back and took two small steps away, then turned to face her again. She saw a hint of a smile in his eyes. "If you're right—though I'm not saying you are—I'd never admit it."

"You must wreak havoc on a jury."

"That's what my clients pay me for."

Jessica looked toward the dance area again and couldn't see Evan and the European woman. When she glanced over at the picnic area, she found the pair sitting at a table beneath a large elm tree munching on barbecue sandwiches.

"She's lovely," Jessica murmured, watching the couple. "No wonder Evan's forgotten me."

"Romilda may be lovely, but so are you," Damian returned quickly, then looked as if he regretted speaking.

"Thank you."

"I shouldn't have said that."

"Why not? That makes me think you didn't mean it."

"I shouldn't be the one saying such things to you," Damian replied. "You're Evan's date."

"He seems to have forgotten, which is just as well. I'd rather spend my time with you."

"With me?" Damian repeated, sounding appalled by the mere suggestion. "Have you eaten?" he asked hurriedly. They were standing next to the dessert table. It was laden with an enormous chocolate cake decorated with fresh strawberries, a lemon torte that would have tempted a saint and a fresh blueberry cobbler, which Jessica knew from years past was the caterer's specialty.

"I'm not hungry just yet," she said, thinking Damian might have used her desire to eat as an excuse to squire her away to one of the tables and conveniently leave her.

Damian eyed her speculatively. "You're sure about

that? I'd hate to see a repeat of what happened the other night."

"Well, yes, I guess I will have a bite…but may I sit with you?"

"If you insist."

She did. Damian handed her a plate. Together they walked along the buffet table. Jessica helped herself to potato salad, baked beans and a generous rack of spareribs.

The band started to play a popular tune, and her foot tapping to the beat, Jessica enjoyed the culinary feast. She was content to sit on the sidelines. Evan seemed to have forgotten her, but far from being offended, she felt only a sense of relief.

Damian's invitation to dance came as a surprise. "Why do you want to dance with me?" she asked. She had a sneaking suspicion it somehow involved his brother.

"Do I need a reason?"

Jessica hesitated, then nodded. "If you're thinking it's a way to get Evan to notice me, then I'd rather sit out."

"What if I said it was because I wanted to see how you felt in my arms?"

Her heart gave a flutter. "Then I'd agree." She met his gaze directly. "So, what's it to be, Damian?"

He took a long time deciding, much longer than should have been necessary. Slowly he pushed back his chair and stood. "Why don't we find out together," he suggested, leading her by the hand toward the farthest reaches of the dance area.

The party was in full swing by now, with a good

number of couples two-stepping around the area. When several old family friends stopped to chat with Jessica and Damian as they made their way toward the other dancers, Jessica could sense Damian's impatience.

They reached the outskirts of the crowd, and Damian turned Jessica in his arms. They fit together nicely, thigh to thigh, hip to hip. Damian was an excellent dancer, his steps easy to follow, his movements smooth and assured. He held her loosely about the waist and gazed down at her as if they'd been dancing together all their lives.

"You're good at this." Her surprise must have been obvious, because he threw back his head and laughed. It was the first time she could ever remember hearing Damian really laugh.

"That amazes you, doesn't it?" he said.

"Yes." It was pointless to deny it. She was discovering that Damian was full of surprises. Just then Jessica felt someone brush against her. She turned to see Evan, partnered with the dignitary's daughter.

"Well, well, if it isn't Damian and Jessica." Evan said with a smile, not sounding jealous in the least.

It hadn't taken long to attract Evan's attention, and Jessica groaned inwardly, wondering if Damian had planned it this way.

"You haven't met Romilda, have you?" Evan murmured. Without waiting for a response, he made the introductions.

Jessica could see that the blonde had fallen under Evan's spell, just like most women did when he'd decided to charm them. His magnetism was lethal. Jessica nearly felt sorry for the unsuspecting woman. Evan did have a bit of a reputation as a playboy.

The two couples moved off to get something to drink. They were making small talk and sipping punch when Damian suddenly asked Romilda to dance. The woman glanced anxiously at Evan, obviously reluctant to leave him. Jessica smiled softly to herself, recognizing Damian's ploy. He'd all but thrown her and Evan together.

Damian and Romilda joined the throng of dancers. "It's a wonderful party," Jessica said to Evan. "I've been having a good time."

"Glad to hear it," Evan commented distractedly, his eyes following the other couple. "Shall we?" he asked, holding out his hand to her.

It became apparent as they moved into the dancing area that Evan was more interested in keeping an eye on Romilda than dancing with Jessica. She and Evan made polite conversation, but his attention wandered as often as her own. The dance couldn't end soon enough for either of them.

When it did, she was grateful Damian and Romilda were on the far side of the dance area, because she needed time and space to put order to her thoughts. When the number ended, Evan was coralled by an older couple who wanted to talk to him privately. He cast Jessica an apologetic look and moved away.

She strolled to the far reaches of the property, near the fence that bordered her parents' home. A white footbridge spanned a good-size pond. She stood in the middle of the bridge, dropping small rocks into the still water and watching the ripples radiate to the shore one after another.

Thus absorbed, she didn't hear Damian approach and was startled to hear him speak. "I wondered if I'd find you here," he said.

"I used to come here a lot when I was growing up," Jessica admitted. "I guess you could have charged me with trespassing."

"Not too likely."

"I know, that's why I used to come. It was so peaceful. So safe." A duck glided past, disturbing the water in the pond, and Jessica wished she'd thought to bring some bread crumbs. The ducks had often been beneficiaries of her trips here.

Damian was silent for a moment, then he said, "You're discouraged, aren't you?"

"About what?"

"It's over, you know," Damian assured her softly. "It was over a long time ago—more than six months now. I thought Evan would get over her, but I was wrong."

Oh, dear, Jessica thought. Apparently Damian believed she was here at the pond brooding about Evan, when in fact nothing could have been farther from the truth. She'd been standing on the bridge thinking about her relationship with Damian.

"Who was she?" Jessica was still curious.

"Someone he met on a beach. No name the family had ever heard of before, not that it mattered. Mary Jo Summerhill."

"What happened?"

"I don't think anyone really knows for sure. What-

ever it was devastated Evan. He hasn't been the same
since. My brother isn't one to burden others with his
problems. He's like that duck down there on the pond—
everything seems to roll off him like water. He'd been
in and out of a dozen relationships, and I assumed he
was never going to really fall for any woman, but I
was wrong."

"You haven't a clue what happened between him
and Mary Jo?"

"No. He changed abruptly after the breakup, started
working odd hours. But his heart clearly wasn't in it,
so I cut back his work load. That helped for a time, but
now I'm not sure it was the right thing to do. I've never
seen him more miserable."

"Have you tried to talk to him?"

"A dozen times," Damian admitted, "but it hasn't
helped. If anything, he's resented my prying. This broken relationship seems to have cut him more deeply than
he's willing to admit."

"He'll get over her," Jessica said reassuringly. "It
just takes time."

"I thought so, too." Damian shrugged. "But now I
wonder. It's been more than six months." He paused,
gazing down at the water. "He needs you, Jessica. You
might be the only one able to reach him."

"Me?"

"I knew the minute Dad mentioned you were coming in to apply for a job that you could well be the answer to our prayers." She started to say something, but
Damian wouldn't let her. "You're just going to need a
lot of patience."

Jessica sighed in frustration. "If I'm going to need patience, it's with *you*. You and your family seem to think I'm still a kid with a crush on Evan."

Damian's eyes darkened. "All right, all right, I didn't mean to offend you. You're old enough to make up your own mind."

"Thank you for that," she said. Turning away from him, she rested her hands on the railing and stared into the serene waters below. "I remember once when I was about six coming to this bridge and crying my eyes out," she murmured.

"What hurt you so badly then?"

"You," she said, turning and jabbing a finger at his chest.

"Me?" Jessica had never seen such an expression of outraged innocence. "What did I do?" Damian demanded.

"Your father was taking you and Evan to the roller coaster at Cannon Beach. My dad was out of town on business, and our mothers were taking the shopping cure. They weren't keen on having to drag me along, and I can't remember who, but one of them suggested I go to the carnival with you and Evan."

"And I didn't want you with us," Damian finished for her.

"Not that I blame you. No fifteen-year-old wants a six-year-old girl tagging along."

Damian chuckled. "Times change, don't they?"

Her mother had said the same thing earlier. *Indeed, times do change.*

To Jessica's astonishment, Damian reached for

her hand. He linked their fingers and tugged her off the bridge. "Where are we going?" she protested. He looked at her in surprise, as though she hadn't already guessed. "Where else? The beach. From what I understand the same roller coaster is still running. The party here is starting to wind down, and I don't think we'll be missed, do you?"

She couldn't help but agree.

Chapter 4

Carrying a sticky ball of pink cotton candy in one hand and a purple stuffed elephant under the other, Jessica strolled leisurely with Damian down the long pier. The tinny music of the merry-go-round played behind them, mingling with children's laughter. The scent of the bay and fresh popcorn swirled around them like smoke from a cooling fire. The night was perfect. The sun had set, and clusters of bright stars blinked approvingly down on them.

"I don't think I've ever enjoyed myself more," Jessica said to Damian. She tipped the cotton-candy cone toward him and he helped himself to a handful. Taking another bite herself, she savored the way the sugary sweetness melted on her tongue.

"We still haven't gone on the roller coaster," Damian reminded her.

"That's because you spent all that time trying to win that silly stuffed elephant." She hugged it against her, belying her words.

"Are you game?" Damian asked, looking toward the huge steel structure.

Jessica hedged. "I... I don't know if that's such a good idea after all the junk we've eaten."

"Trust me." He looped his arm through hers and pulled her along, not giving her a chance to protest.

"Great, first you fill me up with popcorn and cotton candy, then you insist on dragging me onto one of the biggest roller coasters in the country. That's not smart, Damian, not smart at all."

The crowds were thicker than ever, and Damian reached for her hand as he led her toward the ride. The line was long, and the wait was sure to be at least thirty minutes. A list of possible arguments crowded Jessica's mind, but she knew it wouldn't do any good. The determined set of Damian's jaw told her that much.

"What am I supposed to do with the elephant?" she asked, clinging to it tightly, as they edged closer.

"Hold it."

"If I'm holding the elephant, who's going to hold me?"

"I will," he assured her calmly. "Stop looking so worried."

"I should tell you, Damian Dryden, the last time I rode on this thing I had a near-death experience. I don't suppose you know when this ride had a safety inspection."

"Thursday."

"You don't *know* that!"

He laughed, seeming to enjoy her unease. "True, but it sounded good. Listen, this roller coaster has been running for twenty years without a single mishap. Well, there was that one time…"

"Damian!"

"I was joking."

"Don't tease," Jessica muttered furiously. She flattened her palm against her stomach and sighed loudly. "My stomach doesn't feel right."

"You won't be sick."

"How can you be sure?"

"Experience. Anticipation's the worst part. The ride itself is fun. The only problem is that it doesn't last long enough. The whole thing is over in no time."

For all her complaining, as the minutes passed, Jessica found herself beginning to anticipate their turn. At last the silver cars came to an abrupt halt right in front of them.

"Just promise me you won't fling your arms up in the air in that bizarre descent ritual," Jessica murmured as the bar fell into place, securing them in the seat.

"I wouldn't dream of it," Damian said, "not when I promised to hold on to you."

Jessica colored slightly, but didn't respond. She dared not look down. Heights were something she generally avoided, which meant she was trapped into closing her eyes. The stuffed elephant was cradled in her arms, much the same way Damian was cradling her.

The cars slowly made their ascent, chugging up the steep incline, making a straining noise as if the weight was too much to bear. The line of cars topped the peak and started its rapid descent. A scream of excitement froze in her throat as they plummeted downward. Damian's arm tightened around her shoulders. Her free hand gripped his, her nails digging into his fingers, but if she was hurting him, he gave no indication. Just when it seemed they were about to break the sound barrier, they started up another steep grade, which slowed the momentum, but once they reached the top they were cast on a crazy twisting, turning journey that left her stomach far behind. Her eyes were closed so tightly her face ached.

When at last they rolled to a halt, Jessica's shoulders surged forward, righted and then sagged with a twinge of disappointment as she realized the ride was over.

"Well?" Damian asked, taking her hand to help her climb out of the cramped car. "Did you or did you not have fun?"

Her legs felt a little shaky once she started walking. "Give me a minute—I don't know what I'm feeling." Confessing he'd been right was too much to ask.

Damian laughed. "Admit it. Don't be shy. It was fun, wasn't it?"

"Yes," Jessica said with ill grace.

Damian laughed again and tucked his arm around her waist. His action seemed so natural, especially since it was evident that her knees had yet to right themselves.

Although his touch was automatic, it had a curious effect on Jessica. She enjoyed being linked with Damian, enjoyed having his body close to hers. She'd experienced it while they were dancing, too.

"You ready to head back?" Damian asked as they neared the brightly lit arched entryway to Cannon Beach.

She agreed with a nod, but in fact she didn't want the night to end. Their time together had been perfect. Perhaps now Damian would understand that it was *his* company she sought and not his brother's. Perhaps now he'd view her as a woman and not the pesky girl next door.

And maybe Evan's obvious attraction to Romilda would blossom into something more, and the Drydens would stop looking to Jessica for solutions. She sincerely hoped that was the case. A man always enjoyed a challenge, and the dignitary's daughter might be just the thing Evan needed.

Damian and Jessica walked along the sawdust-covered ground of the parking lot until they reached his car. The lights from the carnival lit up the night sky, and the sounds droned on behind her.

"I had a marvelous time," she told Damian as he started the engine.

"Me, too," he said. "It's been years since I've been to Cannon Beach. Years since—" He stopped abruptly.

Jessica was reminded of what she'd heard about Damian's working too hard and not taking time to enjoy life. It felt good to know that Damian had enjoyed her company. The memory of his laughter produced a sudden smile. He didn't laugh often enough, and when he did she felt as if she'd been rewarded with a priceless gift.

Damian drove Jessica to her apartment building. It was after eleven by then, but she was keyed up with excitement. Somehow she felt it would all end when Damian left, and she wasn't ready to let that happen.

"Do you want to come up?" she asked, not really expecting he would, hoping she could change his mind.

He glanced her way as though judging the sincerity of her offer. "All right."

"I'll put on a pot of coffee, and you can gloat over how much I enjoyed the roller coaster."

"I'll gloat, coffee or not." He found a parking spot on the street, got out of the car and then went around to open her door. A true gentleman, she thought not for the first time.

Laughing and joking they strolled toward her building. The doorman held the door for them and smiled at Jessica and the purple elephant.

The laughing and teasing continued as they stepped into the elevator for the ride up to the tenth floor. The doors glided shut and Jessica sagged against the mirrored wall in mock exhaustion.

"You sure you don't want to close your eyes?" he said.

"Why?"

"This elevator is moving at death-defying speeds. Who knows the last time it was checked for safety."

"Thursday," came her glib reply.

Damian laughed delightedly.

"I don't know," she teased. "You might be right."

Jokingly she squinted her eyes closed, but when she did, Damian kissed her.

It took Jessica a moment to realize what had happened. Damian had actually kissed her. It was a simple, uncomplicated kiss, the kind a brother gives a sister. One pair of lips touching another.

Only it didn't *feel* simple.

If anything, it left her longing for much, much more. Dumbstruck, she blinked up at him, not knowing how to respond.

"Don't look so shocked," Damian muttered.

"I..." She closed her mouth to stop herself from asking him to kiss her again.

"It was just a kiss."

"I know," she muttered. She realized he regretted the impulse and wished she knew of some way to tell him how thoroughly she'd enjoyed it. But before she could find the words, the elevator stopped.

Jessica led the way to her apartment and unlocked the door. Turning on the light, she moved into the cheery yellow kitchen and, as was her habit, flipped the switch to her answering machine. Cathy Hudson's voice greeted her.

"Jess. Hi, it's me. I haven't heard from you in days, and of course I want to know how the barbecue went with Lover Boy today. Give me a call when you can."

"So your friend knows about Evan?" Damian asked casually, making himself comfortable at her round oak table. He leafed through a newsmagazine she'd been reading that morning.

"I might have mentioned him, but certainly not as Lover Boy, if that's what you're asking."

"That's not what she said."

"She's teasing," Jessica insisted. She hadn't talked to her friend about her new feelings for Damian and was sorry now, because Cathy, like everyone else, it seemed, was intensely curious about the relationship between Jessica and Evan. "I made the mistake of telling her I once had a crush on Evan and she assumed... Well, you just heard." Jessica took out the coffee canister and poured some grounds into the paper filter. The rich coffee aroma filled the room. "This will only take a minute," she promised.

"Listen, don't bother. It's later than I realized."

"You're sure?" Jessica said, disappointed.

"Positive." He set aside the magazine and stood. Pausing in front of her, he drew his hand against the side of her face. "Thank you for a wonderful day, Jessica."

"Thank *you*," she whispered back.

The apartment seemed unnaturally empty when Damian was gone. She'd hoped he'd kiss her again before he left. He'd been tempted, she could see it in his eyes, but he'd resisted, apparently wanting to keep an emotional distance from her.

Jessica wasn't at all tired and, needing to talk, dialed her friend's number.

A groggy Cathy answered on the fourth ring.

"I didn't wake you, did I?" Jessica said with a giggle, delighted to pay back her friend for all the times Cathy had phoned her in the middle of the night.

"From the dead. What are you doing calling so late

and sounding so damned cheerful? There should be a law against that. Let me guess. You were with Evan."

"No! Damian and I went to the—"

"Damian? You're dating Evan's brother?" Cathy sounded wide-awake now and interested. Very interested.

"I know in that silly romantic heart of yours you figured once I was working with Evan, all the unrequited love I'd stored up years ago would suddenly blossom."

"Those were my thoughts exactly," Cathy said.

"Cathy, listen to me. Evan Dryden is a terrific guy, but he isn't the man for me."

"How can you be so sure?"

"Because…well, because I just am." Even now it was difficult to talk about her feelings for Damian. She wasn't sure how to describe them. "For one thing, Evan's in no emotional shape to get involved in another romance, which is fine by me."

"What happened?" Cathy demanded. "I thought he asked you to his family's barbecue."

"He did, but only because Damian prompted him. By the time I arrived he'd met a lovely European woman and the two were inseparable."

"How rude!"

If she'd had her heart set on Evan it would have been devastating, but she didn't, and as a consequence she'd spent a glorious night in Damian's company. She wouldn't have traded the evening for anything. "No, not at all," she said.

"You aren't disappointed?"

Apparently Cathy wasn't as awake as Jessica had

believed. "Not in the least. Damian and I drove out to Cannon Beach and rode the roller coaster."

"You? The original wimp on that monster ride? You didn't really, did you?"

"Yes, I did," she announced proudly, "and it was fabulous." She spent the next few minutes relaying the highlights of the evening—Damian's winning the stuffed elephant for her and their walking along the pier and sharing cotton candy. When she finished there was a short silence.

"Hmm," said Cathy thoughtfully. "This could be *very* interesting."

Jessica arrived bright and early at the office Monday morning. Evan had apparently been to work at some point during the weekend, for he'd left her a list of instructions. His notes included a series of laws he needed her to research. Jessica got to the task right away.

Damian found her in the library some time later. "So you *are* here," he said, sounding surprised. "Mrs. Sterling didn't think you'd come in for the day. I phoned your apartment and got the answering machine."

Jessica straightened in her chair and arched her back, hoping to relieve the tension in her tired muscles. A glance at her watch told her it was nearly eleven. She'd been so involved in her research she hadn't noticed the time.

"I've been in here all morning," she explained, pinching the bridge of her nose. The words were beginning to blur in front of her eyes. Some of the reading was dull, but there were several cases she found intriguing.

Damian left and returned a moment later with a steaming cup of coffee. "Here," he said, handing it to her. "Take a break before you go blind."

"Has Evan shown up yet?" The coffee tasted like ambrosia.

Damian sighed. "Not yet. But Evan comes and goes at will, or at least he has for the past several months."

"Well, he left me some work to do, so he must have been in yesterday." She paused. "What about him and Romilda?" She sincerely hoped those two were enthralled with each other.

"It's too soon to tell, but maybe there's some hope there." Good. Damian sounded as if he really meant it.

"I want Evan to be happy," she said, not exactly sure why it was important Damian know that.

"Exactly." Damian smiled and got up to walk over to the polished bookcase. He pulled down a well-used volume. "Take some advice," he said tucking the book under his arm.

"Sure."

"Don't skip lunch."

"I won't," she promised.

He left then and Jessica smiled and closed her eyes. After a moment she returned to her research. A long time passed before her smile faded.

As promised, Jessica took her lunch hour and returned to find Evan searching for her. He sat down next to her in the library and reviewed her notes, asked a series of intelligent questions and made comments every now and then about her progress. Several times he praised her efforts. He made a few notations himself, and they spent the better part of an hour discussing different aspects of the Earl Kress case.

After Evan left, Jessica was exhilarated. Damian had revealed a keen insight into his brother's personality by assigning Evan to this important case. Representing Earl Kress had given Evan the challenge he needed; had given him a purpose, a cause. Evan was no slouch. He was dynamic, sharp and dedicated to representing this former athlete to the best of his ability and to the full extent of the law.

Several hours of research remained, and although it was late, Jessica decided to trudge on until she was finished.

"It's six o'clock and time for you to go home," Damian said from behind her in the tone she recognized. It was the one he used when he wouldn't listen to a word of argument. The kind that swayed juries.

"I'll be finished in a bit."

"You're finished now."

"Damian."

"Don't argue with me, Jessica. It won't do any good."

She closed the book she was reading and stood up. Every small movement of her lithe body spelled reluctance.

"Did you take time for lunch?"

"You're beginning to sound like my guardian!"

"I see you didn't eat, otherwise you wouldn't be snapping at me."

"I did so—and I'm not snapping!"

"That does it!"

Was he about to fire her for insubordination? Jessica wondered. She stared up at him, wondering what would happen next.

"We're going to dinner," he muttered.

"Dinner! But Damian, you've already—"

"Pizza," he said, "the deep-dish variety. There's a small Italian restaurant around the corner. I swear it's one of the best-kept secrets in Boston."

"Pizza," Jessica repeated slowly and her stomach growled in anticipation. "Well, if you insist, and it seems that you do." She reached for her purse.

They walked to the restaurant, which was nestled in the basement of one of the older buildings. The marble floors were badly worn, and the architecture showed that the structure had been built in the early thirties. Jessica had passed the building a hundred times and barely given it a second's notice.

"How'd you hear about this restaurant?" she asked.

"From the security guard. He eats here regularly and recommended it to me. I've never tasted better Italian food."

The proprietor greeted Damian as if he were a long-lost cousin, kissing him on both cheeks and speaking in Italian as he looked approvingly at Jessica.

"What did he say?" she asked when they were seated at a table covered with a red-and-white-checked cloth. A candle flickered from inside a small red vase, and shadows danced across the opposite wall.

"I'm not entirely sure. I only know a few words myself."

"In that case you did a good job of faking it."

"All right, if you must know, Antonio assumed we're lovers," Damian said casually, opening the menu.

"You corrected him, didn't you?" she demanded, putting a hand to her chest. She could feel the color rush into her face.

"No."

"Damian, you can't let that man believe you and I…"

"You're probably right, I shouldn't. Especially when it's my brother you're in love with, not me."

Jessica set the menu aside and leaned forward until her stomach pressed against the edge of the table. They needed to get this straight between them once and for all. "I'm not in love with Evan," she whispered heatedly.

"All right, all right."

"You don't sound convinced."

"I'm convinced," he said, without looking at her. Whatever was offered on the menu had apparently captured his full attention.

"Good," she said, reaching for her own menu. She was about to suggest the sausage pizza when a basket of warm bread was brought to their table. The lovely dark-haired woman who'd delivered it caught Damian's face between her hands and kissed him soundly on both cheeks. Jessica must have looked shocked, because the older woman laughed delightedly. "You don't need to worry—I won't steal Damian away from you," she said, then added something in Italian.

Damian seemed to go pale at the woman's words. Jessica's own knowledge of Italian was scant, but she knew what *bambino* meant.

"Damian, tell me what she said."

He was silent while the same woman poured them each a glass of wine and brought a plate of antipasto. Then he sighed. "Nona says you seem good and sturdy."

"*What?* Anyway, she said more than that."

"Jessica, I already explained I only know a few words of Italian."

"You know more than me. She said *bambino.* Doesn't that mean 'baby'?"

Damian sighed again. "Yes. If you must know, Nona said you'll make a good mother to my children."

"Oh." Jessica glanced at the woman, who was standing on the other side of the room, busy ladling minestrone soup into two ceramic bowls, which she then brought.

"I guess we aren't going to get that pizza," Damian muttered after the soup was served.

Antonio returned with the bottle of Italian wine and replenished their glasses with many exclamations of pleasure. Damian thanked him in Italian, then they spoke for a minute or two.

"When did you learn to speak Italian?" Jessica asked.

"I didn't. I picked up a smidgen here and there over the years. I spent a couple of months in Italy before I entered law school and muddled my way through the country. That's about it."

"You're a man of many talents," she said, picking up her spoon and sampling the soup. It was rich and flavorful. In fact, everything was excellent—the meal, the smooth red wine, the cappucino and dessert. Each time she was convinced she couldn't swallow another bite, Nona would bring them something else she insisted they try.

"Either we leave now, or you'll have to roll me out of here," Jessica said.

Damian chuckled, settled the bill, and together they walked back to the office high-rise. The evening was glorious, and Jessica felt wonderful. She wasn't sure if it was the result of the weather, the delicious food and wine or the company—or maybe all of them.

"Thank you," she said in the elevator.

"You're welcome." Damian fell strangely quiet as they walked to the law library. Before she left for the night, Jessica wanted to shelve the volumes she'd been studying. Damian worked silently with her. When they were finished, he preceded her from the room, automatically turning off the light.

The room was suddenly dark and Jessica bumped into a table.

"Jessica."

"I'm fine," she assured him, walking toward the hall light.

"That's the problem," he muttered, reaching for her. She was in his arms before she realized it. "I'm not." With that his mouth came down on hers.

Chapter 5

This kiss wasn't brotherly, nor was it uncomplicated. Damian's mouth fit over hers, warm and coaxing. Jessica sighed and relaxed against him, giving herself up to the sensation. It felt *right* to be in his arms, that was all there was to it.

Her hands gripped the lapels of his jacket, her fingers crushing the soft wool as his mouth moved against hers. Damian's hand curved around the side of her neck, his touch tender as though he feared hurting her.

The kiss was unlike any Jessica had ever experienced. She felt the sensual power of it all the way to her toes, the impact stealing her breath. She moaned and Damian did, too. When they broke apart, neither spoke. Jessica wished he'd say something, anything, to break the silence. She needed him to explain what was happening, because she was lost, taken by surprise, yet delighted to the very depths of her being.

Instead, Damian turned and walked away.

She couldn't believe it. A tear slipped unnoticed down her cheek and dropped onto her silk blouse, the droplet bleeding into a small circle. She raised her hand to her face, surprised by the tear.

Funny that when she couldn't find the words to say what she felt, a tear would speak for her. She'd learned that lesson years earlier. Her mother's tears had fallen onto her grandmother's casket, and they had said far more than a whispered farewell. Tearstains on a letter revealed more than its words.

A tear on her cheek now, after she'd shared a kiss with this man, spelled out volumes. Only to Jessica the language was one she couldn't fully understand.

The sudden need to escape overwhelmed her. Collecting her purse, she stepped out of the library and proceeded down the hallway. She paused outside Damian's open door. She saw him standing in front of his window, looking into the night. His hands were clasped behind his back.

"Good night," she called softly.

He turned and smiled briefly. "Good night, Jessica. See you in the morning."

She wished they could sit down and discuss what had happened, but one look told her Damian was confused and not nearly as delighted as she was. He seemed troubled, burdened somehow. She wondered if he regretted having kissed her.

"Thank you for dinner," she said. "You were right.

It's the best Italian food I've ever had." She didn't want to leave, but didn't have an excuse to stay.

"I'm glad you enjoyed it."

Jessica headed for the elevator. Her thoughts remained so muddled that she nearly missed her subway stop on the ride home. The first thing she did when she walked into her apartment was reach for the purple elephant Damian had won for her. She wrapped her arms around it and hugged it tight. It made her feel close to Damian. All she needed to do was shut her eyes and the memories of their night together at Cannon Beach filled her mind. She could almost hear the sound of the carousel, the echo of her own laughter when Damian insisted on winning her the elephant. She could hear the roller coaster as the riders shrieked past and smell the popcorn, candy apples and hot dogs.

Keeping the elephant pressed to her, Jessica slumped into the overstuffed chair and reached for her phone, dialing the number of her best friend. Cathy was far more insightful in these matters than she was. She would help her make sense of Damian's kiss.

"Hi," Jessica murmured when her friend answered.

Her greeting was met with a slight hesitation. "What's wrong?"

It didn't surprise her that her friend knew her so well. "What makes you think anything's wrong?"

"I recognize that tone of voice."

Smiling to herself, Jessica brought up her knees and rested her chin there as she assembled her thoughts. There didn't seem to be an easy way of explaining what had happened. Best just to blurt it out. "Damian kissed me tonight."

"And you liked it, didn't you?"

Cathy sounded gleeful, as though tempted to break into song. Jessica supposed this was what she got for having a theater-arts major for a best friend.

"Yeah—but I'm totally confused," Jessica admitted quietly. This jumble of mixed feelings was the main source of her troubles.

"Surprises you, doesn't it?" Cathy asked, then chuckled softly, again with that note of delight. "I've seen the handwriting on the wall ever since you mentioned Damian Saturday night. The guy sounds perfect for you."

"Don't be ridiculous."

"What's ridiculous about it?"

"I haven't thought of him…that way. Well, I have recently, and frankly, it frightens me to death. I've already made a fool of myself over one Dryden. I'm not anxious to make the same mistake with another one."

"You were a kid the first time. There's a world of difference between what happened then and what's happening now."

"Maybe," was all Jessica was willing to concede.

"Think, woman," Cathy said dramatically. "The man's obviously attracted to you, too. Otherwise he wouldn't be kissing you."

"I don't know that, and you don't, either. We kissed, and then he acted as if it was the worst thing he could have done. He didn't say a word and he just walked away. I don't know what to think. I'm so confused." She pressed a hand to her forehead.

"So you think he regretted it?"

"He must have. Otherwise…otherwise everything would have turned out differently. He looked at me as if I were a stranger, as if he didn't want to see me again."

"What was he supposed to do? Confess undying love? Didn't you tell me you had the whole situation figured out? The only reason Damian hired you in the first place was to bolster his brother's spirits. Think about it, Jess—the man has integrity. He can't very well start dating you himself if he believes you might still have some feeling for his younger brother."

"It drives me crazy that he'd think that!"

"I know, but you've got to look at it from his point of view."

"At the cost of my own sanity?"

"For now," Cathy said sympathetically.

"I don't know what to do!" Jessica cried, amazed at the amount of emotion that spilled into the words.

"There's more," Cathy said, warming to the subject. "If you're interested in Damian, it makes perfect sense that you're going to have to be the one to make the first move. Damian's hands are tied as long as he thinks there's the least chance you're interested in his brother. The guy's in a real bind here."

"Him! This whole thing with Evan's gotten out of hand. The poor guy's suffocating with everyone's concern. I actually feel sorry for him. He got the raw end of a deal in a relationship, and all he needed was some time to work out his pain," Jessica lamented. "Instead, Damian cut his work load until he's bored out of his mind. His parents, especially his mother, are dishing out sympathy by the truckload, and it's all Evan can do to stay afloat."

She paused for breath, then went on, "The only reason Damian hired me was that he thought I'd pull Evan out of the doldrums. I haven't talked to Evan, but I'm sure he resents all this nonsense. And I don't blame him."

"What about you and Damian?"

"I don't know what to think," Jessica admitted. "I wish I did. If he's interested in me, then surely it's his place to say or do something. Regardless of how he thinks I feel about Evan."

"Oh, come on, Jess!"

"I know Damian."

"Huh. You thought you knew Evan, too."

"I do, or rather, I did," she argued. The conversation was frustrating her more by the minute. "Besides, like I said earlier, I'm not interested in making a fool of myself over another Dryden. I learned my lesson the last time. Good grief, that was years ago and my parents and his *still* talk about it. Just this last weekend my own mother mentioned how pleased she'd be if I married Evan!"

"I have an idea," Cathy said slowly as though the scheme was taking shape in her mind as she spoke. "Introduce me to Damian."

"What possible reason do you have to meet him?" Jessica didn't like the sound of this.

"I just want to. Things aren't going well with David...."

"David?" Jessica cried. "Who's David?"

"The director for *Guys and Dolls.* Now listen, I know this sounds crazy, but trust me, it could work."

"What could work?" Jessica was fast losing what remained of her patience.

"Our meeting. I'll turn on the charm, do what I can to enchant him, and—"

"Just a minute, Cath, you're talking about the man *I'm* interested in."

"I know," she replied as if all this were perfectly logical. "But you want to know how serious he is about you, don't you? Also, maybe watching him with another woman will help you sort out *your* feelings for *him.*"

"Yes, but—"

"Come on, Jess. You said yourself you weren't willing to make a fool of yourself a second time. This way you'll know."

"This sounds silly to me."

"Not only that," Cathy went on as though Jessica hadn't spoken, "it'll give me a chance to practice some of my best lines. Just introduce us, and I promise I won't do anything to embarrass you."

"All right," she agreed without any real enthusiasm. "How do you propose we do this?"

"I could stop by the office one day soon and suggest lunch. It'd be natural for you to introduce me around, wouldn't it?"

"I...suppose, but doesn't that seem a bit obvious?"

"Perhaps. Do you have a better idea?"

"No." She sighed. "Okay. Do you want me to invite Damian to join us? I'm coming into the office this Saturday to catch up on a few things, before Evan's big court case starts next week. My guess is that Damian will be there, as well."

"All the better, then. I'll see you Saturday around noon."

Jessica hedged. "You're sure about this?"

"Absolutely! I have ways of getting a man to talk."

"That sounds like something out of a movie."

Cathy laughed. "It is."

"That's what I thought," she mumbled.

Precisely at noon Cathy arrived at the office. Jessica envied her petite friend her pixie good looks, short dark hair and big blue eyes. Cathy looked striking in her pants, which were black with huge white dots, and multicolored striped suspenders. Her blouse was white with small black dots and she was wearing black high heels. One thing was certain—no one would miss seeing her walk down the street. If Evan had been in the office, he doubtless would have begged an introduction.

"You must have forgotten about our lunch," Cathy said more loudly than necessary, standing outside Jessica's office. Loudly enough for Damian to hear.

Her friend's ploy worked because a minute later he wandered out of his office.

"Damian, this is my friend Cathy Hudson," Jessica said. "I might have mentioned her in passing."

Damian and Cathy shook hands. "Jessica forgot we were supposed to meet for lunch today." Cathy said.

"It isn't a good idea for Jessica to skip meals," Damian said. His eyes twinkled and the effort to suppress a smile caused the corners of his mouth to quiver.

"So you've seen what happens when Jessica's stomach growls. Wounded bears are easier to reason with than Jess when she's hungry."

"Hey, that's not true!" Jessica flared. They were speaking as if she wasn't there. She braced her hands on her hips and glared at the two of them. She hadn't been keen on this idea of Cathy's from the first and her instincts were proving to be right.

Her former roommate eased closer to Damian and was gazing soulfully into his eyes. He didn't seem to mind in the least; in fact, he seemed to lap it up.

"I'll get my purse," Jessica said stiffly, leaving Cathy and Damian gazing at each other while she went behind her desk and dug in the bottom drawer. The whole charade irritated her, and she was furious she'd allowed herself to be talked into it.

Cathy managed to tear her eyes away from Damian long enough to throw visual spikes at her friend. It took Jessica a moment to realize what was being signaled. Oh, yes—she was supposed to invite him to tag along.

"Would you care to join us for lunch?" she asked Damian, managing to sound polite, if unenthusiastic.

"Please, do," Cathy said, her words like warm honey.

Damian looked at Jessica as if seeking her confirmation, and to her credit, she did produce a smile. She didn't know why she'd ever agreed to this.

"I'll be happy to join you," Damian surprised her by saying. She'd never dreamed he would. The man was *full* of surprises.

"Great, just great," Jessica muttered under her breath.

"Fabulous," came Cathy's melodious response.

Jessica rolled her eyes, and together the three of them headed out of the office. Damian suggested a well-known expensive restaurant, and before Jessica could comment one way or another, Cathy had agreed. Jessica snapped her mouth closed before she said something she'd regret. It irked her that Damian would so easily fall into Cathy's snare. It might be just a charade, but she was left more than a little confused.

Outside the building, Damian waved down a cab, and Cathy managed to have Damian in the backseat with her. Jessica sat in the front while her best friend giggled her way through the streets of Boston. They drove past the Boston Common and the Freedom Trail, the winding yellow path that led history buffs and tourists from one historic monument to another.

She was acting like a jealous fool, Jessica realized with a start. Jealous of Damian and Cathy? The fog that had clouded her thinking for the past several days cleared.

She was falling in love with Damian Dryden. It couldn't have been any more obvious. It was one of the things Cathy had set out to prove, and her friend was right—she'd needed this blunt lesson.

Of course she loved Damian. From the minute she'd walked into his office and asked about the job. From the minute he'd stood on the footbridge that forged the pond on his parents' property and insisted on taking her to Cannon Beach.

From the minute he'd kissed her.

This was what Cathy had been trying to tell her.

When they arrived at the restaurant, Cathy excused

herself and Jessica. With her arm wrapped around her friend's, she dragged her to the ladies' room.

Before Jessica could open her mouth, Cathy burst out, "Damian's wonderful!"

"I know."

"I haven't met Evan, but I'm telling you right now if you're not interested in his big brother, I am. He's got a great wit, he's gorgeous, and—"

"I know all that." And a lot more.

"Listen," Cathy said, "I want you to make some excuse and leave."

Jessica was stunned. "You want me to *what?*"

Cathy was refreshing her makeup in front of the mirror, her eyeliner in hand. "You heard me. Remember an urgent appointment, something that will call you away so the two of us can be alone together. Only don't make it sound phony, or Damian will know what we're doing."

"*I* don't know what we're doing," she protested.

"I want you to give me some time alone with him."

"Why?" Jessica demanded. "Listen, you've already proved your point. I do care about Damian. And I'm not interested in sharing him with you."

"I know how you feel about him," Cathy said slowly as if that much had been understood from the beginning. "But my being alone with him will tell us both how he feels about *you,* which was the main purpose of my plan."

"You're sure about this?"

"How many times are you going to ask me? Of course I'm sure."

"I can't help thinking we're both good candidates for psychoanalysis!"

Cathy laughed outright at that. "Don't worry, I'm not going to steal him away from you, although heaven knows I'm tempted. The guy's a hunk. Why hasn't he ever married?"

"How am I supposed to know?"

"Have you tried asking?"

Cathy had a way of making everything sound perfectly straightforward. "Don't worry about it. I'll find that out, along with everything else."

Jessica hesitated. She trusted Cathy—most of the time. She also knew it wasn't beneath her best friend to say or do something sneaky. That was what worried Jessica.

"Go back to your apartment," Cathy instructed, before outlining her lush full mouth with a glossy shade of lipstick.

"I still don't understand what you're doing."

Cathy patiently closed the tube and shook her head as though to suggest the answer was obvious. "You don't need to. When Damian and I've finished lunch I can report my findings to you. Is everything clear now?"

"As mud."

Cathy rolled her eyes. "I'm trying to be a help here. The least you can do is cooperate."

"All right, all right," Jessica muttered, but she didn't like it.

"Let's not keep Prince Charming waiting any longer," Cathy said, taking Jessica's elbow. "Just remember to come up with something brilliant to excuse yourself."

Jessica was feeling anything but brilliant at the moment. "All right," she promised.

Jessica did manage to come up with a plausible excuse. They were seated and given elaborate menus decorated with gold tassels. Jessica set her purse on the floor, and it promptly fell over. When she leaned down to right it, she pulled a small appointment card from the outside pocket. Straightening, she studied the card.

"What's the date today?"

"The twelfth. Why?" Cathy's eyes had never been rounder, or more guileless.

"It says here I've got a dentist's appointment this afternoon." She made a show of looking at her watch. "In half an hour."

"On a Saturday?" Damian asked casually.

"Lots of dentists are keeping Saturday hours," Cathy explained conversationally, spreading the linen napkin across her lap. "I went in for a checkup myself no more than a month ago, and my appointment was on a Saturday."

"It's too late to call and cancel," Jessica said with a defeated air. "It took me months to get this appointment as it was. The Saturday schedule fills up quickly."

"If you made it months ago, it isn't any wonder you forgot." Cathy seemed all too willing to offer Jessica an excuse.

"I'd better see if I can catch a cab," Jessica mumbled. She wouldn't be able to keep up this charade much longer. It'd be a miracle if Damian didn't see through their plot. It had more holes than a golf course.

"I'm so sorry you have to go," Cathy said with enough sincerity to sound believable.

Damian said nothing. If Cathy's theory was true, Damian would reveal some regret at her leaving. Instead, he smiled at her and nodded as if he welcomed the time alone with her friend. Jessica's hands closed tightly around her purse strap as she stood and made her farewells.

Once she was outside, the doorman's whistle hailed her a cab. Jessica climbed into the backseat and gave the man the address of her apartment, thinking this was going to be the longest afternoon of her life.

She was right.

She paced her living room munching on pretzels for a good two hours. Most of the large bag had disappeared before her doorbell chimed. Cathy. In her eagerness to hear what she'd achieved, Jessica nearly jerked the door off its hinges.

Nothing could have surprised her more than to find Damian standing on the other side. She must have looked as dumbstruck as she felt, because he grinned and let himself in without waiting for an invitation.

"How was the dentist's appointment?"

"Ah… I didn't have one."

"I know." He walked over to her bookcase and was examining the titles as if he'd come for that purpose alone.

"You knew?"

"You're not nearly as good an actress as your friend," he said, turning to face her. Jessica tried to read his expression, but found it impossible. She felt rooted to the carpet, unable to move and hardly able to breathe. She wondered if he was angry with her. Perhaps he was amused. She couldn't tell which.

She should have known he'd see through their ploy. "It was a stupid plan," she admitted. Her shoulders sagged with a burden of regrets. She'd allowed Cathy to talk her into this crazy scheme, and she'd followed like a lamb to the slaughter.

"I…we didn't offend you, did we?"

A hint of a smile touched his eyes. "No, it was a very sweet thing to do, but unnecessary."

She blinked, not knowing what to say because she wasn't sure she understood.

Damian walked over to her and reached out a hand to press against her cheek. His touch was gentle, his gray eyes as serious as she'd ever seen them. He spoke as though his words pained him. "I appreciate your efforts, Jessica, but I can find my own dates." Then he bent and gently placed his mouth on hers. The kiss was far too short to satisfy her. Instead, it created a need for more. When he lifted his head, everything within her wanted to beg him not to stop.

"I'll see you Monday morning," he said, turning and heading toward the door.

She opened her mouth to tell him to stay, but by the time she could get the words out he was gone. He actually believed she was setting him up with Cathy. No wonder. That was exactly what it looked like. Why hadn't she thought of this before? Jessica slumped onto her sofa, covered her face with her hands and resisted the urge to cry.

Damian hadn't been gone for more than five minutes when Cathy arrived. Jessica opened her door to find her friend leaning against the doorjamb as if she needed its support. She threw herself down on Jessica's couch and removed her high heels. "That man's a tough nut to crack."

Jessica folded her arms and asked, "What do you mean?"

"I mean he was so closemouthed about you, there's only one sensible conclusion."

"And what's that?"

Cathy stopped rubbing her toes and turned her big blue eyes on Jessica. "You're serious? You mean you really don't know?"

"I wouldn't be asking if I did!"

"He's in love with you."

Jessica didn't believe it. "He can't be."

"Why can't he? Is there a law posted somewhere that says it's a crime to fall in love with Jessica Kellerman?"

"No…"

"He wasn't interested in me, and trust me, I tried."

Jessica stiffened, remembering her reaction to Cathy's attempts to flirt with Damian. She hadn't liked it. None of the crazy stunts her friend had pulled over the years had put their friendship on the line. This one had. Damian was off-limits, and before Cathy left for home, Jessica wanted to make sure she knew it.

"He thought I was trying to set him up with you," Jessica muttered disparagingly.

"What's so tragic about that? That was exactly what I wanted him to think."

"But why?"

Cathy's smile was slow and confident. "This is the reason I'm your best friend. My little performance this afternoon was for both your benefits. You know how you feel about Damian, too. I'm right, aren't I?"

Jessica nodded reluctantly, hating to admit her friend's ploy had worked. But there was a problem. "Damian assumes I was setting him up with you because I'm not interested in him."

"What makes you think that?"

"'Think' nothing. He practically said so."

"When?"

"Just a few minutes ago. He was here. The whole experiment backfired, Cath."

"You straightened him out, didn't you?"

"No… I didn't get the chance." Jessica felt worse and worse. She had no one to blame but herself. She'd allowed Cathy to talk her into this crazy scheme, and now she was suffering the consequences.

Cathy went uncharacteristically quiet. "You'll talk to him, won't you?"

"I… I don't know. I suppose so."

"Good. Explain how you feel, otherwise he'll go right on thinking you're not interested."

Jessica closed here eyes and groaned.

"It won't be hard," Cathy assured her. "He's crazy about you, Jess."

When her former roommate left a few minutes later, Jessica realized what a good friend Cathy had always been—despite her penchant for theatrics.

* * *

Jessica considered Cathy's advice for what remained of the weekend and arrived at the office early Monday morning. To her surprise, Evan was sitting at his desk when she walked in. He smiled broadly in greeting. "Good morning, sweet Jessica." He seemed to be in an awfully good mood. His brown eyes were clear and lively, and his smile was warm. "You're just the person I was waiting to see."

She stowed her purse and moved into his office with a pen and pad, fully expecting him to give her another lengthy assignment.

"Sit down," he instructed, motioning her toward a chair on the other side of his desk. He leaned back in his own chair, looking relaxed. "Now tell me something."

"Sure." Her mind was churning with a possible list of requests.

"I've been something of a bad boy around here lately, not pulling my own weight and the like. You know that, don't you?"

"I... I've only been in the office a short time," she said, not wanting to speak out of turn. "It's not for me to say if you have or haven't been doing your share of the work."

"Really, Jess, there's no need to be shy."

"All right," she said, resenting the fact that she'd been put in this position. "I know you were hurt, but we all face disappointments in life. It's time to pull yourself up by your bootstraps."

Evan laughed delightedly, not the least bit offended. "By heaven, I like a woman who can speak her mind."

Jessica relaxed and uncrossed her legs. "Was that all?"

"No." He tipped back in his chair and rubbed the side of his face while studying her carefully. "There was a time when you were rather...keen on me, wasn't there?"

"Yes." She flushed. "Years ago."

"You worshiped me from afar, so to speak."

She lowered her gaze and nodded.

"You're right about my being disappointed," he went on. "I felt the need to prove myself. In looking back, I realize how shallow I've been. I'm not proud of my behavior these past few months, and I'm hoping to make up for it with the Earl Kress trial."

Jessica didn't know how to comment or even if she should.

"My father and I had a good long talk this weekend," Evan added thoughtfully.

"I understand he's considering running for the Senate."

"Yes, and he's decided to give it a shot. Damian and I will be spending a fair amount of time working on his campaign. The gist of our conversation was simple. He wants me to get my life straightened out and start dating again."

"I think he's absolutely right," she agreed readily, assuming Evan was referring to the diplomat's daughter.

"Great." He beamed her a killer smile. "I was hoping you'd feel that way."

Jessica blinked, not grasping what he meant. "Why's that?"

"Because, my dear Jessie, I've decided I'd like to get

to know you better. You're very sweet and a hell of a good worker. Dad reminded me that you were keen on me a few years back, and I'm hoping to capitalize on your affection."

"Ah…" Now didn't seem the appropriate moment to bring up her feelings for Damian. Then again, she'd better before matters got out of hand.

"I don't mind telling you," Evan said before she could speak, "my confidence has been badly shaken. I feel safe and secure with you. Frankly, I don't know how I'd deal with any more rejection."

Chapter 6

"Aren't you seeing Romilda?" Jessica asked with a sinking feeling. She *had* to say something, set the record straight, but Evan was studying her with an eager intensity, and coward that she was, Jessica couldn't make herself do it. "You seemed to get along so well with her at the barbecue, and her political connections might help your father's campaign efforts."

"She's already returned to Europe."

"I see."

"Don't get me wrong, Romilda's a sweetheart, but she isn't the one for me," Evan explained. "I want an old-fashioned girl, who values the same things I do. Mom, home, apple pie—that sort of thing. A woman who knows what's really important in life. Someone like you, Jessica."

Jessica didn't doubt for an instant that Evan was echoing his father's words. Maybe the sort of woman he described *was* right for him, but Jessica wasn't the one. She was about to explain diplomatically that there was already someone in her life—without telling him who—when he spoke again.

"I've got a ton of work waiting for me this morning, but my parents asked that we meet later, and I thought the five of us could have lunch together."

"Five?"

"Damian will be there, too. Would noon be convenient?"

"Ah…"

"Great." He returned his attention to the papers on his desk. Jessica waited a moment, then got up and went back to the outer office. She felt the blood drain out of her face as she reached her desk and sat down.

"Is Mr. Dryden here?" Jessica hadn't been aware of Mrs. Sterling's arrival.

Jessica looked up and nodded.

"But it's barely nine."

"I know," she murmured.

"What's come over that man?" the secretary murmured, unable to disguise her amazement. "Never mind, let's not question it. I'd rather count my blessings. I was about to lose heart with him. I was afraid Damian had given Evan too much slack the past few months."

Jessica managed a weak smile. Mrs. Sterling moved about the office with the efficiency that was her trademark. She brewed a pot of coffee and the aroma of the rich Colombian helped revive Jessica. When the coffee was ready, Mrs. Sterling poured Evan a cup and carried it into his office. Jessica couldn't hear what was being said, but apparently Evan was in top form, because his secretary returned grinning broadly.

Jessica sat at her desk, too numb to think clearly. She'd missed her golden opportunity, if indeed there'd been one, to tell Evan she was in love with Damian. Yet it didn't seem fair to make such a confession to his brother when she hadn't said a word to Damian. Nor was she convinced Damian felt the same way about her. All she had to go on was Cathy's faith.

Her theatrical friend had a tendency to exaggerate, to expand the truth and fill it with an enthusiasm that simply might not exist. Damian was fond of her, Jessica didn't doubt that, but as for his being in love with her, Jessica couldn't say.

There was nothing to do but sit by patiently and wait to see how matters developed. Evan was making this effort for his father; it didn't mean he intended their relationship to be anything but show. Certainly he wasn't serious about wooing her. Not when he'd cared so deeply for this unknown Mary Jo.

The morning passed quickly as they prepared for the Earl Kress trial, slated to begin the following day. The attention generated by the local television stations was sure to spark interest in the law firm and in Evan's father's bid for the Senate. In addition, the trial had the potential to affect the outcome of education in school districts across the country.

Close to noon, Evan emerged from his office, and with a warm smile at Jessica, said to his secretary, "I'm going to steal this lovely one away from you for a couple of hours."

Mrs. Sterling nodded approvingly.

Jessica reached for her purse and stood, hoping this lunch would afford her a few minutes alone with Damian so they could talk. She desperately needed to discuss things with him, to explain what had happened and seek his counsel.

To Jessica's disappointment, the opportunity never arose. The three met Evan's parents at the Hilton. The meal was pleasant and cordial, and everyone seemed to be in a good mood—with the exception of Damian, who practically ignored Jessica. She might have been invisible for all the attention he paid her.

She decided to make an effort to let her feelings for the older Dryden son be known, and she waited until there was a lull in the conversation.

"Damian and I were out to Cannon Beach recently," she announced brightly after their salads were served. Evan's parents exchanged meaningful glances.

"From here on out Evan will be the one taking you to the beach, isn't that right?" Damian said to his brother.

"You should have said something earlier, Jess," Evan said, picking up on Damian's cue. "I love Cannon Beach. We'll make a point of going there sometime, all right? As soon as the Earl Kress trial's over."

"All right," Jessica agreed, her heart in her throat. She looked to Damian, who was busy eating his salad. From all outward appearances, it made no difference to him whom she dated. Apparently the idea of

Evan's holding her close while they rode on the roller coaster didn't trouble him. Not at all.

After lunch they made their way into one of the meeting rooms on the second level of the hotel, where a news conference was scheduled. There, Walter Dryden, surrounded by his wife and family, announced his intention to run for the Senate.

Mingling in the audience of newsmen, well-wishers and political-party members, Jessica was able to stand back and view the four Drydens. They were a handsome, wholesome family who believed in the American dream. She admired and loved them, and wished Walter Dryden every success.

Flashbulbs exploded around her as she wandered to the back of the room. She wasn't sure why Evan had insisted she attend this affair, other than to reassure his father he'd taken their father-son talk to heart.

Jessica knew that life was often filled with ironic twists such as this, but why did hers have to be so frustrating? She was pretty sure Evan's father had put the idea of dating her into his son's head. And why not? It was well-known she'd once had a crush on Evan. And their families were so close. She was the logical choice, and the fact that she now worked for Evan made it all the more convenient.

The younger Dryden hoped to enhance his image, assist his father in his campaign efforts and prove he was over a painful relationship. What better way to start than with a woman who'd once had stars in her eyes for him?

Except that those stars were focused in another direction now. On his older brother. A man who seemed determined to do the noble thing and step aside for his brother.

For the first time in months, Evan had revealed a willingness to put the past behind him and get on with his life. And Damian believed she was the reason he had. So he would do nothing to change that—even if he did love her himself.

Every day for the next week the Dryden name turned up in all the media. The television and radio stations followed the trial, and each afternoon the newspaper carried an account of what had happened in the courtroom. Jessica met Earl Kress the first time in the courtroom and was impressed with the young man's sincerity. He wasn't looking to cripple the school system with a huge monetary settlement; instead, he sought changes that would help other athletes. Evan had arranged for a private tutor for the young man. Earl hoped to return to college within a year and work toward a degree in education. His goal was to teach high school students himself.

The more she learned about Evan's generosity to Earl, the more impressed she was with the lawyer's generous heart. Earl had been cheated out of his education, and Evan had made it his mission to make sure this didn't happen to future generations.

At the same time, Walter Dryden was making a splash across the various media. It seemed there was a social engagement every night of the week having to do with the upcoming primary. Because of his involvement with the trial, Evan wasn't expected to attend these functions. For that Jessica was grateful, although she knew Damian had become actively involved in his father's campaign. She yearned to talk to him, but he seemed to be avoiding her. She rarely saw him, and when she did he was occupied with someone else.

On Friday the jury convened. Jessica returned to the office, preferring not to wait at the courthouse for the outcome of the trial. Evan had built a strong case and she was confident Earl would win his suit, but waiting for the jury's verdict was agony.

The office buzzed with activity, the way it generally did in the afternoons. There was the hum of computers, fax machines and photocopiers, and messengers zigzagged from one room to the next, crowding the hallways. The whole place was filled with an air of expectancy.

Jessica walked over to her desk, removed her shoes and rubbed her sore toes against her calves. Her muscles ached, and she was mentally and emotionally exhausted. This had been an incredibly hectic week. As soon as she got home, she was going to soak in a hot tub and curl up with a good book. Sleeping until noon the next day held irresistible appeal.

Mrs. Sterling had left on an errand and Jessica had just slumped down in her chair when Damian strolled into the office. He stopped abruptly when he saw she was alone.

Jessica froze, her breath trapped in her lungs.

"Hello, Jessica," he said stiffly.

"Hello," she managed.

"Where's Mrs. Sterling?" he asked, recovering first. He was brisk and businesslike, as if he'd never held her in his arms, as if she'd never been more to him than a friend, a casual one at that.

"Off on an errand," she answered, then added, "The jury's still out."

"So I understand." He walked over to Mrs. Sterling's desk and set a stack of papers in the secretary's in-basket.

"Have you been to that Italian restaurant lately?" she asked, desperate to make conversation. Desperate to remind him of the good times they'd shared—and what had happened afterward. She yearned with all her being that he understood her message—that those times had meant the world to her and that she hoped they'd been important to him, too. She prayed he'd realize how much she missed him.

"I haven't dined out lately." Then he turned abruptly and strode from the room.

Hurt and angry, Jessica wanted to shout at him to come back. But it wouldn't have done any good; she knew that. He'd sliced her out of his life without a second thought, and apparently without a single regret.

About an hour later, Evan burst into the office. He paused just inside the doorway, threw back his head and released a yell loud enough to sway the light fixtures.

"We did it!"

Startled, Jessica looked up from her desk. She stood to offer him her congratulations, and Evan rushed to her, lifting her high off the ground and whirling her around. "We won!" he shouted.

"Evan!" She laughed, bracing her hands on his shoulders. He was spinning so fast she was growing dizzy.

His cries of jubilation had attracted the attention of others in the office, but Evan didn't show any signs of releasing her. He set her back down on the ground and, looping his arm around her shoulders, kept her close to his side. Words of congratulations were enthusiastically offered.

"I couldn't have done it without Jessica," he announced to the gathering. "Her research was invaluable. Damian, too," Evan said, holding his free arm out to his brother. "A man couldn't ask for a better brother."

Jessica was looking at Damian, and whether he'd intended it or not—she suspected he hadn't—their eyes met. His guard had lowered, and his expression was one of such emotional intensity that nothing could have pulled her gaze from his. In him she read pride, loyalty and devotion. In him she saw that there was nothing on this earth he would do or say to hurt his brother, even at the sacrifice of his own happiness.

Tears clouded her vision. Gazing into the faces of those around her, she forced herself to smile, forced herself to look as though this was the happiest moment of her life, when on the inside, she'd never felt more miserable.

Evan insisted on taking her to dinner that night to celebrate. A victory gala, he told her. He chose a restaurant well-known for its superb food and service, and Jessica knew when they were seated that she was the envy of every woman there. Evan had never looked more handsome or been more charming.

They were leaving the restaurant, waiting for the valet to bring around Evan's car, when a news photographer stopped them and took their picture. Jessica protested, but Evan told her that this was the price of fame and she might as well smile.

The next morning, Jessica's mother phoned before she'd had a chance to wake, and hours before she'd intended to. She was extremely depressed, and sleep was the perfect escape.

"Jessica, have you seen it?" Joyce demanded, her voice raised with excitement. "I've already called the newspaper and am having them make copies for Lois and me. You both look fabulous."

"Seen what, Mother?" was the groggy reply.

"The newspaper, sweetheart. There's a picture of you and Evan on the society page with a nice little write-up. In case you didn't see it, your name was mentioned in the gossip column, too, on Thursday, linking you with Evan. Oh, honey, I'm so pleased."

"Oh, Lord," Jessica whispered, her mind clouded with exhaustion. "I remember now. A photographer stopped us last night."

"Yes, I know, that's what I've been telling you. The picture's in this morning's paper. I'm thrilled and so is your father, not to mention Lois and Walter."

Jessica was anything but thrilled. "It's only a picture, Mom."

"It's more than that, Jessica. It's a dream come true for you, and for me, too. You've always felt so strongly about Evan and now, after all these years, he feels the same way about you."

"Mother, you don't understand. Evan and I—"

"You don't know how pleased Lois and I are. We realize it's much too soon to be making wedding plans, but it's the sort of thing good friends love to do when their children are dating. You're our only daughter, and I can tell you right now this will be the gala event of the year. Your father and I insist."

She only paused long enough to take a breath, then rushed on, "We'd be so very pleased if you and Evan decided to have an autumn wedding. Lois has been my friend for so many years, and to think that someday we might share grandchildren! It does both our hearts good."

Jessica rubbed a hand over her eyes, repressing the urge to weep. "Mom…"

"I don't mean to pressure you."

"I know you don't."

"Good. I'm sorry I woke you, darling. I should have realized you'd be exhausted after this last week. Go back to sleep. We'll talk later."

Sleep was impossible now. Jessica padded barefoot into the kitchen and made coffee, standing at the counter until the liquid had drained into the glass pot. Then she poured herself a mug, and cradling it in both hands, sat at her kitchen table. Balancing her feet against the edge of the chair, her knees propped up under her chin, she waited until the coffee had cooled enough for a first sip. It did little to revive her sagging spirits, settling unsatisfactorily in the pit of her stomach while she mulled over what she was going to do.

Already it had started, already she could feel the

ropes tightening around her heart, binding her. She felt imprisoned by what everyone believed was right for her, what everyone believed she wanted herself, when in reality she loved Damian, not Evan.

The phone startled her, and she swore as she spilled coffee on her hands. "Hello," she snapped, grabbing the receiver.

"What the hell's going on?" Cathy demanded, sounding full of righteous indignation.

"Excuse me!" The last thing she needed was her best friend's accusations.

"I picked up the paper this morning, and there's your bright smiling face to greet me."

"So I understand," she muttered.

"There's something wrong with this picture, though. You're with the wrong brother. Care to explain?"

"No."

"Why not?"

Jessica sighed. "It's a long story."

"Condense it."

She sighed again. "Evan's decided to come out of his doldrums—"

"About time, wouldn't you say?"

"Yes, definitely, but he isn't doing this for himself. His father's running for political office and so Evan's making an effort to smile and put on a happy face."

"By dating you."

"It seems so."

"I know all about his father. Walter Dryden's name's been splashed across the headlines all week, right along with Evan's and Earl Kress's," Cathy said impatiently.

"So cut to the chase and tell me why you were out on the town with Evan and not Damian."

A simple explanation was beyond Jessica. This was the most complicated misadventure of her life. "You were wrong, Cath," she said miserably. "Damian isn't nearly as fond of me as you assumed. Otherwise he would have said something long before now."

"Said something about what?" Cathy yelped.

"Caring about me," she whispered miserably. She felt as though she was standing chest deep in quicksand with no chance of getting free.

Cathy groaned. "All right, I can see this tale of woe isn't something you're going to be able to abbreviate. Start at the beginning and be sure you tell me everything."

To her credit, Cathy listened attentively to the events of the week, all that had ensued since Jessica's conversation with Evan on Monday morning. When Jessica finished, Cathy was uncharacteristically silent.

"I see what you mean," she said finally, sounding none too happy herself. "Damian's caught between a rock and a hard place. He's crazy about you, Jess. My instincts told me that the day we had lunch."

"But apparently not crazy enough." Jessica closed her eyes to the sharp pain the thought produced.

"Wrong," Cathy corrected defensively. "Damian's got a sense of family and duty so strong he'd sacrifice his own happiness. That's not loving you too little, my friend, that's loving you—and Evan—too damn much."

"If that's the case, then why do I feel like leaping

off a bridge? My mother and Lois Dryden are talking about a wedding and grandchildren."

Cathy let the comment pass. "How often do you see Evan?"

"Every day—we work together, remember?"

"I meant socially."

That wasn't a fair question. Because of the trial they'd been together for the better part of each evening, as well as every day. Lunch and dinner had been haphazard affairs while they discussed different aspects of the case and their strategies. It was business, nothing more. He hadn't so much as held her hand.

"We've been seeing a good deal of each other," Jessica said, and then explained.

"I see, and how do you feel about Evan now?"

"I'm glad he's trying to get his life together. But he isn't attracted to me, and doesn't pretend to be, either."

"Then why haven't you said something to Damian? Why haven't you explained?"

"How could I?" Jessica protested tartly. It wasn't that she hadn't thought of doing so a hundred times. "First off, we were both heavily involved in the Earl Kress case. The timing was wrong. I might have said something over dinner last night if Damian had given me any encouragement, but he didn't. I can't help thinking you're wrong about us."

"We've already been through that," Cathy muttered in frustration.

"I know Evan is dating me for show. I wouldn't be surprised if he'd arranged for that photographer himself. It's the sort of thing he'd do."

"Aren't you afraid he'll fall in love with you?"

"No. His heart is so battered it'll be a good long while before he takes a chance on love again."

Cathy was uncharacteristically quiet. "His family's important to him, the same way yours is to you. So play this hand close to your chest, Jess. Vulnerable as he is just now, Evan might develop a deep…affection for you. That would be a disaster."

This was something Jessica had worried about earlier, and she was greatly relieved that their relationship had turned out to be strictly platonic. "You're certainly filled with happy suggestions."

Cathy ignored that, too. "When are you seeing him again?"

"Tomorrow afternoon. He's picking me up for a fund-raiser for his father. It's a picnic." She dreaded the entire affair. If it wasn't for the opportunity of seeing Damian, she'd have found an excuse not to attend.

"Have fun."

"Right," Jessica said, knowing fun would be impossible.

After she'd hung up the phone, Jessica took a shower. She stood under the hard spray, letting the water hammer at her face. When she'd finished she felt better—and filled with purpose.

Evan arrived to pick her up early the next day. He wore a white sweater with a blue braid along the V-shaped neckline. He looked stylish and debonair, very Ivy League casual. His eyes lit up when he saw her in her cheery summer dress with the short white jacket.

"I can't get over what a beauty you grew up to be."

"You always were a silver-tongued devil," Jessica teased. He was in a good mood, and he had a right to be after the success of the previous week.

Evan's sports car was parked right in front of her building. He held open the door for her and helped her inside. They chatted amiably on the ride to Whispering Willows, where the fund-raising picnic was being held. The area was decorated with banners and American flags, and there was even a small grandstand and a band.

Jessica was determined to find a chance to talk to Damian, to explain her feelings. He couldn't avoid her forever.

Jessica's parents were there, handing out small American flags to the guests. Rows of folding chairs were set up in front of the grandstand for Walter Dryden's speech.

Everyone was busy with one picnic task or another. Jessica helped where she could, keeping her eye out for Damian.

She was busy dishing up potato salad alongside Evan when she first saw Damian. He was talking to an older woman and happened to look in Jessica's direction. Their eyes met for the briefest of seconds before he quickly averted his gaze. Jessica swallowed the pain that constricted her throat.

After the food had been served, Walter Dryden strolled up to Jessica. He was a big man, strong in build and, she knew, equally strong in character. He hugged her and thanked her for all her help.

"You've grown into a beautiful young woman, Jessica." His deep voice echoed what Evan had said to her earlier.

"Thank you. I don't know if I've had a chance to tell you how pleased I am that you've decided to run for senator," she said.

"I wish I'd started my campaign much sooner. I'm going to be stuck playing catch-up the next couple of months, which means a lot of hard work."

"You're exactly what this state needs," Jessica said sincerely.

"Your confidence means a lot to me." They were strolling together side by side. "I've been doing some hard thinking along those lines myself. About how you're exactly what my son needs."

"I'm sorry?"

"You and Evan."

Jessica didn't know what to say. She should have explained then and there that it was Damian she loved, but her throat went dry and her tongue seemed glued to the roof of her mouth.

"He needs you," Walter Dryden repeated.

"He's going to be just fine, Mr. Dryden. I don't think you should worry about him."

Walter Dryden's nod was somber. "Lois and I believe you're responsible for that."

The taste of panic filled her mouth. "I'm sure that's not true."

"Nonsense. You have to learn how to accept a compliment, young lady. It'll serve you well later in life—Evan, too, for that matter." He paused, his look thoughtful. "I believe my son will eventually enter politics himself. He's a natural, but he isn't ready yet and probably won't be for several years. I've had to bite my tongue not to sway that son of mine, but Lois would never forgive me if I pushed him toward something he didn't want."

Jessica hoped he felt the same way about forcing Evan into an unwanted relationship.

"We're getting off the subject," Walter muttered, with a shake of his head. "I wanted to thank you, my dear, for helping Evan."

"But I haven't."

"Nonsense. You've made all the difference in the world to my son these last few weeks. I'd mentioned to Damian that you and I had talked and you'd be coming in for an interview. His decision to hire you was brilliant. I couldn't have thought of anything better for Evan myself."

"I have a lot to thank Damian for," Jessica said, so softly she doubted Walter heard her.

"Ah, here you are," Evan declared, coming up behind them. "Don't tell me my own father is stealing away my favorite girl."

Walter chuckled. "Not likely, son. You two enjoy yourselves now. You've both worked hard all afternoon. Take a break, sneak away and have fun."

"But your speech…" Jessica protested.

"No matter. You can hear me speak any day of the week. Now off with you."

Evan reached for her hand, and they walked along the outskirts of the grandstand area. They were moving toward a stand of weeping willow trees, and Jessica found that Evan's mood had changed subtly. He seemed troubled. She waited for him to broach the problem.

"Do you mind if we take a few minutes to talk?" he said after a moment.

"I'd like that." Her heart swelled with relief. What they needed was a healthy dose of honesty. She stopped and leaned against the trunk of a tree. They were partially hidden from view, and the privacy was welcome.

"I don't feel that you and I are connecting, Jessica."

"I know." She thought about her mother and all her talk about a wedding and grandchildren. Her mind drifted back to the conversation she'd had with Evan's father moments earlier. Everything had gone much too far.

"I've wanted to talk to you all week, but everything was so hectic, what with the trial and Dad announcing his candidacy."

"It was quite a week," Jessica agreed.

"Our names have been linked in the newspaper."

"Your name's often in the paper." He was from one of Boston's most prominent families, after all.

Evan chuckled. "That's true enough." He reached for her hand then, holding it between his own. "I'd like all that speculation about us to change. I'm ready to settle down with one woman."

Jessica's heart stopped beating. If he proposed marriage, she swore she was going to break down and weep. Everything and everyone seemed to be working against her, including her own parents.

"I… I've always been fond of you, Evan, but I think it's only fair for you to know—"

"'Fond' is such a weak word," he interrupted, frowning.

She didn't want to walk over his already bruised ego. "I know, but—"

"Do you realize we haven't even kissed?" He smiled, his eyes twinkling with boyish eagerness. "That's about to be corrected, sweet Jessica." He placed his hands on both sides of her face and, before she could protest, lowered his mouth to hers.

It was a gentle kiss, undemanding and tender. Jessica felt nothing, except an increasing desire to cry. How could she feel anything for Evan when she cared so deeply for Damian? When she *loved* Damian?

Evan lifted his head from hers and gazed down at her, his eyes now dark and unreadable. He studied her for a moment. "I won't pressure you, Jessica. We'll give this time." He brushed a stray curl from her cheek and kissed her there, his lips warm and moist against her face.

It was then that Jessica saw Damian. He was standing on the edge of the crowd that had gathered to hear Walter's speech. His eyes were on Jessica and Evan. When he realized she'd seen him, he turned and walked away. His steps were brisk and hurried as though he couldn't move fast enough.

For one wild moment, Jessica considered running after him, but Evan had put one arm possessively around her shoulders and was leading her back toward the grandstand.

It was too late.

Chapter 7

"Well?" Cathy demanded without a word of greeting as Jessica opened the apartment door to her friend Sunday evening. Cathy swept her backpack from her shoulder and carelessly tossed it aside. "How'd the picnic go?"

"Politically it was a success. From what I understand, Mr. Dryden raised a lot of money for his campaign." She was avoiding the issue and knew it, but the subject of Evan and Damian had become too painful even to think about.

Cathy knew her well enough to recognize the signs. "Sit down," she instructed, pointing at the overstuffed chair that was Jessica's favorite spot. Her friend became downright dictatorial whenever she felt strongly about something; apparently, she did now.

Jessica followed Cathy's orders simply because she didn't have the force of will to argue. Settling into the chair, she waited while Cathy paced the carpet in front of her. Jessica could almost hear her friend's brain waves crackling.

"I've been giving this matter some thought," Cathy began.

"I can see that," Jessica returned, wondering what Cathy's feverish mind had concocted this time.

"I want you to develop a limp," Cathy said. She sounded as though this was a stroke of pure genius.

Jessica wanted to laugh out loud. "You're joking, right? Because heaven knows I can't take you seriously."

"I'm dead serious, but I only want you to limp when Damian's around, not Evan."

Jessica shook her head, as though that would improve her hearing. For sheer lunacy, this idea ranked right up there with the luncheon invitation. "What possible reason would I have to do something as stupid as fake a limp?"

"Just remember to limp on the same foot," Cathy said, ignoring Jessica's question and looking a bit worried. "This is just the type of thing you'd forget. It might be a good idea if you put a mark on the top of your shoe so you don't goof up."

Jessica held up her hands. "Cathy, have you OD'd on too much sugar or something? This is the craziest thing you've ever suggested!"

"Trust me," Cathy said impatiently. "I'm in theater— I know what I'm doing."

"Your self-confidence doesn't reassure me in the least."

"It should. I know about these things."

"Would it be too much to share the logic of your plan with me?"

"Not at all." Cathy's step was jaunty as she walked over to the sofa, dropped down and crossed her legs. "Sympathy. We want Damian to think you've hurt yourself—a twisted ankle, a trick knee, that sort of thing. If he cares about you half as much as I believe, he won't be able to stand by and do nothing. He'll come to your aid, and the minute he touches you, he won't be able to hide how he feels." She stopped abruptly. "Be warned, though. You should be prepared."

"For what?"

"He might just explode at you. Anger in a man is far more complicated than it is with us women. He'll think you aren't taking care of yourself, and he'll feel responsible for that. Men do that kind of thing, you know. He might even decide to blame Evan, so make sure you take that into account."

"Of course Damian'll get angry!" Jessica cried. "And he'll have every right to be mad once he discovers I'm faking an injury to gain his sympathy."

"Don't let him know that part," Cathy said simply.

"Cathy," Jessica said on the end of a long sigh. "I appreciate your efforts, I really do, but I can't pretend to be hurt. First of all, Damian would know in an instant. I'm not nearly as good an actress as you, and he'd figure out my ploy in no time. You seem to have forgotten Damian's an experienced attorney."

Cathy frowned, chewing on her lower lip as she thought. "Okay," she said after a while. "Forget the limp. The only other thing I can suggest is forthright honesty. You'd be amazed at how well it works sometimes. This might just be one of those times."

"As it happens, I couldn't agree with you more," Jessica said. "This whole situation is preposterous. I'm not any good at charades. I'd like to help Evan, but not at the expense of my emotional well-being."

"Now you're talking." Cathy slid to the edge of the cushion. "What are you going to say to Damian?"

"I…don't know yet." A heaviness settled on her shoulders at the thought. "You know what my biggest fear is? That Damian will smile fondly at me and tell me how flattered and honored he is by my little confession."

"With sadness echoing in his voice," Cathy added, demonstrating her usual flair for the dramatic.

"Right. Then he'll sigh and add that unfortunately he doesn't share my feelings."

"That sounds just like a man," Cathy agreed. "Naturally he'll lie through his teeth, because he's being noble for his brother's sake. Just don't listen to him. Trust me, Jess, this guy loves you."

Jessica wished with all her heart that it was true. She looked over to her friend, realizing how much she treasured Cathy's support, and gave her a thumbs-up. Cathy grinned and returned the gesture.

Evan was in his office working when Jessica arrived Monday morning. "Good morning," he called out cheerfully. "I was hoping it was you."

"Would you like me to put on a pot of coffee?" she asked. Then she glanced toward the machine and noticed Evan had already done so.

He wandered out of his office, mug in hand, and sat on the corner of her desk, one leg swinging like a pendulum. He smiled down on her, his eyes twinkling. "Are you rested and ready to tackle the world?"

Jessica smiled. That didn't describe her even on her best Monday morning. "Not quite. Give me until Wednesday or Thursday for that."

"Then this should help brighten your day," he said casually, withdrawing two tickets from the inside pocket of his jacket and handing them to her. Jessica read the tickets and gasped. "Two box seats for the Red Sox game this evening!"

"I thought you might enjoy baseball."

"I love the Red Sox."

"So your mother told me. Be prepared, Jessica, my lovely, I'm planning to sweep you off your feet."

Her gaze shot up to his. He was sweeping her off her feet all right, but she didn't like where she was landing. She'd awakened that morning determined to resolve this matter between her and the Dryden brothers once and for all, only to be thwarted at the first turn. As if things weren't bad enough, Evan had been conferring with her mother, learning what he could about her.

"Evan, we need to talk," she said, keeping her gaze lowered. All the way into the office she'd practiced what she intended to say.

"I can't now, Jess. Sorry. I'm going to be in court all day with the Porter case. But don't worry, there'll be plenty of time for talking later. I'll come by for you at six-thirty, all right?"

"All right," she muttered, managing a weak smile.

By the time Evan arrived to pick her up that evening, Jessica was determined to have her say—after the game, she decided, when they were afforded some privacy.

Evan was determined, as well, only his determination was to lay on the charm. Their seats were situated directly behind home plate and their view was excellent.

They downed steaming hot dogs, salty peanuts and a glass of draft beer each. Evan was more relaxed than she'd seen him in a long while, cheering on his team and shouting at the umpire. When the Red Sox scored a home run, he placed his fingers in his mouth and let loose with a piercing whistle. In all the years she'd spied on Evan and his brother, she couldn't remember him once whistling like that.

"My mother would've had my hide," he explained when she asked. "Whistling isn't proper behavior," he said, sounding so much like Lois Dryden that Jessica laughed.

"When did that ever stop you?" she teased.

"I found that my yen to whistle was the one thing Dad wouldn't tolerate, either," Evan said, as though cheated out of a normal childhood.

Jessica was amazed. She'd assumed that Evan, who'd always been the fair-haired boy, had gotten away with everything.

In the seventh-inning stretch, Evan reached for her hand and squeezed her fingers. She'd always liked Evan and found it impossible to be irritated with him for any length of time. This was his gift, Jessica realized, what his father had referred to during their talk at the fund-raising picnic. Evan was a born leader. People had always been drawn to him. He'd always been accepted, admired and highly regarded. When uncomfortable situations arose, they viewed him as a problem solver.

Suddenly Jessica felt a change in him. He let her hand slip from his grasp. He stiffened and went utterly still. He gasped, and then seemed to stop breathing altogether.

"Evan?"

His smile was decidedly forced. At that moment the crowd roared and fans got to their feet. Jessica hadn't a clue what had happened in the play. Her eyes and mind were on Evan.

"What's wrong?" she asked when the noise died down.

"Nothing." He attempted to convince her with a smile, but failed. Something was very wrong, indeed, and she was determined to find out what.

"Come on," she said, standing and not waiting for him. "We're leaving."

"Jessica, no, it's all right. I'm fine."

"You're not, and don't even try to tell me otherwise, because I know better."

"It's nothing," he said once more, defensively.

She ignored him, gathered her things and left the box. He had no alternative but to follow her.

"Has anyone ever told you what a stubborn woman you are?" he muttered, racing after her. Their steps echoed against the concrete steps as they made their way out of the stadium. Every now and again they could hear shouts and cheers coming from inside. A couple of times Evan glanced regretfully over his shoulder.

"All right, tell me what happened to you in there," Jessica demanded, as they neared the parking lot.

"It was nothing."

"If you say 'nothing' again, I'm going to scream. Now, who'd you see?" But she already knew the answer. Only one person would have evoked such a pain-filled response in Evan, and that was the woman he'd loved and lost.

"What makes you think I saw anyone?" Evan tossed right back at her, irritated now and not bothering to disguise it.

"Was it Mary Jo?"

He stopped so abruptly she'd taken half a dozen steps before she realized he wasn't at her side.

"Who told you about Mary Jo?" His voice was hoarse.

"No one yet, but you're about to."

"Sorry, Jess, but—"

"Now listen here, Evan Dryden, you need to get this off your chest once and for all. You've nursed the pain she caused you long enough. It's time to let it go. Past time!" Jessica tucked her arm in the crook of his elbow as they wove their way toward his car.

He was silent, his mood dark and brooding by the time they arrived at Jessica's apartment. She wasn't sure if she was helping matters by insisting he tell her about this woman he'd once loved. She feared her insistence might well rip open a half-healed wound, but she also knew he couldn't hold this inside any longer.

Jessica led the way into her kitchen, turned on the light and brewed a pot of coffee. Evan sat down, but grew restless almost immediately and stood, prowling about her small apartment.

Soon Jessica was sitting in her favorite chair, watching Evan pace. She didn't pressure him to talk, didn't try to prompt him. When he was ready, he'd tell her what she wanted to know.

"We met by accident," he said, his voice low and intense, "although I've wondered since if it really was."

"You mean you think she arranged it?"

Evan's eyes widened with surprise. "No...not that. I was thinking that there's little in life that really *is* an accident."

"I see," Jessica murmured.

"I was at the beach with a few friends of mine. We'd played volleyball and had a few beers and were enjoying ourselves—taking a real break from the grind of the office. We soaked up sunshine and laughter and got rid of a lot of pent-up energy."

He stopped moving and turned to face her. "Most of my friends had left and I was winding down by taking a walk along the beach, and that's when I met Mary Jo. She was walking her dog and good old Fighto—bad pun, eh?—anyhow, he got loose. She was chasing him down the beach and, being the heroic kind of guy I am, I caught the leash for her. She stopped to thank me and we got to talking. She's small and pretty with big brown eyes that... Well, none of that matters now."

"You liked her right away?"

Evan nodded. "There was a freshness about her, an enthusiasm that bubbled over. I knew immediately that I wanted to know her better, so I asked her out to dinner. It threw me for a loop when she refused."

That must have been something of a novelty, Jessica mused. "Did she give you a reason?"

"Several, as a matter of fact, but I was able to talk her out of her objections. She had the most marvelous laugh, and I found myself saying the most ridiculous things, just so I could hear it. Being with Mary Jo made me want to laugh myself. It was the most exhilarating day I'd had in years."

"She did go out with you, though?"

"Not exactly." Caught in the memories, Evan didn't seem inclined to say anything more for a minute. Jessica watched silently as the emotions crossed his face. First she saw his eyes light up with the recollection, followed by a pain so deep she yearned to reach out and take his hand. The small movements of his mouth were telling, too. It quivered when he first mentioned meeting Mary Jo, as if that first conversation served to amuse him still. But a moment later, the corners sank as his pain took hold. Jessica longed to reassure him, but knew Evan wouldn't have appreciated it.

"As it happened," Evan continued at last, his tone wistful, "I spent the rest of the day and nearly all of the night with Mary Jo. We built a fire on the beach and talked until morning.

"We started dating regularly after that. I found her refreshing and fun. Our lives were so different. Mary

Jo was the youngest of a family of six. She's the only girl. I met her family one Sunday, and her mother insisted I stay for dinner. I'd never seen such a spread in all my life. There were kids running all over the place. Several of Mary Jo's sisters-in-law were pregnant at the time, as well. I've never known such a family, the joking and the teasing and fun. Don't get me wrong, I've got a great family myself, but Mary Jo's is different. I really loved being with them."

"I'm sure they felt the same way about you."

He shrugged, his look doubtful. "I'd like to think so."

"What happened next?" Jessica prompted when he didn't immediately continue. She was eager now for the details.

"I knew I was going to fall in love with her that first day on the beach," he said, his voice so low it was a strain to distinguish the words. "Love isn't something I take lightly, but it hit me then—and I knew."

"I know what you mean," Jessica offered. She felt the same way about Damian.

"After I met her parents, I realized how much I wanted to marry her, how much I wanted us to have five or six children of our own. The Summerhills' home was full of love and I wanted that kind of happy free environment for my own children someday."

"Mary Jo sounds like a very special woman," Jessica said quietly.

"She is," Evan whispered softly. "Special enough to marry."

"You asked her to be your wife, didn't you?"

He gave an odd smile, one that was a blend of

amusement and pain. "Yes. Afterward I took her to meet my parents. Mary Jo was intimidated by my family's wealth—I realized that from the beginning. Who wouldn't be, seeing Whispering Willows for the first time. My parents had some doubts about our being suited, but once Mom and Dad met Mary Jo, they changed their minds."

"I don't remember hearing about the engagement," Jessica said.

"I wanted to give her a diamond, but she preferred a pearl ring, instead. She'd recently completed her student teaching and been hired as a first-grade teacher. She wanted to delay making a formal announcement until she'd settled into her job, but more important until after her parents' fortieth wedding anniversary celebration that October.

"I wasn't keen on waiting," Evan confessed, "but I agreed, because, well, because I was willing to do whatever Mary Jo wanted." He paused and drew a deep breath, holding it a moment as if he dreaded continuing. "I first suspected something was wrong the first part of October. She kept finding excuses why we couldn't see one another. In the beginning I accepted them—I was busy myself—and although I missed her, I didn't press the issue. I didn't like it, mind you, but I understood how busy she was with school and her family obligations. A couple of times I showed up at her parents' house. They seemed glad to see me, and her mother obviously assumed I was starving and made me stay for dinner." He smiled.

"They sound like wonderful people."

Jessica didn't think Evan heard her. "When Mary Jo mailed me back the ring, I was stunned. I've had some surprises in my life, both pleasant and unpleasant, but none that have shocked me more."

Jessica felt angry at Mary Jo for not having the courage to confront Evan face-to-face. If she wanted to break the engagement, even an informal one, then the least she could have done was have the consideration to tell him in person. Mailing Evan the ring was cowardly and cruel.

"So," Evan continued, "I drove over to her apartment in a fury."

"You had every right to be furious."

He shook his head. "I should have waited until I'd cooled down. I wish with everything in me that I had."

Life was filled with regrets, Jessica thought. She'd been carrying around a fair share of her own, especially in the past few weeks.

"When I confronted her, Mary Jo told me there was someone else," he whispered. "I didn't believe her at first. I refused to entertain the thought that a woman as fundamentally honest as Mary Jo would see another man behind my back. It didn't tally in my mind—but I was wrong." His voice dwindled to a whisper. "Apparently they met at the school where she teaches. He's a teacher, too. The agony of being engaged to me and in love with someone else must have torn her apart."

Jessica dropped her gaze for fear he would read what was in her eyes. She wasn't engaged to Evan, but she continued to see him when she was in love with Damian. While Evan spoke, Jessica had been casting mental stones at Mary Jo, when she was guilty of essentially the same thing.

"You saw her tonight at the ball game?" Jessica gently prodded.

Evan nodded. "She was with him…at least I assume it was him." The pain was back in his eyes, and Jessica felt the urge to weep. For Evan, yes, but for herself, as well. What a couple they made, each in love with someone else, fighting hard to do the right thing and making themselves miserable in the process.

"Mary Jo's a special woman," Evan whispered. "The man who marries her is a lucky man…" He paused again, and that odd smile, the one of blended joy and pain returned. "She'll be a wonderful wife and mother."

"Under the circumstances, that's a generous thing to say."

"You don't know Mary Jo, or you'd think the same thing yourself. In the months since we parted, I've come to realize that my ego played a substantial role in all this. Mary Jo was the first woman to break off a relationship with me." He smiled as he said it, as though it had served him right after all these years. "I guess I'd gotten a bit cocky."

"We're all guilty of that in one form or another," she offered.

He looked at Jessica then, and his gaze sobered. "I've ruined our evening, haven't I?"

"No," she told him, hoping he heard the sincerity in her voice. She understood how passionately Evan had loved the woman, and how deeply the pain of their parting affected him still.

More than ever, after hearing Evan talk about losing the woman he loved, Jessica knew she couldn't allow the same thing to happen to her. She couldn't continue to mislead Evan by letting him believe their relationship would evolve into something it was never meant to be.

A week passed. Every time she was with Evan he told her more about his relationship with Mary Jo. She soon realized that every invitation to dinner or a show was an excuse to talk. Every outing was followed by coffee and a long heart-to-heart. It was as though a floodgate had opened inside him, and the need to release the pent-up emotion was too strong to ignore.

They were friends, nothing more, and Jessica was comfortable with their relationship. With their frequent talks, she was able to open up to him, as well, in little ways.

"Have you ever been in love, Jessica?" he asked her unexpectedly one night.

"I think so," she said hesitantly as they strolled through Boston Common. "Yes," she amended quickly. "And it isn't what you're thinking."

"Oh?"

"It's not you, so don't get a big head." She didn't realize until she spoke how insulting she sounded, and she immediately sought his pardon.

Evan laughed off her apology.

The night was lovely. The stars were like twinkling rows of sequins that hung so close they seemed draped over the upper limbs of the trees.

"You know when it's love, don't you?" he asked after a few moments.

"Oh, yes," she whispered.

"Does this mystery man feel the same way about you?"

"I... I don't know. I like to think so." Although there were more signs to the contrary.

For Damian continued to avoid her. Other than that brief moment when he'd come into her office, she hadn't talked to him once.

He arrived at the office promptly at eight each morning and left at five. She guessed that his involvement with his father's campaign dictated his hours. That meant if she wanted to see him, it had to be during working hours. With his hectic schedule it was easier getting an audience with the pope. Jessica didn't know how Damian managed to cram all he did into a single workday. She'd tried to talk to him, but hadn't found the opportunity when there weren't other people around.

Jessica was fast losing her patience. And then, just when she was about to throw her hands in the air and scream with frustration, it happened. Quite by accident, and where she'd least expected it.

Whispering Willows. His family's home.

Evan had learned from Jessica's mother that she'd played on her college tennis team; he'd been intrigued, and challenged her to a game. It had sounded like an entertaining way to spend a Saturday afternoon, and she'd agreed. Since he'd neglected to schedule time on the courts at the country club, they drove to his parents' home to play.

They smacked the ball back and forth for a solid hour, and Evan soundly defeated her. Not that his athletic ability surprised her, but in her effort to impress him she strained her knee. It wasn't anything serious, but Evan insisted they stop playing.

They made their way to the house, laughing and in a good mood, her knee long forgotten, to discover Evan's mother anxiously attempting to start her car, without success. She needed to be at campaign headquarters within the hour and was fretting about what she should do.

"Not to worry, Mom," Evan said, affectionately kissing his mother's cheek. "I'll drive you."

"Nonsense," Lois protested when she viewed Evan's two-seater sports car.

"Didn't you tell me you gave Richmond the day off?" Evan said, opening his car door. "No more excuses, Mom."

"But what about Jessica?"

"I'm perfectly capable of entertaining myself," Jessica assured her. She stood in the driveway until the car had disappeared, then wandered back into the house, wiping the perspiration from her brow with the back of her forearm. She walked into the kitchen and, finding a cold soda in the refrigerator, helped herself.

She was humming a show tune when the kitchen door swung open. "Mother, what in blazes are you doing here? You're supposed to be at—" Damian stopped when he saw her. "Jessica," he said, his surprise evident.

"Your mother's car wouldn't start, so Evan drove her over to campaign headquarters," she explained. Her face was red with exertion, and her hair fell in damp tendrils about her face.

"Evan drove her." Already Damian was physically withdrawing from her. "I'd better go see what's wrong with Mom's car."

"Damian…" Cathy's suggestion about faking an injury came into her mind like a stone from a slingshot. She was injured—well, only slightly—but there was no better time than the present to make use of it.

She concentrated her efforts on her right foot and limped toward him. She hated resorting to such an underhanded method but she was desperate to talk to him. Surely he'd forgive her once he learned the truth.

His gaze went to her knee, his concern immediate. She was wearing a white top and a short tennis skirt. "You hurt yourself," he said, moving toward her. The kitchen door swung in his wake.

"I'm fine," she whispered.

"Sit down," he ordered, his voice none too tender. "Does Evan know about this?"

"Yes, but it's not all that bad," she mumbled. He pulled out a kitchen chair and eased her into it. His hands at her shoulders were gentle but firm. She closed her eyes at his touch. Lord, how she'd missed him! For days she'd waited for the opportunity to be alone with Damian, and she wasn't about to waste it now.

"We need to talk," she said. "Listen, I—"

"We'll talk after I've seen to your knee. What in God's name possessed my brother to leave you like this?"

"Damian, please listen to me."

"Later." He was busy at work packing ice into a bag.

She was irritated now and leapt off the chair. "My knee will be fine. I strained a muscle or something. It's no big deal."

"You'd better have a doctor check it out," he insisted, positioning her back in the chair, raising her leg and resting it against the seat of a second chair, then balancing the ice pack on the knee.

"I need to talk to you about Evan and me," she said, refusing to be put off any longer. "I'm not in love with Evan and he doesn't love me. We're friends, nothing more. He's in love with Mary Jo and I'm in love with—"

"Keep that ice pack on your leg for a good twenty minutes, understand?"

Infuriated, Jessica rose to her feet and tossed the ice pack into the sink. "You're going to listen to me, Damian, if it kills me! I realize I'm making a mess of this. I should never have used my knee to keep you here, but I was desperate."

"Did you or did you not twist your knee?" he demanded.

"Yes, a little, but it's nothing. I want to talk about the two of us. About you and me."

"Jessica," he said with ill-concealed impatience. "You're dating my brother."

"Your brother and I are *friends,* nothing more. How many times do I have to say it?"

"There's a change in Evan," Damian insisted heatedly. "Do you think I haven't noticed? For the first time in months, he's his old self. My brother's back again and it's all due to you."

"Maybe, Damian, but not in the way you think."

"It doesn't matter what I think," Damian said angrily. "You're dating my brother, so there can't be a you and me. Do you understand?"

"No!" she cried. "No, I don't!"

"It has to be this way, Jessica."

"But why?" Hot tears blurred her vision.

He didn't answer her for several time-shattering seconds. "That's just the way it is."

"Is…is that the way you want it?" Swallowing became impossible. She knotted her hands into fists at her sides.

"Yes," he said after a moment, the longest moment of her life. "That's the way I want it."

Jessica turned away from him, grateful to the very depths of her soul that she hadn't declared her undying love for him. This humiliation was bad enough.

"Jessica." Her name was a plea on his lips.

She hung her head, knowing he would abandon her the way he always did—but he didn't. Instead, his arms came around her and turned her to face him. His touch was as if he had to experience holding her, as if the feel of her was the one thread keeping his sanity intact. And then his mouth came down on hers.

This kiss was hungry and hard, unlike the kisses they'd shared previously. Jessica clung to him, mindful only of this man and the sheer joy she experienced in his arms. She caressed his face with wondering fingers as the intensity of their need increased. He angled her head to one side for a series of short nibbling kisses down her cheek, her throat.

"No more," he moaned, then jerked his head away. But she refused to release him, hugging him around the neck and burying her face in his shoulder. "Jessica, please." When he tugged her hands free, she realized he was shaking as badly as she was. His hands closed around hers and his head fell forward.

The sound of the front door closing echoed like a clap of thunder. Damian moved away from her and had his back to her when Evan strolled into the kitchen, whistling. He stopped when he saw Damian.

"Damian, hello. I'm glad to see you kept my best girl company."

With something less than a curt nod to his brother, Damian strode out of the kitchen, muttering about seeing to his mother's car.

Jessica thought her heart would break.

Chapter 8

"Thank you," Evan said when he dropped Jessica off at her apartment half an hour later. "By the way, there's a formal dinner with three hundred of my father's closest friends Monday night," he said casually. "I'd like you to attend it with me."

Jessica looked up at Evan, realizing she hadn't heard what he'd said. She hurt too much. Damian didn't love her, didn't want her. She'd all but blurted out her love for him, and he'd rejected her, insisted Evan needed her, and then walked away. As he always did.

"Jessica, are you all right?"

"I'm fine." How easily the lie came, even though she was falling apart on the inside.

"I was asking you about the dinner party."

She blinked. Dinner party?

"Monday night," he said slowly, waving a hand in front of her face. "You'd better tell me what's wrong."

"Would it be all right if I go in now?" she asked, instead. She wasn't in the mood to explain anything, least of all what had happened between her and Damian.

"Of course."

Evan insisted on escorting her into her apartment. He placed her tennis racket in the hall closet and stepped into her kitchen to get her a glass of ice water.

Jessica sat at the table and smiled her appreciation. "I'm fine," she said, and this time it was a little less of a lie. Yes, she hurt but it was a clean cut, deep and swift. She knew now what she'd suspected all along. Damian didn't want her, didn't love her.

"Thank you, Jess," Evan said again, and although his words were casual, Jessica sensed a deeper meaning.

"For letting you whop me in tennis?" she asked, knowing it was much more than that.

The smile faded from his eyes. "For that, too, but mostly for listening to me these last few days. Talking about Mary Jo has helped clear my head. It's shown me what went wrong between us and helped me realize how much I still love her." This was issued with a pain-filled sigh.

"That isn't a sin, Evan." Any more than her loving Damian was a sin.

"Talking is what's helped me. Perhaps you should take note and tell me what's troubling you. You can't fool me—those are tears glistening in your eyes."

Instinctively she lowered her gaze, focusing her attention on the water glass. "I... I'm not ready to talk just yet. Don't be upset with me. I have to sort through my own feelings first."

His hand covered hers. "I understand. You will attend the dinner party with me, won't you?"

Jessica's first inclination was to refuse. Instead, she nodded. "All right." Sitting home feeling sorry for herself would solve nothing. Nor would she give Damian the satisfaction. From here on out, she was going to kick up her heels and enjoy life. Even if it killed her, and that was what it felt like just now.

"Damian will be there," Evan said as if he expected her to comment.

She nodded. After this afternoon it made no difference.

"He'll be bringing someone, too," Evan added. "You won't mind if we share a table, will you?"

"I won't mind in the least," Jessica said brightly. "The more the merrier."

"I thought we'd look through your wardrobe before dinner," Cathy said as she entered Jessica's apartment. Jessica realized her mistake the moment she'd mentioned the dinner party to her friend. From that point on, Cathy had insisted she choose the dress.

"I've managed to dress myself without a problem for several years now," Jessica felt obliged to say.

Cathy was sorting through the dresses in her closet, shuffling them from one side to another as if this was a mission of great importance. She paused and tapped her foot impatiently. "I can't tell you how disappointed

I am in Damian. You're sure you didn't misunderstand him?" She sounded as though the fault was Jessica's.

"There was no misunderstanding," Jessica said firmly, wishing she'd never mentioned the incident to Cathy. She wouldn't have except that her friend had been on virtually every phase of this…this mess. "He doesn't want anything to do with me. He couldn't have made it any plainer."

"I don't believe it. There's something very wrong here, and it's up to you to figure out what it is."

"I know what it is," Jessica protested. It wasn't necessary to dissect the problem when the answer was so simple. If Damian *did* care for her, he would have found a way to make things right. He didn't, and he hadn't.

"You're coming to my opening night, aren't you?" Cathy asked as she continued to examine the contents of Jessica's closet.

"I wouldn't miss it for the world." Jessica was proud of Cathy's big career break. She'd gotten the plum role of Adelaide, after all, in the local production of *Guys and Dolls.* Jessica also thought Cathy was sweet on the director, David Carson. Her friend had mentioned his name several times in passing, and Jessica thought there'd been a small catch in her voice each time.

"I think I'll invite Damian to my opening," Cathy suggested nonchalantly. "After all, I have met him."

Jessica wasn't likely to forget. Cathy's eyes shifted in her direction. "You don't have anything to say."

"Do what you want, Cathy."

Cathy's laugh was short and telling. "You can't fool me, Jess, I know you too well. I don't know what's wrong with Damian, but trust me, he'll soon come around."

"I sincerely doubt it." Jessica hated to be so pessimistic, but she couldn't stop herself.

Cathy took three dresses from the closet and laid them across her friend's bed. Her hands on her hips, she circled the bed, then returned two of the dresses to the closet.

Jessica studied Cathy's selection. It was a full-length black dress, sleek and shiny with silver highlights that sparkled in the overhead light.

"Try it on," Cathy insisted.

Mumbling her discontent, Jessica slipped out of her clothes and into the dress, lifting her hair so Cathy could close the zipper properly. Then she regarded herself in the full-length mirror. Her shoulders drooped as she released a slow, defeated sigh.

"I look like Natasha from the Rocky and Bullwinkle cartoon show," she muttered.

"Nonsense," Cathy said. "The dress is perfect."

"For consorting with spies maybe," Jessica muttered. But then again, maybe it *was* right. If she was destined to sit at the same table as Damian and his date, she wanted to be darn sure he noticed her—and knew what he was missing.

Evan arrived to pick her up for the dinner party five minutes ahead of schedule, just as Jessica was putting the finishing touches to her makeup. "Beautiful," he said, taking both her hands in his. "You're absolutely beautiful."

His appreciation lent Jessica confidence—until they reached the table where Damian and his date were sitting. The woman was tall, regal, blonde and gorgeous. Every woman's basic nightmare. So much for the best-laid plans.

"Nadine Powell," Damian said. "My brother, Evan, and Jessica Kellerman."

Jessica's gaze moved to Damian, and she was gratified to discover he was staring at her the way a child gazes into a store window at Christmastime. Cathy had been right—the dress was perfect. Damian abruptly looked away as if angry with himself for being so obvious.

"Nadine," Evan said, taking the other woman's hand and holding it several moments longer than necessary.

Dinner was a drawn-out affair, with speeches from several long-winded politicians. Jessica lost count of the number of speakers and the number of courses served, but they seemed to be running neck and neck. The speeches made dinner conversation almost impossible, but Jessica did manage to learn that Nadine was a longtime friend of Damian's. Friends and nothing more, Nadine went on to explain, reading the situation with amazing accuracy. As for Damian, well, he pretended she wasn't there. He didn't say one word to her the entire meal.

When the dessert dishes were removed, a ten-piece orchestra began to play on a low stage behind the polished oak dance floor.

"You game?" Evan asked, holding out his hand to Jessica. The music was from the forties, the big-band sound she particularly loved. Evan was tapping his foot and swaying his shoulders.

Jessica declined. She wasn't keen on being one of the first ones on the floor. "I think I'd prefer to sit out a few of the numbers, if you don't mind."

"Nonsense. I won't take no for an answer." Evan all but pulled her out of her chair. He led her onto the dance floor, and although the number was fast, he brought her into his arms and held her close.

"Evan," she hissed, acutely aware of the impression they were creating. It looked as if they were madly in love and couldn't bear to be separated.

"Shh," he whispered close to her ear.

"What's wrong with you?"

"Me?" he asked, then threw back his head and laughed as if she'd said something uproariously funny.

"Nothing. I'm having a good time, that's all."

"At my expense," she told him in an angry whisper. "Soon everyone will be talking about us."

"Let them."

"Something is very wrong," Jessica insisted.

He laughed again. "Not exactly, but soon everything should be just right."

Jessica hadn't a clue what he meant, but she wasn't going to continue with this farce any longer than necessary. As soon as the number finished, she broke away from him and returned to their table.

"Jessica's knee is bothering her," Evan explained, and before she realized what was happening, Evan had asked Nadine to dance and the pair stood and left the table. Damian looked unnerved.

"Well," Jessica said dryly, "I guess you can't keep a good man down."

Damian frowned darkly. "He might have asked someone other than my date." His hand closed around his water glass, and he seemed intent on studying the dancing couples. Intent on not making conversation with her, Jessica thought, which was fine. Just fine. Everything had already been said as far as she could see, and apparently Damian felt the same way.

"How's your knee?" Damian asked unexpectedly.

"It's okay. Evan was using it as an excuse to dance with Nadine."

The music circled them in a warm halo of melody. Soon Jessica was tapping her foot, wishing she hadn't been so quick to insist she leave the dance floor.

"Come on," Damian said with a decided lack of enthusiasm. He stood and offered her his hand.

Stunned, Jessica looked up at him.

"There's nothing worse than sitting with a woman who obviously wants to dance."

"I…" She intended to tell him there was nothing worse than dancing with someone who obviously didn't want to be her partner. But before she could speak, he'd taken her hand. He was muttering something under his breath, which she couldn't quite make out. She did hear Evan's name, and she guessed he wasn't pleased with his brother.

Jessica wanted to kick Evan for leaving her alone with Damian. The orchestra had been playing fast-paced songs, but when Damian and Jessica moved onto the floor, the band began a slow dreamy number. The lights lowered and Jessica groaned inwardly.

"Let's sit this one out," she suggested.

"Not on your life," Damian said, easing her into his arms. She didn't understand why he felt obliged to dance with her. He held her stiffly in his arms as though afraid to bring her close. His back was rigid and he stared straight ahead.

"Relax," he whispered impatiently. "I won't bite."

"Me?" she said. "I might as well be waltzing with a mannequin."

"Okay, let's both make an effort."

Jessica hadn't realized she was so tense. Determined to do as he suggested, she closed her eyes and released a slow sigh. She felt the tension ease from Damian, and when she opened her eyes he'd brought her closer, close enough for her to rest her temple against the side of his jaw. The solace she found, as their bodies swayed gently to the rhythm, was worth every minute she'd waited to feel his arms around her.

This was where she belonged, Jessica mused sadly, where she'd always belonged. Surely Damian felt it too. Why else would he be holding her as if she was the most precious thing in his world? Why else would his lips be moving against her hair as if he longed to kiss her.

Neither spoke, she realized, because they feared words would destroy the moment. She clung to him even when the music stopped, not wanting this blissful time to end.

"We should get back to the table," Damian said, and the reluctance she heard in his voice gave her hope.

"I don't see Evan or Nadine. Do you want to dance one more number?" she asked.

He didn't answer her for a long moment, and then said gruffly, "Yes."

"I do, too."

"Jessica, listen…"

She chanced raising her face and looking at him, her eyes filled with a longing so great she couldn't hide it. Pressing her finger over his mouth, she smiled. "Please, Damian, not now."

He briefly closed his eyes, sighed and nodded.

Jessica lost track of time. She knew they danced far longer than they should have, for more numbers than she could count. Every once in a while she glanced at their table, but neither Nadine or Evan were in sight.

It wasn't until the music sped up again, that he revealed any signs of regret. She knew something was wrong the minute he eased her from his arms. His face hardened. She looked up at him and blinked, not understanding.

"I'll have my brother's hide for this," Damian muttered.

"For what?" she asked softly.

A muscle in his jaw jerked as he reined in his temper, but that was the only answer she got.

They left the dance floor and sat like strangers at the table. Jessica couldn't bear it any longer. She stood, excused herself and moved from table to table to greet several old family friends. She returned only when she saw that Evan had joined his brother. Nadine was nowhere in sight. The two brothers seemed to be having a rapid intense exchange of words, but when she approached, Damian clamped his mouth closed and looked the other way.

"I've neglected you," Evan said contritely, claiming her hand between both of his. "I'm sorry, Jessica. Can you forgive me?"

"Of course." What else could she do? Demand that he immediately take her home? That would have been silly. Especially as she wasn't interested in him as anything other than a friend. Besides, his neglect had given her all that time with Damian.

A breathless and laughing Nadine returned to the table a few moments later, and the four of them ordered drinks. The waitress had just brought their order when Walter and Lois Dryden approached their table.

"I hope you four are enjoying yourselves."

Evan said that they certainly had been.

Lois smiled benevolently down on Jessica, then gently placed her hands on Jessica's shoulders, leaning forward so that their heads were close together. "We owe you so much," she said, kissing her cheek.

"Nonsense." The words embarrassed her.

"It's true. Tell her, Walter," Lois insisted. "We were about to despair over what was happening with Evan, and that all changed the minute you started working for the firm."

"Mother..." Evan didn't seem to appreciate this, either.

"It's true. You have no idea how pleased Joyce and I are that the two of you are seeing so much of each other," Lois continued.

"I have to agree with your mother," Walter said in his deep, vibrant voice. "You're a good man, Evan, with a bright future. It was a damn shame to watch you waste your life over a woman you couldn't have. It's much better now that you're seeing Jessica."

A stilted uncomfortable silence followed his father's praise. Within a few minutes of the elder Drydens' visit to their table, Damian made an excuse, and he and Nadine got up and left. After that, Evan didn't seem too keen to stay, either. As for Jessica, she was more than happy to get home. Enough was enough.

She lay awake most of the night thinking, and by daybreak, she'd made her decision. With purpose driving her steps, Jessica walked into the office the next morning, her eyes burning from lack of sleep.

"I need to see Mr. Dryden for a moment," she told Damian's secretary.

The woman, doubtless noting the determination in Jessica's voice, reached instantly for the intercom and announced her.

Jessica strode into Damian's office and stood before him. He was sitting behind his desk reading a file. He glanced up, his expression, as always, inscrutable. "What can I do for you, Jessica?"

Her heart pounding, she said flatly, "I'm resigning from my position with this firm, effective immediately." It was an impulsive thing to do, Jessica realized, considering how difficult it was these days to find a job. But her sanity was more important. She'd do temporary work if she had to. Or work in another field.

If Damian was surprised by her announcement, he didn't reveal it. He leaned back in his chair, calm and composed. "This is rather sudden, isn't it?"

"Yes…but it's necessary." She avoided eye contact by studying the painting on the wall behind him. It was a seascape with the ocean crashing against the jagged edge of a protruding rock. A bird was perched on the uppermost point of the rock, undisturbed by the raging sea. Jessica wished she could be more like that bird.

"Does Evan know?"

"Not yet," she replied. "Since you were the one to hire me, I felt obligated to tell you first."

He paused as if gathering his thoughts. "If you could work out your two-week notice, I'd appreciate it."

Jessica wasn't sure what she'd expected. Nothing, she'd told herself, but she realized now that wasn't true. In the deepest part of her, she was praying Damian would ask her to reconsider, that he'd make at least one attempt to change her mind. Perhaps a raise or some other inducement. Instead, he calmly accepted her resignation as if he was almost pleased to see her go.

That hurt. She held the pain to herself for as long as she could, before turning and walking toward the door.

"Jessica."

She stopped, but didn't turn around.

"You've been a valuable asset to this firm, and we'll miss you."

That was all he was willing to offer. It was damn little.

"Thank you," she whispered, then walked out the door. She was trembling by the time she sat down at her own desk. After taking a moment to compose herself, she reached for the phone and dialed Cathy's number.

"You did *what?*" her friend cried.

Jessica had never used the office phone for personal calls before, but she made this day the exception. "You heard me. I quit."

"But why?"

"It's a long story," she murmured, "but suffice to say, I'm tired of this whole ridiculous charade."

"Damian loves you."

"No," she whispered, "he doesn't." She'd been swayed by Cathy's comments and her own foolish heart, because she so desperately wanted to believe it was true.

"Jessica, Jessica, Jessica," Cathy said in an impatient singsong, "don't be so hasty."

It was either leave the firm or lose her sanity, Jessica mused. It'd been a mistake to contact Cathy; her friend simply didn't understand.

"What did Evan say?"

"He doesn't know yet," she admitted reluctantly. Not that it would make any difference. No argument Evan offered could convince her to change her mind.

"Keep me informed, will you? Following what's going on in your life is more interesting than my soap operas."

Mrs. Sterling came into the office and stared at Jessica, looking as if she were about to burst into tears. "You're leaving!"

This office had an information network the CIA would envy. Jessica didn't bother to ask where Evan's secretary had heard the news; it didn't matter.

"But you can't go now, not when Mr. Dryden's back to his old self."

"I apologize for leaving you in the lurch."

"You won't reconsider?"

Jessica shook her head.

"Personally," said Mrs. Sterling, "I think it makes for bad politics when men and women from the same office date one another. These things have a way of turning sour."

"What does?" Evan asked, stepping into the room, carrying a leather briefcase and looking very much the professional he was. He paused at his secretary's desk and reached for his mail.

"Jessica's resigned," Mrs. Sterling said baldly.

Evan dropped the mail and turned to stare at Jessica. His mouth fell open with disbelief. "Is it true?"

She nodded. Until she saw the look of dismay on his face, she hadn't believed he held any real affection for her.

"Come into my office," he commanded, leading the way and clearly expecting her to follow. When she was inside, he closed the door.

"What's this all about?" he demanded.

To the best of her memory, Jessica had never seen this side of Evan. He looked and acted like Damian. "It's time I moved on," she said weakly, not knowing exactly how much to say, if anything, about the real reason.

"After less than two months?"

She crossed her arms and shrugged.

"Are the hours too long?"

"No."

"We're not paying you enough?"

"I'm receiving an adequate salary," she returned. She didn't like the way he was putting her on the defensive, and she stiffened her resolve. There was a side of her he hadn't seen, either—her stubborn side.

"There must be a reason you find it so repugnant to work for me."

"I never said I found it repugnant to work for you." She dropped her hands and formed tight fists at her sides. Evan was acting every inch the attorney.

"So it's the firm you don't like. Have we done something to offend you?"

"No!" she cried, hating this interrogation. Evan's reaction was certainly the opposite of Damian's. Evan was clearly upset at the idea of losing her.

"Then why? You owe me an explanation," he insisted.

"I don't feel I do…" She hesitated, her stomach in knots.

"Is it something I've done?" His voice was gentler now, as if he was trying to soothe her, to gain her confidence.

"No," she assured him. "You've been wonderful…a good friend. I'll treasure the times we've had together, Evan, but you don't love me and I don't love you. It seems to me that we should appreciate what we do share and not try to make something of it that isn't there." Or allow their parents to do so, either, she added mentally.

He looked puzzled. "That's no reason to quit working for the firm."

"Perhaps not, but it's the right thing for me. Damian

asked me to work out my two-week notice, which I'll gladly do, but I'm not going to change my mind."

"All right," he agreed reluctantly. "In the meantime, you don't mind if we continue to see one another, do you?"

"I'm...not sure it would be wise."

Evan jerked back his head as though her answer amazed him. "You aren't serious, are you?"

"Yes, Evan, I am. I enjoy your company and consider you a friend, but..."

"What about coffee to talk over old times?"

"Perhaps."

Evan grinned then, that devilishly handsome grin guaranteed to stir the heart of any woman. "I'm not letting you back out of our sailing date, though. I've been counting on that. You aren't going to let me down, are you?"

"No, I won't let you down." Nevertheless, Jessica's heart sank as she remembered her promise to go out with Evan on his sailboat in three weeks' time. He'd made the date *before* the formal dinner event. *Before* she'd known she wanted out of the Drydens' sphere.

He beamed her a wide smile.

Jessica stayed late that night, wanting to clear her desk before she headed back to her apartment. Undaunted by her stated reluctance to continue seeing him socially, Evan had asked her to dinner, and Jessica had declined. Besides, she'd been out late the night before, hadn't slept well and was anxious to finish up at the office and head home.

She was leaving just as Damian came out of his office.

"Good night," she said cordially, moving down the corridor to wait for the elevator. Damian joined her there.

The doors opened and they stepped inside together. They stood like strangers while the elevator made its descent. Jessica stared at the numbers above the door as they lighted up one by one. Only a week earlier, she would have been thrilled to have these few seconds alone with Damian, and now she would have given anything to avoid him. Being this close to him physically and so far apart emotionally was agony in its purest form.

The elevator doors silently slid open, and Jessica stepped into the lobby, glad to make her escape. Damian would go about his life, and she would go about hers.

"Jessica." Damian sounded impatient, but she didn't know if it was with her or himself. "Are you taking the subway?"

"Yes, it's right around the corner." She began to move away.

"I'll give you a ride home."

"No, thank you."

"I insist," Damian said in steel tones. "It's time we talked."

If Jessica had thought her heart was beating hard that morning when she entered his office, it didn't compare with the way it thundered against her ribs now.

Silently he led her into the parking garage to his car. He unlocked the passenger-side door and held it open for her, then went around to the driver's side and climbed in. As he inserted the key into the ignition, he asked, "Have you spoken to Evan about your resignation?"

"Yes."

"What did he have to say?"

She gestured weakly with her hands. "He asked me to reconsider."

"Have you?"

"No. I'll work out my two-week notice, since you asked me to, but my decision stands."

Damian's hands tightened around the steering wheel. "Why, Jessica?"

"Why should you care, Damian?" she returned, losing patience with him. "This morning, you couldn't wait to be rid of me."

"That's not true," he said sharply.

"I don't think discussing this will solve anything," she said, reaching for the door handle, intent on letting herself out.

The air was electric. "Jessica, stay for a few minutes. Please." His words were soft, without emotion, and yet filled with it.

Jessica hesitated. "All right." She dropped her hand.

"Did you give your notice because of what happened at the dinner?" he asked.

Confused, Jessica turned to study Damian. "Last night?"

"Evan virtually abandoned you. I know your feelings must have been hurt, but—"

"Just a minute," she said, twisting in her seat to look

at him directly. "You don't honestly believe that, do you?"

A puzzled look crowded his features. "Yes. My brother was rude in the extreme to abandon you the way he did."

She was angrier than she could remember being in a long time. When she let things fester inside her this way, her anger took the form of hiccups when she released it.

"Do you think *hic* I'm so shallow I'd quit *hic* my job in a fit of *hic* jealousy? Is that *hic* what you're saying, Damian?"

He blinked when she was finished, as though he expected more.

Jessica threw open the car door, climbed out and slammed it. "I *hic* don't think this *hic* conversation is getting us anywhere."

With that she marched away. She thought she heard Damian's car door close, but she didn't bother to look back.

"Jessica!" he called, storming into the empty lobby.

She hesitated. The hiccups hadn't subsided, and she was having a hard time breathing properly.

"I'm sorry," he said after a tense moment.

She understood then. He was apologizing for much more than their argument. He was telling her how much he regretted not loving her.

Chapter 9

Other than brief glimpses Jessica didn't see Damian at all during the next two weeks. A new legal assistant, Peter McNichols, was hired, and Jessica helped train the conscientious young man.

On her last day, Damian sent word that he wanted to see her in his office. Mrs. Sterling issued the summons. "I hope you'll change your mind," Evan's secretary said wistfully. "You're an excellent worker and I hate to see you go." She cast a speculative eye toward Evan's closed office door. "I'm sure Mr. Dryden's going to miss you, too."

Evan had made several attempts in the past two weeks to bribe her into staying, but Jessica had stood steadfastly by her decision. Although it had been made impulsively, it was the right thing to do.

Jessica reached for her pad and pen before starting toward Damian's office, although she doubted he expected her to take notes. She was promptly shown in by his secretary.

She found Damian standing at the window, his back to her. His hands were clasped behind him, the pose he assumed when he was thinking or when he was troubled about something. She wondered if he found her departure distressing, then decided if that was the case he'd have said so long before now.

"You wanted to see me?" she asked quietly.

He turned around and offered her a reassuring smile. "Yes, please sit down." He motioned toward the chair, then claimed the seat behind his desk. He reached for an envelope on the corner and handed it to Jessica.

"It's your paycheck," he explained. "I took the liberty of adding a small bonus."

"That wasn't necessary," she said, surprised by the gesture.

"Perhaps not, but I wanted you to know how much the firm appreciated the extra time and effort you put into the Earl Kress case."

"I stayed late because I wanted to."

"I realize that. Now," he said, leaning back in his chair, his posture casual, his eyes curious, "have you found another position yet?"

"No." Working every day had made searching for a job almost impossible. There would be time enough for that later, in the days and weeks to follow.

"I see," he said unemotionally. "If you like, I'd be happy to write you a letter of recommendation."

The offer was generous in light of the fact she'd worked for the firm such a short while.

"I'd appreciate that very much." She'd given considerable thought to the consequences of being out of a job. A letter of recommendation would help.

"There are a number of firms I know who might be interested in obtaining a top-notch legal assistant. I could make a few calls on your behalf."

Damian was being more than generous, she thought. "Thank you. I'd be grateful."

He nodded and she got to her feet. Saying goodbye to Damian was much more difficult than she'd ever expected. When she walked out the door she didn't know how long it'd be before she saw him again. Their families might be close, but Jessica and Damian led very separate lives. It could well be months or even years before they ran into each other. But perhaps that would be for the best. She fidgeted with the yellow notepad. "I want you to know how much I've appreciated working for you and Evan," she said, barely managing to keep her voice steady. "You were willing to give me a chance when all I had was classroom experience."

"You've proved yourself in countless ways since then."

She backed away, taking small steps, until her back was against his door. She felt the wood pressing against her shoulder blades. "Thank you, too," she said, and her voice came out a hoarse whisper, "for everything else."

His brow creased with a frown.

"For the dinners and our time at Cannon Beach," she elaborated. The final words stuck in her throat, and she was sure that if she said what was really in her heart, it would embarrass them both.

His eyes revealed his sadness. "Goodbye, Jessica."

She turned then and opened the door, but before she walked out of his life, before she took that first step, she glanced over her shoulder to look once again, to grab hold of this last memory of him.

Damian was standing there, in the same spot he'd been when she first arrived, gazing out the window, his hands clasped behind his back.

"I can't believe you left it like that." Cathy was outraged, pacing Jessica's living room like a caged tiger. She hadn't been able to stand still from the moment Jessica had told her about her last meeting with Damian.

"What did you expect me to say to him?" Jessica demanded in irritation. The romantic part of her had been hoping Damian would come after her, but he hadn't. Even Evan had seemed resigned to her wishes. She'd spent one of the most emotionally draining days of her life, and the last thing she needed was chastisement from her best friend. "If he had a shred of feeling for me, this would have been a golden opportunity for him to say something, don't you think?"

"You don't want to know what I think about that man," Cathy muttered darkly.

"The best he was willing to do was a letter of recommendation. I don't need to be hit over the head, Cathy. Damian Dryden simply doesn't care about me." Kneeling before the coffee table, she jerked a piece of pizza from the box with such force the cheese slid off the top.

"Does he know you're not seeing Evan?"

"Of course he knows."

"How can you be so sure? Did you tell him?"

"No."

Cathy lifted her hands in abject frustration. "Then that's it. He thinks you're still dating his brother."

"Evan's gone out with Nadine Powell twice this week. Damian knows that. Besides, all Evan and I have ever been is friends. I told Damian that. Obviously he's not interested one way or the other, so there's no point in discussing it, is there?"

Cathy dropped onto the carpet and reached for a slice of pizza. "I'm really disappointed."

"So am I." That was a gross understatement, but Jessica had never been one to dwell on past mistakes. It would be a long time before she could consider loving Damian a mistake. She'd learned several lessons about herself, and love, in the process. When all was said and done she was going to miss him dreadfully.

"I thought you told me you and Evan were going sailing this weekend?" Cathy asked curiously.

"Not this weekend. Next."

"Aha!" Her friend slapped the end of the coffee table with her free hand. "So you *are* continuing to see Evan. Damian must know that, too. No wonder he's—"

"Cathy," Jessica said, cutting her off, "leave it. I probably won't be seeing Damian again, and apparently that's the way he wants it. Heaven knows I couldn't have been any more obvious about how I felt."

Cathy shook her head sadly. "I guess I must be more of a romantic than I realized. I was so sure he was in love with you. I was so confident I was right, I guess, because I wanted to be. I've waited all these years for you to fall in love, and now that you have…" Her voice faded as a frown ruled her features. "I was so very sure," she whispered, the puzzled expression growing more intense as though she didn't understand, even now, what could possibly have gone wrong.

"This is a treat," Jessica said, sitting across the table from her mother in their favorite seafood restaurant. They were given a table that looked out over Back Bay. The waters were green and peaceful, and fishing boats could be seen in the distance, bobbing up and down like corks.

Joyce Kellerman spread the linen napkin on her lap and smiled serenely.

Jessica groaned inwardly. She knew that look well. It was the one that spoke of pained disappointment. Her mother had given her that identical look when she'd learned Jessica had dropped out of piano lessons. The look was there again when Jessica had refused to go to Girl Scout camp when she was twelve; it hadn't helped that her mother had been the group leader. It was her mother's way of saying Jessica's behavior completely baffled her. Jessica didn't pretend not to know what this luncheon engagement was about.

"You think I made a mistake quitting my job, don't you, Mother?"

Joyce looked mildly surprised that Jessica had introduced the subject. "I just don't understand why, that's all. It was the perfect job for you, with old family friends. You and Evan seemed to be getting along so well, and then for no reason I can discern, you resigned."

"It was time for me to move on," Jessica said vaguely.

"But you'd barely worked there two months," Joyce protested. "It doesn't look good on a résumé for you to be hopping from one job to the next. You know what your father has to say about such behavior."

There it was, in black and white, with the emphasis on black. She'd disappointed her father, the man who'd devoted his life to the preservation of her happiness.

"Working for the Drydens had become...uncomfortable, Mom." Jessica didn't explain further. What could she say?

Her mother reached for the menu and focused her attention there. "Lois and I blame ourselves for this, you know. We were both so excited when you and Evan hit it off that we let our imaginations run away with us. Here we were talking about a wedding and grandchildren, and you two had barely started dating."

"Mom, it wasn't that."

Joyce set the menu aside and clutched the edge of the table, leaning toward Jessica. "I feel so badly about all this. I do hope you'll accept my apology, Jessica."

"Mom, listen to me. Evan and I were never romantically interested in each other. He's in love with someone else. We've had several long talks, and he's simply not ready to become involved in another relationship. That's perfectly understandable."

"Oh, dear, I'm sorry I'm late." A flustered Lois Dryden approached their table, surprising Jessica. This was her first week away from the Dryden law firm, and when her mother had suggested lunch, it had sounded like a great way to kill a couple of hours between job interviews, the very ones Damian had arranged for her. Jessica hadn't realized Damian's mother had been invited to this luncheon, as well.

"With the primary less than three weeks away, I don't think I've ever been busier." Lois Dryden pulled out a chair and sat down next to her friend and neighbor.

"Mom didn't mention you'd be joining us," Jessica said, casting a mild accusatory glance at her mother. The last thing she needed now was another inquisition.

"I hope you don't mind," Lois murmured contritely. "It does look as though we're ganging up on you, doesn't it? We don't mean to, dear. It's just that we can't help being curious about what's going on between you and Evan."

So, her mother wasn't the only one looking for answers. Lois Dryden, too. And the pair *were* ganging up on her.

"We're both far snoopier than we should be," Lois Dryden went on breathlessly, setting her small handbag next to her silverware, "but that's just part of being a mother."

"Jessica was telling me that Evan's still in love with someone else," Joyce explained.

"Oh, dear," Lois said wistfully, "I was afraid of that. Is it that Summerhill girl he was so keen on a few months ago?"

Jessica looked out over the sun-brightened waters of Back Bay and sighed. "Please understand, I don't mean to be rude, but Evan and I are friends, and I don't feel comfortable sharing what he said to me in confidence."

Joyce Kellerman beamed proudly at her friend. "My goodness, she sounds just like an attorney, doesn't she?"

"That's what she gets from hanging around my sons too long," Damian's mother replied. She crossed her arms and leaned on the table, her expression regretful. "I'm afraid I made a terrible mistake when Evan brought Mary Jo out to the house to meet Walter and me."

"I can't imagine your doing anything to offend anyone," Joyce said loyally.

"She was a shy little thing, and it was easy to see that Walter and I made her decidedly uncomfortable. After dinner, I tried to put her at ease, and I'm afraid I made a miserable job of it. You see, it's vital that Evan marry the…right kind of woman."

"Right kind of woman?" Jessica echoed, a little confused. She'd known the Drydens most of her life. They weren't snobs. They were two of the most generous conscientious people she'd ever met.

"Sometime in the future, Evan is destined to enter the political arena," Lois explained. "Being a politician's wife is like being married to a minister. I should know. After the last few weeks, I've been left with the feeling that *I* am the one running for the Senate, not Walter."

Jessica looked puzzled. "To the best of my knowledge Evan's never said anything about being interested in politics."

"Perhaps not recently, but he was keen on it before, and we've talked about it a lot in the past. It's only been in the past year or so that his interest has waned."

"You said all this to Mary Jo?" Joyce asked.

Lois nodded, her eyes betraying her remorse. "I've thought back on our conversation a hundred times, and I see now that I did more harm than good."

"Does Evan know what you said to her?" Jessica questioned.

"I'm fairly certain she didn't repeat it. I've thought of contacting her since then, thinking if I apologized she might find it in her heart to forgive me for being so terribly presumptuous."

Jessica groaned inwardly. This new information explained much of what had happened between Mary Jo and Evan, but it was too late. Mary Jo was married now, wasn't she? To that other teacher?

"I feel like I'm responsible for ruining things between you and Evan, as well," Lois went on. "I do try to stay out of my sons' lives, honestly I do, but I don't seem to have much success. I do hope you'll forgive Walter and me for pressuring you and Evan."

"Mrs. Dryden, please, you aren't at fault."

"You're such a dear girl, and Walter and I hoped it would work out between you and Evan." She paused to reach for the menu. "You make a handsome couple."

"Thank you."

The waiter came and took their order, and Lois fully relaxed. "Something's bothering Damian," she remarked. "I've tried to ask him about it, but you know Damian. He's as closemouthed as his father. Evan, bless his heart, is more like me. I've always known what Evan's thinking—well, until recently—because he's so open about his feelings. Not so with Damian."

"What about Damian?" Jessica asked, making the question sound as casual as she could.

"You could probably explain more to me than I can to you, dear," Lois said. "You see him far more often than I do, or at least, you did."

"I... Damian didn't make a practice of confiding in me."

Lois sighed noisily. "I figured as much. Mark my words, there's a woman involved in this. Damian may be as tight-lipped as his father, but I know my son. I think he might have fallen in love."

Jessica glanced back at the water, knowing that if Damian's mother was right, the woman was someone else. Not her.

"Once on board, you can go below and unload the groceries," Evan instructed, as they walked along the floating dock at the marina. When they reached the berth where the thirty-foot sailboat was moored, Evan helped Jessica aboard.

While she went below, Evan moved forward and busied himself with the sails, setting the jib and readying the spinnaker.

"It looks to me like you packed enough food for a week," Jessica shouted through the open stairwell that led to the deck above. The day was lovely, the wind perfect for sailing. Despite all his comments about being the captain while she was the crew, Evan seemed eager to do the majority of the work. Putting away a few bags of groceries seemed a paltry task.

"I'll probably set sail while you're below," Evan

shouted down to her, "so don't be concerned if you feel the boat move."

Jessica's experience as a sailor was limited. Evan had insisted for weeks that he was going to change all that. Before the end of the day, he claimed she'd be a top-notch mariner. Apparently the lessons started in the galley.

Humming as she worked, Jessica unloaded the three large grocery bags. They were apparently going to eat well this weekend. She was busy cleaning radishes when she heard voices up above, but although she craned her neck to see who Evan was speaking to, she couldn't see anyone. It was probably someone standing on the dock, Jessica decided.

A few moments later came the sound of the sailboat's small outboard motor. The boat dipped slightly as Evan moved ahead and raised the sails. When the motor stopped, she knew they were a safe distance from the marina.

She finished her tasks and, bringing a couple of cans of cold soda with her, climbed up from the galley. It wasn't until she looked away from the helm that she realized someone else had joined them.

Damian.

She cast an accusatory look in Evan's direction, but it was nothing compared to the look Damian sent his way.

"I didn't know Evan had invited you," she said.

"I didn't know he'd invited *you,*" Damian returned, his voice cut by the wind. The boat tilted to one side and sliced through the water.

"Evan?" Jessica glared at the man she'd once considered a friend.

Evan was grinning broadly, clearly pleased with his own cleverness. "Didn't I mention Damian would be coming along?" he asked innocently.

"No," she answered, handing each brother a can of soda and retreating to the galley. Evan was pretending the situation was the result of miscommunication, but she knew he'd purposely set it up.

Damian followed her below a few minutes later. She was sitting at the booth, her back against the side of the boat and her legs stretched out on the upholstered seat. Her arms were crossed over her chest as she tried to take in what was happening.

Damian didn't look any happier with this turn of events than she did. Walking over to the refrigerator, he replaced the can of soda she'd given him as though that had been his sole purpose in coming below.

"I think you should know I didn't arrange this meeting, if that's what you're thinking."

Jessica had nothing to say. She wasn't angry with Damian; he'd been just as manipulated as she had. She didn't know what game Evan was playing, but she wanted no part of it.

"I imagine having me around ruins your day with my brother," Damian said in what sounded strangely like an apology. He investigated the cupboards as if searching for something to eat. He brought out a bag of potato chips. "Have you found another job yet?"

"Not yet, but I've been called in for a second interview." She doubted this was news to Damian. From what she'd gathered at the new firm, he'd made her sound like God's gift to the legal profession, which was going to be one hell of a reputation to maintain.

"Do you mind if I ask you something?" she said.

"Of course not." He slipped into the narrow booth across from her.

"If you thought so highly of me, why'd you accept my resignation?" Not an entirely fair question, she realized, since she'd been the one to quit.

"Did you want me to ask you to stay?"

She smiled and shrugged. "I guess in a way I did, although it's difficult to admit that now."

"Why did you decide to quit?" He opened the bag of potato chips and offered it to her. Jessica took a handful of chips and dumped them on the tabletop, grateful for something to occupy her hands.

"Why did I decide to quit?" she said, repeating his question thoughtfully. He wasn't going to like her answer. "Mainly because of what happened at that dinner party."

Damian's dark eyes glittered with indignation. "Then it did have something to do with the attention Evan paid Nadine."

"No," she flared back. "I quit because of the pressure I felt from both sets of parents. They practically had me and Evan engaged."

"You could do far worse than marrying my brother."

"How can you even suggest such a thing?" she demanded, her voice quavering. She'd never marry a man she didn't love. "What's the matter with you, Damian?"

"With me?"

"Did you or did you not hear me in the kitchen of your parents' home less than three weeks ago?"

He frowned. "Yes." The word was clipped and angry.

"Then how can you ask me something so stupid?"

Damian's eyes were furious. He wasn't the kind of man to take kindly to insults.

Jessica grabbed a potato chip and shoved it into her mouth. Crunching down on something crisp and salty seemed to help vent her frustration.

"But Evan—"

"If you so much as suggest that Evan's in love with me," she interrupted, "I swear I won't be responsible for what I say or do next."

Damian looked taken aback by her angry retort. He closed his mouth and frowned heavily. Reaching for the potato chips, he munched on two or three, and for a moment this was the only sound in the galley.

"You know my problem, don't you?" she said.

"You mean you only have one?" Damian asked with honey-coated sarcasm.

Jessica ignored the comment. "It's that I assumed a man who had passed the bar and was one of the most brilliant minds in corporate law in Boston today, would—"

"How's everything going down there?" Evan called down. "Are you two talking yet?"

Jessica looked up to find that the younger Dryden brother had opened the door to the galley and was sitting almost directly above them, his arm on the helm, steering the sailboat. The wind ruffled his hair and flattened his windbreaker to his chest.

"We're trading insults!" Damian called back.

"That's a good place to start." Evan sounded disgustingly cheerful. "There's something you should know," he added. "I don't have any intention of turning this boat around until you two have reached an agreement."

"About what?" Jessica demanded.

"We'll get to that in a moment. Now, Damian, admit you're in love with Jessica and be done with it. Quit playing these ridiculous games."

"Damian in love with me?" she repeated incredulously. "Not a chance."

"So that's the way it's going to be," Evan called down. "Not to worry, I packed enough food to last us a good three or four days."

"Don't be absurd." Damian was beginning to sound impatient.

"Listen up, big brother," Evan shouted. "You didn't think I saw you the day you kissed Jessica in Mom's kitchen, but I did. You're crazy about her. What I can't figure out is why you insist on hiding it."

"You were the one dating her."

"So?"

"I don't get involved with women you're dating."

"There's always an exception to the rule. Jessica's a free woman. If you're in love with her, like I suspect, then why didn't you say something?"

Damian's mouth thinned. "You wouldn't understand."

"Try me," Evan insisted.

"Listen, you two," Jessica said, interrupting the exchange. "If you don't mind, I'd rather you didn't discuss me like I wasn't here."

Both men ignored her.

"Jessica's been crazy about you since she was a kid," Damian declared.

"So?" Evan returned. "She grew up and fell in love with you. A woman can change her mind if she wants. They've been known to do that."

"But you love her!" Damian insisted impatiently.

"You're right—like a sister. She'd make a terrific sister-in-law. We get along great."

Damian's eyes, which were now fixed on Jessica, grew dark and intense. "Were you about to tell me you love me?" he asked her in a husky murmur.

"Yes, you imbecile! What do I have to do—hit you over the head?"

"I don't mean to be offering you advice, big brother," Evan shouted down, "but this might be a good time to kiss her."

"I appreciate the help, *little* brother, but I can take it from here," Damian hollered back and slipped out of the booth. He shut the galley door and bolted it, then turned to Jessica.

He was grinning, she noticed, as if he'd just found out he was holding the winning ticket in the state lottery. "You must have thought I was a stubborn fool," he said, grasping her ankles and tugging her across the length of the upholstered bench. Then he gripped her around the waist and brought her upright and into his arms.

"Do you love me, Damian?" she asked.

"Heart and soul," he admitted as his hands framed her face.

"You might have said something sooner, you know," she murmured, thinking there'd been ample opportunity.

"I didn't dare. I assumed Evan loved you and needed you, but I was wrong, Jessica, very wrong. In the past few weeks I've discovered how very much I loved and needed you myself." He stroked her hair as though he couldn't believe even now that she was with him.

His mouth found hers. She wrapped her arms around him and leaned her weight into his. Damian kissed her again and again, until she was breathless with wonder. Until she marveled at how she'd managed to survive this long outside of his arms.

"I can't believe I'm holding you like this," he whispered between kisses. He couldn't seem to get enough of her, which was fine with Jessica, because she couldn't get enough of him, either.

"You're a fool, Damian Dryden."

"I know, but not any longer. I thought I was doing the noble thing by stepping aside for Evan. I was furious with him after the dinner party, but even more furious with myself."

"Why?"

"For being unable to resist holding you." His grip around her tightened. She felt the even rise and fall of his chest and nestled closer.

"You let me walk out of your life," she said, remembering the pain of leaving the law firm.

"I let you walk out of my office," he said, pressing

his jaw against her hair, "but not out of my life. Never that. I was waiting, rather impatiently, to see what developed between you and my brother."

A loud knock from above finally separated them. Continuing to hold her, Damian raised one arm to unhook the latch and raise the door. "Yes?" he asked impatiently.

"Can I turn this boat around yet?"

"Not yet!" Jessica shouted.

"Give us a few more minutes," Damian added.

Evan chuckled. "Just promise me one thing," he insisted. "No, make that two."

"All right," Damian said, apparently in a generous mood.

"First, I insist on being best man at the wedding."

"Wedding," Jessica repeated slowly.

Damian nodded insistently. "The sooner the better. I've been waiting for you far too long already."

"Am I going to be best man or not?" Evan demanded.

"There's no one else I'd even consider, little brother."

"And second," Evan said with a hearty sigh, "I want to be there when you tell Mom and Dad Jessica's marrying you, instead of me."

Chapter 10

"I'd feel better if you kissed me first," Jessica murmured, looking up at Damian. They'd called the Drydens from the marina and asked Lois to invite the Kellermans over, as well.

"If you don't kiss her, I will," Evan teased, eyeing his older sibling.

"Not this time, little brother." Damian wrapped his arm around Jessica's shoulders and gently kissed her. It would have been easy to continue had they been elsewhere. Being held and kissed by Damian was the closest Jessica had ever come to paradise, and it was difficult to break away from the tender shelter of his arms.

"I don't know why I'm so nervous," Jessica said as they headed, hand in hand, toward the parking lot.

"I do." Of late, Evan seemed to be the one with all

the answers. "Both sets of parents think you're marrying me." He laughed cheerfully. Clearly he was looking forward to this meeting.

Evan had been the one who insisted they talk to all four parents immediately. Damian and Jessica had agreed, but now Jessica wished she'd suggested they return to her apartment first. She needed to change clothes. Her hair was wind-tossed, and her face was red from the sun and wind.

But Damian seemed eager for this meeting, as if he, too, wanted the matter cleared with both sets of parents. He raised Jessica's hand to his mouth and brushed his lips over her knuckles.

"Don't look so worried. Mom and Dad are going to be ecstatic."

She wasn't concerned about his parents' reaction, or hers for that matter. Neither set would object to her marrying Damian. They'd be thrilled. It was just that the idea of Damian's loving her was still so new she was afraid it wasn't real.

Jessica rode with Damian, and Evan followed in his car. They got separated on the freeway, and when they pulled into the long winding drive that led to Whispering Willows, Jessica noticed Evan's car was already parked out front.

"The speed demon," Damian commented with a chuckle. He parked behind his brother, turned off the ignition and reached for Jessica, kissing her soundly. "Are you ready to walk into the dragons' den?"

She smiled and nodded, thinking she'd follow Damian anywhere.

He helped her out of the car, tucking her hand in the bend in his arm, and they walked together into the family home. The elder Drydens and Kellermans stared back at them with a look of anxious interest.

"Hello, everyone," Damian said, leading Jessica to a chair in the massive living room. He seated her and then stood directly behind her, his hands resting on her shoulders. She raised her fingers and placed them over his.

"I imagine you're wondering why we asked you here," Jessica said to her parents. Her mother sat studying Jessica as if trying to figure out what was wrong with this picture.

"Hold on!" Evan shouted from the kitchen. "Don't say another word until I get there."

"Son?" Walter Dryden gave Damian a puzzled look. "What's the meaning of this?"

"Okay, now," Evan instructed breathlessly, carrying in a silver tray with seven crystal flutes and two bottles of champagne.

"I've asked you to be here, Mr. and Mrs. Kellerman," Damian began formally, "to request the honor of marrying your daughter."

Hamilton Kellerman's face wrinkled with confusion as he turned to his wife. "You told me she was marrying Evan."

"She's—I mean, we hoped—" Joyce stammered.

"I'm in love with Damian," Jessica broke in.

Her father scratched his head. "That's not the way I remember it. You were crazy over Evan for years.

Last I heard, you were making a damned nuisance of yourself."

"Daddy, that was years ago."

"She's crazy about *me* now," Damian interjected, lightly squeezing her shoulders. "And I feel the same way about her."

"Oh, Damian." Lois Dryden covered her mouth with her fingers. "We're delighted. Just delighted. Joyce, think of it, we'll be sharing grandchildren, after all."

The two women were hugging each other and dancing around in circles as Evan passed out champagne glasses to the silent, confused fathers.

"You know what this is all about, Walter?"

"Can't say that I do, Ham."

"You object?"

"Hell, no. I haven't seen that much life in Lois in fifteen years. What about you? Would you rather Jessica married someone else?"

"Heavens, no." Hamilton shook his head as if he didn't know what to think. "The wife's been talking about a union between our two families all summer, only she thought it would be between Jessica and Evan. The way I figure it, a union is a union, and the two of them certainly look to be in love."

"Yes, they undoubtedly have the look," Walter said, smiling at them.

The sound of an exploding cork echoed about the room as Evan uncorked a bottle of champagne. "I'd like to propose a toast," he said, walking from person to person filling the flutes. "To Jessica and Damian," he said, setting the bottle aside and holding up his glass.

"May their lives always be filled with happy surprises, and may their love endure for all time."

"Evan, how sweet," Lois said, dabbing the corner of her eye.

"For all time," Joyce agreed.

Everyone raised their glasses, then took a sip of champagne.

"Now, let's talk about the wedding," Lois said, prepared then and there to square away the details. She sat on the sofa next to her husband.

"It'll have to be after the November election," Joyce commented thoughtfully.

"We need to make it through the September primary first," Lois said. "I can't see delaying the wedding when we don't know for certain Walter will be in contention for the Senate."

"Nonsense. Of course he'll be on the ballot."

"Does any of this matter to you?" Damian asked Jessica, leaning so that his lips were close to her ear. A warm tingling sensation raced down her arms.

She smiled softly and shook her head. Nothing mattered except Damian and his love. "I'd marry you tomorrow if we could arrange it."

Damian drew in a deep breath. "Don't tempt me, sweetheart."

"Or in six months, if that's necessary. I've waited for you all my life, Damian. A few more weeks isn't going to matter."

Their mothers would have it all arranged within the hour, Jessica guessed. Their fathers were talking, too, working out schedules and other necessary details. The two families had been friends through all the seasons of their lives. The same way their own love—hers and Damian's—would last, weathering all the ups and downs the years would bring.

Jessica felt as though she'd come to the end of a long journey. She was home now, secure in Damian's love.

Epilogue

As Evan Dryden set aside the brief he was preparing and pinched the bridge of his nose, there was a knock on his door. Glad of the interruption, he called, "Come in."

His brother entered. The changes in Damian in the months since he'd married Jessica were many. Evan remembered a time when practicing law ruled Damian's life. He worked after hours and weekends, rarely taking time away. But now his brother looked younger, happier and so damn much in love Evan couldn't help a twinge of jealousy.

Witnessing the changes in Damian caused him to wonder what his own life would have been like if he'd married Mary Jo. They'd have started a family by now. The glimpse he'd caught of her almost a year ago at the

Red Sox game drifted into his mind, and with it came a stab of pain.

Loving her as he did, even now, it was impossible to want anything but the best for her. He tried not to think about Mary Jo, tried to place her firmly in the back of his mind, but every now and again, the memory of her escaped to taunt him with the might-have-beens.

It had been nearly eighteen months since they'd parted, and she still had the power to move him. He'd dated now and again, but there wasn't anyone he'd gotten serious about. He wished he knew what it was about Mary Jo that he couldn't forget.

Evan envied his brother the happiness he'd found and didn't expect to find the same happiness himself. He could see himself thirty years down the road with white hair, dressed in a smoking jacket, sitting in front of a fireplace smoking a pipe. A black Labrador would lie snoozing at his feet....

"You're looking thoughtful," Damian said, helping himself to a chair.

"Just woolgathering."

Damian was more relaxed these days, Evan noted. His brother leaned back in the chair and rested one ankle over the other knee. "Remember last month when Jessica phoned from the doctor's office?"

Evan chuckled. "I'm not likely to forget." Nor would anyone else in the office. Rarely had he seen his brother so excited, so elated. For days he'd walked around grinning like a mad fool. It wasn't every day, he said, a man learned he was going to be a father.

Funny, Evan thought, his brother was wearing a similar grin now. "What's going on now?" he asked. "Did you just learn Jessica's carrying twins?"

"Not quite. I've been approached by the bar about an appointment as a judge."

"Damian!" Evan rose from his chair. This shouldn't come as a surprise; it was Damian's destiny, just as marrying Jessica had been. He walked around his desk. Damian stood and the two brothers embraced.

"You're going to accept." Evan didn't put the words into a question. It went without saying Damian would and should.

"Yes, if Jessica concurs."

"She will." Evan had no doubts about that, either. "Are you going out tonight to celebrate?"

"As a matter of fact we are. Cathy Hudson, Jessica's friend, is starring in a new play that's opening tonight. Did I mention she recently got engaged to some director friend of hers?"

Before Evan could respond, his intercom buzzed and he reached for the button. "The receptionist called," Mrs. Sterling informed him, "and said Earl Kress is here to see you, Mr. Dryden."

"Earl?" Evan said with surprise. He hadn't heard from him in six months or more. "Send him in."

"We'll talk later," Damian said as he walked out of the office. "Give my regards to Earl, will you?"

Evan went with him, meeting Earl in the hallway outside. The two exchanged hearty handshakes. Evan slapped the younger man on the back as he led him into his office and closed the door.

"It's good to see you," Evan said, motioning toward the chair. "Sit down and make yourself comfortable."

"I can't stay long," Earl said, sitting on the edge of the chair. "I probably should have called, but I was in the neighborhood…"

"I'm glad you stopped in. How's school?"

"Good. I got my general equivalency diploma not long ago," he announced proudly.

"Congratulations." Evan experienced a surge of pride at the younger man's progress.

"I have a lot of people to thank for that, but you're the one who started it all. I don't think you ever realized how afraid I was of having the world know I couldn't read or write. It's humiliating to admit something like that."

"I realized at the time how difficult it was for you."

"Without your support, I don't think I could have gone through with the trial."

"I'm sure glad you did."

"Yeah, me, too," Earl said with a hearty laugh. "My life would certainly be different if I hadn't. Listen, I didn't mean to take up your time, but I wanted you to know how grateful I am for all your help."

"No problem, Earl."

"I'm working as a volunteer myself now with grade-school kids, helping out in the slow-reader program. I wouldn't have grown up illiterate if I'd gotten help while I was in the elementary grades."

Evan smiled broadly. "That's great, Earl."

"By the way, I ran across a friend of yours the other day—another volunteer."

"Oh?"

"At least I assume you two know one another. Her name's Mary Jo Summerhill."

"Mary Jo." Evan realized he breathed her name more than spoke it.

"Funny, she reacted the same way when I mentioned you."

"I thought she was married," Evan said.

"Not as far as I know." Earl stood and held out his hand. "Anyway, I won't keep you. I just wanted to stop in and update you about what's been going on in my life."

"I'm happy you did," Evan said, walking his former client to the door. He stood there for a moment, his mind spinning.

A few minutes later Damian strolled into his office again.

"What did Earl have to say?" he asked.

"Mary Jo isn't married." He said it out loud just to hear the sound of it. Damian wouldn't fully understand the significance of those words, but it didn't matter.

"I see," his brother said thoughtfully. "What are you going to do about it?"

Evan thought long and hard, then a slow smile spread across his features.

* * * * *

Also by Lee Tobin McClain

HQN

The Off Season

Cottage at the Beach
Reunion at the Shore
Christmas on the Coast
Home to the Harbor
First Kiss at Christmas
Forever on the Bay

Safe Haven

Low Country Hero
Low Country Dreams
Low Country Christmas

Love Inspired

Rescue Haven

The Secret Christmas Child
Child on His Doorstep
Finding a Christmas Home

Rescue River

Engaged to the Single Mom
His Secret Child
Small-Town Nanny
The Soldier and the Single Mom
The Soldier's Secret Child
A Family for Easter

Visit her Author Profile page at Harlequin.com,
or leetobinmcclain.com, for more titles!

CHILD ON HIS DOORSTEP

Lee Tobin McClain

To Grace, the inspiration for every child character
I've ever written.

Have not I commanded thee? Be strong and of
a good courage; be not afraid, neither be thou
dismayed: for the Lord thy God is with thee
whithersoever thou goest.
—*Joshua* 1:9

Chapter 1

Professor Corbin Beck stretched his stiff back, then leaned toward the computer screen in his home office. He was so close to figuring out the meaning behind his data points that he could taste it. Feel it. Smell it.

Hear it.

Hear it? He lifted his head. The sound he'd heard was a lot like a little kid crying.

Must be one of Mrs. Hutchenson's grandchildren next door. He refocused on his experimental protocol. If he could understand just where this was leading, he might make a breakthrough with nutritional care for senior dogs. It could have ramifications for other mammals, too. Not only would his position at the university be secured—no small thing for a guy who'd grown up the way he had—but he'd be helping animals. He understood them so much better than he understood people.

He forked his fingers through his hair and leaned closer to the computer screen in front of him, but now that he'd noticed it, the wrenching, sobbing noise couldn't be blocked out.

Definitely a kid. Definitely crying. Definitely not at Mrs. Hutchenson's house; much closer. Somewhere in the vicinity of his front door.

He shook himself out of his academic fog, shoved back his chair and strode to the door. He'd get the unhappy little tyke back to his grandma—hopefully without terrorizing him, as he had a tendency to do with kids—and return to his work.

He opened the front door of his sturdy brick home and reeled back a little. There, right on his front porch, was a scrawny toddler. The boy looked up at him and his squalling subsided for an instant, then started up again with redoubled force.

"Hey, hey, it's okay." Corbin hurried out onto the porch and folded his six-foot-three frame a little closer to the child, peering at him. Yep, super skinny with long, wildly curly hair, just as Corbin had had as a kid. Fortunately, Corbin looked more ordinary now, but he remembered being teased and felt a pang of sympathy for what this child was likely to go through.

He seemed to be quite a crybaby, which Corbin had been as well. Worse and worse for the child. Although since this one couldn't be more than two, he had every right to act like a baby. "Where's your mother?" he asked.

"Mama!" The child wailed louder.

Corbin cringed and squinted toward the house next door, but there was no sign of life there. He vaguely remembered hearing Mrs. Hutchenson and her grand-kids packing up the car with a picnic basket and bats and balls and Frisbees, when he'd come out onto his porch to stretch his back. That must have been around three thirty, just after the time the school bus usually chugged by.

Now, the sun was setting, golden and gorgeous as only an Ohio sunset could be.

The child's wails seemed to be subsiding, probably from exhaustion. His big brown eyes still broadcasting fear and worry, he reached for a stuffed tiger that was lying on top of a superhero suitcase.

Corbin blinked. A *suitcase*? And was that a car seat next to it?

When the boy secured the stuffed tiger and put its toe in his mouth, a piece of paper fluttered to the ground.

Corbin snatched it up, his quick movements caus-ing the child to break into another round of ear-split-ting shrieks.

Could Corbin slip back inside, away from the noise, to read what looked like a letter? No, that probably wouldn't be humane, leaving a crying child alone on the porch. But he couldn't stand to watch the kid get redder and redder in the face, practically choking on his sobs.

He went inside, grabbed a chocolate bar from the stash beside his recliner, and took one longing glance into his study, where his neatly lined-up papers sat be-side his computer.

The sooner you help the kid, the sooner you can get back to work. He went back out onto the porch, the screen door banging behind him. "Here," he said, unwrapping the candy bar and thrusting it into the child's grubby hand.

The child stared at him and kept crying.

"Eat it," he encouraged, and reached out, intending to break off a piece and show the kid how. Come to think of it, he hadn't eaten anything today himself. The candy looked good.

"Mine." The little boy clutched the candy to his chest, then lifted it to his mouth for a cautious lick.

The sobs stopped, and a smile crossed the little boy's tear-stained face. He mashed half the candy bar into his mouth.

Blessed silence reigned. And Corbin remembered the letter he was still holding in his hand. He lifted it and began to read.

Seriously, Corbin—candy? Samantha Alcorn shook her head and shifted positions inside the small copse of evergreen bushes along the side of Corbin's small yard.

She'd taken watch half an hour ago, the longest half hour she'd ever experienced. It wasn't just that the ground was muddy and cold. Listening to little Mikey cry had ripped at her heart. To stop herself from rushing over and scooping him up, she'd gripped the branch beside her so hard she'd gotten red dents in her hands.

It was for Mikey's greater good, though. That was what this whole mission was about. If she could help Mikey find a good home, if she could save him from an awful childhood—all while keeping the truth about him secret from Corbin—maybe, just maybe, she could forgive herself for what she'd done.

She couldn't forget. And she wasn't ever going to have a family herself, didn't deserve one. Helping Mikey, though, would be satisfaction enough. At least, she hoped so. Just like she hoped Mikey would find a happy home with Corbin. Although the full-sized chocolate bar he'd consumed in record time gave her a niggling sense of worry…

Mikey, temporarily sated by the candy, sat cuddling his tiger and studying Corbin.

Samantha studied Corbin too as he stood in the golden light, reading the letter. *My, my, my.*

Tall and muscular, the glasses he'd plucked from atop his head giving him an intellectual air, he looked way more attractive than a former ninety-pound weakling, now nerdy college professor, ought to be.

How was he going to react to the contents of the letter?

And how was she going to take action on the next part of the plan?

He finished reading, and even from across the small yard, Samantha heard his sigh. He took off his glasses and looked into the distance, then frowned at Mikey as if the little boy were a complete mystery.

"Mama," Mikey said fretfully, and looked toward the street where his mother had driven away. "Mama."

The discouraged sound in the toddler's voice brought tears to Samantha's eyes.

"Where's your mama?" Corbin asked, sitting heavily down on the front porch step, marginally closer to Mikey.

Mikey pointed in the direction of Main Street.

"I guess we should go look for her," Corbin said. Again, he studied the boy, his forehead wrinkling. "Can you walk?"

"No walk." Mikey pointed to the rope tied around his ankle. "No walk."

Corbin's whole body stiffened, and then he knelt and rapidly untied the child.

Samantha's face heated. That was the part she hadn't wanted to agree to, but Mikey's mother had casually explained that Mikey was used to it, that she regularly leashed him to a chair leg or doorknob when she needed to keep him safe.

Bringing him to Corbin is for Mikey's greater good. She shifted position and watched while Corbin picked up the little boy and lifted him down the steps. He didn't even seem to notice the chocolatey hands gripping at his shirt.

"This way," he said. "Let's go find Mom." But his voice was bleak.

It looked like he knew he wasn't going to find Cheryl.

But by going downtown, he was playing right into Samantha's hands. As soon as the pair had made their slow way past her hiding place, she checked the area, climbed stealthily out of the bushes, and brushed off her knees.

Enough of playing the role of Moses's sister. She was about to take center stage.

As she headed after the pair, walking at a safe distance, Samantha marveled at the unexpected paths life could take. No one who'd known her in her younger days would have expected her to allude to a bible story, even inside her own head.

What was the world coming to?

As Corbin walked through downtown Bethlehem Springs, he held two-year-old Mikey—his brother, if his mother's note was to be believed—by the hand. The little boy clutched his tiger in his other arm.

How could his mother inflict Mikey on him, and especially, how could she inflict Corbin on Mikey?

She couldn't. She'd just have to take Mikey back.

He blew out a sigh. What was he doing, walking downtown, anyway? Did he really think he'd find Cheryl in one of the cafés? More likely at a bar out by the highway. He'd pulled her out of a few of them in his day.

I have a brother. Corbin could barely take it in.

Suddenly, Mikey pulled his hand away from Corbin's and pointed. "Dog!" he said joyously, pointing across the street.

And then he took off toward it, running with all his two-year-old might.

"No!" Corbin dove after Mikey as time seemed to switch into slow motion.

An oncoming car swerved, its brakes squealing.

Corbin caught Mikey in his arms and crashed to the ground, landing hard on his shoulder to keep from hurting the child. He wrapped his brother in a bear hug and scrambled to the curb.

"My tiger!" Mikey sobbed.

Reese and Gabby Markowski, owners of the dog, rushed across the street with their daughter, Izzy. Gabby picked up the tiger and handed it to Mikey as the driver of the car, Bernadette Williams, parked and hurried back over.

"You almost gave me a heart attack," she said. "Everybody okay here?"

"Yes, thanks to your good reflexes." Corbin flopped down on a bench, Mikey in his arms. "I thought I'd have a heart attack, too." Was he going to have to place his brother in social services? No way could he take care of him. He'd almost gotten the child killed within the first hour of meeting him.

"Somebody needs to teach this little one to stay out of the street," she said. "And keep a firm hold on his hand until he's learned it."

"You're right." Corbin felt completely inadequate. *Was* completely inadequate.

"All right. I'm late to a finance committee meeting. You all take care." And Ms. Williams hurried off.

"Who's this?" Reese asked over Mikey's whimpers.

"Um, it's…my little brother," Corbin said, trying on the words. "I'm taking care of him for awhile." *A very little while.* Cheryl had said a week in her letter, but he'd like to make it shorter. Surely he could find his mother today or tomorrow and force her to take responsibility.

But even as he had that thought, a sick feeling spread through his stomach. Cheryl hadn't been much of a mother during Corbin's childhood, and it was doubtful that she'd improved. Her drinking had gotten steadily worse, to the point where he'd had to cut her out of his life for his own sanity a few years ago; all she ever wanted him for was money, anyway, and all she ever spent it on was booze.

As for their father, he didn't even merit the name.

If Mikey's parents were incompetent, and so was he, then what was going to happen to Mikey?

"If he needs a friend, he can come over and visit with Izzy anytime," Gabby said, ruffling Mikey's hair. "We're running late for play group right now—hey, you should bring him to that next time!"

"Hit us up if you need anything," Reese said, and they were off.

Corbin stared after them, bemused. There was a whole world of parents and kids and activities that he had no clue about. He tended to avoid kids.

And now here was one sobbing in his arms.

Chocolate had worked before. He looked around, spotted Cleo's Crafts and Café, and took Mikey inside. Soon, they were seated at a small table with two mugs of hot chocolate and two giant cookies.

Mikey grabbed at his hot chocolate. The mug tipped onto its side, spilling it onto the table.

Corbin jumped up and yanked Mikey away from the steaming liquid, then held his brother at arm's length to study him. If he'd gotten burned, Corbin wouldn't be able to forgive himself. "Where does it hurt?" he asked.

"Chocolate!" Mikey wailed, pointing at the spilled beverage now soaking the tiger's leg and dripping onto the café floor. "Want chocolate!"

"It's okay, you can have my hot chocolate." He sat

down on the edge of his chocolatey chair and perched Mikey awkwardly on his knee.

"Need some help?" came a husky voice above him, a voice that had always sent electrical sensations up and down his spine.

"Samantha?" Corbin stared at the girl he'd never expected to see again.

"I'm surprised you remember my name."

He squinted at her. How could he forget the name of his secret crush? She'd been a freshman when he'd been a senior, but from the moment he'd seen her in the cafeteria, he'd never been able to get her out of his mind.

She was even prettier than she'd been in high school, where she'd worn nothing but black. Now, she was dressed in slim-fitting jeans and a shirt made of some flimsy, flowery stuff. "I'll get some napkins," she said, and walked up to the counter.

Corbin was sure his weren't the only male eyes that followed her. Even Mikey stopped crying to stare.

She came back and made quick work of cleaning up the table, the tiger and Mikey while Corbin introduced them and explained he was taking care of Mikey for a little while.

She didn't laugh at the notion of him caring for a child. That was kind of her.

"Hot chocolate from a regular cup might not be a good idea," she said instead. "Want me to get him a box of juice or something?"

"Sure," Corbin said. "Here, Mikey, eat some cookie."

"Like cookies." Mikey scrambled off Corbin's lap,

grabbed a cookie and attempted to stuff the giant thing into his mouth.

"Break off a piece." Corbin reached for the cookie to illustrate.

Mikey kicked at him. "Mine."

Corbin winced and lifted his hands, palms out. "Whatever you say, kiddo." He broke off pieces of his own cookie and ate them, realizing he was starving.

And he needed to figure out what he was going to do. Preferably soon, before Monday came along with classes to teach and papers to grade and meetings to attend.

His mother had done a lot of dumb things in her life, but asking—*needing*—Corbin to take care of her child for a week had to beat all. Her excuse, stated in the letter, was that a family member was sick, but she'd been so vague about it that he wondered if that was even true.

"Here. I got him some juice and a cheese stick," Samantha said, slipping into the chair beside him as if they were friends. She opened the cheese stick with a deft flick of her fingers and handed it to Mikey.

Mikey nibbled on the cheese stick and sipped the juice. His face came unscrunched and he relaxed enough to stare into space, clutching his tiger with one arm as he finished the snack.

"Thank you," Corbin said to Samantha. "I'm…not really good with kids." With people, he could have added, but didn't. Something about Samantha made him not want to look quite so bad in her eyes.

"Oh, isn't he *cute*." A middle-aged woman carrying

an armload of shopping bags stopped beside their table, staring at Mikey.

"Hi, Mrs. Diebel," Corbin said. You were supposed to see the light of Christ in everyone, and Corbin tried, but so far, he hadn't succeeded with Mrs. Diebel.

"And this must be your little boy," the older woman crooned to Samantha. "Isn't that funny, how much he looks like Corbin!" She reached out to tickle Mikey under the chin.

Mikey reeled back and batted her hand away.

"He's not my child." Samantha's voice was cool.

Corbin was opening his mouth to explain that Mikey was his brother. Not that it was any of Mrs. Diebel's business, but he didn't like the greedy, gossipy way she was looking at Samantha.

"My mistake!" Mrs. Diebel tittered. "It's just, I remembered that when you left town, you were expecting. Or anyway, that's what the story was. Rumors!" She threw up her hands as if she had nothing to do with the spread of them.

"I miscarried a baby shortly after I left Bethlehem Springs." All the light was gone from Samantha's eyes. "Maybe that's what you heard."

Ouch. Corbin felt a completely inappropriate urge to pull Samantha into his arms.

"Oh, dear." Mrs. Diebel drew back a little.

Color climbed Samantha's neck. She was upset, as upset as she'd been in the high school halls when one of the football players, Brock Markowski, had called her an ugly name.

She'd answered back in kind, thoroughly putting

Brock in his place and making a bunch of the other kids laugh.

But Corbin, standing close behind her, had watched the bright red blotches bloom on her neck and realized there was much more going on inside her than showed in her cocky, sarcastic exterior.

"'Mantha sad," Mikey said now, and held out his tiger toward her. "It okay, 'Mantha."

She took the tiger, hugged it and gave it back. "Thank you, Mikey. That was really nice." She didn't look again at Mrs. Diebel, and after an awkward thirty seconds, the older woman turned and hurried away.

Misery washed over Corbin. Misery for Samantha, who'd lost a child, which had to be one of the worst things a person could go through. And misery for himself, for his complete lack of social skills. Even a two-year-old was better at comforting another person than he was.

"So," she said, twirling a stirring stick around in her cup of coffee, "you said you're taking care of your little brother for a week?"

"I guess I'm going to try," he said. "It's all a bit of a surprise. I'm not sure what I'm going to do about him, and work, and…" He shrugged and blew out a breath, staring at Mikey, who was inexplicably using his tiger to break the rest of his cookie into bits. "I have exactly zero experience with kids."

"Sounds like a challenge."

He nodded, grateful she'd come by. At any other time, he'd have been tongue-tied around Samantha, but right now his own problems overshadowed his social discomfort. He was glad to have someone to talk to. "I guess I'll need to find a temporary babysitter or something. I don't know, do you think I can just drop him off somewhere, like at a day care?"

She lifted an eyebrow, her mouth twisting to one side. "Do you have his medical records?"

"I don't know," he said. "I haven't looked into his suitcase yet."

"I haven't been back in town long," she said, "but I heard there are waiting lists at most of the places. There's a shortage. It's my line of work, is why I know that."

"It's your line of work?"

She nodded. "I'm thinking about putting in some applications."

He shot a glance upward. God did amazing things. He'd caused Mikey to be dropped into Corbin's lap, which seemed like a huge mistake on His part. But then He'd thrown a qualified, experienced caregiver at him. Corbin was smart enough to connect the dots.

"Would you like a temporary job?" he blurted out.

Chapter 2

"It was almost too easy," Samantha said into her phone. Then she put it on speaker so she could lean back against the headboard of the bed in her cousin's guest room. "He was talking about needing a caregiver, and I said it was my line of work, and he asked if I could help out with Mikey."

"I can't tell you how much I appreciate you doing this." Corbin's mother, Cheryl, sounded out of breath. "I was at the end of my rope."

Samantha leaned over to straighten the books on the bedside table, the devotional on top seeming to glare at her. "Are you sure we can't just tell him the truth? He seems a lot more mature than when I knew him before."

"You can't tell him!" Cheryl's voice rose to a squeak. "Please, don't tell him. He'll just send Mikey back to me, or dump him into social services. I—we—couldn't stand that."

"How's Paul doing?" Samantha thought of Corbin's formerly handsome father and bit her lip. As his body had wasted away, he'd gained new faith that had transformed his soul into something beautiful.

"Today wasn't a good day. I think the stress of worrying about Mikey, missing him, set him back." After the slightest pause, she added, "And yes, I still think we're doing the right thing. A sickroom is no place for a two-year-old to live, and Corbin is the only family we have left."

"And you don't think he'd like to see his father? Make amends?"

"He won't. Maybe you haven't seen this side of him, but Corbin is…rigid. He decided he wanted us both out of his life—with good reason, I'm the first to admit that—and now he won't speak to either of us. If we had more time…" Her voice broke. "Please, please don't tell him, just take care of my baby."

The anguish in Cheryl's voice tugged at Samantha's heart. "Of course. I agreed to do that, and I will." And after a few more minutes of trying to soothe Cheryl, Samantha ended the call.

She wrapped her arms around her knees and looked around the small bedroom. Her cousin Hannah wasn't the frilly type. The plain blue bedspread and curtains were serviceable, but there was no other decoration. The room was spotless, though, and Hannah had immediately offered it up when Samantha had told her she wanted to move back to town. That generosity meant a lot to Samantha, especially considering she hadn't stayed in touch with Hannah during the bad times.

The other benefit of staying at Hannah's place was that there wasn't a bar or a liquor store in easy walking distance. That would help.

Her phone buzzed again, and she clicked into the call before registering that it wasn't Cheryl calling back, it was Corbin. They'd exchanged numbers after she'd agreed to help with Mikey.

"He's throwing up," Corbin said without a greeting. "And it's Friday night. What should I do?"

Half an hour later, she and Corbin were pulling into the driveway of an old house on the edge of town. In the back seat, Mikey whimpered.

"The doctor doesn't mind having her evening disrupted?" Samantha asked.

"She's a good person. And she just happened to be here having dinner with Gabby and Reese when I called them."

"I hate to interrupt their evening. I mean, Mikey's probably just got a stomachache from all the chocolate, but since we don't know his medical history..." She trailed off. Corbin had searched Mikey's suitcase and found none of his medical records. He'd told her he had no idea how to get in touch with his mother and get them.

Unbeknownst to him, Samantha *did* know how. She was planning to do it tomorrow.

"It's probably my fault, for feeding him all that junk," Corbin said as he struggled to unfasten the straps of

Mikey's car seat. "Why would anyone think I'm the right caregiver for Mikey?"

Because you're her only option, and at least you're not an alcoholic or drug addict. "Let me help you with that," Samantha said, and reached past Corbin to undo the buckle.

She caught a whiff of Corbin's aftershave, woodsy and masculine. Despite the cool evening air, her face heated.

As they walked into the little house, shyness overtook Samantha. She had never been terribly comfortable with the normal kids in school. She'd preferred to hang out with those like her, the ones who had home problems and reason to be angry at the world.

Of course, Corbin had had home problems and reason to be angry, at least as much as she had. But he'd taken honors courses and won science awards and gotten elected president of the Future Farmers of America, even though he didn't live on a farm. He just liked animals.

He'd been productive and made something of himself, whereas Samantha…

She pushed the thought out of her head as Gabby Hanks, now Gabby Markowitz, ushered them into the house.

"Come in, come in. I'm so glad you called. Perfect timing."

A pretty, slender woman with multiple long braids—she looked slightly familiar, but Samantha couldn't place her—came out into the foyer and reached a hand toward Mikey. "This must be the little boy who's not feeling well."

"This is Mikey," Corbin said. "Hey, Sheniqua, thanks so much for agreeing to take a look at him. He just got here today, and I don't have a way to get in touch with his—with my, our—mother, and I made the mistake of giving him a bunch of chocolate, and…"

"Slow down, Corbin." Sheniqua's chuckle was rich and throaty. "I'm happy to help. And remember, kids are resilient. I'm sure he'll be fine." She laid a hand on his forehead. "A little warm, but I wouldn't say he's feverish."

"Come on in," Reese said, beckoning them out of the foyer. "Sheniqua, this is Samantha Alcorn, a friend of ours. You can use the front bedroom if you want, take a look at him."

Being called a friend of Reese and Gabby took Samantha aback. It felt a little bit good, but it made her suspicious. "Do you want me to come while she checks him out?" she asked Corbin.

He nodded. "Of course."

Good. That was a little less awkward than hanging out with a couple of people she didn't know well, but who probably remembered what a juvenile delinquent she'd been.

Sheniqua listened to Mikey's heart and looked into his ears, asked what he'd eaten recently.

"I'm an idiot," Corbin said. "If it weren't for Samantha giving him cheese and a juice box, he'd have had nothing decent all day."

"You didn't feed him dinner?" Samantha asked.

"I got him a kids' meal out at Burger Bistro, but he didn't like it."

"Toddlers are picky," Sheniqua said. "Mikey, what do you like to eat?"

"Like apples," he said. "And candy."

He was so cute. "And cheese," Samantha prompted. "And…muffins, right?" She remembered Cheryl had fed him pieces of her muffin when they'd talked over their plan.

Which she shouldn't be broadcasting to Corbin. Her face warmed. "I mean, every kid likes muffins, right?"

Mikey saved her by nodding. "Muffins. Mikey like muffins. Mama like muffins." He looked from her to Corbin and back again, his forehead wrinkling. "Where Mama?"

Samantha's throat tightened and she looked away from Mikey's puzzled face. Why had she ever agreed to be a part of this scheme?

"Mama had to take a trip," Corbin said. "She'll be back again soon."

"Okay," Mikey said with equilibrium he shouldn't have had as a two-year-old. How many caregivers had he had that his mom's absence wasn't a big deal to him?

Sheniqua was putting away her equipment. "No fever, no ear infection, no more vomiting. I suspect he's just suffering from some poor food choices and some emotional upset from missing his mama."

"Maybe Reese and Gabby could lend you some food until you can get to the grocery," Samantha suggested. "I'm sure they've got cereal, and crackers and the like."

"Will you grocery shop with me tomorrow?" Corbin

asked Samantha. "I need to buy good kid food, and I don't have a clue what that would be."

"Um, okay." The thought of doing that domestic of a task with Corbin felt concerning in all kinds of ways. "Better yet, how about we hit the farmers' market?"

Corbin shrugged. "Sure. And I'll pay you extra. I know you weren't supposed to start until Monday but—"

"Sure." Was Corbin really as much of a basket case around kids as he seemed? Had Cheryl made a terrible mistake?

"You'll get it figured out." Sheniqua patted Corbin's arm. "Everybody does. You have a PhD, right?"

"In animals, not in babies," Corbin said.

Sheniqua laughed again. "Come on out and hang with us a few minutes, and we'll make sure Mikey doesn't start feeling bad again. I have to go home soon, but it'll do you good to connect with other families of babies. Nobody can go it alone."

"That's for sure!" The voice at the door belonged to a gray-haired woman. "Corbin Beck, have you gone and gotten yourself a baby?"

"He's my brother. Mrs. Marks, this is Samantha Alcorn. Samantha, this is Gabby's grandmother, Mrs. Marks. This is her house."

"Our house, now," the old woman said. "I love having the kids live here with me. Now, why do you look so familiar, Samantha?"

"We all went to school together," Corbin explained. "Samantha graduated a few years after the rest of us."

"Barely graduated, in my case," Samantha said, holding out her hand. "Nice to meet you."

Mrs. Marks looked her over, then nodded as if Samantha had passed inspection. "Come on out. All the commotion has woken Izzy up, I believe."

They walked out to the living room where Reese, Gabby and Sheniqua sat talking. Izzy lay on a blanket on the floor, cuddling a baby doll. A teenage boy, introduced as Gabby's brother, Jacob, was sitting in the far corner of the room; he waved and then went back to his video game.

Corbin placed Mikey on the floor beside Izzy. They proceeded to stare at each other while Mrs. Marks and Reese brought out iced tea and coffee for the adults.

"Nothing like diving right into fatherhood, eh?" Reese said to Corbin. "You said this is a temporary arrangement?"

"Ye-es," Corbin said. "It's supposed to be."

"Sounds like there's a 'but' in there," Reese said.

"My mother isn't exactly dependable." There was unexpected bitterness in Corbin's voice. "I wouldn't count on her coming back for Mikey when she said she would." He looked over at Samantha and smiled, and she felt the warmth all the way to her toes. "I'm very blessed Samantha has experience in child care and was available to help out."

"You do child care?" Gabby looked thoughtful. "You know, if it *does* go on longer…like through the summer… We could talk about some kind of arrangement."

That was puzzling. "What kind of arrangement?"

"Well, Mikey and Izzy are about the same age. And summer is a superbusy time for me and Reese."

"They run a program for at-risk boys," Corbin explained. "After school, and during vacations."

"And we just got funding to do full day programs in the summer," Reese said, lifting a fist in the air. "Thank you, Mr. Romano."

"An influential member of the church board," Corbin explained to Samantha.

"I think Nana had something to do with Mr. Romano's generosity," Gabby said, raising her eyebrows and looking at Mrs. Marks, whose cheeks had gone pink.

"It was your good programming that convinced him to get behind the project," Mrs. Marks said primly.

A smile curved Gabby's mouth. "Anyway," she said to Samantha, "we'll be looking for some help caring for Izzy. Nana takes care of her some, but I don't want her to have to do it full-time. If you're still around, and interested, maybe you'd like to take care of Izzy along with Mikey."

Samantha stared at her. She just didn't get it, how friendly these people were. "Why would you let me do that?"

"What do you mean?" Gabby tilted her head to one side, looking genuinely confused.

"I mean, I was a screwup in school, in trouble all the time. Corbin's desperate, but you guys must have lots of friends, people who'd be willing to take care of Izzy, day care options."

Gabby narrowed her eyes. "Didn't you say you were experienced?"

"Yes, I worked for two years at a day care in Cleveland. They liked my work fine until…" She trailed off when she realized it wasn't just Gabby but everyone else who was waiting for her to go on.

"Did something happen, dear?" Mrs. Marks asked.

"Nothing exactly happened, but…" She sucked in a breath. She might as well be up-front about things. "My boss found out I went to AA meetings. Apparently, that wasn't the kind of person to make the parents feel confident about dropping off their little ones."

She didn't dare look at Corbin. Now she'd done it. She waited, miserably, for him to revoke his offer of letting her care for Mikey.

"Well, that's inappropriate," Sheniqua said.

Ouch. Samantha felt her shoulders slump at the judgment, even though she'd expected it.

"Inappropriate of them, not of you," Sheniqua said. "You were doing something positive for your life and that's admirable. Besides which, attendance at a twelve-step program should be fully confidential."

"I admire you for taking care of your issues like that," Gabby said with a firm nod. "Everyone has problems and mistakes in their pasts."

"That's for sure," Reese added. "If we couldn't overcome the past, where would we be?"

"Thank you," Samantha said doubtfully. These people were nice, but a little too welcoming to be believed, at least in her experience. She definitely needed to stay on her guard.

"The offer stands," Gabby added. "In fact…" She looked at Reese. "Are you thinking what I'm thinking?"

He nodded slowly. "Adding that program for younger kids," he said. "Samantha might just be the person to get it started. Trouble is, my aunt and uncle are the ones who offered to fund it, and my aunt will want to be involved as we get it going."

"Brock Markowski's mom," Corbin clarified to Samantha.

The others were glancing at each other, but Samantha's mind was reeling. Were they offering her work, a responsible job, here in town? "I'd love to hear more about that," she blurted out, forgetting to stay on her guard after all.

The next day, Corbin clung to the fact that he and Mikey were to meet Samantha at the farmers' market at 2:00 p.m. It was the only thing that got him through the morning.

Neither he nor Mikey had slept well. Mikey had awakened, crying, at least three times; Corbin had lost track after that. Mikey wanted his mommy.

Corbin wanted her, too. Wanted her to get back here and take responsibility for the son she'd dumped on Corbin's doorstep. Tied to it, actually, a fact that had brought back dim memories of being tied to the picnic table in the back of their apartment complex when he'd been small.

Who *did* that to a kid?

And that thought made him ashamed of wishing Cheryl would come take Mikey off his hands. Corbin was no prize as a caregiver, but he'd never, ever tie

Mikey in place. There had to be better ways to keep a kid safe and under control.

TV, chocolate and video games didn't work on Mikey, though, not today, anyway. Corbin hoped a car ride would do better—that often worked on dogs he cared for—but Mikey fussed the whole way.

He was definitely a loser in the parenting game, trying dog-handling techniques on a human child.

When he pulled Mikey out of the car at the farmers' market, the kid struggled and nearly slipped through his hands. It was like handling a greased pig. He let Mikey slide to the ground, then turned back to the car for the diaper bag, taking a moment to wipe his forehead with his sleeve. It was hot for April.

Around them, other families were parking in the field or heading toward the trucks and colorful table umbrellas that must be the farmer's market, calling friendly greetings to one another. He could smell good farm smells, earth and hay and green plants.

You can do this. He drew in a deep breath, shot up a quick prayer for help, and turned back to the boy. "Come on, Mi—"

Mikey was gone.

"Mikey!" He looked frantically from side to side, stretching up to his full height and then standing on the door frame of his car, scanning the area.

Finally he spotted Mikey's bright green shirt, and took off jogging toward the spot where the inquisitive toddler knelt in front of a pen containing lambs and baby goats. Putting a leash on the kid was looking better and better.

"Corbin! What's wrong?"

It was Samantha, hurrying up beside him, but he didn't dare take his eyes off Mikey. "He ran away. He's at the petting zoo." He slowed down as he realized the child wasn't going anywhere. "How do parents manage more than one kid? I turned around to pick up his diaper bag, and when I looked again, he was gone."

"At least he didn't get far," she said, patting his arm. "You'll get better at it."

"I hope." They were walking side by side now, headed toward Mikey. His worry about Mikey contained as they got close enough to keep the child safe, he glanced over at Samantha, and his mouth went dry.

She wore a short summer dress that showed she was still as slender as she'd been in high school. Her flip-flops revealed pink-painted toenails, and her long hair hung in a messy braid down her back.

Thankfully, she focused on Mikey instead of Corbin's gawking. "Hey, buddy," she said, kneeling behind him. "You can't run off like that. You need to stick with your grown-ups, okay?"

"'Kay." Mikey smiled up at them and then pointed at the animals. "Lammies and goats, see?"

"They're cute." She stood and winced.

"What's wrong?"

She slid her foot out of her flip-flop. "Blister. Not the right footwear for walking."

He was ashamed he hadn't offered to pick her up. "Do you have a car?"

"I do have a car, but I'm kind of nursing it along," she said. "It didn't want to start this morning."

"Where are you staying?" He knelt to examine her foot, determinedly focusing on her injury rather than her soft skin. "We should get some antibiotic on this, and a bandage."

She hopped backward, pulling her foot out of his hands. It must be the hopping that made her sound breathless. "It'll be fine. And I'm staying with my cousin, over on the east side of town. Remember Hannah?"

"Antonicelli? I remember." Corbin frowned. "That was quite a hike."

"A little bit," she admitted, watching as Mikey toddled closer to the fence, staring in at the animals.

"You should have called me for a ride."

"Oh, well…" She shrugged.

"Well, what?" Since Mikey seemed happy, Corbin wasn't in a hurry to go vegetable shopping. He was rapidly learning that you took advantage of every moment your toddler was occupied and not fussing.

She shrugged again. "It's bad enough that I have to mooch off my cousin. I don't need to be mooching off you, too."

"Does Hannah act like you're mooching?" That would have surprised him. He remembered Hannah as a nice girl.

"No! No, not at all. I just don't like to be dependent." She sighed. "But I needed a fresh start, and this was the only way I could afford to get one."

"Because of the AA thing?" He felt bad as soon as he'd asked it. "Sorry. That's not my business." Except that he'd vowed to avoid involvement with alcoholics, due to his parents. And he had to protect Mikey from going through the kind of thing he'd gone through as a kid.

"Yeah," she said. "That was part of why I needed a fresh start. When you lose your job…" She lifted a shoulder. "But that's a boring thing to talk about. It's a nice day. Let's walk around."

"Okay, sure." Even Corbin could recognize that she wanted to change the subject. "Come on, Mikey."

"Unless…" She looked at him, biting her lip. "I can tell you more about being in AA if you're worried about my helping with Mikey. That would be totally understandable. I mean, I've been sober for a couple of years, but I can understand why it's worrisome to a parent."

"I trust you." It was true, he realized. Despite his lack of people skills, he was usually pretty good at spotting a liar or a fake. Samantha was neither. She hadn't been in high school, and she wasn't now.

Still, the fact that she had a drinking problem meant he needed to be watchful.

"Thanks." She gave him a little smile and their eyes met, and then she looked away, a flush crossing her lightly freckled cheeks.

Quickly, he cast around for some nonpersonal topic of conversation. "Is that kettle corn I smell? Mikey, do you like kettle corn?"

"Whoa, whoa," Samantha said. "We're here for healthy food, right?"

"Like kel-corn," Mikey argued.

"Let's shop for real ingredients," she said. "I'm a pretty good basic cook. If you want, I can pick out stuff for a couple of meals that you could serve several times." She squinted up at him. "Because I get the feeling you don't actually cook meals for yourself."

"You're right." Corbin just couldn't get interested in cooking for himself, and he never had anyone else to cook for. Now that he did, he supposed he should learn, but the notion daunted him.

They wandered through the stands, Samantha picking out the makings of vegetable soup and one healthy-looking oatmeal cookie for Mikey.

"Hello, Corbin," came a voice from behind him, and he turned to see Reese's aunt, Mrs. Markowski, standing behind him. "I'm surprised to see you at the market. How are you?"

"Hi, Mrs. Markowski." He stepped back to bring Samantha into the conversation. "Did you know Samantha Alcorn?"

"Your name sounds familiar." The older woman studied Samantha. "Did you grow up here? You might have known my son, Brock."

Corbin waited for a frown to cross Samantha's face. After all, Brock had tormented her from the moment she'd started ninth grade until the day he graduated, senior year. He'd been pretty awful to most people, right up until he'd died in a single-car accident after leaving a party drunk.

Samantha reached for Mrs. Markowski's hand, clasping it in both of hers. "I did know Brock. I'm so sorry for your loss."

"Thank you, dear." Mrs. Markowski choked up a

little on the last word, her eyes going shiny with un-
shed tears.

Samantha patted her arm. "It must be so hard to lose
a child," she said. For a minute, she looked like she was
going to cry herself.

Mrs. Markowski nodded, cleared her throat and
clenched her jaw, quickly regaining control of her emotions.

Mikey finished his cookie, and Corbin wiped his
face. "This is my little brother, Mikey," he said to Mrs.
Markowski.

"Hi!" Mikey smiled up at her.

"He's come to stay with me for a while," Corbin said.
Really, he just thought he ought to contribute something to the conversation, but as soon as he said it, he
regretted it. The news would shortly be all over town.

But then again, it wasn't something he was ashamed
of, and it wasn't something he could hide. They lived
in a small community. Everyone would find out that
Mikey was staying with him.

Mrs. Markowski smiled at Mikey. "Oh my, aren't
you adorable."

"He's a smart boy, too," Samantha said, ruffling
Mikey's hair fondly.

After saying goodbye to Mrs. Markowski, they
strolled back toward Corbin's car. Mikey got tired, so
Corbin picked him up on the back of his shoulders as
he'd seen other men do, carefully holding Mikey's legs
so he didn't fall. "I'm surprised you could be so nice to
Mrs. Markowski after how mean Brock was to you,"
he said. "I admire it."

"Brock must have been struggling with something, to be that mean," she said. "Hurt people hurt people, like they say in AA. Oh, look at the flowers!" She stopped at a display of orange and yellow daisy-like flowers. At the same moment, they both leaned closer to sniff them. Samantha had closed her eyes to do it, and Corbin could see her lashes, so long, resting against her pink cheeks. He forgot to breathe.

And then she opened her eyes and stared at him, her own eyes wide.

Corbin's heart hammered in his chest. He had to put a stop to this. He couldn't go down that path, not even a little ways.

Samantha seemed great, but she was an alcoholic. Maybe she had a sobriety coin, but so did both of his parents; in fact, they had a drawerful of them.

He'd promised himself to avoid involvement with addicts, and that promise felt much, much more important now, with Mikey at his side. While he had responsibility for his brother, there was no way he could give in to the attraction he felt for Samantha.

Even before he could withdraw from her, Samantha straightened and turned resolutely toward the car. "I'll help you load the things and Mikey, and then I'll be on my way."

"I can give you a ride home."

"No, that's okay. I'll text my cousin. She works close by."

And as she hurriedly helped him and then left, he realized that she was just as eager to get away from him as he was to get away from her.

Chapter 3

Samantha walked into Hannah's kitchen Monday morning and found her petite, jeans-clad cousin pouring a cup of coffee from the old-fashioned coffee maker on the counter.

"Sit down and have a cup," Hannah invited.

"Thanks," Samantha said, "but I'd better not. Don't want to be late on my first day taking care of Mikey." She'd been feeling nervous ever since that visit to the farmer's market. She'd felt almost close to Corbin. When he'd met her eyes and held them, she'd felt a sharp jolt of awareness.

That couldn't happen. She couldn't *allow* it to happen. Not when she was deceiving him about her connection with Cheryl and her participation in the plot to have Corbin take custody of Mikey.

"You are *not* walking all the way over to Corbin's house," Hannah said. "That's like three miles. I'll drive you. Coffee," she added, waving the fragrant cup beneath Samantha's nose.

The thought of sitting down for a cup of coffee before taking on another encounter with the disturbing Corbin, and then a day with Mikey, was tempting.

But Samantha didn't want to put Hannah out. "It's a beautiful day for a walk," she said, looking out the window. It was true. The sun already shone bright on the dewy grass. A gentle breeze rustled new green leaves and an array of spring flowers in Hannah's little garden.

"It's a beautiful day for coffee. Sit down." Hannah pulled a second cup from the cupboard, filled it and handed it to Samantha. "You'll get plenty of time to enjoy the day and use your energy taking care of a two-year-old."

Samantha inhaled the rich scent of fresh coffee again and couldn't stop herself from reaching out for it. "Okay, but just for a minute. I need to get going."

"I said, I'll drive you."

"You've done so much for me already, giving me a place to stay. I can't ask you to do more."

"I have some errands to do over that way anyway," Hannah said. "Besides, I'm glad to have you here."

That was hard to believe.

"I mean it! I've missed you. And it's nice to finally catch up. I don't think we've spent this much time together since elementary school."

"Those long summer days at the park pool." Samantha smiled. Her single mom had struggled to keep food on the table, but she'd done her best. During elementary school, Hannah's mother had taken care of Samantha, which had basically meant sending her and Hannah off to play all day. Pretty sweet.

"Those were fun times. But, honestly, I never thought you'd come back to Bethlehem Springs. I thought you'd be living the high life in some big city, married to a hot guy. They all were crazy about you. Not like me, permanently in the friend zone." Hannah sighed.

"You've got to be kidding. I can't believe you'd be there unless you wanted to be." Hannah was pretty and kindhearted, independent, fun.

"I've always been fine with it, but lately..." Hannah shrugged.

"The right guy will come along. I know it." Samantha hesitated. "Honestly, I wish I'd hung out with you as I got older. Maybe I wouldn't have made as many mistakes." They'd gone their separate ways in high school, Samantha partying and running around with boys, and Hannah studying and volunteering at the Humane Society. As a result, Hannah was a successful dog trainer who owned her own home, while Samantha was struggling to keep her life together.

"You've changed." Hannah cocked her head to one side, studying her. "A lot."

"I hope so," Samantha said.

"What made it happen?"

Samantha hesitated, but her cousin's friendly, open face encouraged her to speak. "I did too much partying. Got pregnant, didn't know it soon enough, and ended up miscarrying the baby." Her throat tightened and she had to force out the last words.

Hannah gasped and then came around the table and hugged her. "That must've been awful. You should have come home then."

She shook her head. "Mom came to stay with me when it first happened. And then…well, I had some growing up to do. Found a church, spent a lot of time talking to the assistant pastor, got a job in a child care program." She hesitated and then added, "Plus, I got into AA."

Hanna's eyebrows rose. "Wow, I didn't know your drinking was that bad."

"It was. I did a lot of things I'm not proud of, hurt some people, too." She drew in a breath, let it out slowly.

"Have you found a meeting here? I think there's one at our church."

"First thing I looked for. I know my limits." She downed the rest of her coffee. "If you don't mind taking me, we better go now. Corbin said he has to go into the office early today."

Hannah stood and carried their cups to the sink. "I'm ready when you are. Corbin's hot now, huh?"

Heat rose to Samantha's face. "He definitely is." She hesitated. "Are you…interested in him?"

"No way!" Hannah laughed. "To me, he'll always be my fellow nerd, good old Corbin."

"He's just a friend to me, too," Samantha said quickly.

"Uh-huh," Hannah said. "You sure?"

"I'm sure." *Because that's how it has to be.*

* * *

That evening, Corbin trotted up his porch steps with his mind still on the comparative physiology course he'd taught that afternoon. The advanced students had been full of questions, clearly engaged in the material. They hadn't wanted to leave when the class was over.

He walked into his house to the sound of Samantha and Mikey laughing together. He followed the smell of hot dogs and baked beans and something else, rich and cinnamony, to the kitchen.

Samantha was at the counter cutting up fruit, the afternoon sun shining on her hair. Mikey stood on a chair beside her, rolling pieces of Play-Doh on a paper plate.

He cleared his throat. "Hi everybody," he said.

Samantha looked over and smiled at him, a little shyly.

Mikey jumped off the chair. "Corbin! Come see!"

"Careful, buddy. What are you doing?"

"Makin' fruit." He handed Corbin a red sphere. "See, apple!"

Samantha scraped a small heap of chopped-up pineapple into a bowl that already held grapes and strawberries. Then she rinsed off the cutting board, speaking over her shoulder to Corbin. "Make sure he eats his fruit before he has a cookie," she said.

Corbin sniffed appreciatively. "Cookies! So that's the good smell."

"Oatmeal raisin," Mikey said, only he pronounced it "waysin."

Samantha was already at the hook by the back door where her coat and purse were hanging.

Corbin didn't know what to make of the squeeze in his heart. "You're not going to stay?"

Her eyebrows lifted. "I wasn't planning to."

Mikey climbed into a kitchen chair. "C'mon, er-rbody. Time to eat!"

"Please stay," Corbin said to Samantha. "I'll take you home after." He'd noticed she didn't drive today, and he certainly didn't want her walking all the way home after a day of caring for Mikey.

She bit her lip, and then a smile lifted the corners of her mouth. "I always did like hot dogs," she said.

"Great." His heart lightened, and he smiled at her.

She smiled back, then seemed to suck in her breath. She rubbed her hands together and looked out the window. "But I think we should eat out in the backyard," she said briskly. "Kind of a picnic."

"Yeah!" Mikey pumped his fist into the air.

"Good idea." Corbin couldn't remember the last time he'd had a picnic.

So they made plates and carried them outside. Samantha spread a blanket and Corbin passed out napkins and they all sat down. They held hands and prayed, and then dug in.

"How'd you manage to make such a good meal out of nothing?" he asked between bites.

She laughed, a sound as sweet and natural as a rushing stream. "It's just hot dogs and beans," she said. "And before you get worried, I cut up Mikey's hot dog so there's no chance he'll choke on it."

"I wasn't worried." He couldn't take his eyes off her.

"Whatcha lookin' at, Corbin?" Mikey asked. "Cookie now?"

Corbin thanked the child, in his head, for providing a distraction.

"Eat your fruit first, honey," Samantha said.

Trying to distract himself from the strange feelings he was having toward Samantha, Corbin looked around the yard. Last year's leaves still clustered behind bushes, and weeds sprouted freely throughout the unkempt flower gardens. "I, um, I'm not the best at lawn care. I mow the grass and that's about it."

She shrugged. "You have a fence. It can't bother anybody but you."

"It pretty!" Mikey jumped up and ran toward a small section of garden, now neatly weeded and tilled. "Look, Corbin!"

Corbin lifted an eyebrow at Samantha and then stood to look more closely. "Did you two do that?"

"Yes. Mikey and I worked hard today, didn't we, buddy?"

He ran to her, and she put an arm around him and smiled up at Corbin. "Mikey had a great time digging in the dirt. He even pulled up some weeds."

"I got dirty," Mikey announced with apparent pride. "Had to take a bath!"

Corbin hadn't even considered the fact that a child would need to be bathed. "I hope you found what you needed for that," he said to Samantha.

"I rummaged," she said with a grin. "And we had fun. It's good for kids to play in the dirt."

They talked a little longer, and then Mikey leaned

against Samantha, rubbing his eyes with the backs of his hands. She glanced over at Corbin. "I think one cookie, and then it'll be bedtime. It's been a long day for this one."

They carried the dishes in and Corbin insisted that she leave them for him to do later. He already felt like she had waited on them enough.

As soon as he finished his cookie, Mikey yawned hugely.

"Come see what I did to his bed," she said. "I hope you don't mind."

They went into the guest bedroom, Corbin carrying Mikey. Two dressers had been arranged to make little walls around the bed. "Good idea," he said. It hadn't even occurred to him that a little boy like Mikey wouldn't be comfortable in a big bed.

"I think he'll feel safer this way. *Be* safer. It doesn't look the greatest, but it's just temporary."

They leaned together over the bed and talked a little bit to Mikey, and within minutes his eyes fluttered closed.

As they walked out of the room, Samantha clapped a hand to her forehead and reached into her pocket. "I forgot to tell you. I found this letter in the door."

He took it and studied it. When he saw the single handwritten line, "For Corbin," his heart pounded harder. "It's from Mom."

He tore into it, scanned the words quickly, and then let out a huge sigh. He'd feared this very thing. "She wants to make this arrangement with Mikey permanent."

Chapter 4

"You're sure about this?" Hannah pulled up in front of Corbin's house and looked over at Samantha, her brow crinkling. "You know you're welcome to stay at my place as long as you want."

"No," Samantha said, "I think Corbin's right. It's easier if I stay here."

"Probably so." Hannah opened the car door. "I just noticed you seemed a little anxious."

"I'm not anxious." Of course, she was, but she'd tried not to show it.

"Your nails," Hannah said as she pulled Samantha's suitcase out of the back seat.

Samantha looked down at her hands and realized she'd picked the polish off her nails. "Oh."

"Do you want me to go in with you?" Hannah offered.

She didn't need her cousin taking care of her to that extent, and she didn't want to impose any more than she already had. She'd left her car at her cousin's already, waiting until she could afford to get it worked on, and Hannah had driven her here. "No, no, I'm fine. I know you have to get to work."

Hannah glanced at her phone. "Oh, boy, I sure do. Anyway, don't be a stranger!" She put down the suitcase and opened her arms, and Samantha went in for a hug. "It's been so much fun having you around. I get a little lonely in my house by myself."

Samantha studied her cousin. Hannah was the nicest person in the world, and really pretty, but she hid that fact behind completely tomboyish clothing. She'd tried, subtly, to find out what was behind Hannah's withdrawal, but so far, she hadn't been able to pierce Hannah's cheery facade.

If Samantha ever got her own life together, she'd find a way to help Hannah be less lonely.

The front door opened, and Corbin came out as Hannah waved goodbye and drove off. His glasses were in his hands and his hair was rumpled. He wore jeans and a T-shirt that fit tight around his biceps. Where did he get those biceps? Did he work out or was it from lifting animals and carrying boxes around his research lab at the university?

Whatever had made him so muscular, she needed to stop staring. "I'm here," she said briskly. "Sure you haven't changed your mind?"

"Have you changed yours?" Corbin came out and picked up her heavy suitcase. "Believe me, I need your help with Mikey. He's scared of the dark and so I didn't get any sleep. With you living in, maybe he'll feel more secure. I'm glad you're willing."

Not just willing, but amazed at how perfectly everything had worked out. When Samantha had called Mikey's mom and told her that Corbin had hired her as a live-in nanny the moment he'd read the letter, Cheryl had been thrilled. And relieved; Samantha had heard it in Cheryl's voice, the release from fear about her son.

Looking at Corbin's kind face, Samantha felt her stomach twist, just a little. He didn't deserve to be lied to and deceived.

But when she'd suggested—again—that they tell Corbin the truth, Cheryl had been vehement. "He hates his father, and me, too, for the way we raised him. If he knew that you and I were friends, he'd suspect a setup and turn you away in a minute, and I'd have no way of keeping track of Mikey." Her voice had wavered a little. "Please, Samantha. I don't think I can survive, nurse my husband, if I don't know my son is safe."

So she'd reluctantly agreed, for Mikey's sake. Now, she stepped over a red plastic trike made to look like a motorcycle. "Where'd you get this?"

"We went to the toy outlet last night, and he wanted it," Corbin said as if he'd buy the child anything he wanted. Typical guy, he probably hadn't bought the practical supplies you actually needed for a toddler. But the trike was sweet. "Where *is* Mikey?" she asked

Corbin as she followed him into the house and up the stairs.

"At Gabby and Reese's," he said over his shoulder. "She offered to keep him for the morning and bring him back when they come to town later. It seemed like it might be good for you to move in without him running around and getting into all your things. Although," he added as he led the way into a little suite and put the suitcase down, "it doesn't look like you have much."

Knowing she was alone with Corbin made Samantha feel inexplicably shy. But the feeling dissolved in wonder as she looked around the bedroom. "Oh, Corbin, this is lovely! It's like living in a treehouse!" She went from the bedroom to the small sitting room. Both had slanted roofs and exposed beams, and triple dormer windows looking out into newly budding trees.

"It's a little dark," he said apologetically, "but you get early morning and late afternoon sun."

She sniffed in a lemony smell. "You've been cleaning."

"I'm pretty good at that, but it doesn't have a woman's touch. Or is that sexist to say? Anyhow, feel free to change whatever you want, make it your own."

Something in his tone made her look at him, and she realized he was sweating. Why was he sweating? Why was he talking so much?

"It's a little warm up here," he said, "but the windows open." He stepped past her and demonstrated, and a cool, damp breeze blew in. "Do you think this will be okay?"

"Corbin." She touched his arm, and the feel of his

skin beneath her fingertips made her want to linger. She pulled her hand away quickly. "Do you remember how we lived when I was growing up? This is a palace compared to our house."

"I remember your place was small," he said, "but I never had the chance to come inside."

"Be glad." She thought of the tiny one bedroom house they'd rented for most of her growing up years. "No shade on my mom. She did the best she could." In fact, when Samantha had been a hormonal teenager, Mom had given her the bedroom to herself, had slept on the couch. Every morning when Samantha had gotten up, there had been a neat stack of blankets on one arm of the couch, and Mom had been in the kitchen, fixing oatmeal or eggs.

I never told her how much I appreciated her. Had never even understood the sacrifices Mom had made. Now, thanks to cancer, it was too late.

"I would have liked to come inside," he said, so quietly she thought she'd imagined it.

"You would?" She stared at him blankly. "Why?"

"I had a major crush on you." Corbin's cheeks flushed but he looked directly into her eyes. "Didn't you know?"

She stared at him, all too aware of his broad shoulders, his steady brown eyes. "No, I didn't. You were a senior, an honors student, way out of my league. I...no."

Their gazes tangled for a moment too long as Samantha thought about what she'd been like back then. Even as early as ninth grade, she'd hung with the druggie kids, stayed out late, dated the boys who had fast cars…how would she have known that nerdy, intelligent Corbin was looking her way?

"Not anymore," he said hastily. "I mean, I like you and everything, but…" He trailed off and looked away.

"It's understood." But she felt deflated. Now that Corbin was successful, and she was anything but, he wasn't interested.

Even if he had been, nothing could have gone forward between them. Samantha was hiding information about herself and Cheryl and Mikey. She'd had a bad lifestyle, done a lot of things she regretted. She didn't deserve the admiration of a man like Corbin.

"If you don't need anything else, I'll head downstairs," he said, backing away as if Samantha were radioactive. "I don't expect you to work all the time. Mikey and I will stay out of your suite. See, it locks." He pointed at the door latch as he slipped out.

"You don't have to…" she said to his retreating back, but he didn't turn to hear what she was going to say. He seemed bent on escaping.

And that was fine. Good, even.

The fact that it left her feeling desolate, well, it didn't signify.

Corbin banged a hand on his desk. He'd made a complete idiot of himself with Samantha. It would be a wonder if she didn't move out.

He sat down at his home computer and logged in to his online class, then got back up again two minutes later. He couldn't focus, and Corbin could *always* focus. And he needed to, now more than ever. He needed to use every spare second when Mikey wasn't here to get his work done.

He looked down at the "Ready to Grade" icon staring at him from his university's Learning Management System. Two sets of exams needed his attention, ideally before tomorrow. The students deserved the feedback. But instead of thinking about his students and their work, Samantha's confused face kept flashing before him.

Why had he told her about his high school crush? She hadn't known, and had never needed to know. High school was a long time ago.

Since then, she'd lost a child and developed a drinking problem. He didn't know which came first. She'd liked to party in high school, but hadn't seemed like one of the truly troubled kids, starting early with an addiction problem. Most likely, then, she'd started drinking too much after she'd lost her baby.

Sympathy tugged at his heart, but he shut it away. He'd vowed never to get involved with someone who had a drinking problem. A counselor at the church had warned him that he might well be extra susceptible to a relationship with an alcoholic, since he'd grown up seeing that type of unhealthy bond as the norm. For that reason, he'd looked carefully at the drinking habits of the few women he'd dated. Maybe he'd even been a little rigid about it. He'd wait for her to order first; if she ordered a drink, it was a red flag to him. If she ordered another to go with dinner, their first date was also their last.

Not that anyone had really clamored for him to change his mind. He wasn't the most popular man in the dating field, once women realized that he spent most of his time working, didn't follow the latest TV shows and could barely remember the names of the local sports teams. To find a partner who liked him despite his esoteric interests had started to look more and more unlikely, especially living in a smaller town. Being judgmental about a woman's desire for a glass of wine didn't help matters any. He didn't like that quality in himself, particularly, but he didn't seem able to change it.

Restless, he walked into the kitchen and got a drink of water, then leaned back against the sink and looked out the window into the green tree-lined backyard.

Now that he had responsibility for Mikey, there was no way on earth he'd jump into a relationship with a woman who'd struggled with alcoholism, even if she claimed to be over it. He couldn't subject a child to that kind of misery. He knew it too well, from the inside out.

Corbin trusted that God had a plan for him, and if that plan was for him to stay single, he would stay single. But following God's will wasn't easy. He got lonely, just like anyone else. Having Samantha—beautiful, lively Samantha—living in his house was going to be tough.

He'd never felt like this about any other woman. His attraction had been strong in high school, but it was even stronger now that Samantha was grown up, nurturing and thoughtful and kind. From the moment she'd walked into the coffee shop and helped him handle Mikey, there hadn't been a day—or a night—when he didn't think of her.

"Corbin?" Her husky voice sounded from the door to the kitchen, and he took a deep breath before turning around.

She'd changed from the flowery, flowy shirt she'd been wearing into a soft, faded T-shirt. She looked even more stunning.

"Mind if I look through the fridge?" she asked.

"Go for it." He had to get himself together, remember that she was just a nanny.

"I was thinking I'd cook some lunch, if that's okay with you." She leaned in and studied the limited offerings. "Maybe sloppy joes and a salad? Mikey will need a good meal, and I'm hungry, too. I think you had sandwich rolls, at least the last time I looked."

"Okay," he said, realizing his own stomach was growling. "But I'm not sure when Mikey is coming home. He might stay there for lunch."

"Oh." Her forehead wrinkled. "Well, if he does, maybe I'll just fix myself some toast. Unless you want... should I fix the sloppy joes anyway? Would you eat one?"

"I'd eat two or three," he blurted out, and then snapped his mouth shut as the notion of sitting down to lunch with Samantha taunted his imagination. "But don't cook. You don't need to cook for me. That's not in the job description."

"Yeah, I guess we should hammer one of those out, shouldn't we?" She opened the food cupboard and scanned it, then glanced back at the table. "I noticed you have a booster seat, but if there's other kid-related stuff you need, I could call around and see what I can borrow for you."

"Good idea. And I'll get around to working up a job description, hours, all of that, to run by you. It's just been so chaotic getting used to taking care of Mikey, it never occurred to me."

"No rush," she said. "And I know I don't have to cook for you, but… I can use the kitchen, right? And if I'm making myself a meal, I might as well make enough for you. We don't have to eat together." She paused, her cheeks going pink. "Not that I'd mind eating together, it's just…you don't need to feel obligated to do that."

"I don't mind," he said quickly. And he didn't.

Except that eating meals at home with Samantha was going to make him hyper-aware of all the things he wanted and couldn't have. He owed it to Mikey to rein himself in. "Maybe I'd better eat in front of the computer at that," he said, gesturing toward his study and looking away from what seemed like hurt in her eyes.

There would be plenty of occasions for eating meals with Samantha in the coming weeks. He didn't need to add to that by sitting down to lunch with her when it wasn't absolutely required.

Chapter 5

The day after the nonlunch with Corbin, Samantha leaned into the red barn that housed the Rescue Haven program for boys and dogs. "Gabby?"

A cacophony of barking ensued. "Over here," came a voice from a row of kennels along the side of the barn, barely audible above the noise of the dogs.

She walked farther in and Gabby came to greet her, wiping her hands on a towel. "Hi! Reese is out getting some supplies and the boys' program doesn't start until after school, so I'm on my own with the morning chores."

"Is it a bad time?" Samantha asked, even though she'd texted Gabby last night to set up this meeting.

"Nope. It's perfect. Come and sit while I finish these last kennels. The dogs will settle down in a sec." And indeed, out of the seven or eight dogs she could see, only one was still barking madly, and another let out the occasional yap.

"They're so cute." Samantha knelt by a reddish pit bull and offered her hand to sniff. The dog came forward slowly, and gave her hand a quick sniff, but when Samantha moved, she jumped back and started barking again.

She looked back at Gabby. "Do you have any treats? If I could make friends with her, maybe I could clean her kennel for you."

"Feed her some treats, but she won't let you clean her kennel." Gabby tossed her a bag. "That's Aurora, and she hasn't had a great life up until now. She's come to trust a couple of the boys, but it takes time."

"Understandable." Samantha tossed the dog a couple of treats and then sidled over to the next kennel. There, a large black longhaired dog panted in a way that made it look like it was smiling. "How about this one?"

"Boomer's super friendly. If you could let him out and change his food and water, that would be great. He can run around the barn a little."

Samantha opened the crate and was nearly knocked over by the giant friendly dog. "Hey, boy!" She rubbed his sides and turned her face so that the dog's kisses landed on her cheek instead of her nose and mouth. "You're beautiful!"

"He is, and he's ready to adopt out, but he's too big and sheds too much for most people. Plus, he's deaf." She tapped Boomer's nose and pointed at the floor, and the dog seemed to laugh over at her before dropping back down on his four feet to greet the other dogs, still secure in their pens.

Samantha found a big bin of dry kibble and filled Boomer's bowl. "So I've been thinking about that idea for a kids' program. Are you still interested in having me get it started?"

Gabby finished wiping down a crate and went to a utility sink to wash her hands, and Samantha joined her to refill Boomer's water bowl.

"Don't you want to settle in as a nanny first?" Gabby asked, her face frankly curious. "Or is it not working out with Corbin and Mikey?"

"Oh, it's working out great!" Samantha said hastily. "Mikey's terrific and Corbin's a very thoughtful employer. He doesn't want to take advantage, and the result is that I have some extra time."

"Where *is* Mikey?"

"Corbin wants to cut down on his hours at the university so he can give Mikey some attention. Today, he said he would keep Mikey at home with him while he grades tests."

Gabby laughed. "Corbin doesn't know much about kids, does he?"

"No, he doesn't seem to." Samantha opened her mouth to say more, then closed it again. She didn't know Gabby well. But she was feeling a little lost, having just moved away from all her friends, and she knew she didn't do well if she let herself get isolated. She twisted her hands together and then looked up at Gabby. "I need something besides being around Corbin all the time. I figure I could do this, at least get something started for you, while I'm taking care of Mikey. Build up my résumé, you know?"

"Makes sense." Gabby frowned. "Is there a reason you don't want to be around Corbin all the time?"

Besides that I keep getting attracted to him? Her face heating, Samantha looked over at the pit bull, now sleeping peacefully in her pen. "It's just better," she said. "Leave it at that."

"Sure." Gabby leaned forward. "I tell you what, it's hard being a working mom at times. I get it that you'd want to escape, have your own life apart from Mikey."

"It's not that." Samantha sighed. "If I could be a working mom, I'd be thrilled, but…" She looked at Gabby, gauging the other woman's capacity to be a friend. "I miscarried a baby right after high school through some not very smart decisions I made. Too much partying," she clarified. She hadn't taken a drink once she'd learned she was pregnant, but she'd spent lots of time up late in smoke-filled rooms, and there had been a lot of drinking in the weeks before she'd known.

"I'm sorry to hear that." Gabby patted Samantha's shoulder, then frowned. "Sounds like you're blaming yourself."

"I guess." And she didn't need Gabby to talk her out of that. A couple of friends and counselors had tried, and that had almost made her feel worse, like they were placating her. "I didn't mean to go into all of that," Samantha said, and ducked her head, her hair falling in front of her face. She reached out a hand to pet Boomer as he bounded by.

"I'm glad to get to know you better," Gabby said,

smiling at her. "I'm glad you're here. Aside from Hannah, I don't have that many friends my age to talk to here in town."

Samantha's heart warmed. Most of her friends in the city were from AA, and they were great. But it would be nice to find friends here who were more her own age, and who had other interests in common with her, not just recovery.

"So anyway, tell me about what you're thinking for a younger kids' group," Gabby said, and they went back and forth with some ideas and found they were on the same page.

"The thing is," Gabby said, "Mrs. Markowski would have to approve it since she's the one funding it."

"Funding what, dear?" came a voice from the barn's doorway, and the dogs' voices rose in a loud chorus again. Samantha turned to see Mrs. Markowski turning away from Boomer's overfriendliness.

The well-dressed older woman didn't look like she'd be very easy to please.

When Corbin arrived to pick up Samantha, he walked into the barn and found her being grilled by Mrs. Markowski. Gabby was there, trying to interject without a whole lot of success.

"'Mantha!" Mikey tugged away from Corbin's firm grip on his hand and ran to throw his arms around Samantha. "Came to get you!" He twisted around and his eyes widened. "Dogs!"

Samantha hugged Mikey back and looked up at Corbin, one side of her mouth quirking, two vertical lines between her brows. He'd never seen *help* broadcast more plainly.

"Say hello to Mrs. Markowski, Mikey," he said.

"'Lo," Mikey said distractedly.

"Do you like dogs, young man?" Mrs. Markowski leaned over to put her face beside Mikey's, pointing at the dogs' crates. "Which one do you like best?"

"That one!" Mikey scrambled off Samantha's lap and ran at Aurora, who cringed back and growled and barked.

Corbin reached Mikey as his mouth opened to wail. "Hey, buddy," he said, swinging him up into his arms. "Some dogs like it when you move slow and don't yell. Aurora is one of those."

"Bite me!" Mikey cried.

Corbin, Samantha and Gabby all looked at each other. Corbin was trying not to laugh at Mikey's statement, and he could tell Samantha and Gabby were having the same struggle. "She won't bite you," Corbin said, trying not to laugh. "Here, let's have you visit Fluffy." He carried Mikey over to another crate, knelt, and opened it. A small scrappy shih tzu rushed out and began running around Corbin and Mikey.

Mikey crossed his arms and shook his head. "Like *big* dogs," he said.

Mrs. Markowski smiled indulgently.

Gabby smiled, too.

But it was Samantha's smile that captivated Corbin. She looked genuinely happy, watching Mikey, sitting between Gabby and Mrs. Markowski, who'd stopped grilling her for the time being.

She whispered something to the other two women and they both began nodding. What were they talking about?

Gabby moved over and sat by Mrs. Markowski, while Samantha tugged Corbin aside, her hand warm on his arm. "We have an idea," she said, laughing up at him, her eyes challenging him to some sort of game.

"Yeah? What's that?" He leaned a little closer and breathed in the smell of flowers from her hair. His pulse quickened.

Her eyes went wide, then dropped quickly as she gestured toward Mikey, who was now standing in front of Boomer's crate, poking his fingers inside. "We think you should get Mikey a dog."

"A what?" He was a little confused because his blood seemed to have sped up its coursing through his veins, and his whole body had heated up.

"A dog." She glanced up through long thick eyelashes and then looked away again. "We think Mikey should get a dog."

"Oh." He tried to process what she'd said, willing himself to cool down. It wasn't his place nor his right to let her affect him as a man, not when he'd never get into a relationship with someone who had her issues. "You think we should get a dog?"

She nodded patiently. "Look at them."

Distractedly, he looked at Mikey, who was giggling as the big dog licked his face through the crate. "I'm only learning how to have a kid under my roof." *And a warm, sweet, gorgeous woman I have to keep my distance from.* "I don't know if I can deal with a dog."

"Just something to think about," she said, and moved away from him to get down on the floor with Mikey.

Reese came in and looked surprised. "What's going on here?"

"Hi, honey." Gabby went to him immediately and wrapped her arms around his waist, and he pulled her close. For a few seconds, they were clearly unaware of anything around them but each other.

A sword of jealousy stabbed Corbin's heart. He remembered when Reese had been single and angry at the world. Now, the man had a wife who obviously loved him madly.

Maybe Corbin would get there, too, but it wouldn't be with someone like Samantha.

"Where's Izzy?" Gabby asked Reese.

"With Nana," he said.

"Well, Samantha came to offer to set up that early childhood program for us," Gabby explained. "But Mrs. Markowski needs to approve it since she's the donor, right?"

Reese nodded slowly and looked over at his aunt. "What do you think?"

She looked up from Mikey and the dog and her face sobered. "I'd like to see Samantha prove her reliability before we trust her with something like this," she said.

Corbin stiffened at the implied insult, but Samantha raised a hand. "She's right, of course," she said. "None of you have any reason to trust me with organizing something so big."

"Why not have her work on something smaller as a sort of test run?" Reese suggested.

"Like what?" Corbin was still defensive for Samantha. "Like…"

"I know!" Gabby snapped her fingers. "How about a Rescue Haven float for the Memorial Day parade? Because we sure don't have time to do it, and it would be organizing something, and working with the kids."

"Would you be willing to do that?" Corbin asked before Mrs. Markowski could respond. He didn't like the way the conversation was more *about* Samantha than including her.

Mrs. Markowski broke in before Samantha could answer. "It's not a bad idea," she said. "I'd like to see that float be very strong, maybe win a prize."

Gabby laughed. "You're so into decorating, maybe *you* should design a float."

"Oh, no, dear, I don't have the time," she said, although to Corbin, it seemed like she probably had nothing but time. "No, I'd like to see how you do with the decorating, of course," she said speaking directly to Samantha for the first time, "but also, how you handle the boys and the dogs. If you can manage that, and manage it well, I'd definitely be more confident to fund your heading up a bigger project."

Samantha looked a little frozen, like a rabbit who'd just spotted a predator. "I, um, I'd like to try, but I don't know anything about how to build a float."

"Corbin does," Gabby said promptly. "He built a great undercarriage for the float the church did last year."

All eyes turned to Corbin, and Reese clapped him on

the back. "Looks like you've got yourself a job, buddy," he said. "If you can handle it."

It seemed to Corbin that his friend had a double meaning to his words. And looking over at Samantha, who was blushing and looking anywhere but at him, he wasn't sure he *could* handle it. But what choice did he have?

"Samantha," Gabby said gently, "what do you think?"

"I'm willing to try," she said. "Are you, Corbin?"

"I'll do it," he said. And wondered what he was getting himself into.

Chapter 6

Samantha and Corbin walked into church on Sunday morning with Mikey between them, each of them holding one of his hands.

Sunshine warmed Samantha's back and a spring breeze cooled her face. Around them, families walked toward the quaint white church, talking and greeting one another.

It felt like Samantha, Mikey and Corbin were a family, too. And it was killing her.

Corbin, tall and broad shouldered in a gray suit, earned several glances from the younger women in the crowd. Understandable. Samantha was having a hard time not staring at him herself.

But she focused on Mikey, whose eyes were wide as they entered the light-filled sanctuary. This whole thing was about him, not her. She wasn't happy with having deceived Corbin about her connection with his mother, but if it allowed Mikey to find a home, if it allowed Corbin and Mikey to become deeply attached, it was worth it.

And because she wanted to make this work so badly, she ignored the butterflies in her stomach. She wasn't comfortable entering the church she'd occasionally attended as a child and teen. She'd hardly been church material, her sarcastic attitude showing, when Hannah's mom, her aunt, had gently forced her to come to church.

She hadn't fit in then, and she didn't fit in now. She might look more respectable, and she, Corbin and Mikey might look like a family, but appearances weren't reality.

Since then, though, she'd come to a new understanding, become a believer. Back in the city, she'd found a large multicultural congregation she loved. That, in addition to all she'd learned about trusting in a higher power in AA, had nudged her in the right direction.

A small-town church was pretty different, but God was unchanging. She hoped she could find a little peace here today.

"Samantha!" Hannah hurried up to her and gave her a hug. "I'm so glad you're here. Come see Mom."

Samantha opened her mouth to protest, to say she needed to be with Mikey, but Corbin's deep, warm voice stopped her, sending a shiver down her spine. "Go. I've got him."

She followed her cousin, waving to Gabby and Sheniqua along the way. When Aunt Becky saw her, she opened her arms wide and gave Samantha a huge hug. "I'm so glad to see you! Don't you look good!" She held Samantha back by the shoulders and looked her up and down. "You've really grown up, haven't you?"

"Tried to," Samantha said, and explained that she was taking care of Mikey and working on another possible job as well.

"That's wonderful." Her aunt, suntanned and fit-looking, explained she'd been away on a trip with her girlfriends. "Now that I'm home," she said, "You'll have to come for dinner."

"I'd love that," Samantha said, and meant it.

"'Mantha." A little hand tugged at hers.

The feel of it warmed her heart, and she knelt to check on Mikey. "How do you like church?" she asked.

"Wanna go play," he said.

Corbin was right behind him. "I told him about the nursery," he explained. "He wants to go. Help me get him settled there?"

"Of course."

As they walked through the church halls, she scanned the familiar banners proclaiming positive messages of faith. One in particular made her stop, wanting to drink it in: "We Are Forgiven," it said, with an image of three crosses on a hill.

Maybe, just maybe, the banner was right. Maybe she *was* forgiven for the sins she'd committed.

It was hard to imagine that the Lord could forgive her for causing the death of her baby. But maybe He'd forgive some of the myriad of smaller sins she'd committed along the way. Like a wave lapping at the shore, forgiveness touched her, receded and touched her again.

They walked into the nursery behind another family. She knelt to show Mikey the bin of stuffed toys, but he wasn't interested. "Blocks!" he shouted, looking beyond the stuffed animals, and started toward them.

She grabbed his shoulders to keep him from escaping. "Wait for Corbin to check you in."

Corbin was discussing Mikey's needs with one of the caregivers as the family who'd been ahead of them turned to leave. From her position kneeling beside Mikey, Samantha caught sight of the father, and her heart stopped as heat flooded her face.

Don't let him see me, please don't let him see me.

He was talking to his wife and she thought she'd escape notice, but then he glanced down. His eyes widened. "Samantha Alcorn?"

"Hi, Jack." She rose slowly, still holding Mikey's hand, and nodded to Jack and his wife. "Nice to see you." She attempted to sidle away, and Mikey helped by tugging her toward the blocks.

Jack touched her sleeve and cleared his throat, stopping her. "Uh, Samantha, this is my wife, Nadine. Nadine, Samantha Alcorn. I met Nadine at college," he added to Samantha, as if she would want to know. Then he looked at Nadine and nodded sideways to Samantha. "Samantha and I were…friends, back in high school."

"Nice to meet you," Samantha said, smiling at Nadine so widely her face felt stretched. "Oops, got to go!" She nodded down at Mikey, who was still tugging, bless his heart. Corbin had sat down at one of the tiny tables and was filling out an index card, no doubt information about Mikey, and Samantha was glad. Somehow, she didn't want him to get involved in any interaction with Jack.

She managed to escape, following Mikey and helping him dig into the block bin as emotions roiled in her chest. Jack Reddin. She hadn't thought about him in quite a while, but she thought about the consequences of what she'd done with him almost every day.

She'd approached him as soon as she'd learned she was pregnant, that crazy summer after senior year, but she hadn't really expected much. They hadn't had a close connection; put baldly, it had been no more than a hookup. Still, she'd felt like he ought to know.

And when he'd started sweating and ran his hands through his hair until it stood on end, when he'd apologized over and over but said he just couldn't become a father right now, that he had one more year of college and a bright future, she'd shrugged and patted his arm and said she'd take care of it.

The relief on his face had been a little sickening, because she'd suddenly realized how that had sounded, what he'd thought she meant.

But explaining that she'd go ahead and raise the baby alone, just like her mom had raised her, well, it hadn't seemed like it was worth her time, given his reaction.

She blinked and brought her attention back to the present, the nursery, as Corbin came over and started talking to Mikey, who'd found a big plastic truck and was crashing it into a heap of blocks he'd made. Jack had obviously married and started a family and moved on with his life, and Samantha was glad. She didn't wish him ill. But she also didn't want anything to do with him.

"Are you okay?" Corbin asked quietly, and she looked up and met his steady gaze and got a little lost. Instinctively she knew that if anything of the sort had happened with Corbin, he would have insisted on taking responsibility for the baby. Just look at how he was embracing guardianship of Mikey.

Corbin's eyes flickered to something behind her just as Samantha heard a throat clearing. She looked up into Jack's distressed face.

"Can I speak to you for a minute?" he asked.

She blew out a breath, thought about refusing, and then decided she'd get it over with. He had a right to know what had happened, if that was what he was after. Maybe he just wanted to make sure she'd keep quiet about it all.

She stood. "I'll meet you out in the sanctuary," she told Corbin.

He stood, too, and took a step closer to Jack. "Is everything okay?" he asked her, putting an arm around her in a way that felt wrong and possessive and wonderful.

"It's okay. I'm fine. I'll just be a minute." She gave him a tiny smile as she shrugged out from under his arm and followed Jack into the hallway, robot-like.

Once outside, Jack gestured toward the church library, where the lights were off and the door was closed. "We can talk in here." He opened the door and held it for her, but didn't flick on the lights.

A small window provided the only illumination, a

twilight atmosphere that felt fitting. Dust motes danced in the single ray of sunlight. She backed against the wall of bookshelves and crossed her arms, hugging herself a little. "What do you need, Jack?"

He opened his mouth, then closed it. Gestured toward the nursery, and then met her eyes. "Is that... Is that little boy ours? And Corbin's helping you raise him?"

"No!" She felt her brows draw together as she tilted her head to one side. Whatever she'd expected him to say, it wasn't that. She was twenty-three and Jack must be twenty-seven, the same age as Corbin. She'd gotten pregnant at eighteen. Their baby would have been four by now. Didn't he know that? "No, that's not our child. That's Corbin's little brother, Mikey. I'm just the nanny."

"Oh!" He glanced over that way again, his square shoulders relaxing a little, then nodded. "Oh, right, I guess I wasn't thinking straight. Um...so where..." He huffed out a breath. "I heard you were planning to keep the baby."

She stared at his handsome face, his creased brow, his slightly receding hairline. She *so* did not want to go into this with Jack. "You heard that and you didn't look me up?"

He met her eyes and then stared at the floor. "I'm sorry. I was a jerk. A complete jerk, and I wouldn't blame you if you hated me, but... I have a kid now, see, and I understand—" He broke off and looked at her again. Outside the library door, more people walked back and forth, their voices slightly audible. In here, though, they were in their own unhappy little bubble of space.

"You understand that kids are important and you shouldn't run away from the responsibility? Yeah." She tightened her arms, still crossed over her chest. "I had a miscarriage at six months."

"Six…oh, man." He took a step closer, then seemed to take in her body language and sank into a chair at the end of a shelf of books instead, dropping his head in his hands. "I'm sorry. That must have been awful."

"It was," she whispered as the blood and the fear and the pain, physical and emotional, rushed back. Mom had come to the city to be with her for a couple of weeks, and that had helped, but her mom had grieved, too. And Mom had died without ever having a grandchild.

It had been her fault. If she'd taken care of herself as she should have…

Her throat tightened to where she couldn't speak. Jack looked up at her, and she saw that his eyes were wet, too.

Whatever their differences and flaws, this loss belonged to both of them. She took a step forward and put a hand on his shoulder, cleared her throat. "We both made mistakes. Lots of them."

He nodded and looked up at her with bleak eyes. "Was it a boy or…"

She cleared her throat again. "A boy."

He stared at the floor again, a muscle tightening in his jaw.

He was processing the loss for the first time, while she'd had years to think about it endlessly, to grieve. And she could hear the organ music starting up. "What's your daughter's name?" she asked gently.

"Misty. She's…she's great."

"Beautiful, too. So's your wife." Samantha patted his shoulder, and even though she ached inside, she swallowed and pulled herself together. "I'm glad you're happy, Jack." She turned away from him and headed toward the door.

It burst open. "Jack, are you—" The woman who had been on Jack's arm stopped still and stared from Samantha to Jack and back again. "What are you doing in here?" she asked, her voice staccato.

Samantha tilted her head, wondering what to say, but there was nothing. And this part wasn't her business. She glanced back at Jack, raised her eyebrows, and shrugged, trying to communicate that the ball was in his court, now.

And then she walked past Nadine out into the hall, and past the nursery and straight out of the church.

As soon as the service ended and he'd picked up Mikey from the nursery, Corbin rushed home and into his house, tugging Mikey along by the hand. His heart pounded. Where was she?

The mouthwatering smell of chicken gave him a clue, and he charged into the kitchen to find her stirring something on the stove. Relief and anger washed over him in equal parts as he surveyed her familiar form, now dressed in faded jeans and an old T-shirt. "What are you doing here?"

She looked at him blankly. "I, um, live here? And I'm making lunch."

His fists clenched, and it was an effort to relax them.

"Don't act like you don't know what I'm talking about."
Corbin heard a sniffle from Mikey but ignored it. "You
left without a word to anyone. I was frantic. Mikey was
frantic!"

She knelt down and opened her arms. "C'mere,
Mikey. Everything's okay."

Mikey rushed to her. "Corbin yell," he said, cuddling up against her.

She hugged him and glared up at Corbin. "Corbin
is mad," she said, "but he's not going to yell anymore."
She narrowed her eyes as if daring him to disagree.

Of course, she was right about that if nothing else.
"I'm sorry I yelled, Mikey. Everything's fine now."
Even though it wasn't. He patted Mikey's back and then
glared right back at Samantha. "Do you want to explain
why you disappeared without telling anyone?"

"I texted you that I wasn't feeling well."

"I didn't get a text." He paced away from her and
Mikey, both of whom were staring at him. She was just
like his mother. Unreliable. Undependable. Always running off when she was needed.

And he hadn't overstated Mikey's upset. When
Corbin had let slip that Samantha wasn't there and he
didn't know where she was, big tears had rolled down
the poor kid's face. He'd already been abandoned once,
by his mother. He didn't deserve to fear abandonment
again, not for one second.

"I'll show you the text." She stood, picking Mikey
up, and walked over to where her purse hung on a hook
by the door. He hated noticing that her T-shirt brought
out the arresting gray-green color of her eyes. Actually,

it was hard to tell *what* color her eyes were—lighter in the middle, darker around the edges and changeable as the Ohio sky. Right now, as she looked back at him, they were stormy.

She tapped on her phone. "See? It's right here… Oh." She bit her lip. "I must not have hit Send. I'm so sorry."

"Why'd you leave church like that?" He couldn't stop his voice from going loud again.

She glanced at Mikey. "Let me get you boys some lunch."

"I want to know."

She opened a pot on the stove, scooped out a taste with the tip of a spoon, and tested it. Then she reached overhead to the salt container and shook a little bit into the pan. Next, she set Mikey down, grabbed potholders and pulled a tray of magnificent-smelling chicken pieces out of the oven.

Corbin's mouth watered, but that didn't halt his irritation. "Why are you ignoring my questions?"

She lifted her chin and looked directly into his eyes. "It's not something I feel comfortable discussing in front of Mikey," she said quietly, then added, "or at all." She nodded her head sideways to Mikey, who stood looking from him to Samantha, his eyes hollow. "And you're upsetting him."

She was the one who'd upset Mikey initially, but now, her dignity brought him to his senses. "I'm sorry," he said. "C'mon, Mikey, let's wash our hands." He took Mikey by the hand, walked him over to the sink and hoisted him up.

Mikey sprayed more water onto himself and the surrounding counters than onto his hands, but at least it made him giggle. Corbin helped Mikey dry off with the dishtowel, washed his own hands and then turned to Samantha, chagrined. "I'm sorry. We made a mess."

"It's okay," she said without looking at him. She was scooping mashed potatoes into a bowl.

He helped Mikey into his booster seat, then held Samantha's chair for her. When he sat down and surveyed the delicious spread, he felt even more ashamed. Chicken, potatoes, fresh asparagus and a fruit cup. Real Sunday dinner, and when did he ever have that?

Mikey reached toward the bowl of fruit just out of his reach, and Samantha took his hand and pulled it back. "Let's pray first, honey."

Corbin reached for Mikey's other hand and then, after a moment's hesitation, reached for Samantha's as well. The feel of her hand grasping his made his prayer fly right out of his mind.

"T'ank you, Jesus," Mikey said.

The sweet, high voice brought Corbin back to his right mind and he uttered a quick addition to Mikey's simple prayer.

As he dished out food for Mikey, then urged Samantha to serve herself, Corbin thought about why he'd gotten so terribly upset.

The truth was, he'd gotten the strange feeling that there was something between her and Jack Reddin. Jack was good-looking, outgoing, active on the finance committee of the church and quite wealthy. None of that had ever mattered to Corbin until he'd seen how Jack was looking at Samantha.

And yeah, Jack was married, but that didn't stop a lot of people from following up on their extracurricular desires.

Even if Corbin had read that right, though, he had no right to think about Samantha in the possessive way he was. He had no business monitoring her personal life.

He took a bite of chicken, then one of mashed potatoes, and his worries started to recede. "This is *good*," he said. "Really good."

"Good," Mikey agreed. He was scooping bites of mashed potatoes with a spoon he held in his fist, and somehow, most of the food was landing in his mouth.

"Try some chicken," Corbin suggested, and reached over to shred a few pieces onto Mikey's plate.

"Chicken goes cluck-cluck," Mikey said as he picked up a piece of meat and stuck his tongue out to taste it. Then he smiled, grabbed a whole fistful, and stuffed it into his mouth.

"Slow down!" Samantha was laughing. She picked up a small piece of chicken from her plate and put it delicately into her mouth. "See? Like that."

Mikey stared.

Corbin did, too.

"And mmmmm, look at the asparagus. It's like a little tree." She held up a stalk, then cut it into small pieces and put a few on Mikey's plate. "Sorry it's a little overcooked," she said to Corbin. "They say you should cook veggies until they're really soft, for toddlers. I meant to take ours out ahead of time, but I forgot."

She'd put real effort into cooking for him and Mikey.

Corbin put his fork down and looked at her. "Why the nice meal?"

"Oh, I thought you and Mikey could use a little lift," she said. "Truth is, I wanted a lift myself, and I like to cook."

"Did it work?"

"Until you came in here like a charging bull." One corner of her mouth quirked up, just a little.

"Yeah." He sighed. "I'm sorry about that. It's not really my business what you do."

"No, but I can see why you got mad when I didn't let you know I wouldn't be riding home with you. That was me being distracted and I'm sorry."

"It's okay. You shouldn't even be working on a Sunday. It's just…" Should he say it? "You seemed kind of stressed out. In the nursery. With Jack."

"I was, a little. Maybe a lot." She didn't elaborate; instead, she turned the tables. "But you seemed awfully upset about my leaving, more than the situation warranted." She raised an eyebrow. "Are you going to tell me what that was all about?"

"When I figure it out," he said ruefully. He didn't want to admit how much he thought about her. That was way over-the-top. But he also had a dim memory of being the last kid at a Sunday school class, waiting and waiting for his mother, his teacher finally driving him to her house until Cheryl could be found.

So maybe being ditched at church had hit him hard in more ways than one. "I hope, sometime, we can sit down and talk about…this stuff."

"What stuff's that?" She toyed with her fork, spun it, put it down.

"This getting emotional and all." He looked into her eyes. Man, did she have pretty eyes.

She looked right back, one eyebrow raised just a little, and his face heated.

Her eyes widened a little and she looked away, her eyes lighting on Mikey. "Someone needs a nap." Samantha stood and nodded over at the boy, who was rubbing his face with the backs of his hands and yawning. She picked him up and he immediately lay his head against her shoulder. "I'll put him down unless you want to."

He stood and came over to them and rubbed circles on Mikey's back, and the words burst out of his mouth: "Let's do it together."

She let out a little sigh. "Corbin."

"What?" He was standing close enough to hear her breathing and to smell the flowery fragrance of her shampoo.

"It just seems a little too…domestic, or something," she said.

He thought about that. "Lunch seemed domestic, too," he said, gesturing to the food-laden table. "Nothing wrong with domestic."

She scrunched her nose. "You sure about that?"

"No," he admitted. "But I know it's more fun to do stuff with someone else than to always do everything alone." Which sounded totally pathetic. He wished he could take back the words. "I'm just not used to it," he added, which wasn't much better.

"I'm not, either," she said softly.

"Do you like it as much as I do?" He was looking down at her, studying her eyes, her face. She looked… vulnerable.

And then he could have kicked himself. What was he doing? He wasn't going to get close with someone unreliable, an alcoholic.

Her eyes darkened. "Corbin…what are you doing?"

It was an echo of his own question to himself. How could he say that he felt like there was a magnet in her, drawing her to him, very much against his better judgment? Mikey rested against her shoulder, picking a little bit at the sleeve of her shirt, his eyes drooping shut. Corbin stepped a few inches closer to brush aside Mikey's hair.

And to breathe in Samantha's perfume, a note of muskiness beneath the floral.

Their eyes met, and it definitely felt like a magnet. The sunlight slanted golden rays over her hair as she ducked her head to brush her lips across Mikey's forehead. The neck of her shirt gaped, showing her delicate throat. Barely aware of what he was doing, he reached out to draw her closer.

When his hands made contact with her upper arms, she let out a little sigh and looked up at him again. Her eyes, up this close, were stunning: huge and gray-green and vulnerable. His mouth went dry.

"Mama," Mikey mumbled, then lifted his head. "Mama at church."

Corbin came back to himself as he realized that Mikey was still awake. He stilled his arms and frowned. "You mean Samantha? She *wasn't* at church."

"Mama at church," Mikey insisted. "Told me to be a good boy."

"You mean your…your real mama?" he asked.

Mikey nodded, then rubbed his eyes and lay his head back down against Samantha's shoulder.

Samantha took a giant step back. "I think it's time for Mikey to go to bed." She held up a hand. "Don't bother. I'd rather do it myself."

That stung, but Corbin was grateful, too. It would give his hormones the chance to calm down. Give him a chance to think better of his extreme desire to kiss her.

As she hurried out the kitchen door and up the stairs, Corbin puzzled over Mikey's words.

Had Cheryl come to church to see Mikey? What had she wanted? What condition had she been in? Why would she do it secretly rather than openly?

And why had Samantha acted so weird about it?

Chapter 7

On Monday morning, Samantha climbed out of Corbin's car at the Rescue Haven barn. She opened the back door and unbuckled Mikey from his car seat.

"I can lift him out," rumbled Corbin's deep voice behind her.

Awareness skittered up and down Samantha's spine. They hadn't cleared the air over what had happened yesterday, Mikey's words about seeing his mother, Corbin's anger that she was missing from church, her own erratic behavior after Jack had confronted her in the church nursery. This morning, though, she'd awakened with the desire to get something done. Mikey had seemed a little restless at breakfast, so they hitched a ride with Corbin to Rescue Haven. He was to pick them up on his way back from the university this afternoon.

Samantha knew her own anxiety had to do with the way Corbin had looked at her. He'd been intense, almost flirtatious. She'd thought he might be going to kiss her. She'd *wanted* him to kiss her.

But Mikey's innocent words had thrown cold water onto that romantic scenario. After she'd put Mikey down for his nap, she'd gone out for a walk and called Cheryl.

"Did you come to the church today?" she had demanded, and Cheryl, after a long pause, had admitted that she had.

"It's hard, that's all," the older woman had said. "I know it's best for Mikey, but he's my baby boy and I miss him so much."

The pain in Cheryl's voice had been real. Samantha's heart broke for her. Cheryl had messed up motherhood badly as a young woman, and admitted freely that she and Paul hadn't been good parents to Corbin. Now, she had a late in life baby and doted on him, but she also had a hard time staying sober. And what energy she had needed to go to her dying husband.

Cheryl's life was a mess, and Samantha couldn't help having compassion for her. Especially since Cheryl was trying so hard to do the right thing, trying harder than she ever had in her life from the looks of things.

Corbin carried Mikey into the barn where Samantha had arranged to meet Gabby and her daughter. The two women were hoping that the babies would entertain each other long enough for Gabby and Samantha to talk over the float that Samantha was going to make for the parade.

Inside the barn, the dogs barked their greetings from their crates that lined one wall. Mikey was already comfortable enough to struggle out of Corbin's arms and run over to visit the dogs. He clapped his hands in front of one crate, riling up the little brown-and-white mutt inside. Then he saw Boomer, the big longhaired black dog, and gave a little jump of excitement. He squatted down and poked his finger into the crate and let the dog lick his face through the bars.

"Looks like he's going to be a dog lover," Samantha said. "He's not showing any fear."

"He sure seems to like Boomer," Corbin said. "For that matter, I like Boomer, too. If I were going to get a dog…"

Samantha glanced over at him and leaned closer to keep her voice low. "Don't you think Mikey would benefit from having a puppy?"

"He might benefit from it, but I wouldn't," Corbin said. "I can barely wrap my mind around the idea of having a child to take care of. Adding in a puppy might put me over the top."

"You're kidding, right?" Samantha asked. "You're doing a terrific job."

"You really think so?" Corbin put his hands on his hips and smiled. "I appreciate that, coming from you. I'm really learning as I go with this."

"So, you admit that it would be great to get Mikey a dog," Samantha said.

Corbin held up his hands like stop signs. "Wait a minute, that's not what I said!" he protested. "You can't seriously think that would be a good idea for me and Mikey at this time."

"Sometimes two are easier than one," she said. "A dog would keep Mikey entertained, and he would grow up learning about and knowing about animals."

Corbin shook his head back and forth, a slight smile softening his refusal. "Seriously, I don't think I could handle it. I know my limits."

"You thought you couldn't handle a child, but you are," she said.

"Why are you so adamant about me getting a dog?" he asked. "Some of the care of it would fall on you, you know."

She wrinkled her nose. "Truth is, I always wanted a dog when I was growing up. Mom was like you. She didn't think she could handle it on top of everything else she had to do, and she was probably right. And I would always say that I would help, but she didn't believe me. And that was probably right, too."

"What was probably right?" Gabby walked into the barn holding two-year-old Izzy by the hand.

"I'm still trying to get Corbin to let Mikey have a dog," Samantha said.

"And I'm ignoring her, because I need to get to the university," Corbin said. "Gabby, please talk some sense into Samantha. Let her know I couldn't handle a dog, too."

As Corbin hurried out the barn door, Gabby turned to Samantha, one eyebrow raised. "You two are arguing like a married couple," she said.

Heat suffused Samantha's face. "Not hardly," she

said. "If Corbin doesn't want to get a dog for Mikey, then he shouldn't get one."

"Get dog!" Mikey said.

He had approached them without Samantha having realized it. "Oh, no," she whispered to Gabby, and then tried to redirect Mikey's attention. "Look, Mikey, it's baby Izzy," she said.

"Want dog," Mikey said. "That one." He pointed at Boomer.

"Come on over here," Gabby said. "Look, Izzy brought her cars and trucks to play with." She led the way to a part of the barn where a square play area was sectioned off with knee-high walls. She plunked Izzy down into the little penned-off area, and Samantha swung Mikey in, too. When Gabby dumped a container of plastic cars and trucks inside, the toddlers gleefully grabbed and banged them.

"We better get done as much as we can while they're interested in each other and the toys," Gabby said. "It won't last long."

"Good idea." Samantha followed Gabby to a bench near the play area. "I just wanted to get a few ideas about the float that I'm going to make for you all," she said. "I feel like it's important to get this right."

"And you won't have an easy judge," Gabby said. "Mrs. Markowski is particular."

"I got that impression," Samantha said. She showed Gabby the drawings she'd made and they talked through some of the techniques that could bring the float to life, as well as budgets and supplies.

Surprisingly, the babies played well together, and

after they'd hammered out the details of the float, Samantha and Gabby sat together watching them. "I hope you're feeling at home here in town," Gabby said. "It can take a while to get readjusted."

"No kidding," Samantha said. "I didn't have the best reputation when I lived here before, and sometimes I feel like I'm in a battle to overcome that."

"With people like Mrs. Markowski?" Gabby asked.

"Her, and others, too." Samantha picked at a loose splinter on the edge of the bench. "The truth is, I made a lot of mistakes, and people know about some of them. I guess it will just take time to see if I can fit in here again."

"Do you want to?" Gabby asked.

Samantha considered that. She had come back to Bethlehem Springs as a favor to Cheryl, to help temporarily with Mikey. She hadn't intended to stay. But if she could get some kind of a career going here, she actually wouldn't mind. "I like this town," she said. "It's peaceful and warmhearted, at least for the most part."

Gabby smiled. "It's not perfect. I've had some issues readjusting because of my past here, just like you. But I'm glad I made the effort. Reese and I have a wonderful life here, and I'm able to be close to my grandmother as well."

"You're fortunate," Samantha said.

"I feel really blessed. But it wasn't always this way, and everything isn't always easy. If you want to make it work here, you can. Just don't let your own attitudes and fears get in the way."

"Easier said than done," Samantha said. "Those old habits of thought die hard."

Gabby studied her, her eyes calm and knowing. "They do. They do die hard. In fact, I don't think we can ever really get rid of our hang-ups on our own strength. Especially if they're pretty significant. It definitely took a leap of faith for me, and by that I mean faith in God."

"I'm a believer," Samantha said quickly. "I wasn't, not in school, but life events brought me close to the Lord, and my AA sponsor helped me figure out some of that stuff."

"That's good," Gabby said. "But that was back where you lived before, right?"

"Yeah." Samantha sighed. "And it takes a while to make new friends, new close friends."

"Well, I hope you consider me a friend," Gabby said. "You know, Hannah and I get together pretty often, and you'd be welcome to join in."

"My cousin Hannah?"

"Yes. We got to know each other over the last year or so, working on some projects for Rescue Haven. She's the main dog trainer we work with, and she's great." Gabby smiled. "I did briefly feel jealous of how close she and Reese were, but I got over it pretty quickly."

"Does Hannah know how you felt?"

"Yes. We had a good laugh over it, in the end. She thinks of Reese as a friend, sometimes even an annoying brother. And Reese and I are...well, we're doing good." A slight pink colored her face.

Jealousy stabbed at Samantha. How great would it

be to have a man who cared about you the way Reese obviously cared for Gabby, and to be secure in his love?

"Anyway," Gabby went on. "Now, Hannah and I walk together a lot. I push Izzy in her stroller. I'm guessing she would love it if you and Mikey came along." She reached out and squeezed Samantha's hand, just for a second. "And I'd love it, too."

They got busy with the children then, and Mikey looked at the dogs some more, seeming entranced with Boomer in particular. Samantha tried her best not to encourage his affection for the big black dog. She had to respect Corbin's stated limits and his rights over Mikey as his guardian.

She felt heartened by her conversation with Gabby. If she made some good friends here in town, maybe she would be able to make some kind of a life here for herself.

One that ultimately wouldn't involve Corbin and Mikey, she reminded herself. That situation couldn't last. Corbin would figure out how to care for Mikey himself—he was already improving at it by the day— and soon, he'd find a daycare spot for when he needed to be at work.

Her heart sank at the thought of their cozy domestic arrangement ending.

But at least she liked this town, which she hadn't expected when she'd come back at Cheryl's request. It was a good place to live. For the most part, people didn't judge her for her past.

Maybe, just maybe, it would work out for her to stay, build a home here.

* * *

When Corbin returned to Rescue Haven to pick up Samantha and Mikey, he sat for a few minutes in his vehicle, getting his bearings. Not physically, but mentally and spiritually.

He didn't know what to do.

He was drawn to Samantha like a horse to sugar cubes. He felt happy going home when she was there. He liked eating meals with her and talking over the small issues of the day. He enjoyed working with her to take care of Mikey.

Unfortunately, that wasn't where it ended. He wanted to hold her in his arms.

But that was the problem. He couldn't in good faith take the relationship any deeper, knowing that he wouldn't even consider making a commitment to her.

He tipped his head back and closed his eyes, wordlessly praying. Wordlessly because he didn't know what to say.

Moments later, a tap on his window brought him out of his prayers. Reese. Corbin climbed out of the car and shook his friend's hand.

"You okay in there?" Reese asked.

"Yes. No. I'm a little unsettled." He wouldn't have admitted that truth to just anyone, but he and Reese were close. Reese had talked over his issues with Gabby when the two of them were falling in love, and though Corbin hadn't had any brilliant insights, he knew Reese had felt better after their talk.

Today might be the day for Reese to return the favor.

By unspoken agreement, they didn't head into the

barn. Instead, they walked toward the outdoor area where Reese was repairing a fence. "Boys don't get here for another…" Reese checked the time on his phone. "Half an hour. Got to fix this so they can bring the dogs out here. Give me a hand?"

"Sure." So Corbin held the wire mesh in place while Reese hammered a frame around it. Reese's service overseas had resulted in the loss of a hand, but with his prosthetic hook, he was better than most people at woodworking and home repairs.

"Unsettled how?" Reese asked as he hammered, adjusted the wood, hammered some more.

Corbin opened his mouth to answer and then shut it again. He'd been in a position to give Reese advice before, but now he was the one who needed help. That wasn't a familiar position to be in.

Reese nodded toward a small box of nails. "Grab a couple of those for me, will you?" After Corbin did and held them so Reese could hammer, Reese spoke again. "Wouldn't have anything to do with Samantha, would it?"

"It's obvious?" Corbin sighed.

"To someone who knows you pretty well, yeah. Never saw you look at a woman the way you look at her."

Corbin blew out a breath and sat back, lifting his warm face to catch the spring breeze. "She's a huge help with Mikey," he said.

"Gabby's grandma is a huge help with Izzy," Reese said, "but I don't look at her the way you look at Samantha."

"Good point." Corbin picked up the repaired section of fence and carried it over to the spot where it belonged, Reese following along with his tools. "Nothing can happen, though," he continued, "so it's tough having her live at my place."

"Why can't anything happen?" Reese lined up the fencing, eyeballed it, made an adjustment.

Corbin frowned. He didn't want to gossip about Samantha's alcoholism, but she'd been open about it when she'd talked to Reese and Gabby before. "She has a drinking problem."

Reese's head snapped around to face him. "Still?"

"No! I mean, I've never seen any evidence of it. She's in AA."

"Okay. I thought you meant you'd seen her drinking or smelled it on her breath or something." He whacked a couple more nails and then stood back to survey his work. "She's been sober for a while, right?"

"A couple of years, to hear her tell it."

"You don't believe her?"

"You can't ever believe an alcoholic," Corbin blurted out with more vehemence than he'd intended. Seeing Reese's raised eyebrow, he tried to explain. "She means well. They usually do. It's just a tough addiction to break. And I promised myself I'd stay away from relationships with women who drink, or who have that tendency."

"Yeah, I heard." Reese sounded almost amused.

"You did?"

"Jen Adams told me you went cold on her the minute she ordered a glass of wine. At first she figured you were just cheap, but after you encouraged her to order the most expensive thing on the menu, she realized it was the drinking that bothered you." He grinned. "She said she ordered a second glass just to test her theory, and you barely said another word to her for the entire meal."

"Jen Adams…oh, yeah." He remembered the petite, curly-haired electrician now. She'd seemed nice enough, until she'd crossed the line he had set for himself.

"You know," Reese said mildly, gathering his tools, "lots of people enjoy a glass of wine. And lots of other people know they can't, and stick with that. If you're cutting out connections with both those groups of people…"

"I know. I get it, I'm being rigid."

"But…" Reese raised an eyebrow.

"But I remember what it was like to get my hopes up about my mom and have her let me down. I can't handle more of that. And no way will I subject Mikey to it."

"Not everyone's your mom."

"True, but how can I know for sure?" Corbin shook his head. "I really think it's best for me just to avoid those women."

"Okay, fine," Reese said, "but you don't seem real happy about avoiding Samantha."

"I'm not." Corbin frowned, leaning against the fence. "It's a problem."

"You're the one who always tells me where to go with my problems," Reese said.

"Right." And Corbin hadn't done that yet, with Samantha. "I've been so preoccupied with helping Mikey get adjusted, I haven't taken the time to pray about it."

"Not to mention you're busy with a big-time job at the university." Reese shrugged. "But you know as well as I do that when you're overwhelmed, that's the time to take it to the Lord. Also..."

"What?"

"You might not remember this," Reese said slowly. "But once, you told me that everyone makes mistakes. When you said that, it made me accept that Gabby had made a few, and I had, too. Ever think about extending that same kind of grace to Samantha? And even to yourself?"

"No. Not really." What did Reese mean, extend grace to himself?

"Think about this, too," Reese went on. "You're trusting Samantha to take care of Mikey when you're at work. So you must believe on some level that she's got her drinking under control."

"She'd never do anything to hurt Mikey." Of that, Corbin was sure.

"So...if she fell in love with a guy, do you think she'd do anything to hurt him?"

Did he? He tried to imagine Samantha drinking and failing to fulfill her responsibilities, breaking promises, maxing out credit cards. All the things his parents had done when Corbin was growing up.

It wasn't a picture that went with the woman he was getting to know.

And as they walked into the barn, just ahead of a busload of Rescue Haven boys, Corbin tried to reconcile the two warring thoughts in his head: the part that wanted to protect himself, and the part that wanted to open himself up to new ideas and possibilities.

Chapter 8

The light was turning golden when the barn door opened to reveal Corbin standing there.

Samantha's heart stuttered.

He wore a long-sleeved dress shirt, open at the collar with the sleeves rolled up, tie stuffed carelessly into his pocket. His hair was a little overlong and his glasses gave him a serious look. Every inch a professor. But the warmth in his eyes as he squinted into the dimness took him beyond the stereotype. Corbin was a major intellectual, but he had a compassionate servant's heart.

"Corbin!" Mikey spotted his brother and guardian. He ran and jumped into his arms, and Corbin's smile got wider and warmer.

As Corbin swung Mikey up high before folding him into a bear hug, Samantha's heart melted some more.

There was no time to explore that feeling, however, because right behind Corbin was a herd of middle-and high-school-aged boys. They must have gotten off the school bus that she'd heard squeaking and creaking its way up the hill.

The boys' noise sparked a virtual riot among the dogs, who barked and jumped inside their pens. The boys seemed oblivious, punching each other good-naturedly, laughing about some joke they'd shared, obviously having a good time and glad to be there.

Mikey tugged Corbin's hand, drawing him toward Samantha. Once safely ensconced between them, Mikey stared round-eyed at the big boys' shenanigans.

A loud whistle pierced the air, and immediately, the boys quieted down and settled into chairs around a long table. To Samantha's surprise, it was Gabby who'd whistled, and who now stood in front of the boys, waiting for their full attention.

"She's got a lot of control over them," Samantha murmured to Corbin.

He grinned and nodded. "Word in the barn is, don't mess with her."

"Okay," Gabby called. "I want to talk to you all about helping with a float for the Memorial Day parade, but first, we need to take care of the dogs. Twenty minutes, walk or playtime, and I want every pen and dish clean."

A couple of the boys grumbled or rolled their eyes, but they all went fairly quickly to the rows of pens that lined the side and back of the barn. That was when Samantha realized that each boy had his own dog to work with, except for a couple of the older ones who had two. Some of the dogs seemed well trained, while others ran wildly, pulling on their leashes and barking at each other. Some were small, most medium-sized, and a couple were downright huge—the fluffy black giant and a mostly white Great Dane mix.

Mikey clapped his hands and laughed to see the dogs all out, and before Samantha could process what he was doing, he twisted away from them and ran at the nearest dog. It reared back, obviously frightened of the shouting little boy. The older boy handling the fearful dog urged it behind him and put out a hand to stop Mikey.

As both Corbin and Samantha hurried toward Mikey, he turned and ran at another dog who began to bark.

"Mikey." Corbin's voice was stern as he blocked Mikey and knelt in front of him. "Stop."

Mikey did stop and stared up at Corbin. Samantha stared a little, too; she'd never heard Corbin's voice this stern.

"Sit down on that hay bale," Corbin ordered, and Mikey did, his eyes welling up with tears.

The boy's contrite expression would have turned Samantha to mush, but it didn't seem to have that effect on Corbin. "Dogs can hurt you," he said. "And you can hurt them. You have to touch them carefully."

Mikey looked confused.

"Use two fingers," Samantha chimed in. It was what they'd told the kids in the day care when any animal had come in. At this age, Mikey needed the specifics, so she held out two fingers and demonstrated on Mikey's arm. "Like that."

Mikey held out two fingers and stroked Samantha's arm, and when she glanced at Corbin, he flashed a smile.

"You always ask the older kid or grown-up who's with the dog first, before you pet it," Corbin continued his lecture. "Understand?"

Mikey nodded solemnly.

"You should get him a dog, Doctor Beck," one of the boys called as he walked past. "We have a lot up for adoption."

Samantha suppressed a smile.

Mikey's expression brightened. "Want dog."

Corbin laughed a little. "Go play," he told Mikey.

"Why are the dogs up for adoption if they're part of the therapy for the boys?" Samantha asked.

"The boys train them to be family pets, if they're suitable for that. There are always more dogs in need when these get adopted out."

Mikey had ventured closer to the pens, and one of the teen boys led the giant fluffy black mutt over to him. "You want to walk the dog?" he asked Mikey.

"Yeah!" Mikey yelled.

Samantha stared for a minute, unable to believe the teenager could be serious. Boomer was twice as big as Mikey was, his giant head at the same level as Mikey's.

"Here you go," the teen said, and handed the leash to Mikey.

"Wait!" Samantha rose and hurried over. That dog was way too big, and with Mikey shouting, he was putting himself in danger. What was the teenager thinking?

"Look!" he cried rapturously to Samantha and

Corbin as he walked straight ahead, the dog plodding slowly beside him. "I'm walking him!"

"You can't yell in his ear, buddy," Samantha said as she caught up to the trio: Mikey, the dog and the teen who'd orchestrated the encounter.

"He doesn't know the difference," the teenager reminded her. "He's deaf."

"Oh, right." No wonder the big dog was so calm around Mikey's loud exuberance.

"Walk him back this way, Mikey," Corbin said.

Mikey turned and walked toward Corbin, and to Samantha's surprise, the dog stayed at his side. "Want *this* dog," Mikey said, his smile huge.

Samantha could see why. How wonderful it would be to a little boy to have such a large, furry companion. And the fact that he was deaf could definitely make it easier for him to be around a shouting toddler. But still, she could see why Corbin wasn't eager to agree. "Mikey, that dog is just so big," Samantha said. "He must weigh over a hundred pounds."

"A hundred and forty," the teenager said, sounding proud.

Reese had come in at some point, and now he approached them. "Boomer is gentle as a lamb," he said. "If you're considering…" He trailed off and looked at Corbin. "We can talk."

"I guess." Corbin looked a little overwhelmed.

"Big dogs seem to be calmer," Reese said. "Less of a bite risk."

Gabby had come over to get into the discussion. "Don't deaf dogs startle easily? And couldn't that lead to problems?" She nodded down at Mikey, who was running his hands through Boomer's fur.

"That's a bit of a myth," Corbin chimed in, his face going thoughtful. "Statistically, deaf dogs are no more likely to bite than hearing dogs. It's always a good idea to approach them from the front, though, and wake them gently. Mikey would have to learn."

"You're considering it?" Samantha's voice rose to a squeak as she considered the bear-like dog.

"All right!" The teenager did a fist-pump. "We've been trying to place him for a long time, but between his hearing and his fur, nobody wants him. Plus, he's old for a big dog."

Obviously, the kid had something to learn about salesmanship, and he wasn't saying anything Samantha hadn't already known about Boomer, but his words tugged at her heart. She reached out a hand to the big black dog, and he sniffed it, then gave it a light lick. Then he flopped down as if all the attention had worn him out.

The teenager patted the big dog's head. "When he was dropped off here, he kinda freaked when you woke him up. But we work on conditioning him every day, making it into a good thing, not a scary thing, when somebody surprises him. Now, he just looks at you when you wake him up, like, 'Where's my treat?'"

They talked a little more about the dog's needs. Corbin hadn't worked with him for his research project, but he'd seen him around. Samantha quickly warmed to the idea of Boomer joining Corbin's family; the dog did seem super gentle, and Corbin was neat enough that he wouldn't mind running the vacuum cleaner every day because of the dog's shedding.

"Love him," Mikey said, his voice rapturous, and they all looked down to see him curled up beside the dog, his head resting on the dog's chest. Samantha's chest warmed, and she glanced over at Corbin.

He was looking at Mikey, the corners of his mouth curling up, his eyes crinkled. "I think that about says it all. I'd like to adopt this dog."

Amazed at how he'd gone from resistance to enthusiasm, Samantha gave him an impulsive hug. He pulled her closer for an instant, and the warmth of his embrace felt like coming home.

And then they were both backing away, and Samantha knew that the uncomfortable expression on Corbin's face was mirrored on her own.

Saturday, between dealing with Mikey's excitement about Boomer and getting the dog settled, Corbin was exhausted. Finally, Mikey went to sleep and Corbin collapsed into a kitchen chair.

He looked over at Samantha, who was across from him at the kitchen table, her shoulders a little slumped. She had to be at least as tired as he was. "I'm sorry you had to work another Saturday," he said. "Be sure to take a day off this week."

"I will, to work on the float," she said. "But I truly didn't mind helping today. It was great to see how happy Mikey was with Boomer." She reached down and rubbed the big black dog's head, and he slid onto the floor beside her, landing with a thump and a sigh. He had to be exhausted, too.

Boomer had proven to be house-trained and gentle, but he had grabbed numerous items off the counters and tabletops before they'd realized they had to further dog proof Corbin's house. It was toddler proof, but when Boomer put his front paws up on the counter, he was way taller.

And although Boomer was an older dog, he'd gotten pretty excited about moving from the Rescue Haven shelter to a house. They had taken him for a long walk in the hope that he'd settle down.

From the looks of things, it was finally working.

"What are you doing tonight?" He wished they could just hang out together, watch a movie or something, but he knew that wasn't wise. "I'm going to prepare my classes for next week."

She smiled tiredly. "As soon as I get a little energy back, I'm going to sketch out a design for the float so the boys can get started on the base of it on Monday."

"Why don't you take a break tonight?"

She shook her head as she stood and headed for the coffee maker. "I have to do a good job on the float. If Mrs. Markowski likes it, she'll support my setting up a kids' program at Rescue Haven. It's my chance to make it in this town, and I like it here."

She liked it here! Happiness bubbled through him as he watched her, and he tried not to think what his own joy meant. "I thought maybe you had some bad memories here."

"Well…" Some of the light went out of her face.

"You never did tell me about Jack." He stopped. "Not that you should." He needed to rein in his desire to know everything about Samantha. That wasn't his right, and it wasn't wise.

She leaned against the counter. "No, it's okay. You might as well know, though this is private."

"Of course."

She studied him for a minute, then sighed. "He's the father of the child I lost."

Really? Corbin was jolted at the thought. Quickly, he reviewed what he remembered about Jack and Samantha from high school days. Jack was older than she was, and Corbin didn't remember them having a relationship. He'd been away at college himself, most of those years, but when he was home he'd paid pretty close attention to Samantha; he would have noticed if she'd had a steady boyfriend. Indignation rose in him, a defensive feeling for a high school student who'd gotten pregnant by a college-aged boy. "Did he take advantage?"

"No." She ran a finger around the edge of her coffee cup. "No, I was a willing participant. I… I didn't know any better at the time, Corbin. I was all about having fun and breaking rules."

"Did he take responsibility?"

She smiled faintly. "No, he didn't do that, either."

Corbin's fists clenched. How could an older, wealthier kid conceive a child with a woman and not take responsibility for it?

"He apologized for that last Sunday." Samantha rubbed at a spot on the table. "I can't fault him for not stepping up, not really. We were both immature and I didn't know how to have a good conversation about responsibility. I didn't push it, because I didn't know men ever really took responsibility. My own father didn't."

Protectiveness welled up in him. "I'm sorry. That must've been difficult."

"It was," she said. "But hey, everyone has tough times." She sighed and pushed away from the counter. "I should get to work."

He couldn't fix what had happened in the past, but maybe he could be supportive now. "Let me help you design the float."

"No! You have classes to prepare."

Boomer lifted his large head, seeming to sense that they were arguing even though he couldn't hear their voices.

"I want to do it," he said. "I've actually done a fair amount of designing in my research, setting up different types of pens and feeding stations. And I'm pretty good with technology. Remember, I helped draw up plans for the Rescue Haven float last year. I already said I'd help build the float, but I'd be glad to give you a hand designing it, too."

She opened her mouth as if to say something, but closed it again, bit her lip, and studied him as if assessing his seriousness.

Finally, she nodded. "I should say no, but I know it would be better if I had some help designing it as well as building it. I don't know a whole lot about designing floats, and I want it to be good enough to pass Mrs. Markowski's test. I have a feeling she's pretty particular."

"Let's have at it." He poured himself a cup of coffee and led her into his office where he had a design table and several helpful programs on his computer.

As they watched some videos about floats and talked about what would show off Rescue Haven to best advantage, Corbin found himself laughing often, joking around, relaxing. Watching her.

He had had a crush on her since he was a high school senior, but he hadn't really known her well back then. Now, he realized that she was quirky and funny, with lots of energy and a good work ethic. Put that together with how nurturing she was of Mikey, and how she stepped in gamely to help him adopt a giant dog, and the package was hard to resist.

"I love the idea of the flashing lights and moving sign," she said, looking over the rough drawing he'd pushed across the table to her, "but I'll definitely need a lot of help with this. Are you sure you and the boys are going to be willing to work on something this detailed? And have the time?"

She didn't know how willing. "Of course. It will be a good project for the boys. They'll learn a lot from working on it. And the more they can have a sense of buy-in at Rescue Haven, the better."

She was looking at him with head tilted, eyes steady. "You really care about that program, don't you?"

He nodded. "They do good work."

"So do you."

The praise, along with the admiring way she looked at him, went straight to his heart. He shouldn't do it, but he reached out and pushed back a strand of her hair.

Her breath hitched and the pulse in her neck throbbed rhythmically, but she didn't look away.

Urgency rose in him as he looked into those gray-green eyes fringed by thick lashes. There was something in the back of his head reminding him that this was a really bad idea, but he couldn't really remember why.

Right now, on this night, it seemed like a great idea to take a step closer, to let his thumb rub along her soft cheek. Her skin felt hot beneath his hand. And when she closed her eyes and tilted her head back, just a little bit, it seemed like an even better idea to kiss her.

Chapter 9

As Corbin's lips brushed gently over hers, Samantha's heart started a steady, pounding rhythm.

His lips were firm, making her want to melt into him, taking her breath away.

He lifted his head and looked at her, his brow wrinkling with concern. "Is this okay?" He didn't move an inch, just watched and waited for her response.

A true gentleman, and that awakened something in her that was deeper than simple attraction. Men had pulled her into their arms before, men had kissed her, but that had been kid stuff compared to how deep and rich and right it felt to be here, now, with Corbin.

She sucked in a breath. It wasn't okay, wasn't a good idea at all, but she wanted him to keep kissing her. So she nodded and let her hand rest, just lightly, against his broad, strong chest.

"Good, because I don't want to stop." He kissed her again, a little deeper and longer and slower this time, and now the rhythm of her heart sped up until it felt like it was knocking against her ribs.

He smelled clean and fresh, and his touch was gentle but assured as he rested one hand on her shoulder and cupped the back of her head with the other. Then he slid his arm around her and pulled her against him. His embrace gave her a feeling of security, like she could rest there, like he could protect her.

She hadn't expected Corbin to be this masterful, to know exactly how to kiss a woman. She hadn't expected his strong arms around her to feel so fantastic, hadn't realized how much she wanted to let go of her worries and just be in the moment with this man.

You can't get involved. He doesn't know about Cheryl.

But that was okay, wasn't it? Corbin was so logical and realistic. He would understand why she'd done what she'd done, wouldn't he?

Besides, she was tired of making good choices and doing the adult thing. She laced her fingers behind his neck and tugged him a little closer.

"Samantha," he said, opening his eyes and looking into hers. "What are you doing to me?"

"I could ask the same question," she murmured. She didn't want him to stop, because she knew that if they did stop, they would both think better of what they were doing. So she raised up on tiptoes and brushed his mouth again.

The office was quiet, fragrant with the smell of the candle she'd set to burning after the quick dinner they'd prepared together. The sun had set, turning the sky outside the window a deep purple.

The world of Rescue Haven and the town and the university, her history here, all of it seemed to recede, leaving only this moment with Corbin.

A car went by, its stereo pounding out a loud vibration that brought Boomer to his feet, barking his deep bark. They stepped apart. Samantha rubbed Boomer and praised him while Corbin checked outside. And then she looked at him and he was looking back at her, and the moment felt confusing and awkward. "This is the kind of time I could use a drink," she quipped nervously.

Corbin's face fell. "Right." He stared at the ground for a moment, and then met her eyes. "That, what just happened, probably wasn't a good idea. I think I'm going to head upstairs. I'm sorry about…" He waved a hand toward the spot where they'd stood kissing. "Sorry about that."

He was gone before she could even respond to him, and the sense of loss she felt turned her bones to jelly. She sank down into a kitchen chair.

"It's just you and me, Boomer," she said, grateful for the large dog leaning against her.

Yes, that had been a mistake. Hadn't it?

But why had Corbin gone from warm to cold so quickly?

* * *

The next morning, things got worse.

Samantha walked across the church parking lot and into the sanctuary through a gray drizzle. How had everything gone so wrong?

Of course, she hadn't slept well last night, torn between worrying about the repercussions of the kiss and remembering how wonderful it had felt. When she'd come down to fix breakfast, Corbin had been sitting at the kitchen table drinking coffee. His eyes, dark with shadows, suggested he hadn't slept well, either. He'd taken off his glasses and rubbed them when she had come in, then looked at her. "Good, I was hoping to see you before church. Why don't you take a couple of days off."

His abrupt words, not a question but a sort of command, startled her. "Why?"

"We've been overworking you." He didn't look at her. "You haven't had a day off since you started."

She tipped her head and crossed her arms and studied him until he met her eyes. "Is that the real reason?" she asked.

He looked away, looked back, paused and then spoke. "Last night shows what can happen when we spend too much time together, and Samantha, that's not the direction I want to go. So I think it's best if we get a little distance."

"Oh." It was all she could get out while her insides processed what felt like a crushing blow. "Do you mind if I go to church, or will that make you feel uncomfortable? I don't mean ride with you," she added quickly.

"Just go to, you know, the same church as you and Mikey."

"Go, go, that's fine." He waved a hand in a way that felt dismissive.

Like he couldn't wait for her to get out of there.

So here she was at church because she didn't know what else to do, where else to go. She was early, so maybe she could spend a few minutes praying quietly in a back pew, getting herself together.

The sanctuary was still dim and fairly empty, and she sidled into a back corner pew. She bowed her head and tried to talk to God, but her worries and hurt feelings didn't seem to want to take the form of a prayer.

Why had Corbin gone so cold on her? She hadn't been the one to initiate that kiss, had she? Hadn't he been into it as much as she was? Maybe even more?

Of course, men were a little more ruled by their hormones than their emotions. She knew that all too well from her dating history before she'd become a Christian. Since then, she'd gotten more careful and aware.

But Corbin was a man, just like any other.

Maybe Corbin was physically attracted to her, but upon reflection, realized he wasn't interested in any other way but the physical. Corbin was too much of a gentleman to pursue a relationship on that basis alone.

Had the emotional connection she'd felt with him been completely one-sided, though? The way they'd looked at each other, the way they'd worked together to get Mikey settled into his new life, their conversations and fun times at home…had it meant nothing to him?

He'd valued her opinion that Mikey should get a

dog, had helped her design the float, had seemed genuinely angry at how Jack had treated her. She'd thought it meant they were having a healthy, full, growing relationship, had started to think that maybe they could get past Cheryl's deception and build something.

But who was she kidding? It wasn't just Cheryl's deception, it was Samantha's deception, too. And Corbin was honorable, yes, but he was also stern. If he learned of the deceit, he was likely to be very, very upset.

He was likely to judge her. So maybe limiting their relationship now was God's way of keeping them both from getting badly hurt.

The problem was, she already felt badly hurt.

A hand came down on her shoulder, accompanied by the smell of expensive perfume. "May I join you, dear?"

Mrs. Markowski. Samantha didn't really want company, but what could she say? Besides, she couldn't feel much worse than she already did. "Of course you can join me," she said, and moved down the pew to make space for Mrs. Markowski to sit.

The older woman slipped into the pew beside her, impeccably clad in a teal skirt and jacket, makeup perfect. Samantha was suddenly conscious that she hadn't changed into church clothes. She was wearing jeans and a flowered blouse. Not terrible, especially since this church welcomed everyone regardless of how casually they dressed, but still, she felt self-conscious. She'd also neglected to put on makeup, and her hair was back in a careless ponytail. Beside Mrs. Markowski, she definitely felt frumpy.

"How are you settling in?" Mrs. Markowski asked.

Was she being kind? Or nosy? It was hard to tell. "I'm doing fine, thank you," Samantha said. Bland and noncommittal seemed like the way to go, given the power Mrs. Markowski had over her future.

Although that future had gotten a little more bleak this morning when Corbin had gone so very cold.

"Living with Corbin is working out okay?" That definitely sounded more on the nosy side.

"It's been convenient living in Corbin's spare suite, since I'm caring for Mikey while Corbin works," she said carefully. If Mrs. Markowski was the type to judge—and she definitely seemed to be—then Samantha wanted to make their chaste living arrangements crystal clear.

At least, the living arrangements had *seemed* chaste, until things had taken a more romantic turn last night.

But this morning, everything had U-turned back to an impersonal, employer-employee relationship.

Sharp eyes seemed to probe into hers.

Samantha looked away. She felt completely ill-equipped to cope with the older woman's prying.

"How about the float?" Mrs. Markowski asked. "Are you making progress?"

Samantha tried to focus. Yes, that was what was important. The float. Because it meant that she could stay here in town. Although she couldn't exactly remember why she had wanted to. If Corbin was going to act like he didn't want her around, staying in town was suddenly a lot less appealing. And that opened her eyes to one of the major reasons she'd wanted to stay, consciously or not.

Mrs. Markowski was looking at her expectantly.

She forced herself to speak pleasantly. "It's coming along well," she said. "We have the basic design, and the Rescue Haven boys are going to help out with it."

"That's fine then. We should set up a meeting soon to go over what you've done so far." The older woman made no motion to leave.

"Is there something in particular you're worried about?" Samantha blurted out the words and then wished she hadn't. But there was some kind of innuendo and what Mrs. Markowski was saying, and she didn't have the patience to try to figure it out, nor to ignore it.

The older woman studied her. "You have a history in this town," she said. "I heard about it from my son."

Samantha blew out a sigh. Brock Markowski had tormented her at various times during high school, maybe because she'd refused to go out with him. But he was gone now. He would never have a chance to make up for past wrongs, and meanwhile, his mother was grieving. Considering how awful Samantha had felt when she'd miscarried a baby, she knew that losing a child you'd raised must be nearly unbearable. "Brock and I weren't close," she said. "In fact, we had our differences. But I'm sure that at least some of what he said was accurate. I made a lot of mistakes back then."

Mrs. Markowski swallowed hard and looked away. "So did he," she said quietly.

So maybe Mrs. Markowski knew some of Brock's issues and failings. That might make it even harder to have lost him, before he could work things out and grow up. "I can't imagine what you went through, losing your son," she said, her own throat thickening. "I'm so sorry."

Mrs. Markowski looked at her sharply, as if gauging her sincerity. Why was that? Had others been less than supportive about her loss, since her son had been unkind to so many people?

She reached out, thinking to touch Mrs. Markowski's arm or squeeze her hand, but the other woman turned away and then stood. "I'll leave you to your prayers," she said stiffly, and walked away.

Another encounter gone wrong. Samantha sank back into the pew and slumped down a little, turning her face away from the aisle where a few more early birds were drifting into the church. It would be best to avoid recognition and sit alone today. That felt safer than trying to connect.

That self-protective isolation felt all too familiar to Samantha. She remembered it from her high school years in this town.

And now, she felt a yearning she hadn't had then: to drink the pain away. Something she hadn't longed to do in months.

She let her head droop down and closed her eyes and prayed, hard.

Corbin stared in dismay at the muddy paw prints that covered his floor, his pants and Mikey's entire church outfit.

When Boomer had stood barking at the door this morning, Corbin had realized it was crucial that the dog go outside quickly. He *seemed* house-trained, but Corbin still didn't feel completely secure in that.

He also hadn't thought ahead. Hadn't realized that such a big dog with such a thick long coat would get completely drenched. That Boomer's paws, like the rest of him, were huge. That the backyard was particularly muddy at this time of spring. And that a very muddy Boomer would bound exuberantly around the kitchen, pausing only to jump up on both Corbin and Mikey.

They were going to be late to church.

"Let's get some towels and clean Boomer off," he said to Mikey. But that meant that Mikey tromped the mud through the rest of the house, as did Corbin and Boomer. Well, that answered the question of how to spend the afternoon: they would be mopping.

"Where 'Mantha?" Mikey asked as they rubbed towels over Boomer. Basically rubbing the mud in. So that further answered the question of how to spend Sunday afternoon: they'd be washing the dog.

"She went to church." He got Boomer marginally cleaner and gated him in the kitchen, then took Mikey back upstairs for clean pants and shirt.

He ended up giving Mikey another bath, which made the toddler's lower lip stick out. Mikey didn't care for baths. "Want 'Mantha," he said.

"We'll see her later." The truth was, Corbin wanted her, too. Wanted to have her help with Mikey and Boomer, and wanted her cheerful attitude about the whole situation.

Not to mention that he also wanted to kiss her again. And again, and again.

Don't go there. He clenched his jaw and focused on getting Mikey dressed and then changing his own clothes. Yes, laundry for sure this afternoon.

As Corbin rushed Mikey out the door and drove to the church, he went mentally over his to-do list for the day. He hoped it was long enough to get him and Mikey all the way through the afternoon and evening, with no time to miss Samantha.

Even when Mikey napped or went to sleep, Corbin could get his schoolwork done. He had plenty of tests to grade. He could work late into the night on them, if he couldn't sleep.

Keeping busy, that was the key, he thought as he pulled into the mostly full church parking lot.

He just didn't know if there were enough chores and tasks in the world to shut a particular pretty brunette out of his heart.

Chapter 10

As the sanctuary started to fill around her, Samantha lifted her head and breathed in the scent of candles and the feeling of peace.

An usher came over and handed her a carnation.

"What's this for?" she asked, smiling at the elderly man.

"Happy Mother's Day, dear," he said.

"Oh…thanks," she said faintly. Mother's Day. How could she have forgotten?

Partly, she'd forgotten because she didn't have a mother to buy a card for or send flowers to. And she didn't have a baby. Pain wrapped around her as she clutched the undeserved flower.

The service started and the theme was "A Mother's Love."

It was nice that the pastor acknowledged that there were many ways to mother, and that the notion of motherhood could bring pain to some. Like those who'd lost a mother—check—or lost a child—check—or wanted a child and couldn't have one. Check again, though that latter was simply because she didn't have the man or relationship that would make it possible to become a real mother.

There was a little disturbance in the back of the church, and Corbin and Mikey came in, looking disheveled. What had happened? Mikey saw her and tried to tug Corbin in her direction, but Corbin pulled him toward the other side of the sanctuary, going to sit with Reese, Gabby and baby Izzy.

Samantha tried to still the ache in her chest with stern admonitions to focus on the service and on God, not on herself.

But when three generations—grandma, mom and baby daughter—made a testimony and lit a candle, sadness overwhelmed Samantha. Her mother was gone, and Samantha had never had the chance to thank her for all she'd done and tried to do, to apologize for not being a better daughter. Mom had been a loving person and had done the best she could, and Samantha longed for a mother's comfort as well as for the chance to be more of a comfort to her mother than she'd been able to be.

Maybe even more, she wished for the baby she'd miscarried. No, she hadn't been ready to be a mother, nor had she had a committed partner to help with parenting, but nonetheless she had been excited about the baby. She had also figured that taking care of the baby would give her a purpose in life, a life that had been pretty aimless thus far. She'd stopped drinking as soon as she realized she was pregnant; not soon enough, as it turned out, but for a while, she had thought that motherhood would mark a wonderful new phase of life for her, more focused on giving and caring than on selfishness and partying.

Oh, she would have loved to have a son. As she looked at the young mother holding her baby at the front of the church, her own arms ached with their emptiness.

She'd been playing family with Corbin and Mikey, had enjoyed caring for both of them, but now Corbin was pushing her away. He didn't want her to take on that role in his family, in his heart.

No point in even pretending she was participating in the church service now, so Samantha slipped quietly out and stumbled down the church hall. She was looking for the ladies' room where she could wipe her tears and wash her face before walking home. But when she found the restroom door and walked in, there was Sheniqua.

"Hey," she said, then studied Samantha more closely. "Are you okay?"

"Not really." Samantha splashed water on her face and grabbed a paper towel to dry off and blow her nose. Sheniqua was still there, so she waved a hand. "Don't worry about me. I'll be fine."

"Let's go sit down a minute," Sheniqua said in that authoritative voice a doctor would use with a patient.

Samantha didn't really want to. She didn't know this woman very well. But following along was easier than making some kind of an excuse.

Sheniqua beckoned her into an empty classroom. "This doesn't have anything to do with the Mother's Day service going on upstairs, does it?"

Not only was Sheniqua a doctor, but apparently, she was good at reading between the lines of what a patient or friend said. "How'd you guess?"

"Because it's tough for me, too," Sheniqua said promptly. "I lost my mom a few years ago, and it's not looking real likely that I'll meet a guy who can put up with my schedule long enough to marry me and father me some babies."

"I'm sorry. It's rough." Samantha tried to focus on the other woman's losses instead of her own, but that backfired; she started crying again.

"It's rough, but I'm handling it. Seems like you're having trouble doing that."

Samantha hesitated, not wanting to admit the truth to the other woman, but she also felt an urge to confess.

And since Sheniqua was being sort of pushy about knowing Samantha's business, she might as well speak up. "I… I had a miscarriage," she said. "My own fault, so it's hard to get past it."

Sheniqua raised her eyebrows. "How is a miscarriage your fault?"

"Before I knew I was pregnant, I lived a party lifestyle," Samantha explained. "Not enough good sleep or nutrition. Staying up too late most nights."

"Sounds like a lot of young people," Sheniqua said.

Sheniqua didn't get it. "I mean really a lot of partying. Including drinking." Samantha stared down at the ground. "I know that's why I lost the baby."

"You *know* it? Do you know how common miscarriages are?"

"I lost my baby at six months," Samantha said.

Sheniqua put a hand on Samantha's arm and rubbed, gently, her dark eyes compassionate. "Oh honey, that must've been so hard. Did they figure out that something was wrong with him or her?"

"They never told me anything like that. The doctor said it was what I deserved, being an unwed mother, and he was right."

Sheniqua's eyes widened. "That was just wrong," she said, and grasped Samantha's hand. "Of him, not of you. Most often, when you lose a baby, it's because there was a health issue. An abnormality, usually genetic, but there are other reasons. They should have gone over all of this with you."

"I was…kind of…a wreck." Samantha hiccupped as she tried to stem the flow of tears. "Maybe they tried to talk to me and I couldn't take it in."

"You should have been offered counseling as well."

Samantha shook her head. "It was a big-city hospital," she choked out. "Kind of impersonal and…and just busy."

Sheniqua's lips tightened and she pulled a packet of tissues out of her purse and passed them along to Samantha. "I'll send you some information about the medical side of miscarriage, if you'd like. It's important you realize that, more than likely, it was nothing to do with your actions."

"That's not what the doctor said." His harsh words still echoed in her head.

"We're all sinners and that's why we need Jesus. You do, I do and that doctor does, too. It's not his place to judge. And as a doctor myself, I have to guess that your losing that baby was just plain old chance. It's sad and awful, but it happens more than you would think."

A little spark of warmth lit in Samantha's chest. Was it possible that she wasn't to blame for losing her baby?

Music swelled overhead, and Sheniqua grasped her hand and pulled her to her feet. "Come on, we both ought to go upstairs and do a little singing and praying. That's what will really help our blues."

"Thank you." Spontaneously she gave Sheniqua a quick hug. And as they walked up the stairs together, Samantha felt like maybe, just maybe, she had made a new friend.

The week after Mother's Day wore Corbin down.

It was final exam week at school, and he had all kinds of paperwork to do with his students. Grades to file. A research project to push through. Lots of committee meetings before everyone dispersed for the summer.

Mikey had been fussy. Maybe the newness of being with Corbin was over for him; he kept talking about his mother in a fretful, longing way that hurt Corbin's heart. Cheryl didn't deserve that kind of loyalty from Mikey.

He did get the feeling that Cheryl hadn't been so neglectful of Mikey as she'd been of him. Mikey was well-fed and, according to the pediatrician Corbin had taken him to visit, hitting all the developmental milestones he should be. He was a typical two-year-old, if not a little advanced. Any crankiness or upset he displayed could be attributed to sadness about moving away from his mother, or maybe just toddler orneriness.

Corbin wasn't used to it, though, and he was uncomfortably aware that he wasn't that good at dealing with Mikey's strong emotions.

Having a dog, a large shelter dog, was proving to be quite a bit more of an ordeal than Corbin had anticipated, and he wished he hadn't let himself get talked into it without thinking through what it would mean. Boomer was a great dog, and Corbin was glad to give him a home, but this might not have been the right time to do it. As witness now: he'd had to take Boomer to the vet after an episode of vomiting had scared Mikey and Samantha this afternoon. Now, after two injections, Boomer was feeling better, but Corbin's wallet was a hundred dollars lighter.

He pulled into the driveway and saw Samantha and Mikey in the yard.

Samantha. That was the real reason the week had been stressful.

He had felt awful about pushing her away, could see that it hurt her. He had always thought he was doing the right thing by taking a vow that he wouldn't get involved with an alcoholic. Prided himself on it, really. But now, his heart was involved, and hers might be, too. So being cold and pushing her away didn't feel like a wise, reasonable decision, but kind of a mean one.

Not to mention that he longed to put his arms around her and comfort her. His brain knew it wouldn't be the right thing to do, but his heart seemed to have another opinion, especially when she looked tired and drawn as she had during the past week.

And now that he knew what she felt like in his arms...

He got out of the car, opened the back door and let Boomer out.

"Boomer!" Mikey yelled, and ran toward the dog.

"Gentle, Mikey," Samantha called.

"Remember he's not feeling well," Corbin added.

But Mikey barreled into Boomer and threw his arms around the big dog's neck. Corbin half expected the dog to growl or snap, but he didn't. He just licked Mikey's face until Mikey fell onto the ground in a rush of giggles.

He looked over to see Samantha smiling at the pair, just as he could feel his own smile. They were awfully cute. "I'm sorry you had to work late," he said to her.

She tilted her head to one side and looked at him. "Don't you remember?"

"Remember what?"

"Tonight's our cookout," she said. "We have people coming over. And we were planning on hosting it together, before..." She trailed off and looked away. "Anyway," she said briskly without meeting his eyes, "I didn't want to leave you in the lurch. So I was planning to stick around and help, anyway."

"Oh, right." Corbin had forgotten. Before that ill-conceived kiss had thrown a wedge between them, they planned a cookout for Reese and Gabby and Izzy, sort of a payback for all the help the little family had given them. Gabby's grandmother was coming too, and then

Samantha had invited her cousin Hannah as well as Sheniqua, that doctor with whom she seemed to be becoming friendly.

"So it would really help if you get the grill going," she said. "They'll be here any minute."

"Any minute?" He ran a hand over his sweaty face. He'd have liked to take a shower, at least. "I wish you'd called me to remind me."

"I tried, but you weren't picking up your phone."

"Oh…right." Now he remembered it buzzing when he'd been talking to the vet. He hadn't looked at it since. "It doesn't matter. What am I grilling?"

"Burgers for the kids, that can wait, but we need to get the chicken on. I got whole pieces because they were on sale, but they take a little longer to cook. I've had them marinating."

She went inside and reappeared a moment later with a tray of chicken, a lighter and some tongs.

Corbin's exhaustion fell away as he started the grill and discussed cooking times with Samantha while Mikey and Boomer played at their feet. No question: being with this woman restored his energy. He loved hanging around with Samantha and Mikey. He loved bickering with Samantha like an old married couple. Loved the idea of hosting their friends together.

Truth was, his life had improved by leaps and bounds since Samantha and Mikey had burst into it. No, it wasn't easy or serene, but it was just so much richer.

Mikey and Boomer rolled around together on the grass with a ball while Samantha brought out dishes and a plastic tablecloth and Corbin got the chicken on the grill. Just in time, too, because Gabby and Reese arrived with little Izzy and Gabby's grandmother and several covered dishes of food.

A moment later Sheniqua pulled up and got out of her SUV with a fruit tray that looked like the ones Corbin bought occasionally from the grocery store. "Yeah, I'm that guest who didn't make anything from scratch," she said with a wry smile. "At least this is healthy."

"This looks fantastic," Samantha said, taking the tray from her and setting it on the table beside Gabby and her grandmother's offerings. "Thank you for bringing it. I'm sure you had a busy day."

"You know it. Home visits." Sheniqua was one of the few doctors in the area who was willing to visit patients in their homes; she considered it part of her Christian outreach, and Corbin admired her for it. She updated them on a couple of patients she'd visited, friends of Gabby's grandmother.

Then Reese and Gabby told them about the Rescue Haven boys and some mischief they'd gotten into today. Glue meant for use on the parade float had somehow gotten into a bunch of boys' hair, with comical results Gabby showed them from pictures on her phone.

"Hannah is on her way," Sheniqua announced, waving her phone. "She just texted me that she's going to be a little late." Perched on the edge of the porch, she looked around the yard. "Where's Mikey?"

"Yes, where is he? Izzy wants to play." Reese spun around with his daughter perched on his hip, making her giggle.

"He was here a minute ago," Samantha said. "He must've gone inside."

Corbin turned down the grill and checked the chicken. When Samantha didn't come out right away with Mikey, a nervous feeling built in his chest. He walked around the yard, checking the spots where Mikey liked to play.

No Mikey.

A moment later Samantha came outside, her face pale. "He's not inside."

Corbin's heart sped up like a galloping horse. "Mikey is missing," he barked out to the group at large. "We've got to get organized and find him before…" He glanced at the sun, sinking lower in the west. "We've got to find him fast."

Chapter 11

Mikey was missing.

Heart pounding, Samantha spun 360 degrees to study Corbin's yard. The trees and bushes that lined it had always seemed to be a good thing, but now they were just so many hiding places.

"He can't have gotten far," Reese said. "Let's search the perimeter of the yard, front and back. And somebody go out front and look up and down the street."

That last idea chilled Samantha. What if Mikey were hit by a car? "I'll take the street," she called, and ran to the narrow lawn in front of Corbin's house. People usually drove slowly around here, but if Mikey ran out suddenly, as he tended to do…

She jogged along the sidewalk, scanning the area. "Mikey! Mikey, where are you?"

How had he gone missing so fast? Reese was right, he couldn't have gotten far. They'd find him any minute, and scold him, and that would be that. Maybe he was just hiding. "Mikey! This isn't funny. Come here right now."

All she heard in response was the caw of a blue jay.

Maybe he'd gone into Mrs. Hutchenson's yard to play on her grandchildren's swing set. He wasn't allowed to leave Corbin's property, but suddenly that seemed like a wonderful thing for him to have done. She ran around behind Mrs. Hutchenson's house.

No Mikey.

All the things that could happen to a little boy flashed through Samantha's mind like a horror movie. He could have run out into the street, gotten hit by a car. He could have made his way into someone's yard who had an unfriendly dog. He could have fallen into a hole, got into a patch of poison ivy. God forbid, he could have been abducted.

But this was Bethlehem Springs. So safe, so little crime. Who would come to a place like this to abduct a child?

Then she thought of the creek that curved from beyond Mrs. Hutchenson's house into the woods behind Corbin's place. Mikey had loved it on the couple of occasions she'd taken him down there to explore.

Why on earth had she done that? What if he'd fallen in? The water was shallow, but everyone knew it didn't take much for a child to drown.

She ran toward the section by Mrs. Hutchenson's, calculating that he couldn't have gotten any farther in the little time he'd been missing. She made her way down one bank, calling his name, looking through the thick bushes that lined the banks. Brambles scratched her arms and legs as she searched. What if Mikey had gotten scratched or hurt? What if he were crying somewhere, all alone?

Her heart ached at the thought, and a sense of failure pressed down on her. She had been a horrible caregiver. She couldn't keep anyone safe. She would have made an awful mother, and maybe that was why God had taken her baby away from her.

This isn't about you. Find Mikey.

She sloshed through the shallow water to the other side of the creek, scanning for his small form in every direction. She could hear the others from various directions, calling Mikey's name.

Her search brought her back closer to Corbin's house, and as she made her way around bushes and boulders, her thoughts flashed wildly, frantically, from where Mikey could be to her own negligence and what it said about her. "Mikey! Mikey!"

Sheniqua had emailed her some articles about how often miscarriages happened and how rarely they were the fault of the mother, even though most women blamed themselves. Before today, Samantha had started to think that maybe, just maybe, she wasn't to blame for the loss of her child.

Be that as it may, she was now responsible for losing Mikey. She was his nanny, and she had let him out of her sight.

She hurried on down the creek, splashing back and

forth through the shallow water, moving aside branches, checking leaf piles and foliage. No success. She started crisscrossing the woods between the creek and Corbin's house.

"Hey, Samantha!" It was Gabby, calling to her from the backyard. "Samantha! Do you know where Boomer is?"

Samantha frowned. She hadn't seen the big black dog for a while. She lifted her hands palms up to indicate she didn't know, and prayed that he was with Mikey.

Because if he was…she got a brief sense of relief. The dog would be a comfort to a child who wasn't all that secure. Cheryl had tried, but she hadn't been consistent in creating a routine for Mikey. When she'd gotten into partying, she'd left Mikey with various caregivers, some reliable and kind, but some not so much. And then she had given him to Corbin.

Mikey needed to feel safe all the time, for an extended period of time, to get past the things he'd gone through.

Being lost and alone would be a terrible setback. Boomer's presence, though, might make it a little better.

People were starting to regather in the backyard and she walked up there to see if anyone had any information or a new idea of where Mikey might be. There was the smell of chicken burning on the grill, and someone turned it off. Corbin and Reese stood together talking, serious, urgent. "They'll figure out the next steps," Sheniqua said, gesturing toward the two men and then patting Samantha's arm.

Gabby's grandmother sat at the picnic table, holding Izzy in her lap. "Can we say a quick prayer?"

So Samantha and Gabby and Sheniqua circled around her. "Father, please keep Mikey safe from harm," Sheniqua said.

"Give us wisdom to think like a little boy and figure out where he is," Gabby added.

"And please," Samantha said, "help us find him fast, so he doesn't get too scared."

"Father, we know Your eye is on every sparrow," Gabby's grandmother said, her voice strong and confident. "Keep watch on Mikey and bring him home safely."

The words brought Samantha a little bit of comfort. The four of them squeezed hands and then Reese and Corbin came back into their midst. "Everybody, listen up."

Reese's military background showed as he gave out assignments to everyone, calm and organized. Hannah arrived, was updated on the situation, and eagerly agreed to check with neighbors up one side of the street while Sheniqua took the other side. "Any neighbors who offer to help us search, send them back here. Nana, you're the command center since you're staying here with Izzy."

"I can call the police as well," she offered.

That silenced everyone. After a moment's hesitation, Reese nodded. "Probably not a bad idea."

The police? What did they all think had happened to Mikey? Dread settled around Samantha's heart.

"I'm still thinking the woods are the spot we need extra help, so—"

"I'll send any additional helpers back there," Nana agreed quickly. "You all go. I've got this part covered."

"Thanks," Reese said. "Gabby and I will take the section to the left. Samantha and Corbin, you take the section to the right."

Samantha glanced at Corbin to find him looking at her. At the same moment, they both nodded and then headed back there immediately, half running.

In that nod had been the silent mutual agreement: *Any personal differences we have, we're leaving them behind until Mikey is safe.*

They reached the back edge of the yard, where several rough paths converged.

"He likes the mud," Corbin said, gesturing at the path that led toward the creek.

"I searched the creek behind our house and the two yards next door," Samantha said. Sometime, in her mind, this house had become her house, too.

"Then let's walk down the main path together and each take a side to search. I don't think he would've gone too far off the path. I always tell him not to."

"Good idea. I tell him that, too." They both headed down the path that was slightly wider and less overgrown than the others. Definitely the one that looked most appealing to a kid; unfortunately, it was also the one that led directly into the deepest, darkest part of the woods. Samantha's heart thudded hard as she walked zigzags on her side of the path, calling to Mikey periodically, listening for any sound that would indicate where he was.

"Do you think Cheryl could have taken him?" Corbin threw the question her way as he did his own zigzag walking pattern on his side.

That notion brought Samantha to a halt. She knew that Cheryl wanted to see Mikey, had tried to see him in church that one day. Could she have taken him somewhere with her?

If so, that was really the best case scenario. No one would be less likely to hurt and scare Mikey than his own mother. "I don't know," she said slowly, conscious that Corbin didn't know how well she knew the older woman. "If she did, do you think she would hurt him?"

Corbin threw up his hands. "I have no idea. I don't understand her."

Samantha was pretty sure that Cheryl wouldn't mean any harm to Mikey, but she couldn't say that, because Corbin didn't know she knew Cheryl.

She should tell him the whole story. Maybe there was some kind of a clue in it that would help them find Mikey.

Then again, the knowledge of Samantha's deception would just add to Corbin's worries and distract him from the search. She couldn't go into it now. But she would, she promised God, if only Mikey would be found safe.

"Over here!" Corbin was kneeling by a fallen log, shoving aside pine needles and old dead leaves. He extracted a red sneaker.

A very familiar red sneaker. Samantha sank down to

the ground beside him and they searched on hands and knees, digging through the debris of the forest, both of them moving frantically. If Mikey had somehow found a hiding place here, if he had gotten hurt or stuck, time would be of the essence.

But he wasn't anywhere in the area where the sneaker had been. "Let's move on," Corbin said, his voice impatient. He tossed the shoe onto the ground and strode on down the path.

Samantha scooped up the shoe before following. "If—when—we find him, he'll need this," she said. "He'll hurt his feet. Tears rose to her eyes at the thought of Mikey limping around, getting hurt and having no one to help him. "Corbin, I'm so sorry I didn't keep a closer eye on him." She dashed tears from her cheeks. There wasn't time for her to have an emotional meltdown.

"I'm at least as much at fault as you are," he said, laying his hand on her shoulder for the briefest of reassuring touches. "But come on. We can't spend time overthinking things. We have to find him."

They hurried on down the path, side by side now, with new purpose. The shoe indicated that Mikey had come this way. And losing a shoe, going half-barefoot, would have slowed him down. He had to be nearby; he just had to be.

"What's that?" Samantha jogged ahead toward something else red. She could hear Corbin behind her.

"His trike!" Corbin said. And indeed, lying there on its side, was the plastic trike he loved to ride, the one that was made to look like a motorcycle.

Corbin bent down and righted the tricycle, a move that nearly broke Samantha's heart. "When I got him this, I was happy about how it would go over rough terrain," he said, his voice bleak. "Now, I realize it's what helped him get so far away. I should never have bought it for him."

"Don't go there." She took his arm and tugged him along the path. "He's off the trike now. Maybe he's close by."

So they continued on down the path. The sun was sinking lower by the moment. The sky had clouded over, and the woods were getting dark. Samantha's stomach knotted. Mikey didn't love the dark, and the woods were full of strange shapes and noises. He would be so frightened.

There was a rustling in the groundcover beside them that made Samantha jump and cling to Corbin's arm more tightly than before. "What was that?"

"A squirrel, I think."

Of course, a squirrel. She shouldn't be such a wimp. All the same, she didn't let go of Corbin's arm.

They walked forward at a slower pace now, scanning the woods more closely and weaving from one side of the path to the other in a methodical pattern. "Of all the days to put him in a camo shirt," Samantha fretted. "He could be anywhere and it would be so hard to find him." She didn't say what they both knew: if he were unconscious somewhere, finding him would be that much harder.

"Mikey!" Corbin had a deep voice and it carried

far. "Mikey, if you're out here, stay still. We'll come find you."

In a small clearing, big birds were visible overhead. They let out an ominous, cawing sound that made Samantha think of scary things, Halloween movies, nightmares.

When they reached the woods on the other side of the clearing, Corbin stopped and shook his head, turning slowly to look in all directions, his shoulders slumped. "I don't think he could have gotten this far."

"You're right." Samantha felt her breath go out like air from a half-empty balloon, and despair pushed hard at her heart and mind. They'd been walking about fifteen minutes since they'd found the trike. A young child like Mikey couldn't stay focused enough to travel steadily in one direction. How could they not have found him yet? Where could he be?

Every moment that ticked away made it more likely that they *wouldn't* find him, that something terrible had happened. The very thought of that made it hard to breathe.

They turned and headed back toward the direction from which they'd come, passing through the clearing and heading back into the woods on the path.

There was more rustling in the leaves. Something alive, and big. Samantha clung on to Corbin's arm. What if there was a bear out here? What if it had attacked Mikey?

Loud, deep barking rang out, and then a giant creature burst out of the trees and ran headfirst into Samantha, knocking her into Corbin so hard that they both crashed to the ground.

It did look like a bear. But bears didn't bark.

Hope rose up in Samantha's heart. It was Boomer.

Corbin scrambled out from beneath Samantha—thankfully, he'd been able to break her fall—and quickly helped her to her feet as Boomer ran in circles around them, barking.

"Boomer!" Samantha tried to get hold of the big dog's collar without success. "Where's Mikey, boy, huh? Where is he?"

"Man, I was hoping Boomer and Mikey were together," Corbin said. In fact, he'd been clinging to that, because he knew that Boomer would be a comfort to Mikey. But now, here was Boomer, alone.

Which meant Mikey was alone, too. Cold air chilled the sweat on his back, making him shiver.

"Boomer! Where's Mikey? Mikey!" Samantha was talking to the dog as if it were a person. How would that help anything? Didn't she remember that Boomer was deaf?

Boomer barked and started running into the woods, and Corbin called to him, himself forgetting for a moment that Boomer couldn't hear.

"He must have caught our scent and come to find us. Maybe he's leading us to Mikey!" Samantha started tromping into the woods after Boomer, who of course had completely disregarded Corbin's command.

"That only happens in the movies," Corbin argued.

"Do you have a better idea?" she snapped over her

shoulder as she struggled through the thick vegetation after the barking dog.

He didn't. So since he didn't know what else to do, he followed Samantha into the woods and then took the lead, walking in front of her, lifting his feet high to stamp down the heavy underbrush. Boomer was weaving a zigzag trail in front of them, still barking, and Corbin was pretty sure that he was after a squirrel or rabbit.

"He's going down into the gully," Samantha cried. The gully was a deep crevice, cut by a larger stream than the creek by Corbin's house, dark and chilly and way too scary for a kid as young as Mikey. Corbin had never even been down there himself. Surely the boy wouldn't have…

"Come on!" Samantha started to scramble down after the dog. But the ground was wet and rocky, and her feet slipped almost immediately. She fell, hard, and although she grasped fruitlessly at tree roots and stones, she couldn't stop her rapid slide down the steep slope.

Corbin rushed forward, made a leap, and with his greater body weight, slid down past her. He braced himself on a rocky outcropping and reached for her, steering her into his arms.

She landed against his chest, safely, making his heart pound with relief. But there wasn't time for a prayer of gratitude. He let her go, and she spun away from him. "Where'd Boomer go?"

"I think that way," Corbin said, pointing upstream. "Mikey! Mikey, where are you?"

Boomer had disappeared, but now, they could hear him barking.

Samantha started to scramble the rest of the way down the gully toward the sound of the barking dog. Corbin took her arm to help her balance on the unsteady ground, and they made their way forward as fast as possible, clinging on to each other. The sound of Boomer's bark was getting closer, and so was the creek, if its rushing sound and the refrigerator-cold air was any indication.

The bottom of the ravine was dark. Down here, the sun had already set.

"I can't see him." Samantha broke away from Corbin and started parting bushes with her hands to look beneath them. "Either of them."

Corbin jumped the creek and started hunting that side. It was nearly impossible to pick out any shapes in the dimness, let alone a black dog, but Boomer was still barking and yelping.

And then Corbin heard it, beneath Boomer's noise: a child's cry.

Corbin's heart leapt. "Did you hear that?" he called to Samantha. He found a narrow spot in the stream and jumped back over.

"Hear what?" She went still, listening, and he did, too.

There it was again: a little boy's cry.

"Mikey!" Samantha rushed toward the sound with Corbin right behind her. They pushed through brambles and kicked aside ferns.

And there, beside a couple of big rocks, was Mikey.

Rubbing his eyes and crying as Boomer stood over him, barking.

"Oh honey, we found you!" Samantha sank to her knees and tugged Mikey into her arms, and Corbin sat down beside her, using the light on his cell phone to examine Mikey's arms and legs.

"Boomer go 'way." Mikey sobbed out the words and clung to Samantha.

She cuddled him close, shifting to allow Corbin to continue his gentle examination of Mikey's limbs. "Boomer came to find us," she explained. "How did you get this far?"

"Lost trike." Mikey's sobs were quieting now. "Boomer run."

Boomer had run, and Mikey had followed the dog.

There was a long scrape on one side of his leg, and when Corbin touched it, Mikey winced. He pointed toward the rocky bank. "Fall down," he said, his face screwing up to cry again.

"It's okay." Samantha gently rocked him back and forth. "Sssh. You're okay now."

The thought of the others, still searching and scared, sent Corbin grabbing his phone again. "I need to call everyone. Let them know he's safe." His hands shook too much to text, so he scrolled to Reese's number and put through a call, asked him to let everyone know.

Samantha rose to her knees, still holding Mikey, and looked up the side of the gully. "How are we going to get him back up the hill and home?"

That wouldn't be a problem. Corbin had so much adrenaline racing through his veins that he felt like he could lift a car and carry it across a football field. "I'll hold him," he said, reaching out.

He was gratified when Mikey settled against his chest just as readily as he'd done with Samantha. "You scared us, buddy," he said.

Mikey rubbed his face against Corbin's shoulder, sliming him with mud and tears. It was a welcome mess.

Samantha rubbed Boomer's sides and scratched behind his ears. "You're such a good boy, aren't you?"

Boomer panted up at her, and it looked like he was smiling agreement.

As well he should, because the big rescue mutt had led them to Mikey. Corbin reached down and rubbed Boomer's head. "Ready?" he asked Samantha.

"I feel like I just ran a couple of marathons, but yeah." Her relieved smile and the happy way she rubbed Mikey's leg touched his heart.

He needed to talk with her, hash things out. Nearly losing Mikey had changed his perspective. "When everything gets settled, let's have a talk," he suggested.

Her eyebrows shot up. "Am I in trouble?" she joked, the concern in her eyes letting him know that she meant the question at least a little seriously.

"Not at all. The opposite." He hoisted Mikey onto his hip, held out a hand to Samantha, and started the climb up the steep hill toward home.

Chapter 12

Samantha could barely believe that only a couple of hours had passed since they'd realized Mikey was missing, found him and got him safely back to the house. Now he was sleepy, fed and warm, cuddled up in a blanket in Corbin's arms.

By mutual agreement, everyone had stuck around; the fear they'd shared seemed to bond them, making them want to stay close.

The chicken was ruined, of course, but Gabby and Samantha rummaged in the fridge and threw together a meal of hot dogs, veggie burgers and canned baked beans. Put together with Sheniqua's fruit salad and the side dishes Gabby and her grandmother had brought, it felt like a feast.

Reese and Corbin built a bonfire, and they pulled up

chairs and blankets around it, roasting their hot dogs and then marshmallows. Soon, both Izzy and Mikey were asleep, Izzy in Gabby's arms and Mikey in Corbin's.

Maybe it was the intense emotion she'd experienced, but Samantha couldn't take her eyes off Corbin. Normally a bit aloof, he'd let his walls down and was talking and laughing, checking often to make sure Mikey was resting peacefully. He didn't seem to want to let the boy out of his lap, which was totally understandable.

"I'm going to take a guess that the two of you are blaming yourselves," Gabby said, looking from Samantha to Corbin and back again. "But it truly was nobody's fault."

"I was supposed to be watching him. I'm his nanny." Samantha scooted closer to Corbin so that she could run a hand over Mikey's hair. He slept, thumb in mouth, his cheeks ruddy, and she shot up another prayer of thanks that he was safely home. "I feel terrible that I let him out of my sight."

Corbin put his hand over hers, a featherlight touch concealed from the others by the darkness and by the angle of Mikey's body. "It was my fault. Once I get home from work, I'm on duty. I fell short."

"Believe me, man, we all fall short," Reese said. "Gabby and I lost Izzy when we went up to Lake Erie. It was only for a few minutes, but…"

"Every possible disaster that could happen flashes in front of your eyes," Gabby finished for him.

"That's exactly it," Samantha said. "The whole time we were searching, I kept picturing…awful stuff." She shivered, remembering.

"Nobody has this parenting thing down pat," Sheniqua contributed. "I see it in my practice all the time. Somebody didn't keep a close enough eye on their kids, and one of them gets burned, or falls off a swing or crashes their bike. And those are the happy cases." She bit her lip and looked at the ground, obviously remembering some situations that hadn't turned out so well.

They were all silent, then, no doubt thinking of how wrong everything could have gone this afternoon.

"Anyway," Sheniqua said, "the parents or caregivers always blame themselves, and in a perfect world, sure, they'd watch their kids every single second. Except if they did that, the kids would grow up neurotic and fearful." She shrugged, raising her hands. "All we can do is our best, and put the rest in God's hands."

"Amen," Samantha said fervently.

"I'll tell you one thing," Corbin said, "I'm happy that we adopted Boomer. Every muddy paw print and late-night bathroom break is totally worth it." He reached down to put a hand on the big dog's head.

"He doesn't want to leave Mikey's side, even now," Gabby said, leaning over to pat Boomer, too. "Good boy, aren't you?"

The dog shifted and let out a sigh, his eyes opening briefly and then closing again.

"I have to admit," Corbin said, "I thought the only time dogs stuck by kids like that was on TV. But Boomer definitely kept track of Mikey and stayed by him."

"Kept him warm, I guess," Reese said.

"And comforted." Samantha couldn't imagine how

much more terrified Mikey would have been if the dog hadn't been there. As it was, the little boy had mostly seemed annoyed that Boomer had left him for a few minutes, which it seemed he'd done only when he'd realized Samantha and Corbin were close by. "He led us right to him. Kept barking until we came. Such a sweetheart."

Everyone was looking at the dog, his black fur rendering him barely visible in the fire's dim light. Boomer started panting, his pink tongue hanging out.

"There's a steak in his future," Corbin promised.

"Honestly, I think he was happy with the hamburger you gave him tonight," Samantha teased. "He ate it a lot faster than Mikey ate his."

Corbin didn't answer, but he gave her a smile that warmed her heart.

Hannah brought out her ukulele, apparently always at the ready in her car, and strummed gently. The stars made a bright, jewel-like canopy overhead. And Samantha felt like she'd never been this at home, this connected, in her life.

Until her phone buzzed. Who could it be, when almost everyone she cared about was right here around this fire?

She looked at the lock screen. Cheryl.

She was sitting right beside Corbin, and she quickly turned the phone so he couldn't see it. Had he noticed the gesture? She didn't dare look at him to find out.

She wanted to decline the call, but she was afraid to, afraid that Cheryl would keep calling. She excused herself and walked over to the edge of the yard. "Hello?"

"What happened to my son?" Cheryl sounded hysterical.

"What do you mean?"

"I heard he was lost!"

Samantha's heart rate sped up. "He's fine now, and how did you find that out?"

"I was driving by," the older woman admitted. "I just wanted to catch a glimpse of him, you know? Paul has an old friend visiting us here, so I could get away."

"If you're doing things like that... Cheryl, don't you think we'd better tell Corbin the truth?" Even as she said it, her heart sank. Corbin had come to mean so much to her. If he learned after all this time that she and Cheryl knew each other and had gone behind his back to set this up, he'd be outraged.

"No, no. I just...it's hard, ya know?" And now Samantha heard the slurring in Cheryl's voice.

"Of course it's hard, but...look, he's fine. Have you been drinking?" she asked bluntly.

"No!" Cheryl's voice was indignant, and that made Samantha's heart sink even more, because she recognized the denial of an alcoholic in active disease.

Recognized it, because she'd been there herself.

And if Cheryl was drunk enough to lie, there was no point talking to her, not tonight. She'd call her tomorrow and urge her to get in touch with her AA sponsor right away.

"Look, Mikey's safe and fine. Please don't drive anymore tonight, okay?"

"I could, but I won't," Cheryl said. "Promise."

"Good. I have to go." Over Cheryl's protests, she

ended the call and stood looking at the circle of dear people around the fire.

She cared about them deeply. Wanted to be a part of the group, of the town.

But was that going to be possible, with the secrets she was keeping pulling her down?

Corbin finally handed off Mikey to Gabby's grandmother to hold. He got a long stick and stood poking at the fire and relishing the company of his friends.

Being here with a group of people who'd unquestioningly jumped in to help him, and then stuck around because they wanted to be here…all of it was new to him. Sure, he had friends at the university, but they mostly talked science and didn't get together just to hang out. And he and Reese were close friends, but as busy as they both were, their chances to spend time together were limited.

This was good, if unfamiliar: he felt like he was a part of the group.

And the fact that Samantha was here, hosting their friends right beside him—that was both *really* unfamiliar, and really good.

Finally, Corbin took Mikey inside and tucked him into bed. When he came back out, Gabby and Reese stood up and scooped up Izzy. "We should get home. It's late."

"You're right." Hannah stood up, too.

Sheniqua stretched and stood, and everyone started collecting the dishes they'd brought and shaking hands and embracing each other. Corbin wasn't a big hugger, but there was no other way to express the gratitude he felt for how they'd all helped him find Mikey.

To his surprise, being affectionate didn't seem awkward at all, and he felt good afterward. Maybe he could be warmer with people than he'd thought. Maybe having Mikey here had pushed that along.

Or maybe it had something to do with Samantha.

She was thanking people for their help right alongside him. And then everyone was gone and it was just the two of them standing there. She looked at him and caught his eye, and all he wanted to do was pull her into his arms. He'd hugged everyone else, after all.

Holding Samantha was something completely different, though, he knew that. He shouldn't. But his emotions felt a lot stronger than his intellect tonight.

Before he could reach for her, she turned away. "Guess we should clean up," she said briskly, and started carrying tongs and bags of leftover buns and dirty dishes into the kitchen.

So much for getting closer. He suppressed a sigh and started to help her clean up.

Between them, they made quick work of carrying everything inside and setting the yard to rights. On their last trip outside, Corbin paused, wanting to drink it all in for just a moment longer: the smell of wood smoke, the buzz of cicadas and the bright tapestry of stars.

Samantha came to stand beside him, close enough that he could feel her warmth. "Do you know the names of the constellations?" she asked.

"I know some," he said, welcoming the chance to be businesslike. "There's Ursa Major. He was my favorite as a kid, because he was easy to find and plus…well, he's a giant bear. What kid doesn't like a giant bear?"

She smiled, at the same time shaking her head. "People always say constellations are easy to find and I don't get it. There are, like, a million stars in the sky tonight. How am I supposed to know which ones to put together and make a bear?"

"It's not that hard," he said, laughing a little. "Do you recognize the Big Dipper?"

"It's there, right?" She pointed upward.

"Uh-huh. The handle of the dipper is the bear's tail, and the dipper part is the back half of his body."

"How do you figure that?"

"Well, trace down from the handle side of the dipper. The two bright stars right below it are basically his feet." He leaned closer to her and pointed so that she could look along his arm. "See?"

"Yeah, I think so." She sounded breathless.

Her voice and the warmth of her made it hard to concentrate. "If you look…past…the dipper," he said, then paused to collect his thoughts. "Look past the dipper to the three bright stars, almost in a triangle. That's his head."

"I see them!" She glanced over at him and smiled, then looked back up. "And the bright ones below that are his front legs, right?"

"Exactly."

"I've never been able to see the constellations when people pointed at the sky before. That's so cool!"

Corbin liked nothing better than an enthusiastic student, so he pointed out several more constellations, showing her easy ways to recognize them and telling her a little about the stories behind them. Finally, he realized he had gone on a little long. "Sorry," he said. "Occupational hazard. I'm always a professor."

"I like that you're a professor," she said shyly. "I like to learn."

The starlight made her face glow as she looked up at him, and the urge to pull her to him was strong. But this was what had gotten them into trouble before. "I better put out the fire," he said.

"Right. I'll get those dishes washed."

"You don't have to do the dishes. You're not working."

She lifted a finger to his lips, barely touching them. "Shh," she said. "You're right, I'm not working. I'm just being a friend."

He'd never felt anything as soft and delicate as that touch, and it paralyzed him. Never before had his brain and his body been so truly at war. He didn't think he was going to be able to stop himself. His hand went toward hers, intent on keeping her finger right where it was.

He wasn't fast enough, though. She pulled her hand away, gave him a little half smile and turned and walked toward the house.

He was so stunned by the intensity of his feeling that he just stood there staring after her, blood pounding in his veins. She was so beautiful, so caring, so loveable. Every new facet of her that he discovered intrigued him more.

Finally, he filled a bucket of water and threw it on

the fire, hearing the hiss, watching the steam and then poking around with a stick to make sure there were no remaining hot coals.

He couldn't cool his own warm feelings nearly so easily. So he stood outside taking deep breaths and looking at the stars and settling himself before he went in.

She was at the sink rinsing and drying dishes, and as he came up behind her, any effort he'd made to cool himself down was instantly gone.

Her skin was so delicate that he could see a blue vein pulsing in her throat. Her lips were full and slightly parted.

He couldn't take his eyes off her. That was how he noticed that her breathing quickened a little under his gaze. She was affected by him, whether she knew it or not, and that made his heart swell with happiness.

At the same time, he felt a huge sense of responsibility.

His own urges were strong, stronger than he ever felt before in his life. If she was feeling something similar, it was even more dangerous.

Because impulsively giving in to those feelings of attraction was what had gotten them in trouble last time, caused a rift between them that had affected their friendship, and more importantly, had affected Mikey. What they needed to do was to talk, not get physical.

So he stepped away from her and leaned back against the counter. "Look, I'm sorry I was distant before. That was just me being foolish."

She didn't ask what he was talking about; she obviously knew. "What was going on?"

He debated finding some intellectual way to say it, but he wasn't thinking straight enough. "I got turned upside down by that kiss."

"Yeah. Me, too." She glanced at him and then turned to put a stack of plates away.

"It was intense."

"Uh-huh."

Now that he had brought up the topic, he wasn't sure where he wanted to go with it. For him to go into the fact that he couldn't get involved with her because she was an alcoholic… Suddenly, that felt judgmental and mean and not how he wanted to talk to her.

Maybe it wasn't how he wanted to be with her, either, but he wasn't ready to make that alteration to his long-held set of values about who he could get involved with. And until he did, he obviously needed to keep a lid on his feelings.

So he talked about something they would probably agree on. "I was never so scared in my life as when Mikey was lost."

"Me, either. It was awful."

He paused, then admitted, "I just don't know if I'm cut out for taking care of a kid."

Her head jerked around to face him. "You're not thinking of sending him back to your mom, are you?"

Was he? He shook his head slowly, letting out a sigh. "No. I feel like I screwed up badly, but I still think he's safer with me than with her."

She let the water out of the sink, not looking at him now. "I think you're doing a great job," she said. "It was just as much my fault as yours. And didn't you listen to what everyone else said? Parenting is a challenge and you can't help but screw up sometimes."

"I guess." He wasn't used to doing things poorly or in a half-baked way. He was used to working at a task until he could become an expert. That had been a great approach in his career, where hard work and long hours at the lab had helped him succeed, becoming one of the youngest faculty members the university had ever hired.

He wasn't arrogant about that; he knew that whatever smarts he had were a gift from God, that other people were smarter and that he'd been incredibly fortunate in getting fellowships and teaching assistant jobs to pay for his graduate work. That was what had allowed him to reach a position of expertise in his field.

But it seemed that nobody was an expert when it came to raising kids, not really.

"Mikey can be a handful, just like any other child," she said.

"He is, but I sure love him," Corbin said. It was the first time he had articulated that, and he realized it was completely true. He loved his little brother as if the boy were his own son.

"I love him, too," she said, almost offhandedly.

She just continued wiping down the counters, not acting like she had said anything momentous, but her words blew Corbin away. She had an amazing ability to love. Mikey wasn't her child, nor her blood, but she felt for him as if he were.

He got the vacuum cleaner and ran it over the kitchen floor, cleaning up dog hair and crumbs, turning it off quickly when it sucked up a little plastic spoon, then extracting it and starting it up again.

If he loved his little brother despite the boy's issues and whining and toddler misbehavior, could it be that he could love another adult who had issues, too? He was definitely starting to care a lot for Samantha. Was he growing, becoming more flexible and forgiving?

He didn't know if he could change that much. He'd been holding himself—and others—to a strict, high standard for a long time. It was how he'd gotten as far as he had after his rough beginning.

Corbin wanted to continue caring for his brother, especially given the alternative, but the fact that Mikey had gotten lost had shaken him. He didn't know if he was good enough to do the job.

He turned off the vacuum cleaner and put it away. Samantha's expression of support soothed his insecurities. He wanted love and acceptance, just like anyone else. And there was a tiny spark inside him that was starting to burn, a spark that wondered if he could maybe fall in love and be loved, even with a recovering alcoholic.

Samantha was wiping her hands on the dish towel. "Everything is cleaned up," she said, "and it's late."

Corbin looked at the clock and was surprised to see that it was midnight.

He didn't want to end this conversation, didn't want to go to bed alone, but he knew he couldn't give in to his desire to get closer to Samantha, not until he had figured things out. "I don't think I can sleep," he admitted to her. "I might watch some TV." He strolled out of the kitchen and into the living room, intent on finding some scientific show that could distract him from his confusing feelings.

She followed along. "I'm too keyed up to sleep, too."

Their eyes met, held, and just like that, something sparked in the air between them. They both looked away.

"Well. Guess I'll go read my book." She turned toward the stairs.

"Do that if you want to," he said. He sat down on the couch and put his arm across the back of it. "Or, you could come watch a movie with me."

She half turned and frowned. "Do you really mean watch a movie, or do you mean something else?"

"I'm not going to lie," he said. "The something else is on my mind. But I really do mean watch a movie."

Her nose wrinkled. "Really?"

"Really. You can even pick it out."

Slowly, like she was walking a tightrope, she made her way over to the couch. She perched in the other corner of it while he scrolled through the guide channel. She chose a goofy kids' movie featuring talking dogs, something he would never have chosen himself.

By the time the movie was fifteen minutes in, they were both laughing hard. Apparently, goofy was just what they'd both needed. About halfway through, she said that she was cold, and he patted the seat beside him.

She scooted over. They put their feet on the coffee table with an afghan over them.

And watching a silly movie, feeling her warm against his side, was one of the sweetest experiences of Corbin's life.

Chapter 13

On Tuesday at precisely eleven thirty in the morning, Samantha pulled up in front of the Markowski home. Really, it was more of a mansion. She turned off her car and sat for a minute, looking around the quiet neighborhood. Each of the widely spaced houses was distinct, some brick, some Tudor style, some, like the Markowskis' place, fronted with classical stone pillars and large urns already spilling beautiful spring flowers. The Markowskis were definitely wealthy.

Maybe there was a servants' entrance in the back. If so, she should probably park there, because her car was a blight on the landscaping. Until this moment, she'd been happy that she had finally been able to get it running. Now, she was uncomfortably aware of how old it was, how loud the engine, how rusty the exterior.

Oh, well. This wasn't a social visit. Mrs. Markowski had asked her to come and update her on the progress of the float. It would be a short meeting. Samantha had pictures of what they'd done so far on her phone and had written down a schedule for how she was going to complete the project. Going through that shouldn't take more than half an hour, and then she could escape this uncomfortably fancy neighborhood and get back to take over Mikey's care for the afternoon.

After Friday's terrifying hour when he was lost, she felt so very fortunate that Mikey was safe and healthy. It wasn't something you could take for granted.

And the new accord between her and Corbin couldn't be taken for granted, either. After the cookout, curled up next to him on the couch, Samantha had felt warm and safe and cared for. No, it wasn't going to amount to anything romantically, but she treasured the sense of connection. Maybe they could be and remain good friends, at least.

She got out of the car and hurried up the brick walkway. She almost expected a butler to answer, but it was Mrs. Markowski who opened the door. High-pitched barking came from somewhere in the back of the house.

"Come in," the older woman said. She wore dark slacks, an elegant long vest and an ornate necklace, and she seemed to be raising an eyebrow at something. Was it Samantha's car, or the way she was dressed? She'd put on khakis and a polo shirt in honor of the occasion. Her hair was tied back, her makeup light. Nothing fancy, but she'd thought she looked professional.

When Mrs. Markowski led the way to the dining

room and she saw the source of the barking, she suppressed a smile. She was definitely way underdressed.

There, yapping furiously from behind a baby gate, was a small white poodle sporting a pink topknot and a sparkly pink confection of a jacket.

Samantha wasn't one of those people who thought it was wrong to dress up a dog; truth to tell, she'd always thought dogs dressed for Halloween were adorable. She knelt in front of the gate. "Hi there! What's your name?" She looked up at Mrs. Markowski. "I didn't know you had a dog." As she spoke, she let her hand rest on the baby gate…until sharp pain made her jerk her hand away. "Ow!" She looked down to see drops of blood. The little dog stood on its back legs, front paws on the gate, baring its teeth at her.

"No, no, Pinky," Mrs. Markowski scolded. "I'm sorry, dear," she added as she stepped over the gate and picked up the dog. "You're going to have to go to your room," she scolded the dog in an indulgent voice. "Gemma?"

"I'm in the pantry."

"Could you please take Pinky upstairs?"

A woman wearing a polo shirt and tan khakis emerged from a door in the back of the kitchen. "You know that little monster's not going to let me carry her upstairs," she said to Mrs. Markowski, and then looked at Samantha. "Did she bite you? Disinfectant soap's under the sink, honey." And she walked back through the door she'd come out.

So apparently, Pinky's biting someone wasn't major news in this household. As Mrs. Markowski carried the barking, growling dog upstairs, Samantha walked into the large kitchen and washed the bite.

She was drying her hand with a paper towel when Mrs. Markowski came back down. "Are you hurt? I'm sorry about Pinky. She's just two years old, and still learning her manners."

"It's okay, it's not a deep bite," Samantha said. When was Pinky going to learn her manners if she hadn't learned them by age two?

"I just adopted her six months ago," Mrs. Markowski explained. "She was found as a stray, all matted and skinny and sick. I happened to be volunteering at the shelter when she came in, and…well, here we are. I guess I needed something to take care of."

That made more sense of it and Samantha smiled. "Dogs are great companions."

Mrs. Markowski nodded and then brushed her hands together. "Gemma is going to serve us lunch in a little while," she said. "Shall we get business out of the way first?"

"Oh…yes, of course." This was a lunch meeting? Now, she felt even more underdressed. In fact, she realized suddenly, she was dressed exactly the same way the housekeeper was. No wonder Mrs. Markowski had looked askance at her.

You're a child of God, just as good as anyone else, she reminded herself. It was something she'd read in a morning devotional and was trying to burn into her mind by repeating it often. "I have photos to show you of where the float stands now, and I can let you know what else we plan to do to complete it. It should be done in good time."

They sat down together on a stiff, uncomfortable sofa. Samantha opened her photos app and showed Mrs. Markowski the first picture. "This is the underlying structure," she said. She swiped to the next photo. "This shows you the background that we'll have and the structures the boys and dogs will sit on, so that they're visible to everyone." She swiped to the next photo. This one she was really proud of. "And this is an internet picture of what the boys and Corbin are going to do to wire up our float, so that it flashes and has a doghouse that opens and closes. The boys are really excited about it."

Mrs. Markowski studied the pictures without speaking. When the silence went on too long, Samantha got nervous. "What do you think?"

Mrs. Markowski shook her head slowly, clucking her tongue. "I'm afraid it's going to be a little...tacky."

That word made Samantha's face heat, because she remembered one of the few girls she'd invited to her house using that word about her mother's decor. Was she hopelessly low-class?

She sucked in a deep breath and consciously relaxed her muscles. *You're a child of God.* A thought came into her mind then, making her smile: anyone who dressed her poodle up in pink rhinestones had no authority to call their float tacky.

Of course, Samantha didn't say that out loud. As her mother would have said, she knew what side her bread was buttered on. "What part feels tacky to you?" she asked, pasting an interested smile on her face and going for a friendly, neutral tone of voice.

"The bright colors, the animation," Mrs. Markowski said. "I was hoping for something a little more tasteful."

Parade floats weren't supposed to be tasteful, Samantha wanted to say, but didn't. "Could you give me an example to go on?" Samantha was kicking herself now. She should have asked for more details, gotten Mrs. Markowski's input earlier.

The woman had given Samantha free rein, but she should've known better. It looked like Mrs. Markowski was the type to test you when you didn't even know you were being tested.

"As a matter of fact, I *can* show you an example." The older woman went to a display shelf and picked up a framed picture. She came back and handed it to Samantha.

Samantha studied it. The high school's football field was in the background, and the float itself looked a little familiar. "Is that from the senior parade at the high school a few years ago?"

"Yes, it is. It's the float representing the football team."

She studied the picture more closely. "I remember that one from watching the parade my freshman year. It was really pretty." But it had looked so different from the decorated cars and scraggly trailer creations the other students had made. Definitely not done by the football players themselves, and she'd even heard some of the gossipy girls making mean remarks about it.

"I was in charge of the football float," Mrs. Markowski said. "I and a couple of the other football mothers spent hours on it." She paused, then looked across the living room at the collection of photos she'd taken this one from.

Samantha looked, too, and realized they were all photos of Mrs. Markowski's son, Brock.

"Those were good times." Mrs. Markowski stared at the photo, seeming to be lost in reminiscences.

Samantha nodded, not sure of how to respond. Mrs. Markowski was a bundle of contradictions, emotionally vulnerable one minute, sharp and businesslike the next. Her heart ached for the other woman's loss. But she wasn't a close friend, so she had better keep it businesslike. "It seems like you want us to make a float that's similar to the one you made during your son's senior year?"

"Well, not exactly, but similar."

"Um, okay." Inside, Samantha groaned. They'd have to redo so much of the work, just because Mrs. Markowski wanted to recreate the past—a doomed effort, since her son was never coming back.

Still, she had to try if she wanted to be selected for the job of starting up a kids' program at Rescue Haven. "Do you mind if I take a picture of that float?" she asked. "Maybe we can incorporate some similar elements."

"If you think it would be useful." Mrs. Markowski handed her the photograph, rose and went to the doorway into the kitchen. "Gemma. We'll take our lunch now."

At first, the meal felt stiff and awkward. Both of

them tried to make conversation, but it was clear they didn't have much in common. Add that to the fact that Mrs. Markowski held the key to Samantha's future, and it made for a lot of tension.

Samantha finally found a topic to break the ice by showing Mrs. Markowski pictures of Mikey and describing some of his antics. She left out the fact that he had gotten lost, figuring that wasn't something she wanted to be judged about.

"Where is the child's mother?" Mrs. Markowski asked. "I'm surprised she would pass off her own child to her son to raise. Is she ill?"

"No, but her husband is. She needs to take care of him." Then she blew out a breath, mortified. Why had she blurted that out? Her face grew uncomfortably hot, and she knew she must be blushing. "I shouldn't have said that. I'm not even supposed to know Cheryl. Corbin doesn't know that I do. Please, don't share this with him."

After keeping the secret from Corbin for all these weeks, why couldn't she keep it in front of Mrs. Markowski? And what must the older woman think of her, hiding something significant from her employer?

Mrs. Markowski was studying her. "I see that things are a little more complicated than they appear to be," she said.

"They are." Samantha's voice came out as not much more than a whisper. The other woman was likely to either fire her or reveal the truth to Corbin.

"Why are you keeping your relationship with Corbin's mother a secret?" Mrs. Markowski asked.

What was the harm in being honest now? "They haven't been close," she said. "His mother was afraid that Corbin would put Mikey into foster care, since he doesn't know anything about raising kids. I was supposed to kind of happen along and offer to help, to keep that from happening."

"So it was for the child's sake."

Samantha nodded. "If Cheryl had sent me in an open way, Corbin wouldn't have wanted anything to do with me. Maybe he'd have found a way to raise Mikey, found another caregiver right away, but Cheryl didn't want to take that risk."

They finished their lunch in silence. The chicken salad was delicious, but Samantha couldn't eat more than a few bites.

They rose from the table, and when Samantha started to carry her dishes to the kitchen, Mrs. Markowski put a hand on her arm. "Just leave them. Gemma will get them." She led the way to the front door and then turned to face Samantha. "I've kept secrets about a child before," she said. "It's not a good idea. You should fix that."

Samantha swallowed and nodded. "I should."

"And I expect better on that float."

"Understood." Samantha waved her phone, which held the picture of the float Mrs. Markowski had made for Brock's senior parade. "Less gaudy. More tasteful."

Mrs. Markowski gave a tight-lipped smile. "I'll be interested to see what you do."

Her stomach tight, Samantha hurried down to her beat-up car.

Would she be able to make a float that lived up to Mrs. Markowski's standards between now and Friday?

And would the older woman reveal her secret to Corbin?

On Friday, the last day before the Memorial Day parade, Corbin stood in the barn staring at the unfinished float.

It was time for the kids to go home, but Samantha had talked Gabby into calling all the parents to see if they'd let their sons work later into the night. The parents had agreed, but the boys were grousing. It didn't help that the pizza she'd ordered was late, and everyone was starving.

Corbin wanted to be supportive of Samantha, but he couldn't believe she had made them recast the whole float. They could have been finished, relaxing with Mikey at home. Instead, here they were staying late, and in sole charge of the restless teenagers. Gabby was nearby at her house, but caring for her grandma, who was under the weather. Reese had taken Mikey and Izzy to an indoor play area in the hopes of tiring them out.

So it was just Samantha and Corbin and a bunch of hungry, cranky boys.

They had already removed the old foil and fringes from the float, even though, to Corbin's eye, it had all looked perfectly fine. They had built up a series of platforms on the float, of graduated heights; each would hold a boy and a dog. That, Corbin thought, was a great idea.

The dogs were to be dressed up in patriotic costumes

as much as they could tolerate, and there, Samantha had gone all out. She'd stayed up late making little hats and shirts and jackets to fit each dog.

Now, they were to replace the foil with the kind of textured sheeting made to look like flower petals. The main colors now were just white and blue, with the dogs' red trimmings providing "pops of color," as Samantha had said.

Corbin wondered where Samantha had gotten the money to buy new supplies. He had a feeling that it had come out of her own pocket, and probably at the expense of things she needed for herself, like another, bigger repair to her car.

One reason the boys were upset was that the plan of animating the float had been nixed. Corbin wasn't altogether sorry about that, since their preliminary efforts had revealed it to be more complicated and unreliable than he'd expected.

"Memorial Day weekend and here we are working," one of the high school boys said.

"This stinks," agreed another boy.

Corbin wasn't thrilled about it himself. He didn't like sending Mikey away in the evening when they had been apart all day, even if Mikey were safe and having fun. He felt like it was important for them to bond some each day.

But one look at Samantha, face sweaty, forking her fingers through her messy hair, and he pretty much felt like he would do anything she said. It was hard, very hard, not to pursue a relationship with her. Corbin had done a lot of thinking and praying about it, but he kept coming up against the alcoholism issue. He was still too concerned to move forward, too full of memories of his past.

His past... Had his own thoughts conjured up the smell of liquor? He turned toward it as a couple of the older boys walked past, coming back in from outside. They melted in with the other boys, and soon there was a lot of whispering and giggling.

And sure enough, that whiskey smell lingered in the air. It brought back so much for Corbin that for a moment, he just sat there, catapulted back to childhood, feeling out of control.

Samantha must have noticed the same smell he did, and unlike Corbin, she didn't hesitate. She waded into the group, plucked the two boys who had been outside by the sleeves of their shirts, and ordered them over to the small office made from one of the stalls in the barn.

He could hear her voice, low and steady, though not the words. And he could catch the emotion, loud and clear, on both sides: Samantha sounded angry and determined; the two boys protesting and upset.

Corbin shook himself out of his funk, made sure the other boys were working at connecting the cloth to the float, and then went over to the stall to see what support he could be to Samantha.

"I can see that you're not actually drunk," she was saying, "and that's the only thing keeping me from calling your parents and the police right this minute. But your parents *will* be notified."

"Oh, man, not fair," the older one, Nick, said. "We barely had a sip."

"Drinking *any* alcohol underage is an illegal act," she said, "and you can be sure the police would jump right on it, especially in a program like this. Don't you know that delinquent behavior threatens the whole program?"

"What are you going to do to us?" the younger of the two boys asked, his voice shaky.

Corbin slipped in to stand beside Samantha, wondering if she'd consider it an intrusion. "You're handling everything well," he murmured to her. And then, louder, "Just wanted to see if you needed any help."

She gave him a grateful smile. "I guess you noticed that Nick and Eric, here, have been drinking"

"Couldn't miss it." He glared at them.

"Eric wanted to know what we're going to do to them. Any ideas?"

He thought a minute. "Since we're not technically in charge of the program," he said, "I suggest we talk to Gabby and Reese. They'll know all the rules and what should be done."

The older boy, Nick, looked relieved; young Eric looked more scared.

Samantha nodded agreement with the plan, and then someone called, "Pizza's here," from the main part of the barn. Corbin went out to pay for it, waving aside the money Samantha pulled from her purse. He figured it was the least he could do.

Once he had opened all the boxes on the long table and they had said a quick prayer, he let everyone fill a paper plate and grab a soda. They started to go off to various parts of the barn in small groups, but Samantha clapped her hands.

"It's break time, but I want you all here at the tables. Sit down." She looked at the two who had been drinking, crooked a finger to beckon them over, and pointed at the table. "You, too. Get some food and then sit down."

"Are you sure you can handle this?" Corbin asked her quietly. "I can talk to them." Though he had no idea what to say. "Or I can call Gabby right now."

"I got it," she said grimly. "Believe it or not, I have some experience dealing with drunks. Enforcing, and reinforcing, rules and reminding them how to be smart."

The boys being boys, they scarfed down the pizza fairly quickly, and Samantha didn't start talking until everyone had gotten at least some food into their bellies. Which was a good move, Corbin thought. They couldn't talk back if their mouths were full, and they'd be more reasonable if they'd eaten something.

"Most of you already know that people were drinking here today," Samantha said. That surprised Corbin. He hadn't expected her to be so blunt.

"Aw, we weren't really drinking," Nick said.

"Uh-uh," she said, shaking her head. "You can't kid a kidder, and you can't out-lie an alcoholic."

"Who's the alcoholic?" Eric asked.

She looked around, making eye contact with the boys one at a time. "I am," she said.

Suddenly, all the boys were silent.

She sat down on a high stool at one end of the table, a piece of pizza in her hand. "Yep, I have a drinking problem. So I don't drink. And guess where it started?"

"At a bar," Nick said, grinning, and a couple of the other boys laughed.

"Nope. It started with me sneaking outside during high school with some other kids who wanted to get wasted, too." She took a bite of pizza and wiped her mouth. "Just like you guys, it seemed like harmless fun to me. But it wasn't."

"Did you get in trouble?" one of the younger boys asked, and Corbin wondered how much she'd tell them.

"I did get in some trouble, messed up some classes in school," she said. "But I didn't take it seriously." She paused. "Until I had to."

"When did you have to?" one of the older boys, Wolf, asked. "Did you hit bottom? My dad did."

She nodded. "I did hit bottom. I lost…" She paused, and Corbin held his breath. "I lost people who were important to me. Ruined some things that really mattered." She bit her lip and put down her pizza slice half-eaten. "I'm going to be going to meetings and being careful the rest of my life. That could be you, too." And here she pinned the two offenders with a steely glare. "Or you could decide that you're not going to take another drink until you're of legal age and can think it all through, make a smart decision."

"I won't," Eric, the younger boy, said immediately.

Samantha shook her head. "I'm glad, but I'm not asking you to make any kind of commitment now. Just giving you something to think about. Promise me you will?" Eric nodded, and after a minute, Nick did, too. And then she looked around at all the other boys. "You, too. You need to be smart about alcohol, because it can really bite you. It's not just something funny."

She went on talking for a few more minutes, answering questions, self-possessed and honest. Her connection with the boys was solid and sincere.

Obviously, she was committed to staying away from alcohol.

Corbin knew that wasn't completely to be trusted, that a recovering alcoholic was always at risk. He'd learned that at his mother's knee. But Samantha might be different because she knew the dangers, acknowledged them to herself.

Samantha stood up and brushed crumbs off her jeans. "Now we have a lot to get done and it's important to me and to Rescue Haven, but anyone who doesn't want to stay can call your folks and go. Do it now, because if you stay, you're working hard. And anyone else who breaks the rules—well, you're done."

The murmurs he heard now were of wanting to stay. The boys seemed recommitted to the float and the parade; indeed, they hurried over to finish the float right now.

As for Corbin, he sat watching Samantha as she talked to them and supervised their work, and an overwhelming feeling of admiration and caring came over him.

Yes, she had a drinking problem, but she admitted it, was doing something about it. Maybe that was good enough for him.

Maybe he should do something about his feelings for Samantha.

In fact, there was no maybe about it. He was going to talk to her, see how she'd feel about going out on a real date, figure out how to manage the fact that she was working for him and living in the same house. Not tonight, since they'd be working so late, but tomorrow, right after the Memorial Day parade.

Chapter 14

The next day, Saturday, they arrived early at the parade grounds to set up, get organized, get ready. Samantha couldn't help focusing on the high stakes of the float to her personally, even as she directed boys and dressed dogs and chatted with their parade neighbors.

She kept scanning for Mrs. Markowski, but so far, there had been no sightings. She *thought* the woman would love the new float, made much simpler and classier along the lines of the one she'd designed for Brock in his senior parade. But she couldn't feel sure. She'd thought the previous float was good, too.

It was looking around at the townspeople getting ready for the parade that finally made her relax. There was Sheniqua, participating in a medical display that encouraged people to stop by for free blood pressure and cholesterol tests. Hannah was helping her mother to put the finishing touches on her cupcake stand, which seemed to already be doing a brisk business. Reese was chatting with some veterans who weren't able to march in the parade; they were all riding together on a military float.

She heard a discordant sound, the high school band tuning up, and looked ahead in the parade line to see a small but enthusiastic group of young musicians and a few majorettes. Small towns like Bethlehem Springs didn't have the ability to choose only the crème de la crème for the band and sports team; they encouraged everyone to participate. Even Samantha had had a brief run as a majorette, and when she'd quit, several teachers had sat her down and questioned her, encouraged her to stay involved in something positive. She hadn't listened, but she'd appreciated the effort.

People *cared* here. And that was what she wanted, for herself and those she loved, going forward.

Corbin stood talking to some of the Rescue Haven boys, holding Mikey firmly by the hand. Corbin. He'd looked at her with such intensity last night and again this morning. And he'd said he wanted to talk to her after the parade. She didn't know what that was about, but he'd assured her it wasn't something bad.

Maybe he wanted to get closer with her. That was the vibe she got, and the notion made butterflies flap wildly in her chest. Was it possible that she and Corbin could have something, build something?

But if anything along those lines were to happen, she'd have to tell him the truth. She still quailed at the thought, but he *did* seem a lot warmer and more understanding lately.

If telling him the truth would give her even a little bit of a chance at a relationship, at an ongoing family connection with him and Mikey, she'd do it. Plus, she remembered uneasily, she'd made a bargain with God while hunting for Mikey, promising that she'd tell Corbin the truth.

She should have done it before now. It wasn't right to postpone fulfilling your commitment to the heavenly Father.

She felt a tiny hand in hers. "'Mantha?"

It was Mikey, and she rested a hand on his shoulder, loving his cute little face. "Are you ready to get on the float with Corbin? You're going to be way up high."

"Weady," Mikey said, his voice solemn, eyes wide.

"I'm still not sure why you think we should be in the place of honor." Corbin stood beside her, his nearness setting her nerves afire. "Shouldn't we feature boys from the shelter?"

"But the float is about trying to find homes for some of our dogs." That had been the turning point in the revision of the float: figuring out a purpose bigger than just advertising Rescue Haven. "You're the success story, because you adopted Boomer. Half the town knows that he stayed with Mikey when he ran away. Besides, Boomer looks adorable in his stars-and-stripes ruff."

"I guess." He picked up Mikey, gestured to the teenager who'd been holding Boomer's leash and climbed easily to the top level of the float. Samantha beckoned to the other boys, and they all took their places, dogs beside them. Samantha took a seat in the back, mostly out of sight. The float wasn't about her.

Behind them, a group of veterans were getting organized into their formation, carrying flags and a sign telling people to remember the reason for the holiday. After that group, a couple of giant tractors gunned their motors. Next was a line of antique cars, something of an obsession with the older men in town.

Bringing up the rear was a fire truck, and even though the parade hadn't started moving, its occupants were already showering the spectators with candy. Kids ran and dove for it, shrieking their delight, while parents and grandparents looked on, smiling from the folding chairs they'd set up early, curbside. This was a town where everyone wanted a front row seat to cheer their kids and friends along.

Samantha saw that she wasn't the only one with the idea of dressing up dogs. Several of the spectators had brought costumed pets, most decked out in red, white and blue. For that matter, most of the spectators wore patriotic colors, too.

The high school band began to march and play up ahead, sounding very respectable now. Along the sidewalks, proud parents snapped pictures: of the band, the flag team and then the scouts.

Suddenly it was their turn to start moving, and Mrs. Markowski was nowhere in sight. "Here goes," Samantha thought, her heart racing as she gave the signal to start.

The oohs and aahs of the crowd were gratifying. They'd put the smallest dogs at the bottom, held carefully by some of the younger boys. Both the boys and the dogs got bigger in size on the higher platforms. And at the top were Corbin, Mikey and Boomer.

She heard people calling questions out to the boys on the float, asking whether this dog or that one was available for adoption. The boys were ready: they held out informational signs about each dog: how old they were, any issues they had and their breed, if known. "Available for Adoption!" proclaimed the headings on each sign, and large lettering at the front of the float repeated the message.

Large, *tasteful* lettering, per Mrs. Markowski's preferences. Samantha could only hope it was classic and classy enough to meet her approval.

When the float driving the older veterans reached the center of town, the entire parade stopped, and spectators shushed each other. The band played taps as a white-haired man wearing a World War II veteran cap, whom Samantha recognized as the grandfather of one of her classmates, put a wreath on the statue. He took two steps back, bowed his head for a moment, and then saluted.

There was utter silence, and Samantha wasn't the only one wiping tears. Another veteran gave a short speech about what Memorial Day was really about, not the veterans so much as the soldiers who had given the ultimate sacrifice: their lives. It was serious and moving.

As more people stood up to speak, Samantha got a little nervous wondering how the boys and dogs would manage the lack of action. But the boys were quiet and respectful, and they kept the dogs in line. Even Mikey kept his cool, thanks partly to the candy Corbin kept handing him. Once, Samantha met Corbin's eyes and shook her head, fighting a grin. They'd pay for Mikey's excessive sugar consumption later.

After the speeches were over, all the veterans saluted the statue again. Then the crowd burst into applause, and the band moved into a rousing rendition of "God Bless the USA," and the parade started up again.

And there was Mrs. Markowski, standing in the midst of a group of her friends. Thankfully, at least Samantha hoped, the parade wasn't up to full speed yet, giving the women a chance to study the work they'd done.

Heart in her throat, Samantha leaned out from her perch at the back of the float. "What do you think, Mrs. Markowski?" she asked as they drew up alongside her. "Do you like it any better than the design I showed you before?"

Mrs. Markowski studied the float for a minute longer, and Samantha held her breath. And then the older woman smiled, nodded her head and looked at Samantha. "It's very pretty," she said, "and one of the classiest in the parade."

One of her friends, similarly dressed in elegant clothing, studied the float and nodded. "Very nice, dear," she said.

"I have to admit you were right," she said to Mrs. Markowski. "Your ideas are what took it above and beyond. That, and the work of all the Rescue Haven boys."

Mrs. Markowski smiled at Samantha before turning to speak more with her friends.

And Samantha dared to hope that the older woman would be pleased enough to recommend her to develop the program for younger kids at Rescue Haven.

Mikey must have heard her talking, and he struggled to get down from Corbin's lap and come to her. Since the parade had come to a halt again, she went over and got him and then sat down on the edge of one of the platforms, pulling him into her lap. As she cuddled him against her chest, her heart filled. She loved him so very much.

She really, really wanted to keep mothering him.

"'Mantha," Mikey murmured sleepily, "will you be my mommy?"

His high voice was loud enough for several of the women around Mrs. Markowski to hear, and there were smiles all around. Samantha just rubbed Mikey's back and didn't answer. She couldn't be his mommy, not really…but oh, how she wanted to.

Her heart was full as she looked around at the Rescue Haven boys, and her friends and the townspeople. She felt like she had a role in this town. Maybe, just maybe, she could stay.

The parade started up again, so Samantha carried Mikey back up to Corbin.

"It's going well," he said, smiling at her. "I heard what Mrs. Markowski said to you."

"I know. I'm so relieved. I hope it means what I think it means."

"I'm not at all surprised. You worked really hard on

this project. And you had the foresight to redo it, even though it was a lot of extra work." His eyes were warm with approval and she couldn't seem to look away.

As she climbed down from the top of the float after leaving Mikey with Corbin, Samantha noticed a small crowd gathering on the edge of the village green. Was someone lying on the ground? It was hard to see, so she climbed back up a few steps to where she could see past others. Yes, someone was definitely down.

Wondering if there was something she could do to help, she shaded her eyes against the sun and watched the drama unfold.

And then her heart stopped.

Among those gathered was *Cheryl*. She was talking and gesticulating and pointing at the person on the ground. The group of people around them parted a little and Samantha could see the person lying in the grass.

Cheryl's husband. He must have collapsed. And it looked like Cheryl was panicking. Samantha hopped down from the float and hurried over. Cheryl was a stranger in town and might not know how to get the help she needed.

"What's wrong?" It was Gabby, coming up beside her.

"Could you go make sure the boys on the float are okay?" She was peering past the small circle of onlookers to see how Paul was doing. She could hear Cheryl speaking, her voice high and shaky, nearing hysteria.

"Of course." Gabby went back over to the float. She knew the boys well and was basically familiar with their plan. She would do fine.

Samantha made her way through the little crowd and reached Cheryl. "What's going on?" she asked, putting her arm gently around the woman. Paul lay unconscious, and a woman who seemed to know what she was doing was loosening his collar and taking his pulse.

"He just collapsed," Cheryl's voice was tight, panicked. She clutched Samantha's arm as if it were a lifeline. "I know I shouldn't have brought him, but he wanted to see Mikey. I'm afraid—" her voice broke "—and *he's* afraid, it could be the last time."

Samantha blew out a breath. *Think*. "Somebody try to find Sheniqua. And did you call an ambulance?"

"Some people did." They both sank down on the ground beside Paul. He was breathing shallowly, still unconscious.

"I wish the paramedics would get here," said the woman who'd been taking his pulse.

"I shouldn't have brought him," Cheryl lamented. "He hasn't been out of the house in weeks."

"You probably shouldn't have. It may have been too much for him. But the paramedics will help." The sirens were close now, and she saw the ambulance, lights flashing, pull up on a side street right next to them. The paramedics knelt down to do their work, questioning Cheryl, and the crowd moved back to give them room.

Only then did Samantha look back toward the float.

At the top of it, Corbin was staring in their direction. He looked furious.

From the top of the float, Corbin stared at the cluster of people in the crowd. He couldn't believe his own eyes.

There was his mother, being melodramatic as usual. Apparently, his father was on the ground. Being worked on by paramedics.

That was shocking enough. But what was more shocking was that Samantha stood talking to Cheryl as if they were old friends.

Could she just be being nice? But why had she abandoned the float to go over there? As he watched, she put an arm around Cheryl and the two talked as if they were old friends.

Anger filled him and all his muscles tightened. The parade was starting up again but he couldn't participate; he eased off the top of the float, Mikey in his arms, Boomer beside them.

"Where are you going, Dr. Beck?" one of the boys asked. "You're supposed to stay on the top of the float."

"Here, want to take my place?" He thrust Mikey toward the boy.

The teenager shook his head. "No, not me. I'm bad with kids."

"Take Boomer, then." He handed over Boomer's leash. Probably not a good idea to leave Mikey with someone else, anyway, so Corbin jumped off the float with Mikey on his hip.

Mrs. Markowski rushed up to him. "What are you doing? You and Mikey are the focal point of the entire float."

"There's someone I have to talk to." He plowed through the crowd toward his mother, his father and the woman he'd thought he knew.

Maybe it was because his father sat up, but no one

noticed his approach. Mikey was sleepy and leaning his head against Corbin's shoulder.

His father was struggling to say something. He reached out toward Samantha. "Thank you…" he said weakly.

"That's part of why he wanted to come," his mother said. None of them had spotted Corbin yet. "He wanted to thank you himself for helping us get Corbin to care for Mikey. It seems like it's working really well, but we never could have done it without you."

Corbin's whole chest went tight. What was his mother talking about?

"I was glad to help you," Samantha said to his father, who'd sunk back down on the ground. "It's worth it for Mikey."

Corbin had hoped his parents had it wrong, that Samantha wasn't involved, but her words made it clear that she was.

Someone tapped his shoulder and he turned, still reeling, unable to believe what he'd heard.

It was Mrs. Markowski. "I guess you know her secret now," she said.

Wait. Mrs. Markowski knew that his parents had somehow set him up? Who had told her?

Did everyone know but him?

Betrayal, aching and hard as a stone, grew in his chest. The people who should be close to him had been talking together behind his back, lying to him. Anger surged as he pushed his way closer to the group of medical professionals surrounding his father.

* * *

Relieved that Corbin's father seemed to be doing better, Samantha leaned back so the paramedics could get to him. She stood. And found herself facing a furious Corbin.

"So you helped my parents scheme against me?" He didn't bother to wait for an answer, but went on. His face was red, his hands clenching and unclenching, even the one that was holding Mikey. "Did it occur to you that I should know the truth about my own family? How long was this going on? Were you fooling me, lying to me, from the start?"

"Excuse me, sir," said a paramedic, who was pushing a stretcher through the crowd.

Samantha closed her eyes briefly. She had hoped to be able to tell him in her own way, hoped that Cheryl would tell him the truth. She'd known he would be upset. But upset didn't even begin to describe the emotion she saw flashing over Corbin's face.

"You are a liar," he said, enunciating each word, his voice like thunder. "Same as she is." He gestured at his mother, contempt in every line of his face.

Mikey started to cry. "Corbin not yell," he wailed.

Samantha reached for him. So did Cheryl, and Mikey's eyes widened when he saw his mother. His face broke into a smile.

Cheryl cupped Mikey's cheek and then put a hand on Corbin's arm, stepping in front of Samantha. "This was my idea and my fault, honey," Cheryl said to Corbin.

"Don't call me honey." Corbin glared at her. "And

don't ever send one of your alcoholic friends to try to pull one over on me again."

"But I needed to have you take care of him so I could—"

"I really don't want to hear it." Corbin's hands were planted on his hips. "I don't want to hear it from either of you. I'm keeping custody of Mikey, obviously, but I would be fine if I never saw either of you two again."

Samantha's heart turned to stone inside her, because he wasn't referring to his parents. He was referring to his mother and Samantha.

He never wanted to see her again.

She had screwed this up royally. Of course she had. She was the kind of person who screwed things up. She had had a little interlude of joy and family life in this town, but now, it was over.

"Ma'am, you're his wife, correct?" the paramedic said to Cheryl.

Cheryl nodded, bit her lip as she looked at Corbin, and then turned back to focus her attention on her ailing husband.

"You can ride along in the ambulance if you'd like," he said. "We're getting ready to take him now."

Cheryl squeezed Samantha's hand, mouthed the word *sorry* to Corbin, and followed the stretcher to the ambulance.

Mikey thrashed and cried in Corbin's arms, and Samantha reached for him again, instinctively wanting to provide comfort. But Corbin turned away so she couldn't reach him.

"'Mantha!" Mikey tried to reach for her.

She couldn't stop her hand from stretching toward him again. Just like she couldn't stop her heart from pounding and her throat from aching.

"Leave him alone," Corbin said, his voice icy. "I won't have his life corrupted by an alcoholic the way mine was."

Corrupted? Was that true, that she was corrupting Mikey's life?

She'd wanted to help him, but hearing the sweet little boy cry now, she just felt like she'd ruined everything.

Some people in the crowd averted their eyes and turned away, leaving them to their argument. Others stayed, whether to help or collect gossip, Samantha didn't know. What did it matter?

"I'll leave now," she said, feeling numb.

"What do you mean, you're leaving?" Where had Mrs. Markowski come from? "You have a float to take care of. And Corbin, you and Mikey are supposed to be at the top of it. There's still half of the parade route to go!"

"I can't," they both said simultaneously. It was just a little irony that they both reacted the same way. They did have a lot in common.

Just not enough.

Samantha stood on tiptoe to see the parade float, feeling guilty that she was letting Rescue Haven down. But it looked like, between Gabby and the boys, they had just reorganized how the dogs and boys were arranged on the float. There wasn't an obvious gap where Corbin and Mikey should have been.

They would do fine without her. As would Corbin and Mikey.

Mrs. Markowski continued to scold them. Corbin ignored her and Samantha, both; instead, he stared in the direction the ambulance had gone with something in his eyes that looked a lot like hate.

She turned and made her way through the crowd toward Corbin's house. She would gather her stuff and leave. Escape, just as she had done once before, pregnant and scared, after high school. She'd go back to the city, she guessed. Nowhere else to go.

Her chest hurt so bad that she wrapped her arms around herself. She would've liked to just double over, but she couldn't. Had to keep moving. Had to leave so she didn't hurt Corbin anymore.

Why hadn't she told him the truth? Why had she let it go on this long?

But she knew why; she was bad at relationships and she always messed everything up.

There was a glimmer inside of her, something she hadn't felt before on that long-ago day when she had left Bethlehem Springs. It came from the signs in the church: you are forgiven. It came from Sheniqua's words and the articles she'd sent, about how miscarriages usually happened because of an abnormality in the fetus.

It came from the bible reading she'd been doing at night when she managed to stay awake.

The glimmer wasn't much, but it did make her want to pray, so she walked along down the residential street toward Corbin's house, mouthing the only prayer she could think of. *Help me, Father.*

Chapter 15

As the parade ended and the crowd dissipated, Corbin got himself together enough to help Mikey calm down. He'd learned that distraction worked wonders, so he took Mikey over by the Rescue Haven float and let him visit with the dogs.

Seeing the float made his chest seize up. Samantha had worked so hard on it. She and Corbin had worked together. And it had looked like it was going to be a success.

But *why* had she worked on it? That was what he didn't understand. Why had she come to stay with him, deceived him about her relationship with his mother, made him think she cared? What was in it for her?

He thought back to the first time he'd seen Samantha back in town. She'd shown up at the café where he'd been struggling with Mikey on that very first day, rescuing him from his own ignorance, making everything better. She'd seemed like a gift from God.

She *wasn't* a gift from God, though. Quite the opposite. For some inexplicable reason, she'd arrived on purpose to deceive him.

Corbin was no expert on people. He understood animals and numbers and charts so much better, and he'd never felt his deficit as much as he did now.

But watching Mikey's tears dry as he cuddled with Boomer and laughed and shouted at the other dogs and boys, Corbin grew determined.

He wasn't going to let Samantha into Mikey's life anymore, nor Cheryl, either. Look how Cheryl had given up her son so coldly. And look how easy it had been for Samantha to lie to Corbin, to pretend she was just showing up in Mikey's life by happenstance.

Mikey was an innocent and didn't deserve to face that kind of duplicity. No one had been there to protect Corbin as a kid, but Mikey's situation was different. He had a big brother who had the means and the desire to take care of him, raise him, love him.

Corbin would do that to the best of his ability. He didn't know exactly *how* he'd manage, without Samantha, but he would figure it out. He took a couple of deep breaths. He needed to settle himself and think.

Reese approached, frowning. "I got a call from Samantha."

Emotions exploded inside Corbin, wrecking his attempt to calm down. Jealousy that she'd called Reese and not him. Worry that something was wrong, that she was in some kind of trouble. And swirling all around those feelings, anger at what she had done. "I'm not on speaking terms with Samantha right now," he told Reese.

"So I hear." Reese frowned. "I'm questioning your intelligence."

Corbin's lips tightened. "You don't know what she did."

"True, I don't. But I know her, and I know she's a good person."

Corbin let out a disgusted snort.

"She knew you wouldn't answer a call from her, and that's why she got in touch with me with some bad news to pass along." He paused. "It's your father. He had some kind of attack on the way to the hospital. There's a chance that he might not survive it."

Corbin blew out a breath. His stomach twisted and roiled. "That's nothing to do with me."

Reese stared at him. "It's everything to do with you, man. It's your father. You need to go to the hospital right away."

Corbin crossed his arms, looked away, checked that Mikey was still safely playing with Boomer and a couple of the Rescue Haven boys. "He wasn't a father to me."

Reese studied him for a minute, thoughtfully, and then spoke. "Look, I don't know what that would be like. All I know is, once your parents are gone, there's no more chance to make it up to them, or forgive them, or even ask them why they did what they did. Death is the end, my friend, and you might want to rethink letting your anger be the last feeling you have toward your dad."

Coming from someone else, those words would've infuriated Corbin. But Reese was his best friend. Not only that, but Reese had lost both of his parents at a young age, so he had some authority. He knew what he was talking about.

Corbin stared at the ground and wondered if he wanted to say goodbye to the man who had disappointed him so often, who had knocked him around, who had made his mother into the flighty and incompetent woman she was. "I just don't know," he said.

"There's something else." Reese was watching him, eyes steady and compassionate. "Your mom is losing it. Apparently, she was hysterical when she called Samantha."

Again, Corbin was irrationally bothered by the fact that his mother had called Samantha and not him, even though he probably wouldn't have spoken to her if she'd managed to get his number and make contact. "My mom's always losing it about one thing or other."

Reese frowned. "All I know is, this time, she may be facing the death of her husband. She needs her son."

Corbin's stomach twisted. So apparently, he still couldn't hear that his mother was struggling without having some desire, however unrealistic, that he could help her. Ridiculous.

Mikey came rushing over then and wrapped his arms around Reese's legs.

"Whoa, little man, wrong guy," Reese said with a chuckle.

Mikey looked up, realized his mistake, and spun to cling on to Corbin.

There was Corbin's excuse not to get involved with his mother. "I can't take Mikey into the hospital. He's too little."

"I'll go there with you and watch over Mikey in the waiting room. I'll bring Izzy along to keep him company. Pretty sure they have a play area for kids there."

"You don't have to do that, man," Corbin protested.

"It's not a problem. Come on." And Reese took Mikey's hand and led the way toward the parking area, leaving Corbin nothing to do but follow along.

Samantha didn't want to answer the pounding on the door. She'd planned to come here and grab her things and go, but she just didn't have the energy. She wanted to stay in her little suite, curled up in a ball, under the covers. She didn't want to face anyone ever again.

Every time she thought of Corbin's anger, she physically flinched. He would never lift a hand to her, but his words had hurt like blows. Because they were true.

She *was* a liar. It was no wonder he never wanted to see her again.

The thought of that void in her life—never seeing Mikey, never seeing Corbin—made her whole chest ache.

But the pounding continued. She pushed herself up out of the bed and made her way down the stairs. She would get rid of whoever this persistent person was—they were probably here to see Corbin anyway—and then she could go back to nursing her misery.

She opened the door, her mouth open to explain that Corbin wasn't in, and then snapped it shut again.

There stood Sheniqua, Gabby and Hannah, and they pushed and hugged their way past her before she could send them away.

"Girl, you look terrible!" Sheniqua studied her face and then took her hand and led her toward the living room. "Make her some hot tea," she called over her shoulder. "See if you can find some carbs, too."

"What are you guys doing here?" Samantha asked, confused, as she obediently followed her friend. They must not know what had happened, how she'd been exposed as the fraud she was.

"We're saving you from yourself." Hannah perched on the end of the couch and patted the cushion beside her, and Sheniqua led her to sit down there and then took the armchair across from the couch. "I've known you practically from the day you were born, remember?" Hannah continued. "I knew you would be sitting in here beating up on yourself. And you shouldn't be. None of this is your fault."

Her cousin was so sweet. Samantha tried to force a smile in her direction and failed miserably. "You don't know what I did."

"Honey, the whole town knows what you did," Sheniqua said. "Corbin's got a pretty loud voice when he's mad."

Samantha ought to be embarrassed, but what did it matter? She was leaving Bethlehem Springs as soon as she could muster the energy to pack her things.

"He has a lot of nerve," Hannah said. "Blaming you

for something his mother did. All you were doing was trying to help, right?"

Samantha blew out a sigh. She could tell from the way her friends were settling in that she wasn't going to get out of this conversation without telling them at least some of what had gone on.

"Water's heating," Gabby said, and plunked four mugs onto the coffee table, placing a teabag into each one. She disappeared into the kitchen and returned with a ziplock bag full of homemade sugar cookies. "Look, you guys, I scored!"

Samantha had planned to surprise Corbin and Mikey with them after dinner tonight. She bit her lip and looked away.

Once the other three had passed around the cookies, Gabby took charge. "First off, you'll want to know that your parade float won a prize."

"It did?" Samantha stared at her blankly. She had thought that when she left the float unattended, when Corbin and Mikey had climbed down and followed her to Corbin's parents, the whole thing was a bust. "Mrs. Markowski said we ruined everything."

Sheniqua lifted her hands, palms up, and rolled her eyes. "I'm a medical professional, but sometimes that woman stretches my vow to do no harm," she said. "It wasn't ruined. Those boys are passionate about what they're doing and about Rescue Haven. They made a few adjustments, and the float continued on in the parade, and everyone loved it."

"Not only that," Hannah said, "but there are at least

three pending dog adoptions based on spectators at the parade filling out paperwork."

"That's wonderful." Again, Samantha tried to force a smile. It really was good that the boys had taken charge and that the dogs were the beneficiaries. At least something had come out of their work.

"But I know," Gabby said, "that you're not going to rest easy until you make things up with Corbin."

"Not gonna happen." Samantha pulled her knees to her chest and wrapped her arms around them. "I tried to call him to let him know about his dad—did you know his dad is in the hospital and not doing well at all?— but it went straight to voice mail. I had to get word to him through Reese."

"Could be that he's just busy," Sheniqua said. Her voice was doubtful, though.

"I don't think so. At the parade, he said—" She swallowed hard. "He said he never wanted to see me again. So when he didn't answer, I asked Reese to let Corbin know about his dad. Hopefully, he'll at least go to the hospital and see his father one more time."

"Reese is trying," Gabby said. "That's all I know."

"Corbin could stand to learn a lesson or two about forgiveness," Hannah said. "And you know what?" she added, turning to Samantha. "You could, too."

"What do I have to forgive?" Samantha asked. "Corbin didn't do anything to me. He's been nothing but upright and honorable. He's a..." She cleared her throat and willed herself not to cry in front of her friends. "He's a good man," she finished.

Gabby moved closer and patted Samantha's arm. Samantha didn't trust herself to say any more, so she just squeezed Gabby's hand. She appreciated her friends' kindness, but they were about to turn her into more of a ball of mush than she already was.

"If you're not angry at Corbin's mother, you should be," Hannah said. "She put you in an impossible position. She knew you cared for Mikey and wanted him to be safe, and she took advantage of that."

"I don't think it was that, exactly," Samantha said. She took a sip of her tea. "Cheryl was desperate, and I agreed to help. I didn't have to."

"She should've found another way. She shouldn't have gotten you involved." Hannah crossed her arms in a way that reminded Samantha of how she had acted when she was angry as a child. That, plus the way her friends were so stalwart in her defense, made her smile for the first time since she'd seen Cheryl at the parade.

Gabby leaned forward, putting her mug down on the coffee table. "We can't forget the main thing," she said, and they all looked at her.

"What's the main thing?" Samantha asked, still smiling just a little. "Because I know you're going to tell us anyway."

"I sure am." Gabby put a hand over Samantha's, briefly, and then looked at each woman in turn. "The main thing is that even if you *did* do something wrong— and we all do, just about every day—you're forgiven."

"That's right." Sheniqua nodded. "Father God knows us. He knows we're human and imperfect, so He made a way for us to start over, be new creations."

Starting over. Being a new creation. Samantha's

heart seemed to reach longingly for the words. "I never really got that," she admitted. "I know it makes me a bad Christian, but I never really understood the whole idea of getting our sins forgiven."

Hannah shook her head. "Don't be so down on yourself," she said. "You're not a bad Christian. It's a tough concept for all of us, because we want to do the right thing, and we're so conscious that we fall short."

"And as women in this society," Sheniqua added, "we tend to take all the blame, all the time. But we don't have to."

"We can feel bad about whatever we've done wrong, and try not to do it again," Gabby said. "That's important. But once we've made that decision, we can be free." She leaned forward, elbows on knees. "I can't tell you how much that meant to me, when I figured it out. Despite my mistakes—and I've made a lot of them— I can be free to go on and live my life. I don't have to wallow in shame."

"That does sound wonderful," Samantha admitted. "I just don't know quite how to get there."

"He'll help you if you pray," Sheniqua said. "Matter of fact, I think we're about at the point of too much talk and too little prayer."

"So let's pray," Hannah said, "and then, let's order pizza. Those cookies made me hungry!"

Samantha laughed at her cousin as they all joined hands to pray. Her heart still ached, and she wasn't through crying. She'd still probably leave town, if not right away, then soon. But as she bowed her head, before asking anything for herself, she silently thanked God for three wonderful, warm, loving friends.

Chapter 16

Corbin let his mother hug him and then walked out the hospital room and down the hall, feeling numb.

Seeing his father, pale and unconscious and hooked up to multiple machines, had shaken him. For the first time, he had internalized the fact that his father might actually pass on.

It didn't negate all the many issues Corbin had with his father, all the painful memories. But it did illustrate, starkly, the fact that life was short. His father would soon face judgment, judgment from a God so much wiser than Corbin that there wasn't even a comparison.

Maybe that meant that Corbin didn't need to do all that judging himself.

After all, despite the difficulties of his childhood, Corbin had gone on to achieve more success than anyone had thought possible. He had a good life. Now, he had Mikey.

His mind skittered away from thoughts of Samantha, because he didn't have her. He had pushed her away, judged her harshly and openly. He felt like he'd been right, but he also felt awful about it.

"Wait, Corbin!" His mother ran after him along the intensive care hallway, disregarding the frowns of the nurses. That was Cheryl, not thinking of anyone but herself.

Except that wasn't quite true, because when she reached him, she took both of his hands into hers. "Thank you for coming," she said. "It means the world to me to be able to speak with you. I'm sorry for pushing Mikey on you the way I did."

"It's okay. I love Mikey." He found himself squeezing his mom's hands back, just a little. "In fact... I know this isn't the time to talk about it, but I hope I can continue to be his guardian, whatever happens here." He waved his hand toward his father's room.

She studied him, eyes filled with tears and love. "You always were a good boy," she said. "I'm proud of you. So very proud of you." She squeezed his hands once more. "I don't know how your father and I, mixed up as we are, made two boys as wonderful as you and Mikey." She paused, then added, "If Mikey can turn out to be half the man you are, I'll be happy."

She studied his face as if she was searching for something. Whatever it was, she didn't seem to find it. She gave him a half smile, turned, and walked back toward Corbin's father's room.

Looking after her, seeing the slight stoop of her shoulders, watching her straighten up before entering the room, Corbin found his own eyes growing wet.

She was proud of him. She wanted Mikey to be like him.

The family lounge right outside the intensive care unit was empty. Dimly lit, and quiet. Corbin ducked inside.

He texted Reese that he would be down in a few minutes. Reese was great with kids, but it was way past Mikey and Izzy's bedtime. Corbin needed to resume his responsibilities.

But first, he'd take a minute to put himself together. Because it felt like his whole world, the world he had ordered so carefully to keep control throughout his adult life, was flying apart.

His parents were mixed up, no doubt about it. They both had drinking problems, and in his father's case, it had led to bigger health problems that might end up taking him young. His mother was healthier physically, but seemed always to be on the verge of some kind of a mental breakdown. No wonder she drank.

Those were the genes Corbin carried, and maybe that was why he felt the need to keep such rigid control. Maybe he was afraid that if he didn't, he would end up going down the same path his parents had.

But the truth was, despite his efforts, he wasn't in control. That had become glaringly obvious when Mikey had shown up on his front porch.

Ever since then, Corbin had had to let go, not just at home but in all parts of his life.

He had let go of his need to meticulously prepare every lecture, to spend hours grading each lab report.

To his surprise, his students didn't even seem to mind. There had been more laughter in his classes lately than ever before, because he had had to improvise on some of his lectures, and in one case, he'd had to wing the whole thing because he'd been so distracted that he had deleted his PowerPoint slides. That had made him pay more attention to the students, ask what they wanted to discuss more, answer their questions. As a result, he was actually enjoying his job more and feeling closer to his students. Between that and the Rescue Haven experiments he'd been writing up, it looked like his position at the university would be secured.

With Mikey, every day brought some new surprise, some unexpected happening that kept Corbin guessing. But he had managed it. Thinking back now, he was shocked to realize that he didn't have to maintain perfect control to have a good life. He was able to go along, caring for Mikey, and figure out solutions as he went.

Of course, a big part of that was Samantha. He couldn't have done any of it without Samantha.

She had done a bad thing, deceiving him as she had; there was no question about it. He was angry at her. But he couldn't muster the rage he had felt even a couple of hours ago.

His mother was difficult, but persuasive. She had explained that she and Samantha had become friends in an AA meeting, and that Samantha had babysat Mikey a few times, because she loved kids and worked in child care, and Cheryl had needed her help.

When Corbin's father had gotten so sick, it had made some kind of twisted sense to Cheryl to ask Samantha to help in the elaborate ruse they had cooked up.

A ruse that wouldn't have been necessary, Corbin realized, if he himself hadn't been such a rigid, unforgiving person.

"I just knew if I came and asked you myself, you would turn me away," Cheryl had explained. "So I had to use Mikey. He's… He's just so adorable. I knew even you couldn't resist him."

Even you couldn't resist him. Shame wound its way through Corbin's chest.

His thoughts spinning, he dropped his head into his hands. Maybe Cheryl needed forgiveness. Maybe Samantha needed forgiveness. Maybe they had both done wrong.

But, Corbin realized, he had done wrong, too.

He prayed with a heart that felt like it had been broken open. *Father, forgive me.*

Even fortified with prayer and the friendship of good Christian women, Samantha was a little scared to put her plan into action. That was why she'd figured out a way to do it when Corbin and Mikey wouldn't be home.

It was Monday, and a rainy day, and Corbin had sent her a brief text explaining that she didn't need to work today, since the university was closed. He'd taken Mike with him on a few errands.

So she was free to pack her few belongings and carry them out to the car without the emotional intensity of doing it all in front of Corbin and Mikey. It didn't take but half an hour to pack all of her things into four boxes. Which was a little pathetic, she thought as she stripped the bed and put her sheets and towels into Corbin's washing machine.

She was a woman in her twenties with a job—well, she had a job for a short time more, at least—and yet her whole life could be packed into just a few boxes.

As she walked back up from the basement, every room she passed through seemed to hold strong memories. Here was the kitchen where she and Corbin and Mikey had shared so many meals, talking and laughing. That gave her a real pang.

Mikey loved to have the attention of both her and Corbin, needed it. It would be hard on him that she wouldn't be sharing in those experiences anymore, even though she'd agreed to remain his nanny until Corbin could find someone else. Just not live in, not anymore. She had to respect herself enough not to do that.

She passed the study where Corbin spent so much of his time. Though not as much as he had probably spent before taking Mikey in. She admired him for his vast intelligence and for how hard he worked. There was no question about it, he was a brilliant man and did important work at the university. More than that, he focused some of his research on rescue animals, showing something about his big heart.

All the same, despite her admiration for him, she couldn't live with his attitudes toward her. Yes, she had deceived him, and she was sorry for that. She had told him so right away, but he hadn't listened. He had been too caught up putting her into the same category as his mother and condemning her.

Corbin had a lot to work out, and Samantha sincerely hoped he would work it out before his father passed on or, hopefully, got well enough to move back to the city in Cheryl's care.

She couldn't wait, though, for Corbin to work through his issues. Even if she did, it was doubtful that he would want anything to do with her. They were too different. They had shared a wonderful six weeks, had found more in common than she would have ever dreamed possible, and yet a friendship just wasn't going to work between them.

She couldn't be with someone who didn't accept her for who she was, who didn't allow her to make mistakes without turning on her, judging her, yelling at her. She knew, now, that she deserved better.

And the fact that her tears were spilling over as she climbed the stairs to get her things—well, it didn't mean she was going to change her mind.

She was huffing and puffing as she carried the first box down the stairs and through the living room.

Suddenly the front door opened, startling her into dropping the box. Her clothes spilled out as she stared at Corbin and Mikey. "What are you doing here?" she asked. And then she saw Mikey tense, just a little, and modulated her tone. "I thought you had errands to run."

"I finished them faster than I expected." Corbin tilted his head to one side. "What are you doing?"

She knelt down and started scooping up her spilled clothes and jammed them haphazardly back into the box. Fortunately, that gave her something to do as she spoke. "I'm taking some things over to Hannah's." She smiled at Mikey. "Hey buddy, come here," she said, opening her arms. He ran to her, and she swung him up onto her hip. "I'll make him a snack. Turn on his audiobook to help him settle down, because after running around with you all morning, he's got to be almost ready for a nap."

Sure enough, Mikey was rubbing his eyes with the backs of his hands. "No nap," he said, and then yawned.

"Snack first," she agreed, and set him up in his booster seat with some cereal pieces and fruit. As she fetched him a sippy cup of water, her throat tightened.

She was going to miss living here with Mikey, having the chance to take care of him all the time. She had grown to love him as if he were her own son.

But she knew it was the right thing to do, so she flipped on his audiobook and got him started on his snack. Then she sucked in a huge breath and walked back out into the lion's den.

And there stood the lion himself, arms crossed over his chest, looking from her to the messily repacked box of clothes. "Looks to me like you're moving out," he said quietly.

She held out a hand like a stop sign. "You're right, but before you start judging me, you need to know I'm not abandoning Mikey. I'm going to keep taking care of him, at least until you find someone else who suits."

"How will you keep caring for him if you're not living here?"

She lifted her chin. "We'll trade him off, and I'll care for him where I'm staying while you're at work."

"Where are you staying?" His face seemed made of stone.

"At Hannah's. I've already cleared it with her. She's delighted to have Mikey spend time at her place."

"So, we'll be like divorced parents?" Now, his stone face betrayed a little expression, a tightening of his jaw.

"Something like that." Her throat closed again and she had to suck in a breath and let it out slowly before she could speak. "When you...when you find another caregiver, of course, I'll withdraw."

"I'd like to talk about all this." Now his hands were planted on his hips.

She closed her eyes briefly, shutting out his stern visage. *Remember, you are a child of God. You're worth a lot, even if you make mistakes.*

"Can you come into my study so we can hash this out?" he asked.

She looked at him, at his dear, confused face, a face she had come to care so deeply for. But she had to take care of herself, respect herself. She drew herself up and willed herself to speak clearly, without wavering. "I don't think I can handle another talk with you. But if you'd like to carry my boxes out to the car, you can certainly do that."

He looked a little surprised, and she realized that she wasn't usually quite so directive with him. Even through her pain, that part felt a little good. She spun and went back into the kitchen to check on Mikey, and when she returned, Corbin was coming back into the house and the box she had spilled was gone. He headed toward the stairs. So it looked like he was going to take her at her word and help her move her boxes.

Was that because he respected her, or because he wanted her out?

Before she could figure out an answer to that question, her phone buzzed, an unfamiliar number. She could have let it go to voicemail, but for some reason she clicked on the call. "Hello?"

"Samantha. It's Catherine Markowski."

"Hi," she said, and sat down abruptly on the couch. *I don't think I can handle this, not today.* But then again, what choice did she have? There was no use putting off this latest rejection. Best to get it over with.

There was a short silence, and Samantha opened her mouth to fill it, to spare Mrs. Markowski the difficulty of telling Samantha she'd done a terrible job on the parade. But she couldn't muster the energy to help the woman out. So she just waited.

"I've been doing some thinking," Mrs. Markowski said, "and I decided you are actually just the person to juggle all the different demands that a new program for young children will involve."

Samantha waited for the punch line, but there was just another moment's silence. "I'm sorry, what did you say?"

"I'd like to offer you the job."

Samantha flopped back against the couch. "You want to offer me the job," she repeated without really being able to process the words.

"Yes, dear, that's right."

"You don't mean you want me to start a program for kids at Rescue Haven." Surely she had imagined what the other woman had said, or misunderstood.

"I *do* want you to do that."

Corbin must have heard her last comment, because he came into the room holding two of her boxes and stood, listening.

Still with those crazy nice muscles that weren't what you would expect of a professor. And why was she noticing that, even now?

"What do you think?" Mrs. Markowski asked briskly. "Any questions?"

"Um… Can I ask why? I thought you were upset about how everything went at the parade."

"I was, dear. But as I said, I've done some thinking. Starting a new program will require juggling a lot of different demands and responding to emergencies. That's exactly what you managed to do on Saturday."

"Uh, thanks?" She leaned against the back of the couch. "Can you tell me more about what would be involved?"

She raised an eyebrow at Corbin, who was openly eavesdropping, and he shook his head and carried the boxes outside.

She listened as Mrs. Markowski explained her offer in more detail. Yes, she really did want Samantha to start the program, and the sooner the better. She named a salary for part-time, and another one for full-time, depending on whether Samantha wanted to keep working as a nanny or to make the Rescue Haven job her main source of income.

The salary Corbin gave her was generous, but Mrs. Markowski's offer was even more so. She'd be able to pay off her small amount of credit card debt, start an emergency fund, maybe even buy a new car.

It was a dream come true. Except that, when she'd dreamed it, she'd imagined a loving man at her side here in Rescue Haven. Corbin, to be specific. She wasn't sure when that had become part and parcel of her staying here, but it had, and his rejection of her had changed everything.

He came back into the room with her last box just as Mrs. Markowski wound down.

"I'm very grateful for your putting your confidence in me," Samantha said. "But I'll need some time to think about it."

"Oh," Mrs. Markowski said. "Of course, dear, but don't wait too long." In her voice was something like respect.

They said goodbye and she clicked out of the call and stared directly in front of her. She didn't want to look at Corbin, didn't want anything he said to influence her decision.

The thinking and praying she had been doing sat around her like a mantle.

It didn't matter what Mrs. Markowski thought. It didn't matter what Corbin thought. What mattered was what God wanted her to do, because she was a child of God. She didn't have to constantly apologize for herself and try to manage other people's feelings.

She was a child of God.

It didn't give her a feeling of exuberance. She was

still sad, very sad, at the prospect of leaving Corbin and ultimately Mikey. But she was all right. It was well with her soul, as the old hymn said, or it would be.

"She offered you the job?" Corbin asked.

She looked at him. "Yes, she did."

"That's great! I'm happy for you." He took a step toward her.

She hunched a little and turned away. He had hurt her too badly to come back in as a friend, even a seemingly supportive friend.

And if she let him come to her, maybe even hug her, her heart would be broken all over again. "Thanks for loading my boxes, Corbin," she said, keeping her voice formal. "I'll be in touch about a schedule for Mikey's care."

His face looked stricken. Maybe he wasn't used to her standing up for herself. Well, he would figure out how to manage.

She walked out of the house, got into her car and drove as far as the little park in town.

There, she pulled into a parking space and broke down.

Chapter 17

When Corbin pulled up in front of his parents' home in Buckeye Acres Mobile Estates, a feeling he'd had way too much lately washed over him again.

Shame.

He was a successful man with a house and a savings account and a good job. What did it say about him that his parents were living like this? That his little brother had grown up in a rusty trailer where the dumpster was overflowing with trash and broken glass littered the road alongside the house?

There were plenty of nice trailer parks in the area. This wasn't one of them.

He made his way up the front walkway, nearly tripping over some overgrown bushes. He rapped on the tarnished screen door.

Beating himself up was starting to be a familiar occupation of his. He was certainly doing it in relation to what he'd said and done to Samantha.

For the past two days, she had cared for Mikey, but the exchange with Corbin had involved only a couple of polite, shallow sentences. When he tried to say more, to really talk to her, she turned away.

He felt like a jerk. And since he couldn't get through to Samantha, he had decided to go visit his mother and tell her that he had forgiven her.

Now, noticing the rip in the screen, he wondered who really needed forgiving.

When Cheryl opened the door and saw him, her mouth dropped open. She pressed a hand to it as tears sprang to her eyes.

"Hi," he said, feeling awkward.

"What am I thinking? Come in, come in," she said, opening the door wide.

He had to stoop his head to walk through the doorway. As soon as he was inside, she wrapped her arms around him in an embrace he didn't feel like he deserved.

She took his hand and pulled him into the small living room. "Come in, sit down, I'll make you some coffee."

The couch was covered with a throw, and when he sat down and sank into the saggy cushions, he understood why. There was another chair, a newer-looking recliner. Most likely, that was where his father sat. A small TV completed the furniture in the living room, which was a good thing, because there wasn't room for much else.

The place was clean, though. There were curtains at the windows that looked homemade and a colorful rug on the floor. Cheryl had made an effort.

Restless, he stood and wandered into the back hallway.

"Need to use the bathroom?" Cheryl's voice behind him was anxious. "The door doesn't close real well, but if you put that little stack of books in front of it, that will hold it."

"I was just looking around. I shouldn't have done it without your permission."

"Don't be silly." She waved a hand. "You're family. Make yourself at home."

"If you have a toolbox, I can fix that door for you," he said.

"Really? You'd do that?" She hurried off toward the kitchen and came back with a couple of screwdrivers, a hammer and a little box of nails. "Your dad would've fixed it, but he hasn't been feeling well for a while now," she said. "Will this stuff do? We don't have a real toolbox. And you don't have to fix it. I'm just glad you're here."

She was talking so quickly that he realized she was nervous. He put a hand on her arm. "Mom. It's okay. I should've come around before now to help you." He knelt down and studied the lock mechanism on the door, then selected a screwdriver.

Cheryl leaned against the wall in the hallway. "No," she said, "I was a bad mother and I know it."

Corbin had come here to forgive her, but saying that explicitly just now didn't seem quite right. "Water under the bridge," he said as he readjusted the mechanism and doorknob, tightened the screws. "You seem to be doing a lot better now."

"I wish I could say that I am," she said, "but truthfully, I've been having a hard time staying away from the liquor store."

He looked at her, curious. She didn't seem to have been drinking already this morning.

"It's just so hard, with Mikey gone and your father at that rehab center. I know it's wrong, but sometimes a drink helps dampen down the feelings."

He nodded, stood and demonstrated that the door mechanism was fixed. "Do you need to call your sponsor?"

She bit her lip. "I probably should."

"You do that," he said, "and I'll trim those bushes outside your door so they don't trip you and Dad, when he comes home." *If* he comes home.

He left her scrolling through her phone and went outside, where he found some clippers in the little storage box at the end of the trailer.

You and Dad. Mom and Dad. It felt surprisingly good to say. They weren't perfect; in fact, they were a mess. But God specialized in messes. He, Corbin, was a mess, too. Just in a different way.

There was a cool breeze, but sunshine warmed his back. He looked around the little lot thoughtfully. If the bushes and grass were trimmed, if he swept up the glass in the street in front, it would be a decent place for Mikey to come and visit.

In fact, as he clipped, he came upon a little plastic

push mower under one of the bushes, the kind designed to help a kid learn to walk.

His throat tightened. Mikey had spent his first two years here. And Cheryl had done her best.

A little later, after he'd tossed the branches he'd cut into the dumpster and swept up the glass, his mother came out. "Thank you for suggesting I make that call," she said. "I'm better, but… I still hope you'll take care of Mikey because I don't trust myself."

"I will," he said, patting her awkwardly on the back. "I'll raise him up to adulthood if you need. But there's no reason he shouldn't come and visit you."

Her face lit up. "I'd love that better than anything," she said. "Especially if you would bring him. My two sons." Her voice broke on the last word, and then she sank down onto the porch steps and let her face drop into her hands and wept.

Some things never changed. His mother was *very* emotional. He comforted her, awkwardly patting her back. Told her he loved her, because that was true despite everything. Promised he'd bring Mikey to see her real soon.

Once she'd finally stopped crying, she went into the house for some tissues, came back out again, and sat beside him. "What about Samantha?" she asked.

"What about her?" he asked, wary.

"You like her, right?"

"I do," he said, "but…"

She seemed to read his mind. Maybe it was a thing mothers did. "You know, she's a lot further along in her recovery than I am. She never was anywhere near as bad as I was, drinking-wise. She helps other members all the time. I don't think she'll relapse, not like me."

He thought about that. "You're probably right," he said, and realized that he meant it.

"And the whole thing of her pretending she didn't know me, that we hadn't set things up with you and Mikey... You need to know that she begged me to tell you the truth. Not just once, but a lot of times. I wouldn't."

"Why not?" he asked.

She shrugged. "Afraid, I guess. Afraid you'd turn around and dump Mikey into social services. You can be a little..." She hesitated.

"Rigid? Judgmental?"

She studied him, eyes clear. "Yes. Understandable, considering the way I raised you, or didn't raise you. But I didn't have a lot of confidence that you'd understand." She patted his hand. "I just want you to know that the deception was more me than Samantha. And it was all for Mikey's sake."

Any remaining anger he'd felt just floated away with her words, leaving him with a strong sense of regret. "Samantha isn't speaking to me. Not after the things I said. I really hurt her."

His mother nodded. "People hurt each other. But that doesn't mean you can't pick up and start again. At least, I hope not."

So if he was forgiving his mother...and if she was forgiving him...then maybe... "I love her," he blurted out, his face heating. "I'd like to marry her, but I've made a mess of the whole thing."

Cheryl nodded, thoughtfully, and they both sat for a few minutes, watching a bird flit from branch to branch. In the street, a little girl rode her trike in circles. Suddenly, his mother snapped her fingers. "What you need," she said, "is a big fancy marriage proposal. And I have just the plan."

He tilted his head, looking at her, as he remembered something he hadn't thought of in years: Cheryl was great at planning surprises and parties and events, at least when she was sober.

"I'm not doing something in front of a bunch of people," he warned her. "That's not my style." Besides, odds were at least fifty-fifty that Samantha would turn him down.

"I get it," his mother said. "We'll make it suit your personality."

Corbin thought about it. If Cheryl had a plan, well, that was a lot more than Corbin had.

"You'd help me like that?" he asked. "Even when I haven't been the greatest son?"

"You're a terrific son," she said, her easy forgiveness of his failings stunning him. "I'd be honored." She patted him on the arm and ran inside for a memo pad and started talking and making lists.

And as they worked together, he and his mother, Corbin felt a warmth he hadn't felt in years.

As Samantha parked her car in front of Corbin's house on Friday night, emotions threatened to overwhelm her.

Corbin had texted her yesterday, asking if they could

switch times: he'd care for Mikey during the day if she could come pick him up and take him for the evening.

That had been convenient for Samantha, because it had given her a day to get started on planning the program for younger kids at Rescue Haven.

But she had to wonder why Corbin had requested it. Did he have a date with someone else? Already?

That shouldn't matter. This was a chance to hang out with Mikey for an evening. She figured she'd take him back to Hannah's house and feed him dinner, let him play a little bit outside, then get him into his pajamas. They'd cuddle up and watch a kids' movie until Corbin came to pick him up.

It sounded wonderful to her, and it didn't matter that Corbin had been vague about what time he'd get there. It didn't matter what Corbin was doing.

If she told herself that often enough, maybe it would start to feel true.

Looking at the house and yard, though, made her chest ache with nostalgia and regret. They had had something wonderful there for a little while.

She got out of the car, and only then did she see Mikey, sitting on the porch by himself, carefully holding something in his lap.

"Mikey!" she said as she hurried up the walkway. "What are you doing out here by yourself?"

"Present for you," he said. He glanced back into the house.

That was when she saw that Corbin was standing just inside the screen door.

She couldn't quite face him, not yet. She sank down onto the steps beside Mikey. "What is it?"

"Candy." He thrust the bag into her hand.

"Well, thank you." For Mikey to share candy instead of eating it himself... She hugged him. "You're a great kid."

Probably, soon, Corbin would find someone else to help care for him. Another nanny, which would be bad enough, or a girlfriend.

That's not your business.

But still, it would be hard to face. She had agreed to stay in town long enough to get the program at Rescue Haven started, but she didn't know if she would continue for the long term. Didn't know if it would be too painful.

When she didn't open the gift bag right away, Mikey thrust it at her again and she peeked inside. It was one of those candy rings.

She pulled it out and held it up in the sunlight. "Look how pretty it is! Thank you!"

"Welcome," he said, looking longingly at the candy, and she laughed and handed it to him.

There was a sound behind them, dog claws on the screen. Boomer was trying to push his way out. Corbin scolded him and then slipped out, leaving the big dog inside.

"Hi," she said, feeling unaccountably awkward. You'd think they would have perfected the exchange of Mikey by now, but it still felt strange every time.

"There's something else in the bag," Corbin said.

She frowned. "What is it?"

"Look."

She did, hesitantly, and when she found a small velvet box, her heart hitched. What in the world?

"Go to Mom, like we talked about," he said gently, and Mikey scrambled down the steps. Corbin took Mikey's place beside Samantha.

Cheryl came out of the same bushes where Samantha had hidden all those weeks ago, watching over Mikey until Corbin found him. "Come on," Cheryl said, holding out a hand to Mikey. "Let's go for a walk."

Cheryl was here?

But she couldn't think about that because now Corbin was taking her hand, holding it in both of his. "Open the box," he said.

She stole a glance at his face and then looked down at the box, withdrew her hand from his, and carefully opened it.

Inside was a beautiful square diamond in an antique setting.

Samantha couldn't breathe. She couldn't think. She just stared at it as the world seemed to spin around her.

"I want you to marry me."

The spinning got faster as she looked from the ring to his serious, handsome face.

"Don't answer. Just think about it." He sank to his knees on the step below her. "I made so many mistakes, said such awful things, but I was wrong. I love you, Samantha. I've loved you since high school, and I'll always love you. So I just had to try."

"To…to try." She couldn't believe what she was hearing.

"Samantha," he said, his voice sounding dogged now, like he was getting to the end of a speech he'd rehearsed, "will you marry me?"

Now her heart was hammering so hard that she couldn't have stood up if her life depended on it. She stared at Corbin's dear face and didn't dare believe that he was serious, that this was really happening. "But you're angry with me."

"I'm not, and I was wrong to feel that way even for a minute. You did what you had to do for Mikey, and I love that about you. I'm the one who was wrong."

"And you really want to…to marry me?" He actually seemed to mean it, seemed to be proposing marriage, and underneath her shock, a thrilled kind of excitement was starting to rise. "Shouldn't we date first?"

"Yes!" He eased onto the steps beside her and took her hand in his. "Yes, we should, and we will. We'll go to movies and nice dinners and…and bowling and…"

"Bowling?" she asked, her mouth curving up into a smile. "Do you *like* bowling?"

"With you, it would be fun. Anything would be fun. Samantha, we've lived in the same house and eaten together and cared for a child together—"

"We've screwed up and lost him together," Samantha interrupted.

"And found him together. And I want to keep doing things together. So yeah, let's date. But I already know how I feel, and nothing's going to change it."

She stared at him, getting a little lost in his eyes.

"You can take as long as you need," he repeated.

She sucked in a breath and finally let herself believe

this was really happening. Joy exploded like fireworks in her chest. "I think I know, too."

"You do?"

She nodded. "I'm saying yes. I'll marry you."

"All *right*!" There was joy on his face as he drew her into his arms. He held her against him for a moment, their hearts beating together, and then he took her chin in his hand and kissed her with all the tenderness and all the promise in the world.

A while later, there was a shout, and Mikey came running into the yard, Cheryl right behind him. "Gotta get truck!" he yelled as he ran into the house, accidentally letting Boomer escape. So Boomer ran around the front yard in circles, and Mikey came back out and zoomed around with his big plastic truck, and Cheryl laughed and tried to catch them both. Of course, Corbin and Samantha helped, and soon the whole crowd was safely on the front porch and they were able to tell Cheryl their good news.

It was fitting that she was there, because she had been instrumental in their getting together. Not that she intended it, but maybe God had intended it.

Whatever the case, they were going to be a family. A happy family, together.

Epilogue

One Year Later

Samantha walked into the Rescue Haven barn with Corbin's arm around her. Mikey ran in front of them.

"I still can't believe they don't want me to do something. I feel like I should've helped set up, made some food."

"They want to celebrate you, not work you to death," Corbin said. "Besides, your aunt Becky was thrilled to do the food. Between them, Gabby and Sheniqua and Hannah are pretty well organized, and Mrs. Markowski ruled over the whole thing. Just relax and enjoy it. His arm tightened around her.

Samantha's heart still pounded a little when she stood close to her new husband. They had gotten married at Christmastime, a little over four months ago, and being a married woman still felt new.

Mrs. Markowski swept over to them, dressed in her usual classy clothes, a maroon-colored blazer and slacks. "We've been waiting for you," she said.

"Sorry. I wasn't feeling well." She glanced at Corbin.

Corbin looked at his watch. "I thought they were supposed to start at three," he said, raising an eyebrow. "I believe we're actually two minutes early."

"Oh yes, yes, it's fine." Mrs. Markowski drew them over to the table where a punch bowl full of something pink—nonalcoholic, of course—stood waiting. She filled punch glasses for both of them.

Gabby and Reese were giving tours of the barn to the guests and benefactors, many of them from the church. Gabby's grandmother handed out flyers about the various programs Rescue Haven now offered, assisted by a wealthy church board member, Mr. Romano. Some of the louder dogs had been moved to their new second kennel, but the best-behaved ones had remained, and the boys were putting them through their paces for the entertainment of the guests. Mrs. Markowski had even brought her poodle, who was learning better socialization skills by spending a little time at Rescue Haven each week.

Sheniqua sat on the floor, a handsome, dark-haired man with a touch of gray in his beard beside her. They had a collection of toys, and Mikey, Izzy and three other toddlers were already playing, making exuberant noise.

Hannah came up beside Samantha as Corbin went off

to talk with Cheryl. They both watched him approach his mother. "How is Cheryl doing?" Hannah asked.

"Better and better. It was tough on her losing her husband, but she didn't fall off the wagon. I think she's going to love living on the same street as me and Corbin and Mikey."

"And you're going to love having your mother-in-law there?" Hannah raised a skeptical eyebrow.

"I really will. She's been a wonderful help with Mikey already." She paused, then added, "I'm just so glad that Corbin was able to mend fences with his parents before his dad passed."

"For sure."

They stood watching the children. Hannah let out a sigh, and Samantha looked over at her cousin. "Something wrong?"

"No. Yes." She ran a hand through her hair. "I'm so happy for you and Corbin. I really am. And I'm happy that Sheniqua has found someone she cares about, too."

"But you're lonely?" Samantha asked bluntly. She and Hannah had gotten closer in the past year, and Samantha tried to include her in lots of activities. Moreover, Aunt Becky had been dealing with problems with Hannah's sister, so Hannah was spending a lot of time helping her mother at her bakery and generally calming her down.

Between that and her dog training business, Hannah was plenty busy. But it would be nice for her to find love, too. "You know," she began, "you could—"

"Don't say it." Hannah held up a hand. "I'm totally fine. Don't go suggesting that I do online dating or some ridiculous thing like that. No way. I just..." She smiled a little crookedly. "I sure do like those kids. Wish I could take them all home."

Mrs. Markowski clapped her hands, calling everyone to order. "No big speeches," she said, "but I think we should all give our thanks to Samantha, who has worked tirelessly to get the Rescue Haven Learn-and-Play up to full capacity."

They had started with a pilot preschool throughout the winter and spring, two days a week. Now, they would have the children every morning during the summer. The children got a farm experience, and learned about animals, and still fit in plenty of active play. Samantha loved planning the curriculum as well as working hands-on with the kids.

"In fact," Mrs. Markowski was finishing up, "we may need to hire more staff and go to a full-day program come fall."

Samantha raised her eyebrows and looked at Corbin, who'd returned to stand beside her. "News to me, but I guess I'm game," she said.

"A full-day program for little ones will be just in time," he said, smiling and brushing back a lock of her hair.

"Shh! Don't tell anyone yet!" But she couldn't restrain her own smile.

"I know. I'm just happy," he said. "Mikey will have a little brother. Or sister. Whatever. It doesn't matter."

That was true, Samantha thought, putting a hand on her belly where new life was just starting to grow. Boy or girl, their new baby would be deeply loved, a wonderful addition to the family they had formed together.

She leaned into her husband and shot up a silent prayer of thanks.

* * * * *

*Amish bachelor Mose Klassen wants a wife who is quiet
and traditional—the exact opposite of his childhood
friend Naomi Peachy. But when she volunteers as his
speech tutor, Mose can't help but be drawn to the outgoing
woman. Could an unexpected match be his perfect fit?*

Read on for a sneak preview of
The Amish Matchmaking Dilemma
by Patricia Johns, the first book in her new
Amish Country Matches miniseries.

"I'm not easy to match, and I know it," she replied. "My
sister is a matchmaker and even she had trouble with me.
That should tell you something. Maybe it's why I want to
drag some *Englishers* into our midst."

His stomach dropped, and he shot her a look of surprise.

"T-to marry?" he asked.

"No!" Naomi rolled her eyes. "But next to a bunch of
Englishers, I'm downright safe, you know?"

"*Yah.*" He wasn't so fortunate, though. Standing him
next to *Englishers* wouldn't fix what made him different.

"I'm joking, of course. But I do give that impression,
don't I?" Naomi asked with a sigh.

"What?" he asked.

"Of being a rebellious woman, of wanting to jump the
fence," she said. "I don't think I'm actually so different from
the other women—I just don't hide things as well! They're
better at keeping their thoughts to themselves, and mine
come out of my mouth before I think better of them."

"That's…a blessing," he said. At least she was honest.

Naomi put the pitchfork down with a clank of metal against concrete floor. "We're polar opposites, you and me, Mose. I talk too fast, and you aren't able to say everything in your head."

Mose met her gaze. "It's h-hard being d-d-different."

"Amen to that," she murmured. Then she smiled. "But a good friend helps."

Yah, a good friend did help. With Naomi and her wild hair and even wilder way of thinking, he didn't feel so alone—she'd always had that effect on him.

But she was right—Naomi was an example of why the *Ordnung* was so important. Everyone needed to be reined in, given boundaries, made to pause and think. Because if everyone just swung off after their own inclinations, there wouldn't be any Amish community anymore. Everything they valued—the togetherness, the simplicity, the traditions—would be nothing but a memory.

But looking at Naomi, catching her glittering green eyes, he couldn't be the one to hold her back. He could try, but in the end, he wouldn't be able to do it because she'd always been his weakness.

Mose felt his face heat and he wheeled the barrow off toward the door to dump it. She was helping him get more comfortable with talking. That was all. And he'd best remember it.

Don't miss
The Amish Matchmaking Dilemma *by Patricia Johns,*
available September 2022
wherever Love Inspired books and ebooks are sold.

LoveInspired.com

Love Harlequin romance?

DISCOVER.

Be the first to find out about promotions, news and exclusive content!

[f] Facebook.com/HarlequinBooks

[y] Twitter.com/HarlequinBooks

[o] Instagram.com/HarlequinBooks

[p] Pinterest.com/HarlequinBooks

[You Tube] YouTube.com/HarlequinBooks

ReaderService.com

EXPLORE.

Sign up for the Harlequin e-newsletter and download a free book from any series at
TryHarlequin.com

CONNECT.

Join our Harlequin community to share your thoughts and connect with other romance readers!
Facebook.com/groups/HarlequinConnection

HARLEQUIN

HSOCIAL2021

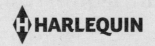

HARLEQUIN

Heartfelt or thrilling, passionate or uplifting—Harlequin is more than just happily-ever-after.

With twelve different series to choose from and new books available every month, you are sure to find stories that will move you, uplift you, inspire and delight you.